FORGOTTEN

The Lost Children Trilogy
Book One

KRISTA STREET

DEDICATION

To my sister, Marla, my first fan and

for many years my only fan.

Thanks for believing in me!

CHAPTER ONE

The cowboy's cloud danced and swayed around his shoulders, its color pure white. Clouds didn't get much better than that. He'd be a safe ride.

"Where you headed?" The cowboy's arm draped across the steering wheel in the old diesel. The truck grumbled softly in the quiet morning.

"West." I snapped my vision back to normal. His cloud disappeared.

"Well, that's where I'm goin' too. Hop in if you want a ride."

I pulled the door open and slipped inside. With relief, I dropped my backpack at my feet. "Thanks for picking me up."

"Not a problem. I'm Pete."

Smiling, I shook his hand. "Nice to meet you, Pete. I'm Lena."

I guessed Pete to be in his early sixties. He had darkly tanned skin and dressed simply in jeans and a red patterned flannel shirt. A large cowboy hat covered his head. He even had a big belt buckle.

I settled into the seat. The soft fabric felt wonderfully

comfortable after the hard, cold ground that had been my night's bed. Pete didn't seem in any hurry to drive despite a lone car honking when it passed. The old cowboy hadn't completely pulled onto the shoulder.

"You thirsty?" He popped the top off a thermos. The delicious scent of hot coffee wafted my way. "It's already sweetened with cream and sugar. Want a cup?"

I perked up. "Are you sure? Is there enough for you?"

He poured a cup. "There's plenty."

My fingers curled around the mug. I gulped the coffee. It burned my throat, but I kept swallowing. The wonderfully rich brew filled the clawing hole in my belly.

Pete finally put the truck into drive and pulled back onto the road. The truck rumbled every time it switched gears.

"Music too loud?" Pete asked. Soft country music strummed through the speakers.

I smiled and set my empty coffee cup in the console. "No, it's fine."

"You from these parts?"

By *these* parts, I assumed he meant here, in eastern Colorado. Good question. If only I knew. "No. How about you? You grow up around here?"

"Sure did. Lived just outside Little Raven my whole life, just like my father and his father before him. We've been ranchin' that land since the eighteen hundreds."

"That long?"

"Yeah."

"You have kids?"

"We got three girls. All the girls settled in the state. Fiona married a farmer, and Shelby married another rancher, but Haley, she moved to the city. Denver." He shook his head. "I can't imagine livin' in a city that size."

I nodded, pretending to understand, even though I had no idea if I'd ever lived in a city or not.

"Now Val and I," Pete continued. "She's my wife. We've

lived out here our whole lives. Can't imagine livin' anywhere different. It's like what they say about puttin' down roots. When they grow, it's hard to pull 'em up…"

I fingered my snarled red curls as I listened to the old cowboy. A content feeling washed through me. I liked Pete. He hadn't commented on my dingy appearance or skeletal figure. That was a first.

"What 'bout your family? Any of 'em live out here?"

I tensed, sitting straighter. "Oh. Um…"

A long moment of uncomfortable silence passed before Pete reached into the backseat. "I've got sandwiches too. What do ya prefer? Beef or ham?"

While Pete was rummaging for sandwiches, I turned toward the window and took a deep breath. The sliver of peace and happiness that the cowboy's kindness and generosity had provoked faded like the sun behind storm clouds. I hated personal questions. They put me in an awkward position and reminded me how scary my life was. The only thing I knew about myself?

My name. That was it.

I stared out the window as the landscape flew by. Fields of wheat surrounded us. Their tall tawny stalks rolled in the summer breeze like gentle swells in the ocean. Mountains loomed in the distance, their snowy peaks promising cooler temps to come. I concentrated on the landscape. My breathing still came too fast. Pete hummed along to the music, oblivious to the unease and fear bubbling up inside me, like a geyser that threatened to blow.

Not knowing my identity, and being reminded of that, brought back that terrifying day in April.

I closed my eyes and took a deep breath. I hated thinking about that day. *Hated* it.

Four months ago, I woke up *outside* on the street in Rapid City, South Dakota. I still remembered that day like yesterday: the cold, hard pavement chilling me through my jeans, the smells of rotting garbage from a nearby dumpster and the absolute panic that made my eyes widen in terror. I had no idea where I was or how I got there. The scariest thing, though, was when I realized I had no memories. None. I didn't know my age, who I was, where I came from, how I got in that alleyway, nothing. And strangest of all – I had a supernatural ability.

So that was the beginning of everything. Now, I was trying to figure out what happened to me.

Luckily, Pete had stopped this morning as I stood alongside the barren county road, my pale skin burning in the hot, unforgiving sun. The desolate road wasn't an ideal location to find a ride. Unfortunately, the trucker I'd been hitching with last night turned south. My instinct told me to go west. So I got out.

In the middle of nowhere.

Not my smartest move, but I hadn't known what else to do. At least, it had turned out okay. Once again, I was traveling in the right direction. My gut instinct, that steady subtle feeling I'd been following since leaving Rapid City weeks ago, told me to go west right now. So west I went. If only I knew what west was leading to.

Pete set a sandwich in my hands. The soft feel of bread snapped me back to reality. "Oh, thanks."

"Hope ham's okay."

"Yeah." My mouth watered. Mayonnaise and lettuce accompanied the meat. I took a bite and lost all control. Wolfing it down, I smiled sheepishly when finished. Pete just handed me a second sandwich.

"Try the beef. Val smokes it herself. It's darn good."

I took a big bite. "Wow, this is fantastic." I took another bite and said in between chews, "So, tell me more about your ranch."

Pete's eyes lit up. "Well, we got about ninety thousand acres, although some is leased from the National Forest Service. We raise mainly Black Angus…"

IT WAS LATE afternoon when we approached a small town. A sign declaring *Little Raven* passed on the right. Large mountains framed the community, their tips covered with snow. My eyes wandered across the buildings. It didn't appear to be a big town. Maybe a few thousand people.

"Last stop before my ranch," Pete said. "Or if you'd rather, you're welcome to stay with us for a while."

Stay at a home? Under a roof? His words were so foreign it took me a moment to process them. For four months, I'd slept outside as I searched for answers to what happened to me.

"Really?"

Pete tipped his hat up. "You look like you could use a good night's rest and some decent food."

"That sounds great, although I don't want to burden–" My breath stopped short when the strangest sensation grew inside me.

"Is that a yes?"

"Um." I gripped the door handle tightly. The feeling grew. It felt like someone banged a tuning fork inside me, the strong vibration demanding my attention. *What's happening?*

We'd almost passed Little Raven, when an abrupt realization came to me. *Is this the instinct?* That possibility occurred to me just as we pulled onto a county road heading out of town. It made me grow cold.

"Can you stop?" I blurted.

Pete slowed and pulled onto the shoulder. I scanned our surroundings. Little Raven was probably a quarter mile behind us already. Distant rooftops shimmered in the sunlight. My eyes darted back and forth. *Do I know this place? Have I been here before? Is that why I feel this?*

I unbuckled my seat belt and tentatively opened the door.

"Lena?"

I stepped out, closed my eyes and concentrated on the feeling. I took a step toward town. The feeling grew exponentially. My breath stopped, and my eyes flew open. That had *never* happened before.

I whirled around. "I think I'll check out Little Raven."

Pete propped his arm across the steering wheel. "You sure? My ranch isn't too far up this road. You could stay with us for the night. Even a couple if ya want. Little Raven's not goin' anywhere."

Just at the mention of Little Raven, anticipation oozed through me like warm honey. Something was waiting for me there. I could feel it. "Thanks, but I'm going to head into town."

"All right, but you come up to our place if you need somethin'."

"I will. Thank you."

Pete tipped his hat back into place. "Best of luck to you, Lena, was nice meetin' ya."

"You too, thanks."

After I slammed the door, the old diesel rumbled off. I spun on my heels in the direction of town and reached down to grab my backpack. Once it was strapped to my back, I'd be off, striding toward the town center, searching for the cause of this feeling, maybe finding the answers I so desperately sought.

But my hand only grabbed air.

There was nothing but dirt and dust around my worn shoes. I twirled in a circle. "You've got to be kidding me. Lena, you idiot!"

Pete was already a half mile away. His rumbling truck headed into a thick forest. I knew exactly where my bag was. Sitting on the floor of the passenger's seat, right where I'd left it.

I cupped both of my hands around my mouth. "Pete!"

Of course, he didn't hear me. I started running.

"Pete!" I yelled again. I waved my arms overhead. The old cowboy continued driving. A second later, his truck rounded a turn and disappeared into the forest. I kept running, as if by some miracle I'd eventually catch him.

CHAPTER TWO

I didn't catch him. Obviously.

Of course, that reasonable thought didn't prevail until I'd been running after him for at least half an hour. By the time I reached that point, I figured I might as well keep going. He said his ranch was up the road. *That means it's close. Right?*

I kept telling myself his ranch was probably around the next bend. Only thing, it'd been at least ten bends now with no sign of it.

If it was anything but my backpack, I wouldn't be doing this. But I needed my bag back. It held everything I owned. My cash, clothes, map, water bottle…everything. All of those things would be essential if it took me a few days to understand why the instinct led me to Little Raven.

However, that wasn't the real reason I wanted my backpack. That stuff could be replaced, but what I had in the small, zippered front pocket could never be replaced. The irony was that I took it off and put it away to *not* lose it.

Typical.

I kept walking. And walking. The evening passed slowly with no sign of Pete's. It wasn't until the sun descended behind a mountain that I began chewing my lip. I pictured the ditch I'd slept in last night. It'd been cool but sheltered. Now? I was at high altitude in the mountains. I stopped in the road. Wind whistled through the trees. Dying sunlight peeked over a mountain. No sign of civilization appeared anywhere.

Great, Lena. Well done. Nothing like being lost at high altitude with no food or water. Or shelter. Or any idea of where you're going for that matter.

I picked up my pace and ignored the searing pain from a blister on my heel that burst wide open. The aggressive pace wasn't easy, but I kept it up. My dry mouth and sandpaper tongue weren't helping. My focus kept drifting from finding Pete's to dreaming of water. At least it kept me from worrying about dying from exposure.

Yep, great logic, Lena. Instead, you'll die from dehydration. Much more painful.

I rounded another bend in the road when a sound reached my ears. Dust swirled around my shoes when I abruptly stopped. I cocked my head and listened. A second ticked past. The sound came again. A faint, distant rumbling. I grinned.

That only meant one thing.

I twirled in a circle and tried to decipher from which direction the vehicle came. The rumbling grew louder. Behind me. I turned and searched for the vehicle in the evening twilight. Eventually, I spotted what made the noise. A shiny, new Suburban rounded a hill in the distance. Its headlights pierced the dim light and wove in and out of view as it snaked through the forest.

Relief poured through me.

When the Suburban rounded the final turn, I ran into the middle of the road and waved both arms overhead. Thankfully, the vehicle slowed as it neared and ground to a halt about ten yards away. I jogged to the vehicle, but the driver's door was already opening.

Dark boots with two-inch heels emerged. I stopped by the

hood, tried to calm my breathing and waited for the driver to get out. When she extracted her long limbs, I examined her tall frame. She wore black from head to toe. Black boots, black pants, and a long-sleeved black shirt. Even her hair was black, and from the looks of it, she also had olive skin. Everything about her hinted at a Hispanic or Mediterranean heritage.

"Hi," I said.

"Evening," she replied.

I reached up to smooth my hair and hoped it wasn't too wild. That always gave off a bad impression. "Say, you couldn't give me a ride, could you? I'm trying to find a guy's ranch, but I don't know how far it is. I don't think I'll find it before dark."

She didn't respond.

I briefly wondered how I must look through her eyes. I hoped my lack of deodorant wouldn't stop her from helping me. It had stopped more than one person in the past. "Um, would you mind?"

The silence stretched.

"You're walking to a guy's *ranch*?" she finally said.

"Yeah."

She shook her head, her short black hair swaying. Her brow furrowed. "Why?"

Why? Does it matter? "Well, he gave me a ride, and I left my backpack in his truck. I need to get it back."

She cocked her head. "You forgot your bag in some guy's truck." She seemed to be saying it more to herself, but I nodded anyway.

"That's why you changed course again."

Her words were so quiet I barely heard them, *if* I heard them. What I thought I heard didn't make any sense. "Huh?"

"Nothing." She stood quietly for a moment, still frowning. Finally, she sighed. "Okay, get in the back. We'll take you to this ranch."

For a brief moment, confusion filled me, but I was so grateful all I did was mumble thank you.

It was only when I reached for the door that I realized I'd broken my cardinal rule. Before she climbed into her seat, I switched my vision. Her cloud readily appeared.

My mouth fell open. I made my gaze shift back to normal and then switched it again. The same image glowed around her. *What the...*

Blue and gold swirled around her shoulders.

"Are you okay?" She sat in her seat, the door still open as she peered out at me. For all intents and purposes, she looked like a normal twenty-some-year-old woman. However, the cloud that billowed around her spoke otherwise.

I switched my vision back to normal. "Uh, yes?"

She quirked an eyebrow and slammed the door. I took a deep breath, my hand still on the door handle. *Get in or keep walking?* I frowned. It's not like her cloud seemed bad, just...different, not the white, gray or occasional black I was used to seeing.

You really want to spend tonight alone in the Rockies with no shelter? I grasped the handle and pulled it open.

THE SECOND THE interior was visible, my mouth fell open. Five other people sat in the Suburban. Three in the very back, one in the middle, and one in the front passenger seat. How had I not noticed that? I glanced at the windows. They were tinted, not to mention the interior light was off. No wonder I hadn't seen them.

"Hello," a girl exclaimed. She sat in the far back right. Unlike the driver, she had a bright friendly smile. Her button nose and shoulder length brown hair gave her a healthy, wholesome look.

"I'm Mica," she waved.

"I'm Lena," I replied automatically. I shifted my vision until her cloud appeared. Once again, the image completely blindsided me. Pink and blue hovered around her. I almost snapped my sight back to normal, but then assessed the two guys sitting beside Mica, the woman sitting in the middle row, and the guy looking out his window in the front seat.

They were all different.

Each person had colors in their cloud. All of them had the same blue but then everyone had a unique color. I'd never seen anything like it.

"Are you getting in?" Mica asked.

I shifted my sight back to normal. Mica still smiled brightly.

"Um," I mumbled.

I wasn't sure if I should. I'd seen hundreds of people, no, *thousands* of people, since that first morning in Rapid City. Every other person I'd met had similar appearing clouds. Dark, gray or white. The darker the cloud, the more evil a person was, the lighter, the more kind, but these guys? Not even close to normal.

"There's plenty of room." Mica still smiled.

I reminded myself their clouds didn't appear bad, just inconclusive. "Right. I mean thanks."

"Move your stuff, Jet." Mica elbowed the guy sitting beside her. The guy reached forward and grabbed a duffel bag off the empty seat.

The two men beside Mica were obviously twins. Both had dark curly hair, stocky builds and bright blue eyes. Each of their biceps seemed as big as both of my thighs. The one by the window regarded me warmly. The one in the middle, Jet, smirked. I smiled tentatively in return before turning my gaze to the woman in the middle row.

She was stunning and for a moment, I just stared. She had to be some kind of supermodel. Her long blond hair flowed down her back in soft waves, and she had one of those hard-to-forget faces. Hollowed cheeks, a full mouth, and honey-brown eyes so piercing I couldn't look away. Suddenly, I felt very self-conscious with my snarled, dark red hair and dirty, pale skin.

"So, get in…" Mica said slowly.

"Sorry." I climbed in and closed the door. New car smell filled the cab. Whoever owned this vehicle must have recently bought it. When I sat, my knee banged into a huge suitcase in the aisle.

"Sorry about that." The blonde supermodel shifted the luggage.

"Ready?" the driver asked.

I clicked my seat belt in place. "Yes."

With a spin of tires, we were off. The driver eyed me in the rearview mirror. "I'm assuming this ranch is in the direction you were walking?"

"Yeah, if you don't mind dropping me off when we get there, that'd be great."

"Hmm," was all she replied.

The Suburban picked up speed as we traveled down the bumpy road. The forest grew darker by the second, and the air flowing in through someone's open window dropped in temperature. I sighed. Despite this group having strange clouds, I was glad to be in a vehicle. Turning away from the window, I was startled to find the supermodel watching me.

"I'm Jacinda." She extended her hand. Her nose wrinkled slightly. I knew she'd detected my stench.

I shook her long, fine boned hand, and felt the usual embarrassment at my lack of hygiene. "Lena. It's nice to meet you."

"That's Jet and Jasper," Jacinda said, her face impassive again. She glanced toward the curly haired twins behind us. Jasper smiled, but the one in the middle, Jet, winked.

"In the front is Di and Flint," Jacinda continued.

The woman in black, Di, eyed me in the rearview mirror as she drove, but the guy, Flint, sitting in the passenger's seat, still stared out the window.

"Flint?" Jacinda said.

He didn't move.

"Flint?" she called again.

He still didn't move.

Jacinda frowned and shrugged, but my gaze lingered on the back of Flint's head, not because he ignored me, but because there was something…about him. An emotion flickered through me, like a sense of déjà vu, but it passed too quickly for me to identify.

"So, you're going to some ranch?"

I could feel Jacinda watching me and forced my attention back to her. "Yes."

"Because some guy has your backpack that you left in his truck?"

"Yep."

"Is he your friend?"

"Kind of."

"Kind of?" she said.

I did an abrupt shake. "Wait, how did you know I left my backpack in his truck?"

"Isn't that what you told Di?"

"Oh, right."

"So this guy is *kind of* your friend?" Jacinda's eyebrows rose.

"Yeah. I just met him today."

She eyed me, her light brown eyes curious. "Then how were you riding with him?"

"I was hitchhiking. He picked me up this morning."

"Hitchhiking?" Her tone told me exactly what she thought about that.

"Yep."

"Do you hitchhike a lot?"

I assessed my filthy clothes and skeletal frame. I certainly didn't look like someone who owned a car, or took the Greyhound for that matter. "Yeah."

"Where were you going?"

"Little Raven." Just thinking of the town made my breath

quicken. I needed to get back there.

Jacinda's smile widened. "So you *were* going to Little Raven." She glanced toward the driver again. Di was still watching me in the rearview mirror. A small, almost smug expression shone in her reflection.

My brow furrowed. They knew I was going to Little Raven? But how could they know that? *I* hadn't known I was going to Little Raven until this morning.

I shook that thought off. Of course, they didn't know I was going there. I probably misunderstood, but then I remembered what Di murmured before I climbed in the Suburban, about how I'd changed course again. At least, that's what I thought she'd said. But how did any of that make sense? I sank back into my seat as an uneasy feeling settled in me. They all did have strange clouds…

"So, Leeena," Jacinda said, taking her time pronouncing the *e*. "Where are you from?"

"Rapid City." It was the answer I gave everyone. After all, it was the closest I had to the truth.

"South Dakota?" Jasper called from the back.

"Yes."

"How long have you lived there?" Mica asked.

"A while." I turned in my seat to better assess everyone. Jasper and Jet stared at one another, their expressions twitching a few times. They seemed oblivious to me studying them.

"A while?" Mica said, forcing my attention to her.

"Yeah."

"And you hitchhiked from Rapid City all the way to here?" Jacinda asked.

"That's right." For whatever reason, that statement made the entire Suburban fall eerily silent. I tried to keep my breathing even, but this group got weirder by the second. Between the strange clouds, probing questions and bizarre comments that I couldn't possibly be hearing right, I didn't know what to think of them.

Okay, it's not the first time you've been in a strange situation. Just get control of the conversation and get out when they stop.

I smiled tightly and clasped my hands together. "Enough about me, where are all of you headed?"

I waited for someone to say something. Nobody did. Instead, the only reactions were a few, subtle glances to one another. The hum of the engine filled the void.

"Or, are you all from Colorado?" I asked.

"Oh…" Jacinda finally replied.

I followed Jacinda's gaze. Di was eyeing me again in the rearview mirror.

"Well, we're…" Mica cut in, but then she stopped and glanced at Di too.

"Ah–" Jasper said.

"We're from all over," Di interrupted. After that statement, the silence resumed.

"Oh, okay."

A minute passed, and then Mica pulled a book out of her bag. A second later, Jet and Jasper turned on an action movie in the headrest's TV. The sound of gunfire and screeching tires filled the back. As for Jacinda, she smiled sweetly and extracted a nail file from her pocket. Lifting her hand, she squinted in the dying light and began filing.

I frowned and sank back into my seat. I eyed everyone suspiciously. They all seemed busy, except for Flint. Not once had he shifted. There was just a tenseness around his shoulders that hadn't abated since picking me up. It was the only indication he was actually alive. Otherwise, I'd probably assume he was their last victim. A dead body in the front seat, me soon to be the second.

Stop it, Lena, now you're talking crazy. They're not going to hurt you. They're just strange.

I tried to convince myself of that as I leaned back in my seat. It didn't help that someone's water bottle lay on the floor.

The sloshing sound beckoned me.

To ignore the water, I switched my vision. All of their clouds appeared, dancing and flowing together. They were incredibly beautiful in their own, unique way, but they were still different.

Very different.

CHAPTER THREE

About five minutes later, Mica lurched forward in her seat, her eyes glued out the windshield. "It's just up ahead, a mile on the left."

"What is?" I snapped my vision back to normal.

"The ranch you're looking for."

I eagerly peered ahead, but all I saw was road and dark trees illuminated by the headlights. "Are you sure?"

"Yep."

A few minutes later, just as Mica promised, a ranch appeared. Moonlight illuminated vast open fields that seemed to stretch for miles. Fences lined the perimeter. Large, black specks dotted the distant hills. I guessed those were the Black Angus Pete told me about. Di slowed the Suburban.

"Is this it?" Di asked.

"I think so. Pete said his ranch was up this road, and it's the only ranch so far."

"Do you know what the name is?" Jasper asked.

Cocking my head, I paused. "Um, I think it was Holloway Hills or Hideaway Hills or something like that."

"The entrance is up there," Mica pointed.

I looked through the windshield again. "Where?"

"Up on the left."

"Are you sure? I can't see a thing."

"I can see—" A thud sounded, and Mica's voice died in a muffle. I snapped my gaze to her, but she was rubbing her arm and glaring at Jet.

"You can see what?" I asked.

"Nothing." A strained smile covered her face. "But I think the entrance is up there."

Before I could reply, Di sped up, and a classic arched timber entrance appeared like a giant mouth beckoning us to enter. A sign perched at the top. *H… H something.*

"Can anyone see the name?" I asked excitedly.

"Hideaway Hills," Mica answered promptly.

I grinned. "Thanks a lot for the ride. You can drop me off here. I'll walk up the road."

"No!" Mica and Jacinda shouted at the same time.

I leaned back, wide-eyed.

"We'll drive you up there," Di interjected. "It'd be rude to leave you in the dark."

"Okay," I said. Jacinda and Mica now smiled sweetly as if their loud outburst never happened. I reminded myself *nothing* about this group was normal.

We crept slowly up the drive. Lights shone at the top, illuminating a few buildings. Gravel crunched under the tires, and the breeze coming in through someone's window carried sounds of chirping crickets and a distant owl.

When we reached the top, Di put the Suburban into park. Off to the right stood a large, well-lit two story house with a wide, wraparound porch and a hanging swing in the corner. A sign over the front door read, *"Y'all come back now, ya hear."*

"That looks like the main house," I said. "I can get out here. You really don't need to wait."

Di's dark eyes flashed in the rearview mirror. She turned off the Suburban. "We'll wait. Just in case you can't find your friend." From her tone, I knew there was no point arguing.

Mica grinned as I opened the door. She tucked a strand of brown hair behind her ear. "Want me to come with you?"

"If you want."

We jumped out and walked along a stone pathway cut into the yard. Nighttime crickets chirped, and the wooden steps creaked softly underfoot when we climbed the porch. Once at the front door, I knocked and fervently hoped I'd find Pete. If I didn't, I'd likely never see my backpack again. My stomach plummeted. I didn't want to consider that possibility.

Muffled footsteps sounded on the other side. The door opened, revealing an older woman wiping her hands on an apron. Her gray hair was wrapped in a bun. Several wispy strands escaped to frame her cherub cheeks and warm, hazel eyes.

"Hello." She smiled and opened the door wider. The smells of home cooking wafted in the air. Roast beef and freshly-baked bread. I licked my dry lips. I didn't think I'd ever smelled anything more appetizing. Her eyebrows rose. "Can I help you?"

Focus, Lena...

"I hope so." I slapped a hand over my stomach when it rumbled loudly. "I'm trying to find a man named Pete. Does he live here?"

The woman smiled brightly. "Pete Henderson? He certainly does. And who may you be?"

I sighed in relief. "I'm Lena. Pete gave me a ride into Little Raven earlier today, but I left my backpack in his truck. I'm hoping he still has it."

"Lena!" She opened the door wider and looked me up and down. "Pete told me about you. Said you traveled all the way to Little Raven by hitchhiking. Such a bold thing to do these days, m'dear. You're lucky to have made it in one piece."

She ushered us inside and closed the door behind us. The heavenly scents floated stronger in the entryway. "I'm Val, by the way, Pete's wife." She held out her hand. "It's lovely to meet you."

Everyone thought hitchhiking was dangerous, and they were right. I wasn't so stupid I didn't know that, but I did have an advantage. I switched my vision as I took her hand.

Val's cloud appeared as we shook. I almost gasped. Long and thick, like a cloak, her white cloud swept around her shoulders and trailed down her back in a waterfall. I'd never met anybody with a cloud like that. I smiled. I couldn't help it. Val had a rare soul: kind, pure and with no hint of malice. I sighed in relief. I knew Val would never hurt me, but more than that, I knew she'd *help* me.

"Are you okay?" Val dropped my hand.

I switched my vision back to normal. "Um, yes, fine."

My stomach rumbled again as a hint of dizziness swept through me. It suddenly felt very hot, but I shook it off. "And I'm sorry for interrupting your evening, but I need my bag back. I hope you understand."

Val swished her hand in the air. "Of course, it's all right. I'm just sorry you had to come all the way out here to get it." Val turned to Mica. "And who may you be?"

Mica said something, but I barely heard her response. I felt so light headed. I put a hand on my forehead and took a deep breath. *Is the room spinning?*

"Come on in," Val said. "I'll go find Pete."

I took a step but swayed. It felt like the entire earth moved. Reaching a hand out, I grabbed hold of a small table in the entry.

"Are you okay, dear?" Val stepped closer, frowning. "You look so pale."

"No, I'm always pale," I mumbled, but I swear the room really *was* spinning.

"Lena?" Mica said. "Are you all right?"

Her voice became distant, muffled. Everything went fuzzy. I blinked rapidly a few times, but my vision wouldn't focus.

The next thing I knew, the floor rushed up to greet me and then...

Blackness.

CHAPTER FOUR

I floated in darkness. I figured I must be dreaming. For starters, I was warm and wonderful smells surrounded me. Normally, my unwashed skin, exhaust, and the unique scents that came with vehicle interiors were what I lived with. But this smell was pleasant. Cooked food, an undercurrent of pine-scented cleaning detergent and...tangerines?

"Lena?" a deep voice said. "Can you hear me?"

My body stiffened. Awareness slid through me like a gentle caress. That voice. I *knew* that voice.

I opened my eyes, but any hope and longing I'd felt vanished. An entire circle of people stared down at me. I would have jolted back, but a hard surface pressed against my head.

"Lena!" Mica exclaimed.

I blinked a few times and tried to comprehend what I was looking at. The ceiling light gave it away. It seemed I was lying on a floor, and a crowd of people circled around and above me, like a football team huddling.

"Lena, are you all right?" Di asked.

I frantically searched their faces. That voice. The deep one.

Whose had it been? Did I dream it?

Lifting a palm to my head, I tried to figure out who was who and what happened. The huddling group was from the Suburban. I remembered that much. Di, Jacinda, Mica, Jet, Jasper and a man I didn't recognize. My eyes widened when I saw him. He abruptly pulled back.

I tried to sit up to see where he'd gone, but my head pounded.

"Take it easy." Di forced me back down. "You fainted and hit your head."

I rubbed my temple. *Fainted? Hit my head?* Well, that explained the pounding headache. I tried to see past her to where the man had gone, but she blocked my view.

"Do you remember what happened?" she asked.

I continued rubbing my head as memories surfaced. Meeting Pete. Traveling to Little Raven. The instinct roaring to life. Walking along the county road. Meeting this group. Finding Pete's ranch. Feeling lightheaded in the entryway. Falling.

I groaned. I *had* fainted.

"Do you remember now?" Di asked.

"Yeah."

"Good. Now tell me, when did you last drink something?"

I propped myself up on my elbows, wincing. "Um, this morning. I had a cup of coffee."

Di's frown deepened. "A cup of coffee? That's it?"

I nodded.

Her eyes widened. "You mean you walked all that way today without one drink?"

"Um, yeah." My water had run out last night, and while dehydration was nothing new for me, I'd certainly never fainted before.

"We need to get her some water." Di reached down and pinched the skin on the back of my hand. It left a tent of skin poking up. "She's incredibly dehydrated. My guess is her blood pressure is low. It's probably why she fainted."

Val wrung her apron between her hands. "Let's get her to the kitchen."

"Flint?" Di looked at someone behind Val. "Will you carry her?"

"I don't need to be carried…" My words died when the strange man appeared again. He hovered above me, just like the others. My gaze widened as I stared up into his deep set, dark eyes. They were so dark they were almost black, but flecks of brown speckled the irises. I scanned the rest of his face. Tanned skin, a smooth brow, firm lips and a straight, if long nose. Chestnut colored hair streaked with gold covered his head.

He was *beautiful*.

"Do you mind if I pick you up?" he asked.

The deep tone of his voice reverberated through me. It was *him*. The one I heard when I thought I was dreaming. His voice raised goosebumps along my arms.

"Um…no…I mean, sure."

He reached down and cupped his arms under my back and knees. My eyes widened. I knew who he was. Di had called him Flint. Flint was the man from the Suburban. The one in the front seat who'd refused to acknowledge me.

He lifted me without the slightest hitch and walked toward the kitchen. I was acutely aware of every inch of him, the hard feel of his arms, the steady thud of his heart, the way his fingers curled gently yet firmly around my legs. His scent fluttered to me as he walked liquidly across the floorboards. Val walked ahead, nervously chatting. I barely heard her since I was so consumed with Flint. Leaning closer, I hesitantly inhaled his scent. Spice, wood, and something else. I inched closer.

Tangerines.

My body jumped to life, like someone ran a jolt of electricity through it. I studied him wide-eyed, but he continued walking, apparently oblivious to my erratic reaction.

I searched his face, looking for something, anything, that would trigger a memory. *Do I know him?* No, that wasn't possible. He'd never mentioned us meeting before.

"She can have a seat here," Val said as Flint strode into the kitchen.

He walked to a kitchen chair. I already dreaded when he'd set me down. I didn't know why, but I didn't want him to let go. An emotion I'd never experienced before was growing steadily in me with each step he took. His warm arms and steady breathing only made it increase. It wasn't until he leaned down to set me on the chair that I finally understood what it was.

I'm safe. Flint makes me feel safe.

Still refusing to meet my eyes, Flint let go. An emptiness consumed me.

"Thank you," I managed.

He didn't reply. Instead, he walked to the opposite wall and leaned against it, looking anywhere but at me. It was like in the Suburban. Once again, he ignored me.

My stomach plummeted. The high that coursed through me vanished like a fire being doused with water. Why was he ignoring me? His behavior shouldn't hurt but it did.

Maybe I hit my head harder than I thought.

Everyone else crowded in the kitchen. Val retrieved a glass from a walnut cabinet and hurriedly filled it. I forced myself to ignore Flint and drink. I emptied the glass in mere seconds, my gulps audible.

"Thank you." I wiped my mouth.

Di placed her hands on her hips. "She needs more than that."

Val grabbed the empty glass. "I'll get another."

Three glasses later, I finally felt sated. Just as I was about to thank Val again, Pete walked in.

"Well, I'll be." Pete put his hands on his hips and eyed

everyone in the kitchen. Di stood beside me while the twins, Mica and Jacinda hovered near the counter. Flint still stood by the opposite wall. It didn't escape my notice that Flint's location was the one place in the kitchen that put the most distance between us.

When Pete's gaze met mine, he grinned. "Lena, what the heck are you doin' here? Did you decide to take me up on my offer?"

I smiled. "Not exactly."

Val gave Pete a scolding look. "No, dear. She forgot her backpack in your truck. She walked almost all the way here to get it."

Pete's expression fell. "You did?"

My eyes darted toward Flint again. The ceiling must be fascinating since he now stared at that. "Yeah, I walked for a few hours, but then this group came along and picked me up."

Pete sighed. "Darn, that's a long walk."

Before I could reply, Di interrupted. "Lena, when did you last eat?"

Flint's gaze shifted to me. Once again, that unreadable expression covered his face.

"Lena?" Di prompted.

"Um, this morning. I had two sandwiches."

"And before that?" Di asked.

"When did I eat before that?"

She nodded.

I cocked my head, trying to recall. Yesterday I'd been riding with a trucker from Nebraska. Before that, I'd spent five days wandering around the plains since the instinct had led me astray for a while. During that time, I'd eaten at a diner with a nice woman named Cindy. I perked up. That's when I'd last eaten.

"Maybe two or three days ago."

Di's eyes widened. "Two or three *days* ago? You've barely eaten anything for the last three days?"

"That's right."

She rolled her eyes. "Well, no wonder you fainted and are so skinny. You're not only dehydrated, but you were probably ketotic prior to this morning."

"Ketotic?"

Di sighed. "Glucose is the sole source of energy for your brain, so in the absence of glucose in your diet, your body is forced to find an alternate food source. It converts fat cells into ketones—"

"Huh?" I interrupted.

"Never mind. You should eat something."

"That's something we can take care of!" Val bustled to a large, six-burner stove and pulled on a pair of hot-mitts that were sitting on the stone countertop. "Have the rest of you eaten supper yet?"

One by one, everyone shook their heads.

"In that case, you're all going to eat. I have plenty of leftovers from the supper meal. Now, go on out to the dining room. Pete will show you the way. Go on now, out you go!" She made a swishing movement with her hands before opening the oven. More heavenly scents emerged from it.

"Come on, Lena, let's go." Di pulled out my chair.

I concentrated on standing since I still felt embarrassingly weak. It was probably all the walking at high altitude this afternoon. Placing my palms on the table's smooth surface, I tried to cover up how shaky I felt.

"Are you okay?" Di's long, tanned fingers reached out.

I pulled away. "Yeah, I'm fine."

"Okay, but take it easy."

Despite my protesting muscles, I stood. That was a mistake. It felt like the entire floor moved beneath me. The next thing I knew, hands were on me. Very large hands. They were warm and rough and felt oddly pleasant.

Flint stared down at me as he gripped my upper arms. He'd moved so fast I hadn't seen him coming. I had the

27

ridiculous urge to stare at him but managed to avert my gaze to his nose.

"Thank you."

He didn't reply.

"Do you need Flint to carry you again?" Di asked.

Her question snapped me back to reality. Even though I'd loved the feel of Flint's arms around me, it was embarrassing that he'd carried me. Normally, I was quite capable of taking care of myself.

"No, I'm fine," I replied.

The instant I said that, Flint let go. My entire body screamed in protest, but then a sudden sense of self-consciousness filled me. I looked down and saw myself the way he must be seeing me.

Greasy crimson curls, pale grimy skin, and an undernourished almost skeletal frame. Not to mention, my clothes were too big and horribly dirty. I was a mess and I smelled. No wonder he'd let go.

My cheeks burned.

"Come on, let's go," Di said. "Clear the way."

THE ROOM WE entered was huge. I guessed it wasn't really a dining room, though. It'd probably once been a large living area or even a ballroom.

The vaulted roof had large wooden support beams. A huge chandelier made of antlers hung from the ceiling. The room was decorated in traditional western theme. Framed pictures of horses, Native Americans, and mountain landscapes hung on the walls. Various types of ranch equipment decoratively garnished the shelves and corners. Dozens of tables and chairs filled the room. Some tables could only sit two or four, others sat twelve to fourteen.

I knew the tables were for the guests. In addition to running cattle, Pete had told me they ran a guest ranch. Every night the guests ate in their home.

It felt like a lightbulb flipped on.

I knew why Val had such large appliances in the kitchen and why she'd had enough leftovers to feed all of us. Pete said their ranch could accommodate thirty guests. Val probably did all the cooking.

"Come on, have a seat over here." Di steered me toward the table Pete stopped at. It was one of the larger ones. She plopped me down on a middle seat and walked around to the opposite end. Jacinda pulled out the chair beside me. Mica took the chair on my other side.

"I'll go find your bag." Pete hooked a thumb on his jeans. His belt buckle gleamed in the light. "I'm real sorry about that, Lena."

"No big deal. Thanks, Pete."

He walked back to the kitchen.

"So you really haven't eaten much for three days?" Mica asked.

"Yeah. Two, three days, something like that."

"Wow," she murmured. "I've never gone a day without eating, except for that first day. That day—"

"So, Lena!" Jacinda interrupted. She said it so loudly I jumped. An overly bright smile covered her face. "Tell me more about yourself. What do you do when you're not hitchhiking?"

Great. More personal questions. Just what I need.

"Um, nothing really," I replied.

"But before you started traveling, you must have done something," she persisted, still smiling. The twins pulled out the chairs directly opposite to me. Di still sat near the end.

One of the twins met my gaze. I switched my vision. From his cloud's yellow color, I knew it was Jasper. Snapping my sight back to normal, I let my eyes wander toward the kitchen, but my gaze didn't get far, since a few chairs down was *him*. At some point in the past few seconds, Flint had sat at the very end of the table, beside Di.

I reached up to straighten my hair. My fingers threaded through thick curls but got stuck in a snarl. I tried to gracefully extract them but ended up pulling out a few strands. If anything, I made my hair messier.

Not that it mattered.

Once again, Flint ignored me. He and Di had their heads dipped toward one another as they whispered. A brief surge of envy pummeled me. It was not an emotion I was used to feeling.

"Lena?" Jacinda asked.

"Oh, um, not really," I finally replied to her question about my personal interests.

Jasper eyed my left, inner wrist and cocked an eyebrow. "Surely, you've got some hobby? Tattoos maybe?"

I shoved my hand under the table. "No. I'm not into tattoos."

"Wasn't that one on your wrist?" Jet eyed his brother and Jacinda.

"Oh, well…" The tattoo on my wrist was another thing I couldn't explain. It was a symbol. A circle divided into four quarters. I hadn't noticed it until the second day after I woke up.

"It's nothing," I finally said. "Just a pen mark."

Jacinda frowned. A myriad of expressions crossed the twins' features – a tilt of a smile, the slight nod of a head, a quirked eyebrow. A second later, it stopped.

"Whatever you say." Jasper smiled, his blue eyes twinkling.

"Yeah," Jet smirked. "Whatever you say."

Thankfully, before anyone could ask anything else, Mica approached the table with glasses and a pitcher of water. I hadn't noticed she'd left. She practically slammed the drinks down. "Drink up, everyone," she said cheerfully.

I didn't need the encouragement. I gulped down another full glass. It hit my empty stomach like a water balloon splatting on a sidewalk. I filled it again and avoided the urge to study Flint and Di over the rim of the glass. They were *still* whispering.

"So, Lena." Mica angled her chair my way. Her brown hair brushed along her shoulders with the movement. I cringed inwardly, wondering what she'd ask. "Is your bag all you're traveling with?"

I made a noncommittal noise and took another drink.

Mica frowned. "That's all you have?"

"Yep."

I felt more eyes at the table assess me. Jacinda frowned, the expression causing tiny wrinkles to mar her otherwise smooth forehead.

"How many clothes do you own?" Jacinda asked.

"Um, a few shirts and two pairs of pants."

"That's it?" Jasper said.

"That's it."

Jet leaned back, frowning. A dark curl fell on his forehead. He pushed it back.

Thankfully, before the Inquisition got into full swing, Val appeared. "Here you go, m'dear."

She placed a steaming plate of food in front of me. Roast beef, mashed potatoes, an assortment of roasted veggies and a large, soft roll. A hefty portion of gravy covered the meat and potatoes. The smell was unbelievably appetizing.

Val pulled plates off the tray she carried and served everyone else, but I couldn't wait for the entire table to get their meals. My focus became entirely on the food. I picked up my fork and took a big bite. Rich gravy and mashed potatoes coated my tongue.

It was quite possibly the best moment of my life.

The next ten minutes were a blur. I had no idea what the group talked about, maybe the food, or the weather, or whatever people normally spoke about at dinner. As for me, all I saw was my fork and the food in front of me. I'd never tasted anything so good, or so satisfying, and it disappeared much too fast.

"Hungry?" a voice asked.

I snapped my head up.

Jet watched me, a smirk on his face.

My cheeks flamed. I'd probably just resembled a front-end loader hard at work shoveling.

"Yeah," I replied sheepishly. I peeked at *him* again, but Flint was still oblivious. I tried not to stare, but he was so gorgeous, it was hard not to. Once again, I wondered at my strange reaction to him. Even though he ignored me and sat at the end of the table, I still felt safe. *Bizarre.*

Jacinda eyed my empty plate. "You really have been starving, haven't you?"

"Obviously," Mica snorted. "Look at her."

I shrank inwards, pulling my thin arms and lean legs into a pretzel. "Well, that's what happens when you're homeless."

A few pieces of cutlery fell from people's grasps. The clatter when it hit the table echoed in the room.

"But how can you not have any money for hotel rooms?" Mica asked.

"Yeah," Jet piped in. "Surely, you have *money*?" He waggled his eyebrows.

The questions started up again, yet this time focused on finances. Why in the world would they ask me about money? Did I look like someone with rolls of hundreds in my pocket?

Sinking into my seat, I wished I could disappear underneath it. Suddenly, I felt very tired. The entire day had been completely exhausting, and this group wasn't helping.

"Enough." Flint stared at everyone through hard, dark eyes.

For whatever reason, the mood around the table abruptly changed. Jacinda smiled brightly and told me she loved my top, but since it was full of tattered holes I wondered if I heard her right. Jasper offered me the rest of his potatoes, Jet continued to smirk, and Mica spooned her zucchini onto my plate before

I could protest.

"I don't like zucchini." She set her plate down.

I shook my head and finished the rest of her unwanted vegetables. However, I declined Jasper's continual offers to give me his food. As hungry as I was, I wasn't that pathetic.

Throughout it all, Flint watched everyone. His hard, dark gaze was unsettling and comforting at the same time. It was entirely bizarre. When the conversation switched to tomorrow's forecast, he rose and slipped into the kitchen. I watched him go, my eyes traveling up his strong legs and wide shoulders.

"You done?" Val smiled down at me. She held out a hand, her hazel eyes sparkling. A light sheen covered her forehead.

"Yes, thank you." I forced my gaze to stop following Flint.

Val moved around the table, collecting everyone's dishes.

Just as she finished, Pete walked into the dining hall with my bag and Flint in tow. I stood so abruptly my chair scraped loudly against the floor. I raced to Pete, grabbed my pack before he could say anything and knelt down. I opened the zippered front pocket.

A relieved sigh escaped me.

It was still there.

My fingers curled around the smooth metal. I carefully extracted the white gold chain bracelet. It glinted in the light. My eyes misted over when I grasped the small charm dangling from the chain. It was in the shape of a heart with an inscription reading, *Love You Forever*, etched into its side. It was the only piece of jewelry I'd been wearing when I woke in Rapid City.

The only proof that someone, somewhere, cared for me.

An emotion, so deep it was silly, coursed through me. In reality, this was simply a piece of metal. Useless. Unable to serve me in any way. But to me, it was so much more than that. Someone in this world knew me and was possibly looking for me. This proved that I wasn't completely alone.

I blinked back the tears before anyone saw them. Putting the bracelet back in the pocket, I zippered it carefully closed. I did that every time after I admired the small piece of jewelry, so I knew I wouldn't lose it. The chain was so fragile. A sharp snag and I knew the clasp would break.

I stood and slung my backpack over my shoulder. It was time to head out. Little Raven waited. "Thank you, Pete and Val. I really appreciate the great meal, but I best be going."

"Go where?" Val asked.

"Back to Little Raven."

"But your friend just booked two cabins for the night," Pete said. "Besides, I told you that you could stay here."

"What friend?" I asked.

Flint crossed his arms. My body turned toward him, as if on its own accord. I felt it again, that strange feeling of safety. *What is it about this guy?*

"I booked cabins for all of us," Flint said. "Including you."

All I did was stare. My tongue refused to work.

"You don't need to leave," Flint added quietly. Something flickered in his gaze, but it disappeared before I could decipher it. "You can stay here tonight, and we'll give you a ride back into town tomorrow."

"You will?"

"Yes."

My will instantly crumbled. I was surprised at how quickly it happened. I forgot that I was dirty and unsightly, and I completely forgot how important it was for me to get back to Little Raven. Unconsciously, I took a step toward him. Realizing what I was doing, I stopped myself.

"Um, okay." I tried to sound more coherent, but his eyes disrupted all electrical activity in my brain.

"Glad that's settled," Pete sighed. "Now, if y'all follow me. I'll take you to your cabins for the night."

One by one, everyone stood. Slowly, the tension eased. I didn't know why everyone was so tense to begin with. I sneaked a glance at Flint again. Even though he walked on the other side of the group, I still felt him, actually *felt* him, like a subtle undercurrent of energy flowed out of him.

I shook my head. I must be more sleep deprived than I thought. Nobody could pour out energy, and whatever it was that caused my strange reaction to him, it couldn't create energy between us.

Or could it?

CHAPTER FIVE

After Pete led us to the cabins, he bid us goodnight. The entire group crowded into the living room of one cabin, even though the guys had rented the cabin next door.

I shuffled uncertainly among them and tried not to admire Flint's height. He was easily the tallest in the group. I barely came to his shoulders. Luckily, he and Di were whispering again so he didn't notice my curious stares. Everyone else eyed me, though. Mica seemed particularly interested in cornering me, if her grin and shining brown eyes were any indication.

I scooted out of the room to check out the sleeping arrangements before Mica could pounce.

There were two bedrooms. One with two sets of bunk beds, the other with two queen beds. Plenty of room for Jacinda, Mica, Di and me. I spent longer than necessary in the bedrooms, giving everyone time to break up for the night. When I returned to the living room, though, they were still there. Except now everyone sat. Apparently, nobody was turning in.

Mica and Jacinda *both* looked up expectantly when I stepped into the room. Jacinda even scooted over to make room for me on the couch.

Great. Now what do they want to know? I groaned inwardly thinking about the questions to come.

"Um, I think I'm gonna clean up." I made a beeline for the bathroom and closed the door behind me. Part of me wanted to sink against the door and crumble to the floor. Between the stress of today, my reaction to Flint, and this strange group, I was exhausted. However, if I did pass out again that would bring the cavalry running.

I sighed and pushed away from the door.

The only good thing about being trapped in this tiny room? I could shower. Crisp, white towels and complimentary soaps and shampoos garnished the shelves. My eyes landed on the tub, shower combo.

I didn't waste any time stripping my clothes. When I stepped under the shower's hot spray, I understood for the first time what bliss felt like. I was currently well fed, had a roof over my head and was now taking a hot shower. Never in the four months of my known existence had I ever experienced any of those three.

I showered for a long time. Longer than I needed to. Partly, because it felt so good, but also because I wanted to avoid more probing questions.

By the time I got out, the water had cooled and thick steam covered the mirror. I ran my hand over the glass. The image staring back at me left me dumbstruck.

I was clean, actually *clean*.

My complexion was paler than I'd realized. White skin with a dusting of freckles across the nose and large green eyes stared back at me. I turned my head a few times. It was the first time I'd been able to study myself like this. Before, I'd always been covered in dirt and grime.

Turning my torso, I was surprised at how long my hair was. Long, crimson locks hung down my back in damp waves. Without filth coating them, they sprung up when I pulled a few strands. Since I didn't have a comb, I ran my fingers through my hair. Luckily, since I used so much conditioner, they easily threaded through.

Despite being clean, my face was still frighteningly thin and my ribs and hip bones jutted out. Sighing, I put my filthy clothes back on, turned off the light and eased the door open. I stopped short when I rounded the corner. *All* of them still waited in the living room, even Flint.

Jet let out a whistle. "Look at you, Red. You sure clean up well."

"Oh, um, thanks."

Di sat near Flint. Her dark eyes trained on me. "Want to talk for a little bit?"

I gulped. *Talk? Is that what they call the grilling questions?* "Ah…I'm going to turn in. It's been a long day."

I hurried past them and escaped into the first bedroom off the hallway. It was the room with bunk beds. Stripping everything off except my shirt, I leaped onto the top bed and dove under the covers. The feel of them temporarily distracted me. They were soft and smooth. I sighed. They felt so nice.

Turning on my side, I stared at the wall. A few minutes passed and my heart rate slowed. My lids actually started to close as exhaustion set in when I heard the door open. I stiffened but made myself relax and fake a few snores.

"Lena?" I recognized Mica's voice. Quiet footsteps approach the bed.

"Lena?" she said more loudly.

I let out a few deep breaths and another snore or two. I felt her presence close to the bed and had no idea what she wanted. I wasn't sure I wanted to know.

Mica eventually sighed and turned. She padded to the door and closed it. Darkness once again enveloped the room. I let out a sigh of relief. A few more minutes passed and when I realized nobody would be bothering me again, I sank into oblivion.

I BOLTED AWAKE. Darkness surrounded me. It took a second to get my bearings. I wasn't outside. That was obvious from the lack of wind, smells and nighttime sounds. So if I wasn't outside, where was I?

I ran my fingers along something rough yet soft. Whatever it was, I lay on it. Frowning, I felt the bumps and grooves and eventually deduced that I was on a couch. *How the heck did I get on a couch?*

Fumbling in the dark, I found a light switch on a table lamp. The room flooded with harsh light. I was in a living room.

The cabin!

It all came crashing back. The ride with Pete, meeting the group and going to sleep in the cabin. But I'd gone to sleep in a bed. I was sure of it. The top bunk in one of the bedrooms to be precise. I groaned as I realized how I'd gotten out here.

I sleep walked again.

Over the past four months, I'd sleep walked a few times, usually when I went to bed late in a particularly strange place. I sighed. At least I hadn't wandered outside.

I turned the light off and fumbled my way back to the bedroom. Soft snores greeted me. It appeared Mica was asleep in the lower bunk. Red, glowing numbers on the bedside clock drew my attention. 2:17. It was essentially the middle of the night.

Instead of returning to bed, I paused. My thoughts drifted to what I'd discovered only twelve hours ago.

Little Raven.

I knew Flint said they'd give me a ride into town this morning, but morning felt like a long way off. Answers possibly lay in Little Raven roughly fifteen miles away. *Fifteen miles.* That was it. That distance would only take about five hours of walking, maybe a little more since the terrain varied so much. And even though this group said they'd give me a ride, what if they slept in? Or, what if they changed their minds?

Then what? I'd have wasted another half day waiting for others to help me when I could have done it myself. Five hours from now, the group probably wouldn't be up, but *I* could be striding into the town center.

I silently collected my things.

THE WALK BACK to the county road was cold and filled with nighttime sounds. Crickets, distant owls, an occasional coyote or wolf. The chilly breeze felt alive in its own way. It caressed my skin, getting shivers out of me until I set a steady pace. I'd put my warmest clothes on. A ragged sweatshirt, knit cap and my worn jeans. They kept me warm enough until I disappeared into the forest. Then, darkness was everywhere and the temperature plummeted.

I kept my eyes on the light colored line in front of me. Moonlight filtered through the canopy, illuminating the road. Still, it was so dark. Without city lights and interstate traffic headlights, the world became an inky sea at night.

As gravel crunched underfoot with every step I took, my thoughts inevitably drifted to Flint. His image swam in my mind. That beautiful, chestnut colored hair, those dark eyes flecked with gold, and a firm mouth that seemed ready to tense at any moment. I sighed. I had no idea why he pulled at me like he did, but there was no use thinking about him. I'd never see him again.

I abruptly stopped. My feet skidded in the gravel. *I'll never see him again.*

I breathed in and out deeply a few times. I even closed my eyes. Cold air pierced my lungs and eventually cleared my head.

Just forget him, Lena! The instinct had led me to Little Raven. Therefore, answers lay in Little Raven. It didn't matter that my heart wanted to run back to the ranch. What mattered right now was finding answers. I *needed* to know what happened to me.

I resumed walking and pushed thoughts of Flint farther

and farther behind me with every step I took. When dawn finally crested the horizon, the blister on my heel split wide open again. The pain helped. It kept me from thinking of him.

About an hour later, the end of the forest appeared. I hurried until the tree's branches and canopy released me. Morning sun shimmered off the town's rooftops in the distance. I grinned.

I was here.

I PICKED UP a jog and didn't stop until I reached the road going into the town center. A few cars passed me on the street. The sound of distant vehicles starting filled the quiet. People were waking up, getting ready for work, heading out for the day. The town was coming to life once again as a new day was born. A day full of possibilities.

I turned down the first street and ducked into a store. A clock hung on the wall. Just past eight. For a brief second, I pictured Flint waking up, stretching in bed, his large hands running through his hair. I pushed the image away. *Not important, Lena!*

Bright sunlight pierced the store's eastern windows. It appeared I was in an outdoor store. Bicycles, kayaks and rows of gear stacked the walls.

An eager shop assistant approached me when I stood there, unmoving. She was dressed in a navy vest sporting the store's logo. She didn't look older than sixteen.

"Morning," she said.

"Good morning," I replied.

"Can I help you with anything? We have sales stuff in the back."

"No. I'm not here to buy anything."

"Oh."

She turned to leave, but I reached out. *She'll do.* "Ah, wait, can I ask you something?"

"Sure!" Her smile revealed a mouth full of braces.

"Do you recognize me?"

Her head cocked. "What do you mean?"

"I mean," I leaned closer. "Have you ever seen me before? Or do you know anyone that looks like me?" I pulled my hair around my shoulders. It's color was pretty noticeable. Maybe she'd recognize that.

Her eyebrows rose. "Um, no. I guess I don't know what you mean."

"Well, do any of your parent's friends have a daughter, or sister, or niece, or know someone, that *looks* like me?"

She shook her head. "Uh, no."

"Are you sure? No one even remotely like me?"

She shook her head again.

"Do you know everyone in town?"

"Yeah. Except for the tourists." She hooked a thumb at a couple standing in front of a mirror. They were trying on hats. Rather large hats.

"But you don't know *me*?" I persisted.

"No," she said firmly.

Her answers weren't what I hoped for, but I smiled brightly and reasoned she was too young. She probably didn't know *everyone*.

"Okay, never mind. Thanks for your time."

"Sure!" She scurried away.

I frowned at how stupid I'd been. It would be someone older, who'd been alive longer than a decade, who would know me. All I needed was one local who recognized me and could tell me where my family lived. I spun around and searched for another employee.

Not spotting anyone, I wandered through the store, dipping between racks of outdoor jackets and peering around walls of biking equipment. At the back of the store, a sales assistant was stocking tent bags into cubby holes. Gray hair peppered his head. He also had glasses. Failing eyesight was a good sign.

"Um, excuse me." I tapped his shoulder.

He turned and smiled pleasantly. The movement lifted his bushy mustache. I waited for recognition to spring into his eyes, but he maintained the same bland expression. "Yes, can I help you?"

"Um, I just wondered, if…you…err, recognized me?"

He frowned and pushed his falling glasses up his nose. "Sorry, no. Should I know you?" His wrinkles deepened into a frown.

Perhaps I'd gone too far in the opposite direction. Maybe he had Alzheimer's, so didn't recognize *himself* in the morning. I paused. I knew I was being ridiculous. The guy couldn't be older than sixty. He obviously didn't know me, and he obviously didn't have Alzheimer's.

"No. I thought I recognized you. My mistake," I replied.

He smiled again and turned back to the shelf he was organizing.

I didn't move. Surely he would know something. I waited a moment and then tapped his shoulder again.

He turned. "Yes?"

"Can I ask you something else?" I asked bluntly.

"Okay."

"This is a small town, right?"

"Yes."

"Where everyone knows everyone?"

"Yes."

"But you don't recognize me?"

He shook his head warily.

"And nobody has gone missing here?"

He shook his head again. "No. Miss, what are you talking about?"

I could tell he was trying to stay polite. "So nobody that meets my description went missing about four months ago?"

"No, not that I know of."

"No? Are you sure?"

43

"I'm fairly sure."

I paused for a minute. *No? Really?*

"Miss, are you okay?" His voice took on a concerned note. He stepped closer.

I forced a smile and backed up before I made a bigger fool of myself. "I'm sorry. I'll let you get back to work."

I turned and ran to the front and out the door. The morning air hit me with cool force. I inhaled a few deep breaths and told myself that maybe the sales assistants at this store were new to town. Maybe they weren't from here despite what they claimed. That had to be it.

I waited on the sidewalk and tapped my foot on the ground. Surely someone would know me. I knew this place held something. It had to.

I just had to find it.

CHAPTER SIX

An hour later, I stopped asking people if they knew me. I'd wandered into coffee shops, restaurants and other stores, intersecting dozens of people, some tourists. I only talked to the locals. They all claimed to not know me.

I'd kept trying regardless, hoping those I asked had simply forgotten me. However, when I practically scared the socks off an elderly woman, who claimed she'd been born in this town, had never left it, and didn't recognize me or anyone who looked remotely like me, I gave up. Apparently, my anxiety was starting to show. People took one look at me and hurried away.

Fresh air carried in the morning breeze as I stood on the sidewalk. Biting my lip, I considered my options. Maybe Little Raven *didn't* hold people I knew. Maybe there was something else here. Perhaps an object that I was supposed to find?

My shoulders slumped as a pang of remorse struck me. I had hoped for something else entirely, something much more precious.

I had hoped my family lived here.

I buried that longing as deep as it would go. Another sharp stab rocked my core. I ignored it.

It had to be mid-morning by now. Patio furniture was being set up outside at the café across the street. Doors were being propped open to touristy shops, and chatter from people talking within filtered out. With each second, the foot traffic increased as the town grew more alive.

Taking a deep breath, I focused. So if it *was* an object I was supposed to find, the only way I could possibly locate it was through the instinct – that subtle feeling that had led me hundreds of miles from Rapid City to here. I could only hope it would lead me to whatever I was supposed to find.

Closing my eyes, I waited for that hum to resonate.

It didn't.

I concentrated harder, searching for something, *anything* that would lead me in the right direction. Nothing happened.

A car honked. My eyes snapped open, and I jumped back. I'd almost wandered into an intersection. I hurried back to the sidewalk and retreated into an alleyway by a brick building. Pungent scents from a nearby dumpster filled the air. I wrinkled my nose but stayed put. Away from the commotion, I closed my eyes. This time I retreated to that calm place within. The place that always made the instinct hum to life.

Breathe in, breathe out. It's got to be in here somewhere.

Nothing.

Clenching my hands into fists, I took another deep breath. Hyperventilating wouldn't help. I tried again. Still nothing.

"No!" I whispered.

I dropped my backpack and sank to the ground. Gasping breaths shook me. I huddled on the pavement against the brick building. The ground was cold through my jeans as I drew my knees up. I didn't care.

Where was the instinct? Did Little Raven hold nothing for me? Had the instinct been wrong? Had *I* been wrong? Had there ever *been* an instinct? Or was it something I made up to give me purpose?

Tears sprang into my eyes as I cradled my head in my

hands. This time, I couldn't stop them. I had no idea what I was going to do. I had counted on finding something here, feeling something, or at least recognizing something, but nothing like that had happened.

I began crying in earnest, silently at first but then my whole body shook. I was completely lost. Lost with no answers, no home, and no way of knowing what to do next.

Wrapping my arms around my shins, I laid my head against my knees and sobbed. Cold tears streamed down my cheeks. A shuffle of feet on the sidewalk sounded, as if someone skidded to a stop.

"Thank God," someone murmured. "Shh. It's okay."

The next thing I knew, strong warm arms encircled me. Before I had a chance to react, I was lifted from the ground. I began to flail and opened my mouth to scream, but the sight that greeted me left me speechless.

Flint's dark, bottomless eyes gazed down at me. "You don't need to say anything."

I didn't comprehend his words. I just saw his eyes and focused on his voice. I needed to. My insides reeled. I had nothing, absolutely *nothing* and I didn't see any way it would ever come right.

Flint carried me to the Suburban parked several blocks over. He placed me in the passenger's seat. I was like a useless doll in his arms, but he folded my limbs carefully and clicked the seat belt in place before tossing my bag in the back.

We were already driving through the forest before I realized we'd left town. I didn't know how long it took us to return to the ranch. The entire journey was a blur. When we arrived at Hideaway Hills, Flint parked the Suburban outside the cabin, and before I knew what was happening, he was carrying me up the front steps.

I vaguely heard voices around me. A mix of male and female voices with different tones and pitches.

"Lena, are you okay?"

"Thank goodness she didn't get far!"

"Where'd you find her, Flint?"

Jacinda appeared in front of me. I tried to smile. She looked so pretty in her pink top. I reached out to touch it. So soft.

"Silk," she whispered and winked.

I was set down on something. It was soft but then something hard pressed against my side. I sank into it. An arm encircled my shoulders and pulled me into the hardness. The next thing I knew, a woman was kneeling in front of me.

"Can you hear me?" Di asked.

I nodded.

"Tell me your name."

My name? "Lena," I mumbled.

"Can you tell me where you are?"

Slowly, my foggy brain began functioning. The living room was familiar, and I sat on a couch. *When did I get back here?* "Um, I'm in the cabin."

"What cabin?"

"The cabin on the ranch."

"And what day is it?" she persisted.

I frowned and slowly the wheels in my mind sped up. "Sometime in August?"

She seemed happy with that answer and glanced at someone beside me. "It's time."

"Yeah," a deep voice rumbled. "I know. We should have told her last night, even when she pretended to be sleeping."

Whoever had spoken was seated right beside me. I slowly became aware that I was pressed into his side, his warm arm around me. I leaned closer. His scent registered. Spice, wood and tangerines.

Flint.

His dark gaze met mine. "Everything's going to be fine. You'll see." His arm tightened around my shoulders, but for the life of me I didn't understand what he meant.

CHAPTER SEVEN

"Is everyone here?" Di asked.

Jacinda, Mica, Jet and Jasper scooted closer. They'd moved the furniture to form a half circle around me. When had that happened?

"Lena?" Di said. Her dark eyes were so serious. She always seemed serious.

"Yeah?"

"Are you doing okay?"

"Sure." But I wasn't okay. I was anything but okay. Everything I'd been working toward for the past four months had been for nothing. Absolutely nothing. My throat tightened.

"You need to focus," Di said. "This is important. We have something to tell you."

"What?"

She paused. "Let's start with this, what brought you to Colorado?"

What brought me to Colorado? Are they really going to start with the questions again? For a moment, I didn't answer, but Di's gaze held mine and she eventually raised her dark eyebrows.

"I dunno. Just traveling around." I gave her the response I

gave all strangers when asked that question. Soon, I'd be saying things like that again. Just as soon as I figured out what to do, or where to go from here. The tightness clenched around my throat again.

"So, there wasn't a special reason?" Di persisted.

I shook my head.

Her frown deepened. "I know it's hard to tell the truth. We all felt like you when we met the group. Untrusting. Guarded. Scared of so many unknowns, but there's something you need to know. We all came here for the same reason as you. To find something."

I stiffened. "What did you think you'd find?"

"Answers that would explain who we are and what happened to us four months ago."

I stared at her. Numb shock crept through me.

"Did you really come out here to travel? Or were you hoping to find something too?"

I shook my head, the movement clumsy. *How does she know?*

"Trust us," Flint whispered. His scent swam around me. Something in me calmed. The feeling of being completely safe cloaked my skin, and I floated back to the surface of reality.

"How did you know?" I asked Di.

She smiled. "Because you're one of us."

"One of you?"

Di took her watch off. The others did the same. It struck me how this group seemed very concerned with keeping time. They all wore watches on their left wrists.

"May I see your wrist?" Di asked.

I held out my left arm. My thin, white limb appeared ghostly beside Di's olive complexion.

Di pulled my forearm into her lap and flipped it over. She traced the tattoo on my left inner wrist. The small symbol a perfect circle divided into quarters, like a pie cut into four pieces. The tattoo I'd had since that first morning. Another mystery I couldn't solve.

"Where did you get this?" she asked. The tattoo was small, maybe a centimeter in diameter and done in fine print, dark ink.

"Um, I don't know," I answered honestly. "I've always just had it."

"I've got one too." She flipped her left wrist over, the one she always wore a watch on. Her left, inner wrist revealed a different symbol. It was also done in the same fine print ink and about a centimeter in diameter. Hers was different. Instead of a circle divided into quarters, it was a full circle with a cross attached to the outside circle's perimeter.

"You have one too?" I asked incredulously.

"Yes."

"Isn't that the symbol for a female?"

"It is."

"And I've got the symbol for a male." Flint flipped his left arm over, revealing a tattoo like Di's, but instead of the cross attached to the circle, there was an arrow.

"When did you get those?" I asked.

"We've always had them," Di said. One by one, Jacinda, Mica, Jasper and Jet flipped their wrists over. I leaned forward, shaking my head. They all had tattoos. Tattoos similar in size and ink to mine.

"Mine's pretty intricate." Jacinda leaned closer. She had two brackets, back to back, connected by a cross – the cross had a small circle at the bottom of it. Unlike Di and Flint's, I didn't recognize hers.

Jet and Jasper had similar symbols. Jasper's was a curly shaped 4, and Jet's was a curly shaped lowercase H, except the vertical line in the *h* had a horizontal bar through the top. I didn't recognize theirs either.

Mica's shining brown eyes met mine when I studied her symbol. It was a U with an upside down cross slashed through it vertically.

"Do you see what I'm trying to tell you?" Di said. "You're one of us. We're just like you. We all woke up four months ago in various cities around the U.S. with no memory of who we are or where we came from, and we all had these tattoos. Isn't that what happened to you?"

My eyes widened.

"You felt the *pull* too, didn't you? The desire to search for something, ever since that first morning?"

I sat numbly, too shocked to speak. *The pull? Was she talking about the instinct?*

"We all felt that *pull* to travel here and search for answers. That's what brought us here," Di continued.

I paused and stared at her warily. Was it possible this wasn't a game? That what she said was true? I glanced at Flint. His dark, solemn eyes regarded me steadily, and I knew, *knew* to the deepest part of my soul that he wouldn't lie to me. I didn't know how I knew that, but I did. What Di was saying was real.

"But how does that make any sense?" I asked.

"It doesn't," she said. "We were hoping to find answers here too, but so far, we haven't found anything."

I shook my head. "Wait a minute. How did you all find each other? How come I've been alone all these months but none of you have been?"

Di put her watch back on. "We were alone too, at first. When we woke up we were hundreds of miles away from one another, but then we found each other."

"How?"

"Is there something you can do, that makes you different to everyone else?" she asked, ignoring my question.

"What do you mean?"

She waved her hand. "Like an ability? Or a gift? Something that's unique to you, that only you can do?"

I knew what she was asking. I thought about what I could do, the thing that made me different. I let my gaze go fuzzy.

Colorful clouds appeared around all six of them. I snapped my vision back to normal. "How do you know about that?"

"We all have special abilities, gifts, as I've started to call them. It only makes sense that you have one too."

"So, what can you do?" I asked warily.

"I can see the future."

"What?"

"I know, I can't explain it either, but it's true. I saw you coming here. Do you understand? I *saw* you. I've been seeing you for months, and I knew that you'd be coming to us, here, in Colorado." She paused. "I thought we'd find you in Little Raven. Yesterday, when we picked you up on the road, it was sheer luck we found you. If Flint hadn't suggested we drive around, it may have been weeks before I'd been able to pinpoint a location on you again."

My mouth dropped. The image of their Suburban driving on the county road flashed through my mind. That hadn't been a coincidence?

"How is that possible?" I asked.

Di shrugged. "How is anything possible?"

"And the rest of you can do other things?"

Jacinda nodded. "For me it's hearing. I could hear this conversation up at the house if I wanted to."

"You could?"

"Or I could ignore it. I can turn it on and off."

"Really? What can you hear now?"

She closed her eyes, her long lashes resting on her cheeks. "There's a scratching sound under the front porch. It's small, maybe a mouse." She cocked her head. "Several conversations in the cabins across the driveway. They're talking about tomorrow. A humming sound in the distance, it's a bird flying—"

"She could go on all day," Mica interrupted.

Jacinda's eyes flashed open. She shrugged and smiled.

"For me, it's sight!" Mica said, pulling my attention to her.

"I can see better than any other human." She grinned.

"How well can you see?"

"I can read twelve point font from three hundred yards."

I gaped.

Mica grinned broader. "We tried it."

"If it's Courier she can read it at three hundred and ten yards," Jet stated in a bored tone. "But if it's Perpetua, it's only two hundred and eighty."

"*And* I can see in the dark," Mica added.

"And you two?" I asked the twins.

"Jet and I are telepathic," Jasper said.

"Telepathic?"

"Yeah, we can read each other's minds," Jet explained.

"I know what it means."

Jasper laughed, apparently finding my stern expression funny. "Jet and I have always been able to communicate with each other, right from the moment we woke up."

"Seriously?"

"Yeah," Jasper said. "Imagine how it felt to wake up, not knowing who you are, where you came from, or what you were doing, and to have a voice in your head. Jet even called me *The Voice*. He wouldn't believe I was a real person until we met."

Jet rolled his eyes.

I shook my head and thought about that first morning. The cold alleyway, the smells of rotting garbage. I shuddered. I hated thinking about that day. "So what is he thinking right now?"

Jasper eyed his brother. "Right now, he's wondering how long this will take since we never ate breakfast."

I glanced at Flint. My breath hitched at the sight. "And you?"

Flint shrugged. "I'm strong and fast."

Mica laughed loudly. "That's the understatement of the year."

Meeting Flint's gaze, my concentration waned. Once again,

I wanted to sink into him. Like Alice tumbling down the rabbit hole. I shook myself and then remembered that strange feeling of power I'd sensed in him last night.

"How strong and fast?"

He smiled, affording me a glimpse of perfect, white teeth. "Maybe I'll show you some time."

I snapped my gaze away. I needed to be in control of my senses right now. It still hadn't sunk in, though, what everyone was telling me, that I wasn't alone. That I wasn't the only one who'd woken up with no memory of who I was or where I came from. That this strange ability I had didn't make me unique. That there were others like me.

"What about you, Lena?" Jacinda asked. "What can you do?"

Di leaned forward. Her short dark hair fell across her cheek. She tucked it behind one ear. "What's your gift? I've been dying to know."

I smiled faintly. Had it really only been eight hours ago that I'd left this cabin to walk back to Little Raven? That now seemed like days.

"Wait a minute," I said. "Why was I drawn to Little Raven? That's where the instinct led me, but when I returned this morning, there was nothing there. I couldn't feel it anymore."

"We were all drawn to this general area," Di said. "Although, none of us know why. Once we all found each other, though, the pulling feeling disappeared."

"So, now that I'm in this area and I found all of you, I *have* found what I was searching for?"

"As far as we can figure, yes," Di replied.

That would explain why nobody in town knew me and why the instinct had disappeared.

"Well?" Di said impatiently. "What's your gift?"

I took a breath. "I see clouds, or at least, I call them clouds."

"Like in the sky?" Jet asked.

"No, around people. I call them clouds because they're like a haze that surrounds people's shoulders. They're not really opaque, more like a wispy fog. It tells me if they're good or bad, if I can trust them."

"Like an aura," Di said, "And you can see that in all of us?"

"Yes, but with all of you it's different. Normally, people's clouds are white, gray or black. The whiter the cloud, the better a person's soul is, the darker the cloud, the more evil a person is. But you're all different. You all have colors." I remembered my reaction when I'd first met them on the county road. I'd been so confused by it.

"We do?" Di said.

"Yeah, nobody else has ever had colors before."

"What colors are we?" Mica asked.

I switched my vision and again marveled at the rainbow display.

"You all have blue in your clouds, but everyone also has a unique color. You have pink mixed with the blue, Mica, and you have violet." I turned to Jacinda.

"What about mine?" Di asked.

"Gold and blue."

"And the guys?" Di asked.

"Jet's blue is mixed with red, Jasper's with yellow, and Flint's with orange."

"So blue mixed with all the colors of the rainbow," Di commented.

I flipped my vision back to normal. The colorful clouds disappeared.

"Interesting." Di tapped her finger to her chin.

"What color are you?" Jasper asked.

His question took me completely by surprise. "My color?"

"Yeah. What color's your cloud?" Jet asked.

I frowned. "Um, I don't know."

"How can you not know?" Jet asked.

"Because I've never looked at it."

"You haven't?" Mica said.

I shook my head, not believing I'd never bothered. "I always assumed it was white. I know I'm a good person, and I never had any reason to think my cloud would be different from anybody else's."

"Well, don't dilly dally!" Mica said. "Go look!"

I got up and raced to the bathroom mirror. As soon as I switched my vision, what billowed around my shoulders made me smile. A beautiful bright green mixed with blue stared back at me. Any doubt I may have carried over being connected to this group vanished. Di was right. I was one of them.

I returned to the living room, smiling.

"Well?" Mica asked.

"Green and blue."

"I knew it'd be like ours." Mica grinned.

I sat beside Flint. His arm once again settled over my shoulders. I liked the weight of it. I also liked its possessive feel.

"Okay," Di said. "Now that you know about us, there's no need to hide things from you."

I frowned. "Why did you hide this from me? Why didn't you tell me right away?"

Jet quirked an eyebrow. "Do you not remember your reaction to us?"

"Yeah," Jasper agreed. "It was pretty obvious you didn't know what to make of us, and I've never seen someone hide her tattoo so fast when we asked about it."

I ducked my head sheepishly. They were right. After months of hitchhiking and lying about myself to strangers, it'd been an instinctual reaction to guard myself against others.

Jacinda put her hand over mine, her honey brown eyes soft. "What they're trying to say, is that we've found it's easier to wait before we tell a new person. Most of us had similar reactions to yours when we met the group, although, not quite as severe." She said the last bit in a very soothing voice and patted my hand.

"Sorry," I mumbled. Maybe if I hadn't thought they were so strange, I would have been more open to trusting them.

"Don't be," Jacinda said. "We all felt untrusting initially."

"You did?"

Jasper smirked. "Jet punched me when I told him it was me in his head. It's not like me being his twin gave it away or anything."

Mica laughed. "He seriously freaked out!"

"We did try to tell you sooner," Di interjected. "Last night, we wanted to tell you when we got to this cabin, but then you bolted for the bathroom and pretended to go to sleep right after that. It was obvious you weren't ready."

"Yeah," Mica piped in. "They tried telling me right after they picked me up, but I almost jumped out of the vehicle." She tucked a strand of short, brown hair behind her ear. Apparently, she found this funny now because she grinned.

"I didn't take it well either," Jacinda said. "I was told ten minutes after I was picked up, and it was a lot to take in. Can you imagine how you would have felt when we picked you up? If the second the door closed, we showed you our tattoos, or told you we had no memory of who we were, and had been waiting and looking for you? How do you think you would have reacted?"

I tried to picture it. I couldn't. I was already uncomfortable from what I'd seen in their clouds. Having them spill all of that information on me would have probably had me running for the hills. Literally. I shrugged. "Yeah, I guess it would have made it harder."

"So we started waiting a few hours, sometimes a day," Di explained. "Just so the newbies could become used to us and know we're not crazy."

I started putting two and two together. "You all arrived

here at different times then?"

Di nodded her head. "I got here first, maybe two weeks after I woke up. I kept seeing this place and images of everyone. I knew I needed to find you all and pull us together. After me it was Flint, then Mica followed by Jacinda. After her, it was Jasper, then Jet a few days later. The twins got here about two weeks ago."

"And now we don't need to hide anything from you!" Mica stated loudly. "Now we can be ourselves again."

"That is, until the new girl gets here," Di warned.

I cocked my head. "The new girl?"

"That's the other thing," Di said. "There's another one of us. She's coming in a few weeks. She's the last."

CHAPTER EIGHT

I sank into the couch. *There are more of us?*

"There's another girl...like me? Who's out there right now, trying to follow the *pull?*"

"Yes," Di replied.

"Who is she? Where is she? What's her name?"

Di shook her head. "I don't know her name or who she is, but she looks young and always appears afraid."

"Where's she's coming from?"

"I think Texas, but I'm not sure. She's been on the road for so long, but she's always on a form of public transport. She's done a lot of traveling in the wrong direction."

I frowned. Poor girl. I knew how she felt. It was awful, traveling alone, with no one to help you. The added stress of not having an identity or any idea of *why* you were traveling made it harder.

"I hope she gets here safely," I said.

"She will." Di leaned back and crossed her arms. "In two to three weeks, she'll be here. And unlike you, she doesn't seem impulsive."

"How do you know I'm impulsive?"

Di rolled her eyes. "My visions of you changed rapidly. Every time you made an impulsive decision, my hold on you would disappear. You've been very hard to track."

"Oh." That did sound like me.

"You know, you did disappear in the middle of the night," Mica added.

I remembered my sudden need to find answers, *now*. I nodded sheepishly. "Yeah. I did."

Mica sighed. "Don't make a habit of it. You're not easy to find."

"How did you find me this morning?"

"Flint," Mica said.

Flint shrugged. "I guessed you went back to Little Raven, so I went looking for you."

"More like freaked out, jumped in the car and drove off before any of us could join you," Mica retorted. "I've never seen you panic like that."

Flint tensed.

He panicked that I disappeared?

"Anyway," Di said. "Now, that we know you're safe and we've told you about us, we can get on with things until the new girl arrives."

"Hmm." I was still reeling that Flint had panicked about me being missing. A warm feeling coated my insides.

"Do you have questions about anything else?" Di asked.

I shook myself, trying to clear my head. "So if you can see the future, do you know what happens to us?"

Di frowned. "Unfortunately, no."

"No?"

She shook her head. "I've seen snippets of the eight of us in the future, brief visions here and there. In most of them we're here, on the ranch, so I know we're not leaving anytime soon, but I know that will eventually change. I've had a few visions of us in some desert, but I'm not sure where, and I've seen us in a large city or two, but I wasn't able to see enough to know what cities they were."

"Oh." So we'd leave here eventually and all travel somewhere together? "Do you know anything else about our future?"

Di shook her head. "Not at the moment, but that could change. I can't control my visions. They come as they want and show me things unreliably."

"Maybe the new girl will know more." As scary as everything was, I felt better that I wasn't alone.

"Yeah, don't count on it." Jet lounged back in his chair and ran a hand through his dark curly hair. Some dirt fell off his boots when he propped them on the hassock. "Personally, I think we're all screwed. There's nothing normal about any of this, and the fact that we can all do something no other human can, seems like a bad omen to me."

"What do you mean?" I asked warily.

"Jet," Di interrupted. "We don't know anything. No need to get anyone worried."

"Yeah." Jacinda clasped her hands tightly in her lap. Sharp blue veins stuck out from the backs of her hands. "Di's right. No one needs to be worried."

"But don't tell me you haven't wondered?" Jet persisted. "Eight people with no memories, matching tattoos and this messed up desire to flee to the same region in Colorado? Not to mention unusual, even unique, physical abilities? And what about the fake ID's? Or the money? Or the fancy condos? You're not gonna tell me that's not a bad omen. And you're not gonna tell me it's all an innocent coincidence. Something's going on here and if you ask me – it's not good."

I swallowed uneasily while Jacinda looked ready to pass out. Di was scowling, but then something Jet said caught my attention.

"Wait. ID's? Money? *Condos?*"

"Right, that's something I wanted to ask you," Di said. "Didn't you wake up in a luxury condominium with money and identification?"

"Um, no, I pretty much woke up opposite to that."

She frowned. "We've been wondering how you were homeless. It doesn't make any sense when we woke up with money." She shook her head. "If you didn't wake up in a condominium, where *did* you wake up?"

"In an alleyway in Rapid City."

Di's eyes bulged. "In an alleyway, *outside?*"

"Yeah."

Perplexed expressions covered everyone's faces. "And you didn't have any cash or personal documents on you?" Di asked.

"No, nothing."

Di cocked her head. "I wonder why that is, since the rest of us all woke up in similar conditions. Except Flint. His was a little different."

Before I could ask what was different about Flint's, Di said, "That's bizarre that you woke up outside."

"So, the rest of you woke up in a condo? With money?" I felt strangely left out.

"Yes," Jacinda nodded. "We all woke up in furnished luxury penthouses or condos, with money, identification and cell phones on the kitchen counters."

"Of course, none of us knew how we got there or why we had those things," Di added, "but that's how we woke up, and even stranger, the properties *belonged* to us. The legal paperwork was also on the counter. The deeds were in our names."

"Why did you all have money but I didn't?" The feeling of being excluded grew.

"I don't know," Di said, "but we all had ten thousand in cash, a bank card with five million dollars in our accounts, a driver's license, a social security card, a birth certificate and the paperwork for the condos we owned. It was all neatly arranged on our kitchen counters in our mysteriously owned homes."

I thought back to that morning when I'd woken by the

dumpster in the alleyway. It would have been much less stressful if I'd had resources like that. "Jeez, that would have made life easier."

"But at least you were able to make your way here, without money. That's what matters," Jacinda said soothingly.

"I have some money." Granted, it was from people who gave it to me out of pity, insisting I take it, but it was still money. I paused as another thought struck me. "If you all have ID's then you do know your identity, right? You just don't remember it?"

Di eyed Flint. "No. I wish it was that easy, but all of our identification is fake. High quality fakes, but still fakes. Flint and I looked into it and found that the hospitals of our supposed births have no records of us, not to mention our Social Security numbers all belong to dead people."

My mouth dropped as I finally understood the enormity of what she was saying. "So, you're saying that something or someone set this all up?"

"It's the only way to explain it," Di said. "If we all woke with money, similar ID's and tattooed symbols, then we're obviously connected and someone knows about us. I doubt one of us did this. How could we?"

I was too shocked to move.

"See what I mean?" Jet said. "Bad omen."

I shivered.

Flint's side warmed beside me. "That's enough. I think we've explained what we need to right now. It's been a tough morning for Lena. She doesn't need to worry anymore."

"No." I shook off the bad feeling. "I want to know. Can I see the stuff you guys woke up with?"

Flint grunted in disapproval, but Di walked into her bedroom and returned with a large duffel bag. "Here." She handed it to me.

I unzipped it. My eyes widened when I saw the considerable amount of cash. "How much is in here?"

"Forty-eight thousand, eight hundred and four dollars. Plus or minus a few pennies," Flint replied. "We combined all of the money each of us had after we found one another."

"We call it the *pile*." Mica grinned. "There'd be more if Jet and Jacinda hadn't blown so much of theirs."

Jet held his hands up. "Hey, what's a brother supposed to do when he wakes up in Vegas?"

"Gambling and designer clothes are not a good way to spend our cash," Di said sharply.

Jacinda sighed. "I did buy most of my things on my debit card."

"Also not a good idea," Di replied. "Bank transactions can be tracked."

"Anyway, as I was trying to say…" Mica said loudly. "We also have almost thirty million in our bank accounts, minus what the Suburban cost and what Jacinda spent. And it grows by the day with all the interest!"

I pulled out a Ziplock bag that held the licenses and social security cards. Opening the bag, I thumbed through them. "Flint Smith." I studied Flint's license. The address was some rural route in Wyoming. "Di Johnson." I flipped to hers. Her address was in Wichita, Kansas. "Jacinda Jones from Phoenix, Arizona." I kept flipping. "Jasper Brown from Salt Lake City, Utah; Jet Davis from Las Vegas, Nevada; and Mica Wilson from El Paso, Texas." I frowned.

"Are those the cities all of you woke up in?" I asked.

"Yep," Mica replied.

I scanned the cards again. Each seemed to have a current picture along with fairly accurate height, weight and eye color. I studied all of the last names again. "Why do these last names seem familiar?"

"Because they're in the top eight most common last names in the U.S." Flint replied. "The other most common last names are Williams and Miller. My guess is your missing ID had one of those names. If you ever had an ID."

I thumbed through the cards again. "There are birth dates on these!"

"Yes," Di replied. "If those are correct, Flint's the oldest at twenty-four, followed by me at twenty-three, then Jacinda and the twins – also twenty-three. Mica's the youngest at twenty-one."

"You're all roughly the same age?"

"If those ages are correct, yes, we're all within a few years of one another," Di replied.

"So I'm probably around that age too? Maybe early twenties?"

"You look to be in your twenties," Jasper said.

"Yep, no wrinkles yet," Jet added.

I'm in my early twenties? Granted I didn't have proof, but most likely I was around the same age as everyone else. More than anything, I wished I knew why I'd woken outside and not in a condo. What I'd give to have documents like these! At least some identity semblance, even if it was fake, would be comforting.

"So this new girl is probably around our age too?" I asked.

"Most likely," Di replied.

I dug through the bag again. "Where are the cell phones?"

"We got rid of them," Di said. "Cell phones can be tracked. We didn't want to take the risk."

I gaped. "Right."

"See?" Jet said. "Can't be anything good."

I felt the blood drain from my face.

"Okay, we're done," Flint said. "This meeting's over. Everyone up."

The tone of his voice surprised me. It was almost protective sounding. His arm was still around me too, and I once again sensed that strange energy coming off him. It felt like heat mixed with power. I shook my head. *Weird.*

"Flint's right," Di said. "I think we've given Lena enough to think about."

Flint stood. His arm dropped from around me. "Jet, Jasper and Mica, I need you guys to stand up."

He moved away. Within seconds, the furniture was back to where it'd originally been. I stared in stunned disbelief. It was like a tornado ripped through the room. His movements were so fast he'd actually been a blur. I'd never in my life, well in the few short months of my known existence, had *ever* seen someone move so fast.

"How'd you do that?" I asked.

Flint shrugged. A lock of chestnut hair fell across his forehead. My pulse quickened. "I honestly don't know," he said. "If I don't keep it in check, I'd probably move that fast all of the time. It hasn't been easy to adapt to."

"Huh," I managed.

"Well if we're all done here, I'm heading up to the house for lunch." Jet stretched and yawned loudly. "I'm starving."

The thought of food made my mouth water. "I'll join you." I eyed Flint and wondered what he'd do.

"Di?" Flint said. "You want to…" He didn't finish his sentence. Instead, he nodded toward the door.

Di stood. "Yeah."

Without another word, the two of them left. A rush of air entered the cabin when the door shut behind them.

I watched through the window as they took off down the driveway. They walked closely, their heads dipped toward one another. A brief swell of disappointment filled me. Flint hadn't said goodbye or looked at me since rearranging the furniture. I tried to shrug that feeling off.

"I know you're hungry…" Jacinda's comment snapped me back to my surroundings. "But how about you come with me first. You can't go up to the house wearing that." Her nose wrinkled as she assessed my clothes.

"But I wore this last night," I replied.

"We're heading out," Jet said. "You guys coming?"

Jacinda shook her head. "Lena and I will be up in a

minute. You three go ahead."

Mica, Jet and Jasper walked out the door. I watched them enviously. "Can't we eat first?"

Jacinda eyed my pants. "This will just take a minute. Follow me."

CHAPTER NINE

I reluctantly followed Jacinda down the hall. Her long blond hair swayed between her shoulder blades. My stomach protested the entire way.

"Don't worry," she called over her shoulder. "I know you're hungry."

We walked into her room. She nodded at a neatly made bed. "Have a seat."

I plopped down.

Jacinda grabbed a very large suitcase from the corner of the room. It was the one that took up so much space in the Suburban. She pulled the gold zipper. The metallic scratch sounded in the room. I eyed the material. It looked like genuine leather. She must have noticed me staring because she smiled.

"It's a Louis Vuitton. A gift from Huxley."

"Huxley?"

"The man I was with before I came here."

"You had a boyfriend?"

She shrugged. "I guess you could call him that. We kept each other company for a few weeks, until we arrived in

Colorado."

I sat farther forward. "How'd you two meet?"

"At some hotel. We actually met the first night after I woke up. I wandered around my neighborhood that entire first day, trying to recognize something. Anything. When that didn't happen, I kept walking. I ended up at a hotel, went inside and sat at the bar in the lounge. Huxley came in a few minutes later. He approached and we got to talking, and the rest as they say, was history."

"So, did you drive up here with...what was his name...Huxley?"

Jacinda snorted delicately. "Drive? No, we flew in his Gulfstream IV."

"You flew in a *Gulfstream IV?*"

If I was right, that was a private jet that could seat close to twenty people. As soon as I thought that, my mouth fell open. *How do I know that?* Once again, a random bit of knowledge popped into my head for no reason. It wasn't the first time it happened.

Initially, when I woke up, I thought everything in my memory was gone but then things slowly filtered through. Things I'd apparently once known.

I'd never forget the first time it happened, when I was walking down a street in Rapid City. I passed a used book store, and from the corner of an outside bin, I spotted a paperback of *Canterbury Tales*. As I continued on, it came to mind that Chaucer was considered the father of English literature. As for where that thought came from, I had no idea.

After that, more and more things materialized in my foggy brain. Such as the chemical composition of methane was CH_4 or that Edvard Munch painted *The Scream*. Just random bits of information. It was incredibly disconcerting to say the least, and it just happened again. Apparently, I knew a thing or two about private jets.

"Jacinda, I know what a Gulfstream IV is. *How* do I know

that?"

Jacinda took out a few clothes from her suitcase and examined them. "I don't know. We're all like that. We just know things. Isn't it weird when it happens? When you're talking to someone and some detail comes up and just like that," she snapped her fingers, "a hundred things appear in your brain and you know what they're talking about?"

"Yes!" I breathed.

Jacinda continued to rifle through her clothes. Every now and then, she pulled out a shirt, turned it back and forth and then refolded it back into her suitcase.

"So, where's Huxley now?" I asked.

"I don't know. I guess he went back to Phoenix. I broke up with him shortly after we landed." She held up another top. It was frilly and made of shiny material. "What about this one?"

I made a face. No doubt it would look great in a photo shoot, but it didn't seem useful for anything else.

"This will be a little big on you, but it should work."

"Um, it's nice but I think my t-shirt is better."

She eyed my shirt. I could tell from her expression that she didn't agree. She fumbled through her suitcase again and pulled out a long-sleeved shirt with splashes of color and some logo stitched on the bottom.

"How about this one?" She threw the shirt at me. "One hundred percent Peruvian cotton, eight hundred thread count."

"Hmm." I fingered the fabric.

"Well? What do you think?"

"This might work."

I rubbed it between my fingers again. It was incredibly soft cotton, smooth as silk and almost plush. All of the clothes I owned came from Salvation Army. Most of them had holes and were ingrained with dirt.

"Try it on."

"What if I get it dirty?"

Jacinda shrugged. "Then we'll wash it."

I stood and peeled my shirt off. Jacinda's top fell below my waist, and the arms were too long, but the fabric felt good against my skin. It was soft, clean, and it didn't smell.

"Thanks, Jacinda!" I grinned and pushed the sleeves up.

Jacinda stared at me, her mouth open. "You really have been starving, haven't you?"

I felt my cheeks heat. I wondered how much of my skeletal frame she'd seen.

She gave me a sympathetic look. "You poor thing, but don't worry, that'll all change now. You're not alone and homeless anymore. You don't need to hitchhike or go hungry again."

Her soft words and encouraging smile caused a warm feeling in me.

She appraised my lower half. "Now, what are we going to do about your pants…"

JACINDA AND I finally walked up to the main house half an hour later. I was ready to bang Jacinda's suitcase over her head I was so hungry, but she insisted I be 'presentable' before I left the cabin.

Consequently, my now clean hair was pulled up into a stylish ponytail. I also wore clean clothes from head to toe. We'd settled on a pair of jean shorts that practically fell off me since they were so big, but Jacinda decided it was the best she could do. My shoes were another story. I wore a pair of her slip-ons that were too big and kept falling off. I asked her why I couldn't wear my worn sneakers. Her response was to pick them up and throw them in the garbage.

Jacinda sighed heavily as I walked beside her. I could tell from her disapproving glances every time I hiked the shorts up or tripped over the too big shoes that she didn't approve.

"We're going shopping after lunch," she said. "You need

your own clothes."

"But I don't have any money." I held up a hand to shade my face in the bright sun. I could practically feel my pale skin burning.

She rolled her eyes. "Weren't you listening when we told you about us? Money isn't an issue."

"But it's not *mine*."

"Yes it is. You're one of us. Therefore, you're entitled to the *pile*."

I didn't bother arguing. We were almost to the porch and scents from lunch drifted outside. I lifted my nose and let the scent lead the way.

When we entered the dining hall, music strummed through the speakers. Several tables in the dining area were occupied with other guests. The entire scene was quaint and pleasant. I spotted Mica, Jet and Jasper at a table in the corner. Mica smiled and waved us over.

Jet smirked when we approached. "You're looking as good as Jacinda."

My cheeks heated as I pulled up the shorts again. "Thanks."

"You've got to try this food. It's amazing!" Mica spooned a huge bite of some kind of berry pie and vanilla ice cream to her mouth.

I watched Mica eat. My mouth salivated.

Jet rolled his eyes. "Good one, Mica. Torment the starving girl."

Mica's brown eyes widened. "Sorry," she said through a mouthful of food. "Buffet's over there." She pointed to the corner. "Help yourself!"

I made a beeline for the buffet and almost cried in happiness when I saw the selection. A large stack of tortillas and taco shells, bowls of taco meat, cheddar cheese, diced tomatoes, lettuce and olives. Cups of sour cream, guacamole and salsa sat at the end. I piled four tacos on my plate. Jacinda only took one.

When we joined the others, Jasper quirked an eyebrow at my heaping meal. "Looks like you've met your match, Mica."

I didn't care how much teasing the twins gave me. Like last night, all I saw was the food in front of me. When I finished, I slowly realized everyone was staring.

"What?" I asked.

"There's sour cream all over your cheek," Jacinda whispered.

Heat crept up my neck. I hastily wiped my mouth. Mica grinned and dabbed some guacamole on Jasper's nose. "Should I lick it off?" she asked.

Jasper grabbed a napkin but a smile tugged at his lips.

"Or I could?" Jet leaned over with his tongue out. Jasper smacked him.

Jacinda snorted delicately as I muffled a laugh.

"Mica will eat anything," Jet said as Jasper cleaned his face. "Next time, leave the sour cream. She'll probably scrape it off with a tortilla chip or two."

Mica slugged him playfully in the shoulder. "Okay, who wants dessert? I'm thinking of having a second helping."

"See what I mean?" Jet said dryly.

I smiled again and joined Mica at the dessert table.

THIRTY MINUTES LATER, I was so stuffed, movement seemed impossible. I groaned in pain. Jet and Jasper laughed while Jacinda clucked her tongue.

"Next time, slow down. Your body isn't used to all of this food," she said.

"You gonna be okay?" Mica asked as she polished off her second bowl of ice cream.

Jet clapped me on the back. "You'll survive." He turned to his brother. "I heard they're having a trail ride for the guests this afternoon, and those ladies over there," he nodded toward a group of four women seated at another table. "I overheard them say they're going."

Mica laughed. "Are you already over that girl you took on a few dates last week?"

Jet shrugged. "She left, remember? Her Colorado trip had come to an end. It's time to move on."

"Didn't she cry when she kissed you goodbye?" Mica replied.

"She may have shed a few tears." Jet smiled devilishly.

Mica laughed.

"So you want to go?" Jet asked Jasper.

Before Jasper could respond, Mica said, "I'll go! And I promise not to interfere when you're making your moves on the ladies."

Jasper chuckled, his eyes twinkling when he glanced at Mica. "Jacinda? Lena? You want to come too?" he asked.

I was about to stand when Jacinda shook her head. "We're going into town to buy Lena clothes. Has anyone seen Di or Flint? We'll need a ride."

"I haven't seen them since the *grand revelation*," Jet replied, making air quotes around the words. He eyed one of the four women when she stood. She was a cute blonde with curvy hips. "So are you two coming or not?" Jet asked. His eyes stayed on the blonde.

"No," Jacinda said sweetly.

I sighed in exasperation. "Riding horses would be more fun than shopping."

Jacinda merely quirked an eyebrow and appraised my bare feet under the table. I hadn't bothered trying to keep her shoes on while we ate.

"You can ride horses later," she said gently yet firmly.

"All right." Jet stood and then smiled when he and the blonde made eye contact.

"See you later," Jasper called. Before I could argue, the three left. Mica's excited chatter trailed through the dining hall.

I sighed in disappointment but knew Jacinda was right. I

couldn't go horseback riding in flats that kept falling off. "Okay, let's get this shopping trip over with."

She grinned. "Perfect. Now, we just need to find Di or Flint."

Hearing Flint's name made my stomach flip. "Why do we need to find them?"

"I don't drive. Do you?"

For a moment, I just sat there. Could I drive? "Um, I have no idea."

Jacinda pursed her lips. The glossy sheen from her lipstick – that amazingly didn't seem to wear off despite eating – reminded me of raspberries. "We should find one of them. Just to be safe. Come on."

My stomach felt like a jumbled mess when we stood. I wasn't sure if it was from overeating or at the thought of seeing Flint again. Regardless, I followed Jacinda as we left the main house. On the gravel drive, I kept tripping and almost fell because of the blasted shoes.

I finally gave up. Pulling the flats off, I ambled down the drive in bare feet. Jacinda clucked in disapproval, but I didn't care. Even though the gravel hurt my soles, I was still ready to throw the damned shoes in the pasture.

IT WASN'T HARD to find Di and Flint. Both were in our cabin. They jumped up from the couch when we walked through the door, as if we'd caught them doing something. My stomach sank as a new thought occurred to me. Were Di and Flint *together*?

I didn't get a chance to think about it since Di asked what our plans were. Jacinda gave a pointed look at my bare feet. Di merely assessed my dirty toes with a heavy sigh, while Flint's lips quirked up in a smile. It vanished when he caught me watching him.

"She needs clothes," Jacinda said. "Can one of you drive us to Little Raven?"

Flint stepped forward. "I'll take you."

Jacinda smiled sweetly. "I'll get my purse."

Without Jacinda in the room, silence fell. Being so near Flint did funny things to my heart rate. He didn't seem to notice. Instead, he and Di were doing that subtle communication again. Di raised an eyebrow, and Flint nodded slightly at which she made a motion to her wrist. I had no idea what we'd walked in on, but I felt acutely aware of it in that moment.

I tried to ignore them. Fresh scents of eucalyptus subtly tinged the air. A dried wreath hung on the wall. I concentrated on that. It smelled nice. Unfortunately, the scent did little to distract me. Flint's towering presence and dark eyes continually pulled at me.

I shuffled my feet and stuffed my hands in my pockets. That was a mistake. The shorts practically fell off. Luckily, I caught them before they fell to my knees.

"Ready?" Jacinda reappeared with a fresh sheen of lip gloss on her lips, and a pink purse clutched in her hand. A metallic Prada label gleamed.

I nodded eagerly. "Yes!"

She grinned, obviously mistaking my enthusiasm for the shopping trip versus wanting to flee the uncomfortable environment.

"Let's go," Flint said.

The sound of his deep voice made me jump. *Calm down, Lena!* It wasn't good to pine for a guy that was already taken.

Or were he and Di *not* together?

I briefly pictured Flint's arm around me this morning when the group revealed who they were. Di hadn't seemed to care that Flint sat so close to me. Although, that didn't necessarily mean anything. Flint's intentions could have been to help me mesh with the group. Or maybe he'd been afraid I'd bolt or pass out. He simply could have had his arm around me to stop me from fleeing. I could be reading into something that wasn't even there.

I sighed. I was putting way too much thought into this.

"Lena?" Jacinda called. She and Flint were standing by the door.

"Oh, sorry," I mumbled.

Flint didn't say anything as we left the cabin. He also wouldn't meet my gaze. Once again, his face was completely unreadable. Di, on the other hand, called out to not spend too much money. Jacinda just waved and acted like she didn't hear.

Our car doors slammed in the quiet afternoon. Flint sat in the driver's seat, Jacinda took the passenger side so I hopped in the back. Sitting right behind Flint offered a very nice view of his beautiful hair and broad shoulders. They were so broad they extended past the seat. A pool of heat filled my core. I squirmed uncomfortably as Flint started the engine. *What the hell is the matter with me?*

Before long, we were in the forest driving toward Little Raven. A breeze trailed through Flint's open window, carrying scents of pine. My thoughts drifted to everything I'd learned this morning. Was it really only this morning?

I rubbed my tattoo. The perfect circle divided into four. Since the silence was killing me, I said the first thing that came to mind. "What do you think our tattoos are symbols of?"

Flint's dark eyes drifted to the rearview mirror. "Di and I have a few ideas."

Jacinda clasped her hands tightly together. "How many shirts do you think you'll need?" she asked. She flashed me her supermodel smile.

Shirts? "Oh, um. I don't know. Three or four?"

"That's it?" she replied.

I leaned forward so I could better meet Flint's gaze in the mirror. "What do you think the symbols are of?"

"I really don't think three or four is enough," Jacinda cut in. "I was thinking you need at least a week's worth at the very minimum. You'll also need hiking boots, if you want to join in the activities. Not to mention jeans, shorts, shoes..." Her list grew.

I leaned back in my seat. Jacinda's nervous energy bubbled around her. Giving Flint a questionable glance, he subtly shook his head in the mirror. I took the hint. Jacinda obviously didn't want to discuss our situation. I remembered what Jet said. How all of this was a bad omen. But still, didn't we need to talk about it? Burying our heads in the sand, pretending like we were normal people, wouldn't help us.

When we got to town, Jacinda gracefully extracted herself from the Suburban.

"Come on, Lena." Her energy had returned to its usual subdued state. I hadn't mentioned our tattoos again.

Flint and I stepped out of the Suburban. We stood beside one another on the sidewalk. He towered over me. In jeans and a t-shirt, he looked incredibly sexy. I tried not to notice.

"I'm going to the public library to use the computers," he said to Jacinda.

A swell of disappointment strummed through me. "You're not coming with us?"

He shook his head without meeting my gaze. "Pete and Val don't have Wi-Fi. Besides, public computers are safer when we're doing internet searches."

"Searches for what?"

"I want to research a few things, now that we know where you woke up. I'll be back in two hours." He still wouldn't meet my gaze.

"Let's get going, Lena." Jacinda reached down and clasped my hand.

"Right, err, okay," I replied.

Flint turned. With the sun glinting off the natural highlights in his hair, and the way his shirt hugged his broad shoulders, I never wanted to look away. However, I wasn't the only one admiring the view. He passed a group of young women sitting at an outside café table. All four watched him.

The sound of giggles and whispered comments followed.

Jealousy raced hotly through my blood. Its intensity surprised me. Feeling my cheeks flush crimson, I did my best to keep my breathing even.

"Everything all right?" Jacinda asked.

A breeze ruffled her long, blond hair. A knowing twinkle glinted in her light brown eyes. I ducked my head and brushed past her into the store. Seriously, I needed to stop making a fool of myself.

THE NEXT TWO hours were entirely painful. I kept thinking about Jet, Jasper and Mica on a trail ride. They were currently enjoying the outdoors, whereas I was stuck trying on piece after piece of clothing. Jacinda dragged me from store to store. The pile of bags grew in our wakes.

It didn't help that some of the shopkeepers recognized me. I'd asked a few of them this morning if they knew about a missing girl matching my appearance. Every time I got recognized, a wary look would flash across their eyes. Luckily, Jacinda did most of the talking and all of the explaining.

"She was looking for us." Jacinda handed a male shopkeeper several hundred dollar bills as he rang up our latest purchase. He'd visibly flinched when I'd walked in. "Silly thing, she was so tired," Jacinda continued. "That's probably why she was saying that stuff."

She gave me a sympathetic smile and winked.

The store owner just stared at Jacinda. I swear he was about to drool. "That's good to hear. My wife...um, I mean...my shop assistant was worried about her."

Jacinda looked at him demurely through her full lashes. "Please let your *shop assistant* know that she's just fine."

The man smiled and almost tripped when he came around the counter to hand us our bags. "You ladies have a nice afternoon. I hope to see you in here again." His eyes stayed on Jacinda.

I almost threw up in my mouth but neither seemed to notice. "Are we done?" I asked.

Jacinda gave the man her supermodel smile. He almost knocked over a rack of sunglasses when he turned. I smothered a gag and followed her out of the store.

Once on the sidewalk, I glanced at Jacinda's watch. We still had thirty minutes until Flint returned. I spotted an ice cream shop on the corner. "Do you want to get some ice cream while we wait for Flint?"

Jacinda's expression told me exactly what she thought of that. "There's a shoe store down on that side. Follow me."

I rolled my eyes and followed her once again. It was hard not to smile, though. There was a bounce in Jacinda's step. I had a feeling this was the most fun she'd had in a while.

When Flint finally returned, we had over ten shopping bags full of items. In my opinion, I didn't need over half of them. Jacinda, of course, didn't agree.

Flint eyed the mountain of items. "How much did you spend?"

Jacinda merely put the bags in the back of the Suburban. "Not much."

"Jacinda…" he said, his voice deepening.

"Only two thousand. Really, it's not a big deal." Worry flashed through her eyes before she smiled brightly. Flint, however, seemed immune to her charms.

He raked a hand harshly through his hair. "Have fun explaining that one to Di. You know we need to conserve the *pile*. What if it takes months or years to find answers? We're dependent on that money."

Jacinda stuffed the rest of the bags in the back. She hurried to her door. It wasn't lost on me that she never replied.

"Did you find anything at the library?" I asked.

Flint gave another angered glance toward Jacinda's door. "Not really."

I stepped back as a slow wave of power hit me. Once

again, that feeling radiated from him. I crossed my arms. "Um…what were you looking for?"

"A connection between our cities, or some kind of connection between us and our cities." Again, he wouldn't meet my gaze.

I wanted to ask more but got the impression this wasn't a good time. Flint was angry. That was apparent.

"Should we head back?" I asked.

He nodded curtly and got in the vehicle. I buckled myself in the back again as he started the engine. We peeled out of the parking spot. A few people stared at the shiny, expensive Suburban. I'm sure the two front occupants were partly to blame. Flint and Jacinda were as good looking as any Hollywood A-list couple.

Jacinda smiled as we drove into the forest. "Lena and I had fun. Didn't we?"

I made a noncommittal noise and muttered something about the experience being akin to dying slowly.

"What was that?"

I knew from her annoyed expression she'd heard me. *Of course* she'd heard me. She could have heard me a mile away. I smiled brightly and berated myself for forgetting her ability. "Nothing. Yes, it was very fun. The time of my life."

Flint's lips quirked up in the rearview mirror.

"Well anywho," Jacinda said. "We'll probably need to go back into town tomorrow or the next day. I'm running short on my favorite nail polish. Since we didn't have time to pick it up…"

I stopped listening as Jacinda rattled off the other things we 'needed.' Instead, I watched Flint's forearms as he gripped the steering wheel. They were well muscled with thick rope veins. That strange feeling of safety washed through me again. I just hoped it wasn't a false security. Jet's words still haunted me. *A bad omen.* I shivered.

CHAPTER TEN

We quickly fell into a routine on the ranch. Since Flint had paid for our cabins through the week, we didn't need to leave anytime soon.

Each day started with having breakfast at the main house. From there, Di and Flint would disappear. I had no idea where they went. We usually wouldn't see them again until evening, and since Di wasn't a talker and Flint seemed intent on ignoring me, I had no idea what they spent their time doing. Consequently, I spent most days with Jacinda, Mica and the twins.

It was fun yet frustrating. Four *days* had passed yet we still knew nothing about our situation.

I sighed heavily and took a drink of orange juice. We were currently eating breakfast. Di and Flint had already left. Country music strummed through the speakers. Guests chatted and silverware clanked. Everything about our stay had been nothing but pleasant. Yet all I could think about was how this felt like some bizarre vacation that was completely avoiding the reality of our lives. We still had *no* answers.

"What do Di and Flint do all day?" I asked Mica.

She took a huge bite of pancakes. Syrup practically drowned them. "I dunno for sure, but I do know they spend a lot of time talking about what happened to us and why."

"But why aren't *all* of us talking about it?"

She shrugged. "Hey, you wanna go on a nature walk? They're having one this morning."

"Um, sure, but why don't we all talk with Di and Flint? Wouldn't it be smarter to have us brainstorming together?"

Mica took another huge bite. "I dunno."

She turned her attention to Jasper and laughed at something he said. Meanwhile, Jet sat with the curvy blonde and her friends at their table. The twin's arm was draped across the blonde's shoulders, his thumb making circles on her upper arm. She inched closer to him.

I sighed in frustration. Over the past four days, I'd also learned that Jacinda wasn't the only one who wanted to avoid our circumstance. Mica seemed completely oblivious to the fact that our lives started four months ago. The twins seemed more open to talking about our situation. However, Jet acted more interested in hooking up with other guests. I didn't mind, though. Each time I'd approached our situation with Jet, he started murmuring about aliens and kryptonite.

I understood why Di and Flint ignored him.

"What about you?" I asked Jacinda. "Do you know why we don't all discuss it?"

The blond beauty's hand stilled as she brought her napkin to her lips. Her face paled. She gently dabbed at the corner of her mouth. "I'm going to get another cup of coffee. Would you like one?"

She stood before I could respond.

I finished my breakfast as Jasper and Mica got into a discussion about Sriracha sauce – to put on eggs, or to not put on eggs? That was the question. My eyes drifted to the window. Were Di and Flint currently discussing our memory loss? Perhaps searching the area for answers? I pushed my chair back.

"I'm gonna pass on the nature walk, Mica. I'll see you all later." I bolted before she replied.

I RETURNED TO the cabin. First ours, then the guys. Neither Di nor Flint was in either. Scents of coffee lingered in our cabin, though. In other words, they *had* been here. Nobody had made coffee this morning before we walked up for breakfast. I'd probably just missed them.

Back outside, I jogged down the porch steps and plopped my hands on my hips. A breeze fluttered my hair around my shoulders.

Where would they go?

Mica had said there was a nature walk today, and there were always trail rides. However, I'd never seen Di or Flint partake in any group activities. In fact, I'd never seen them on the ranch during the day. Not even at lunchtime.

The sound of a car engine starting broke the quiet. My eyes widened. I sprinted to where the Suburban was parked. White tail lights were alight as I careened to a stop at the bumper. I hurriedly knocked on the back window. Red tail lights flashed.

Without bothering to ask if they minded, I opened the back door and jumped inside. Flint's dark eyes met mine the second I did. He sat at the driver's seat, Di on the passenger side. She whipped around just as I clicked my seat belt in place.

"Mind if I join you guys today?" I asked.

They glanced at one another. An unreadable expression covered Flint's face. My heart quickened at the sight. He looked devilishly handsome, even more so this morning. His hair was still damp from his shower, and his unique scent drifted toward me. That bizarre feeling of safety once again cloaked me. I almost sighed in contentment. Just being around him made me happier.

Di finally shrugged. "Three heads together is better than

two. Let's get going." She reached for her coffee. Two steaming mugs sat in the console. "Just no talking about aliens and superman. Got it?"

"No aliens and no super heroes," I replied. "My lips are sealed."

Flint's hands merely tightened around the steering wheel. He didn't say a word.

I couldn't tell if he was unhappy about me joining them or not. I clasped my hands tightly together. His eyes wouldn't meet mine when he looked over his shoulder to reverse.

The drive on the county road wasn't any better. Neither Di nor Flint said a thing. It was very different from hanging out with Jacinda, Mica and the twins. Gone were the joking quips and easy laughter. I felt acutely aware of my presence with these two.

"Where are we going?" I finally asked. We were driving through the forest. Pine trees and aspens flashed by my window.

"Little Raven," Flint replied. "To the public library."

"To use the computers again?"

"Yes."

"What are you trying to find?"

"Today we're going to—"

"Ah!" Di exclaimed. She grabbed her head and leaned forward. Flint slowed the vehicle and pulled to the side of the road. The Suburban stopped abruptly when he threw it into park.

"Di?" Flint reached over and put a hand on her back. My eyes glued to his large palm resting near her shoulder. My stomach plummeted. *Yep, they're definitely together.*

I shook off the intense pain that realization brought. Di was currently holding her head between her hands, and all I could think about was how Flint touching her ripped a hole in my heart.

"What do you see?" Flint's words were soft and gentle.

"A city," she said. "It's…there are skyscrapers and a body of water…maybe an ocean. No…" She shook her head. Her fingers wrapped so tightly around her skull they dug into her hair. "Not an ocean. A lake? No, that can't be right. It's a huge body of water."

"Maybe the Great Lakes?" Flint asked.

"Maybe," she panted.

My eyes widened as it dawned on me what was happening. Di was in the midst of a vision. She leaned forward, slightly rocking as she gripped her head. I wanted to ask questions, but I didn't want to interrupt whatever was happening. From how they acted, I guessed this wasn't the first vision Di had experienced in Flint's presence.

"Try to make out a detail," he coaxed. "Can you see something on a building that stands out? Or a pier in the water? Something we can identify?"

"There's a park. I see lots of grass and people walking and–" Her breath whooshed out of her. She sat up abruptly. "It's gone."

She still held her head. Flint rubbed her shoulder. "Did you see anything on a building? Any glimpse of a street sign?"

She shook her head. "No."

"Concentrate. Try to remember."

"There was…um…one of the buildings was black. It was the tallest one."

"Good. What else can you remember about it?"

"The black building was by the water. Kind of."

"Anything else?" Flint asked gently.

She was silent for a moment and eventually shook her head. "No. That's it."

"We'll see what we can find based off that. Thirsty?"

"Very."

He reached into the back. His gaze again wouldn't meet mine. Heat raced up my neck as he fished a water bottle from under the seat. When he turned back around, he unscrewed the cap and held the bottle to Di. She took it with shaky fingers and drank greedily.

I swallowed uneasily.

An air of intimacy hung in the cab. I'd never seen Di so shaken or Flint so attentive. Regret pulsed through me. I shouldn't have come. This was too intimate, too intense. I was forcing myself on them and it was obvious they were sharing something that wasn't meant to be witnessed by others.

"Are you okay?" Flint asked.

Di nodded. "Let's go."

He put the Suburban back in drive. With a spin of tires, we once again sped down the gravel road. None of us said anything for the rest of the drive. When we pulled up to the public library and parked in the small lot, Flint turned.

His gaze softened for the merest second when our eyes met. "We'll spend most of the day here."

I nodded mutely.

The three of us climbed out of the vehicle. Di stood straight, her head held high. If I hadn't witnessed her vision, I'd have never guessed any bone of vulnerability lay inside her.

"We'll search cities today," she said. "Specifically cities by the Great Lakes with parks by the waterfront. Let's get a move on."

She strode forward. The stoic, resolute Di I was slowly coming to know was back.

WE SPENT THE morning on the computers. One of the librarians smiled at Flint and Di when she passed us. Neither of them smiled back. I wondered if Di or Flint had considered the staff here may begin to recognize them. It was my understanding neither Di or Flint wanted to draw attention to us.

Flint leaned closer to Di just as the woman passed. "We may need to start scoping out the internet cafes," he murmured.

"I was just thinking the same thing," she said.

I almost rolled my eyes. Of course they'd considered it.

Di sat in the middle of us. Her fingers flew across the keyboard as images from her Google searches came up. I was glad for the distance from Flint. I tried to concentrate on what I was supposed to be doing – searching for cities that matched Di's vision – but it was hard. My body was so in tuned to Flint's. Every time he took a deep breath or hunched forward, I perked up. Or whenever he leaned back to stretch, I couldn't help but glance in his direction to admire his strong forearms and rounded shoulders.

Each time he moved, my body betrayed me. I berated myself internally. He and Di were together. So what that he'd put his arm around me four days ago when the group revealed who they were? For the past four days, he'd ignored me. In other words, that comforting arm had obviously been a tactic he used to help new members mesh into the group. I swallowed the lump in my throat. It was crazy how much that realization stung.

Don't think about him, Lena.

I made myself type in a new search and forced myself to ignore the pain ripping through my chest.

THE REST OF the day passed in a blur. We found a few cities that matched the description from Di's visions and narrowed it down to three: Chicago, Cleveland and Buffalo. Chicago seemed the most likely since its black skyscraper, the John Hancock building, was the tallest.

"Does that mean we'll go to Chicago?" I pulled open the door to the Suburban as we all climbed in. It was almost six in the evening. Supper was served at 6:30 at the ranch. We'd probably make it back just in time.

"Not necessarily." Di clicked her seat belt in place. "We need to stay here regardless until the new girl arrives, and we won't leave until I'm positive that Chicago is in our future."

"You mean it could be a fluke?"

"I can't say for sure. So far, my visions haven't been wrong, but we're not about to travel across the country until I'm sure it's right."

Flint started the engine. I tried not to let it bother me that Flint hadn't said a word to me since lunch. More than ever, I felt like a third wheel.

I *had* caught him watching me a few times throughout the day, though, that unreadable expression on his face. However, each time our eyes had met, he'd hastily looked away as if embarrassed that I'd caught him. Those awkward moments wreaked havoc on my nerves. All day my body strummed in awareness for him, and all day, he'd only spoken to me when necessary.

"Thanks for your help today, Lena," Di said as we drove up the ranch's driveway. "It was nice to have another set of eyes."

"Um, sure," I replied.

It wasn't lost on me that Flint didn't voice his agreement.

CHAPTER ELEVEN

That evening Flint retreated to his cabin even though Jet and Jasper joined us for a movie in ours. It was another thing I'd noticed over the past four days. Flint rarely joined the group when we hung out in the evenings.

The next morning, Di, Jacinda, Mica and I all walked up to the main house for breakfast. Our feet shuffled quietly on the gravel as a mourning dove crooned in the distance.

"What a beautiful morning," Jacinda murmured.

"Hmm," was all Di replied.

Normally, Di joined Flint first thing, but since he wasn't waiting on his porch for her, she'd continued on with us. I couldn't help but think the reason for Flint's absence was because of me. Maybe he didn't want me joining them again today. Maybe, he'd whisk Di away when I wasn't looking. I bit my lip as the main house came into view.

When we entered the dining room, soft country music floated in the air. The thought of a big breakfast had my spirits rising. I still felt perpetually hungry, even though I'd probably gained a few pounds. All thoughts of food vanished, though, when I caught a glimpse of Val.

I immediately knew something was wrong.

Pete's wife stood in the kitchen wringing her hands in between frantic movements to the stove, oven and dining room. The room was also suspiciously empty. Not a guest to be seen.

"Where is everyone?" Mica asked.

Jacinda put her hands on her hips. "Good question."

Since nobody was in the dining room, I wondered if we were early. The clock on the wall read just after eight. We weren't that early.

"Oh!" Val stood in the entryway to the kitchen, her eyes wide. "You're here!"

"Is everything okay?" I asked.

"Yes!" Val turned and hurried back to the counter. She picked up a bowl and beat something furiously. "Everything's fine, nothing to worry about! Just give me a little more time!"

"No, everything's not fine," Pete said. I almost jumped when he appeared behind us.

Di's gaze narrowed. "Why? What happened?"

Pete sighed. "It seems Sheena and Mary Beth ran off with two of the cowboys."

"Sheena and Mary Beth?" I said.

"The two girls that helped Val in the kitchen," Pete explained. I vaguely recalled the plump blonde and skinny brunette that often frequented the dining hall.

Di crossed her arms. "They didn't give you any notice?"

Pete shook his head. "No. They took off in the middle of the night. Val found a note from the girls. One of our guys, Tyler, found a note from the cowboys. They've all cleaned out, gone to Vegas. Something about getting married." Pete shook his head. "I doubt they'll be back."

"That sucks," Mica commented. "Does that mean no breakfast today?"

Before Pete could respond, Jacinda said, "Is there anything we can do to help?"

Val stopped her frantic beating. Her cheeks were rosy, and her eyes glowed with fatigue. "Don't be silly. You're our guests here."

"It'll go much faster if you let us help," I said.

"Yeah," Jacinda added. "We're not busy."

A shrewd expression covered Di's face. After a moment, she said, "We'd be happy to help."

Her admission surprised me. I figured she and Flint would disappear regardless of what the rest of us did.

"Oh, you couldn't possibly want to spend your time doing this!" Val cried.

Pete walked to Val and put a hand on her shoulder. *"The Lord works in mysterious ways."* He said it so quietly, I almost didn't hear him.

Val's gaze softened. Her shoulders relaxed. "Okay, thank you." She nodded toward a mountain of fruit. "You can help cut that up."

After getting situated, we formed a line along the counter. I had the oranges, Mica had the pineapple, Di, the strawberries, and Jacinda, the melons. I glanced at Di curiously as we cut up the fruit. Her movements were quick and methodical. She seemed to be thinking about something from the concentrated expression on her face.

A few minutes later, she wiped her hands on a towel. "I'll be right back."

"Where are you going?" I asked.

"To talk to the guys. If two cowboys also quit, Pete may need their help." She was about to turn when I grabbed her arm. Her muscles tensed and her gaze drifted to my hand. I hastily let go.

"You're going to ask the guys to help too?"

Di's gaze shifted to Val before she turned back to me. In a quiet voice, she said, "If they've had workers quit, they may need to hire more help. The new girl's not coming for at least another week, possibly two or even three. We need to stay in this area until then and the more we conserve the *pile*, the better. An income would help."

"You mean you're hoping they'll *hire* us?"

"Keep your voice down!" she hissed. Mica glanced over her shoulder but went back to cutting the pineapple. Jacinda meanwhile, pretended like she hadn't heard a thing even though it was impossible she hadn't.

"Maybe," Di said. "I need to run it by Flint to see if he agrees."

She strode out the kitchen's screen door before I could ask anything else. It banged loudly behind her.

With Di gone, Jacinda and I took over the strawberries since Mica seemed to have her hands full with the pineapple. Mica winced when one of the thorns pricked her finger.

"Damn fruit." She cut into another piece, again with too much force, and grimaced when another thorn stuck her.

"You want to trade?" I asked.

"Thought you'd never ask." She dumped the remaining fruit in front of me.

As I cut carefully through the rough skin, my thoughts drifted to what Di said. She was going to try to wheedle us into jobs on the ranch if Flint agreed. Flint's image popped into my head. Those dark eyes, his tanned face and perfect lips. I almost dropped my knife. *Perfect lips? Really, Lena? The guy's got a girlfriend!*

"It's crazy that Val's workers quit," Mica stated.

"What?" My knife almost slipped.

"I'd never give up a job on this ranch," Mica sighed. "Well, if I worked with the horses. I'm not much for cooking, but working outside would be great." Mica's chatter soon helped distract me. She talked about rounding up cattle, taking the guests on trail rides and lassoing calves. I smiled at some of her ramblings.

Di returned a while later, stating the guys went in search of Pete to offer what help they could. She didn't fill me in on what she and Flint decided, and I didn't ask. It was becoming obvious that putting distance between myself, Di and Flint was probably best. Even though I wanted answers at any cost, my heart still ached knowing that Flint was taken. Perhaps a little distance would cool my feelings.

Mica, however, grumbled enviously. "Couldn't I join them instead of doing this?"

"If Val needs help here, than that's where we'll help," Di said sternly.

Mica rolled her eyes.

About an hour later, the kitchen returned to normal. With Val's direction, we finished preparing the food and arranged the buffet table. With all of us working, we soon had a mountain of food prepared.

"We did it!" Val said, as she topped off the coffee.

"Of course, we did it." Mica put her hands on her hips. "Now, we just need people to eat it."

"When are the guests coming up?" I asked.

Val wrung her hands in her apron. "I don't know. Pete went to their cabins first thing this morning to tell them breakfast was delayed. He must have forgotten about all of you." She gave us an apologetic smile. "I was so flustered. I told him to have them stay put until I finished. I guess they're still waiting in their cabins."

"They must be hungry," Jacinda commented.

Val nodded. "I'm sure they're all ravenous. Not to mention, the activities have been held up because of this."

"They can all come up now, right?" I said. "We could get them for you, couldn't we?"

"Sure!" Mica replied. "We'll get 'em." She tromped out the door before Val could respond. Dirt flaked off her boots, and the door banged loudly behind her.

"Oh…" Val paused. She eyed the dirt and reached for the broom in the corner. "If you don't mind. I've got a bad knee and walking up and down the gravel drive flares it up."

"We don't mind," Jacinda replied.

"Be back before you know it," I added.

Val gripped the broom tighter. "Well, I still need someone to carry a few things out."

"I'll stay," Di said. "Just tell me what to do."

Val let out a sigh. "Bless your souls."

Outside, Jacinda and I caught up with Mica. The three of us walked to the cabins. In the daylight, the ranch stretched as far as I could see. Pastures and fields traveled for miles. The main house sat at the highest point and overlooked the valley that dipped down in front of it, although a barn off to the west sat a little bit higher.

Twenty minutes later, we had all of the guests in the dining hall. To say that Val was over the moon would be an understatement. She also practically kissed us when we offered to refill the buffet as things ran out. Di of course had been the one to insist we help. Val seemed completely oblivious to every calculating move Di made.

When the guests finished, Val dished us all large plates of food. The four of us sat in the empty dining room while Val washed a mountain of pots in the kitchen. Banging from the pots echoed into the hall. Jacinda nibbled a piece of fruit. Di merely watched Val, taking bites of toast every now and then. That gleam was back in Di's eyes.

Turning toward us, Di set her toast down. "New plan. We're going to try to get jobs on this ranch."

Jacinda set her fruit down and wiped her hands. "Jobs doing what?"

"This." Di held up her plate of food. "If Val and Pete are willing to hire us, it'll not only give us a steady income so we don't have to use the *pile*, but it'll also give us an excuse to stay in this area while we wait for the new girl."

"Does that mean we'll be cooking *every day*?" Mica complained.

"If they hire us, yes," Di said.

Mica groaned dramatically. Jacinda patted her on the back.

Di stood and approached Val. They fell into conversation. I watched through the open area into the kitchen. From Val's shaking head and fluttering hands, I guessed she was saying no, but then Di said something else, and after a few more exchanges, Val smiled again and seemed contrite.

Di sauntered back. "Get your cleaning gloves ready ladies. Looks like we'll be cabin cleaning all morning."

"Cleaning?" Mica stated. "Seriously? Can't I go with the guys?"

Di crossed her arms. "That'd be up to Val. I told her we could all help until they find new staff."

Mica's eyes brightened. She raced to the older woman. After a few quick exchanges, Mica squealed in delight and disappeared out the screen door.

I cocked my head. "Until they find new staff? But I thought we were trying to get their jobs?"

A glint shone in Di's eyes. "All in good time."

I had no idea what that meant, but I did know one thing, Di had a plan and the only person who knew about it was Flint.

CHAPTER TWELVE

We spent the morning cleaning. Apparently, the normal staff routine consisted of breakfast prep, followed by cabin cleaning and then lunch prep and serving. Following that, it was lunch cleanup and supper prep. After Val wrapped the pans of lasagna we'd made for the supper meal, she put them in the fridge.

Her cheeks were still rosy but the frantic movements were gone. "I can't thank you all enough. Now, you girls go enjoy your afternoon. There's archery down by the pond this afternoon. Perhaps you'd like to try that?"

"What time should we be back?" Di asked.

Val wiped down the last counter. "Oh no, you've done enough."

Di crossed her arms. "I thought we talked about this. We're happy to help until you find more staff."

Val wrung the washcloth out a bit longer than necessary. "But I hate to ask that of you. This is your vacation."

Di smiled. The expression looked entirely out of place on her face, but my guess was that Di found the description of this being our *vacation* as amusing as I did. Since when was trying to find your identity and forgotten memories a vacation? Of course, Val didn't know about that.

"We're really just aimlessly traveling right now. No plans. Just tell us when to be back," Di said.

"Well, if you don't mind, are you able to come back at six?" Val folded the washcloth neatly on the counter. "I really hate to ask it of you, but if you're willing..." She wrung her hands again.

"We'll be back then," Di said.

Val nodded contritely. "Bless you, girls."

The three of us left and ambled back to the cabin. I glanced at Di's watch on her swinging wrist. Two in the afternoon so four whole hours to kill.

"Won't us getting jobs cut into your and Flint's research time?" I asked. The sun shone down as our feet crunched into the gravel.

Di eyed me coolly. "Yes and no. If you hadn't noticed, only four of their staff quit, yet there are seven of us. That means we won't be working full time."

I bit my lip as I realized she'd already worked out all of the details. "In other words, you'll still have time to search for answers even if four of us are on the clock every day."

"Exactly."

"Is that what you're going to do now?" I asked as our porch came into view. "Are you going back into town for the afternoon?"

Di shook her head. "Not today. I'm going to try to see her again."

With that, she climbed the steps to the cabin and retreated inside. My guess was to her bedroom. If Di's visions were always like what I'd witnessed yesterday, I wouldn't be surprised if she preferred having them in private.

"What about you?" I asked Jacinda. "What are you going to do?"

The panicked expression that coated her face, the

expression that always seemed to appear when our situation was mentioned, slowly disappeared.

"How about a manicure?" She picked up my hand. The panicked look was replaced with a horrified one when she got a look at my nails.

I glanced at the upper barn. It was one of the few places I hadn't explored. I pulled my hand back. "I was thinking about going up there." I nodded toward it.

"Why?" The horrified expression remained.

I shrugged. "Want to join me?"

"No thanks."

"Okay, see you later."

I took off toward the upper barn before Jacinda could insist my nails came first. Ever since noticing the barn, I'd been curious what lay behind it.

I struggled up the large hill, cursing the thin air. I still wasn't used to the altitude. Huffing, I reached the top.

The view around the main house had not prepared me for what resided beyond the ranch. Distant mountains gleaming with snow shone on the horizon. Rolling, forested hills stretched for miles. An abundance of wildflowers littered the perimeters of the surrounding pastures. It was like something off a postcard.

"It's Lena, isn't it?"

His voice startled me. One of the cowboys stood at the entrance to the barn. He dusted his hands off on a leather apron that covered dirty jeans. Sunlight gleamed off his faded cowboy hat.

I cocked my head. "Do I know you?"

He shook his head, smiling. "No. Mica told us your names when she started helping this morning. She said the redhead was Lena. I'm guessing that's you?"

"Oh, right." I realized I'd seen him before in the dining hall. He'd never helped in the group activities, though.

"You lookin' for someone?" he asked when I didn't say

anything.

"No. Just looking around."

"I hear your helpin' Val in the kitchen?"

"Yeah, until she can find more help. I don't have to be back till six so thought I'd take a walk."

The cowboy stepped closer, and I was able to see him in more detail. He had hazel eyes. Dark blond hair peeked out from under his cowboy hat. His face was angular but had soft contours. I guessed he was young, probably in his early twenties and those soft lines would harden with age. He grinned and held out his hand.

"I'm Dean Stewart. It's nice to meet you."

I returned the smile and shook his hand. Something about Dean pulled at me. He seemed so genuine and friendly. I switched my vision. When a white cloud appeared, I wasn't surprised.

"So what are you doing in there?" I snapped my sight back to normal.

"Just shoddin' one of the mares. You can watch if you want. Pete has me do all the horses."

We walked into the barn. Scents of hay and horse hung in the air. I blinked at the light adjustment. A mare in cross ties peeked over her shoulder when she heard our voices. She was a pale golden color and nickered when Dean got closer.

"Hey, Giselda." He bent down and lifted a front hoof. Alongside the mare were a number of metal tools.

"Is this your horse?" I asked.

"No." Dean smiled again. "My horse is in the pasture out back. The big gray gelding with the black mane. I've had 'im since I was a teenager. He's a great cattle horse."

Every time Dean spoke, his voice became more animated. I was beginning to understand why he'd been so welcoming to my company. He seemed to enjoy meeting new people as much as I did.

I smiled back. "What's his name?"

"Coal."

"Can I meet him later?"

His eyes lit up. "Yeah, I'll get Giselda done and then we can go out back. You can even ride 'im if you want."

I leaned against the workbench. The hard wood pressed into my back while I crossed my ankles. Dean's hands moved quickly and efficiently over Giselda's hooves. His hands weren't as big as Flint's and watching Dean didn't make my pulse quicken. As soon as I thought that, I wanted to slap my forehead. *Now, you're comparing guys to Flint?*

"So, you grow up around here?" I asked.

"No, I grew up in Wyoming. Just outside Laramie. My parents died a few years ago and left our family ranch to my oldest brother. I've got a share in it, but Joe can be hard to work with, so I thought I'd come ranchin' somewhere else for a while. Pete here was nice enough to offer me a job."

"So, how'd you meet Pete?"

Dean continued filing Giselda's hoof. The scraping sounds echoed in the barn. "He and Dad knew one another. I've known Pete since I was a boy…"

I listened contentedly to Dean's story. A while later, he finished up with Giselda. "Come on, girl." He led the mare out back. "Follow me, Lena," he called over his shoulder.

I followed him until we got to a pasture. Dean removed Giselda's halter and turned her loose. "So you want to get on Coal?" The bright sunlight reflected off his hat, shading his face, but I could still see his sparkling hazel eyes.

"Um, I don't know."

"Oh, come on," Dean said good naturedly. "I'll take care of ya." He guided me to another pasture and whistled sharply. In the distance, a large, beautiful horse lifted his head. He whinnied before breaking into a gallop. My eyes widened at the sight.

When Coal reached us, he slowed to a trot and then stopped a few feet from Dean. He blew forcefully through his nose. My eyes traveled up his height and widened even more. He was huge, much bigger than the trail ride horses.

"Ah…" I took a step backward. "I don't need to ride him. I can just pet him."

Dean grinned. "You'll be fine. Trust me. Coal's real good with beginners."

Dean proceeded to show me how to groom and saddle a horse. He then spent the next hour teaching me how to ride. It was a lot different from the trail rides. Coal didn't have a horse in front of him to follow, therefore, I had to tell him what to do. Riding was also tiring. By the time the lesson finished, my legs felt like Jell-O.

"You did great!" Dean said when I steered Coal to his side. Dean grinned ear to ear, his eyes twinkling in the sunlight. He pulled off his hat and wiped the sweat from his brow.

"That was fun." I patted Coal's neck. The large gelding breathed heavily. Sweat shined on his coat. I was sweating too. A salty trail slid past my ear.

"Should I walk him?" I asked. "He feels really warm."

"Yeah," Dean said. "Yeah, of course, take 'im back out to the ring."

I walked Coal around a few times. It wasn't until I was on my fourth cool-down lap that I realized we weren't alone. My eyes widened when I saw our audience. Standing beside the barn were two other cowboys, Pete, Jet, Jasper and Flint. My eyes went to Flint's. I thought a small smile covered his lips. With a blink, it was gone.

His averted gaze felt like an arrow through my heart. Five days of this and I still wasn't used to it.

"You ready to get off?" Dean asked.

I slid off Coal's back easily enough, but once I hit the ground, my legs buckled. Luckily, Dean caught me. A blush crept up my cheeks. Of course, everyone had seen my stumble, including Flint.

"Thanks," I mumbled. "That was more work than I

thought it'd be."

"You'll probably be sore tomorrow."

"You're most definitely going to be right."

Dean took Coal's reins and led him to the barn. I followed. The group still watched. Jet smirked and Jasper grinned. I had no idea what Flint was doing since I made myself avoid him.

"Have ya met Tyler and Aaron?" Dean asked.

I shook my head.

The two cowboys stood beside one another, watching us. Tyler had a wiry build and skin that looked like he spent all day in the sun. Aaron was meaty looking and big. I got a feeling off Tyler that was similar to Dean, but Aaron...

I frowned.

Something about Aaron's gaze made me nervous. I switched my vision and tuned into the clouds that surrounded them. Tyler's appeared normal. Aaron's, however, made me pause midstride.

My mouth went dry.

Dean turned, seeming to notice I wasn't beside him. I snapped my vision back to normal and began walking again. A sheen of sweat erupted across my body that had nothing to do with the bright sun.

When we reached everyone, Dean introduced me. "Lena, this here is Tyler and Aaron. Tyler's been ranchin' here with Pete for years but Aaron's a bit new."

Tyler held out his hand for me to shake. I shook it readily. Aaron did the same, but I hesitated a fraction of a second. I didn't want to touch him. I didn't want to be anywhere near him.

Swallowing, I took his palm. It was hot, big and felt like a vise seizing mine. When my eyes reached his, I had to stop myself from visibly flinching. There was a hunger in his gaze that made me squirm. I withdrew my hand as quickly as I could.

I sought Flint. Relief poured through me when I found

him watching me. That safe feeling once again settled over me, like a massage easing away the tension. Flint's gaze flickered to Aaron's before coming back to mine. I unconsciously took a step toward Flint. At the last minute, I stopped. Once again, my reaction to Flint baffled me. I wasn't a child. I'd grown used to taking care of myself. So why did I seek his comfort? And *why* did I feel so certain he would never let Aaron hurt me?

"You did pretty good on that horse, Lena," Pete said, interrupting my thoughts.

"Oh." I mentally shook myself. "Thanks, Pete."

"First time riding outside of a trail ride?" he asked.

Since I had no idea how to answer that question, I nodded.

"You could give Mica a run for her money," Tyler added. He sounded amused.

"Speaking of which, where is Mica?" I asked.

Jet rolled his eyes. "She's off with Jessie, the other cowboy. The guests are on a big trail ride this afternoon. She was so eager to go, Pete let her. The rest of us have been moving cattle around."

"Mica must be doing all right," I replied. "If she's helping Jessie on the trail ride."

"Yeah, she's been a great help this morning." Tyler grinned. "She's very enthusiastic." There was a smile in his voice.

Coal pawed the ground behind us. "Should we unsaddle Coal?" I asked Dean. Even with Flint present, I still didn't like being so close to Aaron. I also didn't like that his eyes hadn't left me since I joined them.

Dean and I walked inside the barn. I breathed a sigh of relief when Aaron finally disappeared from view. Thankfully, Dean's infectious good nature soon took hold. As the minutes ticked by, I felt more and more like myself. By the time we had Coal ready to turn to pasture, I was smiling again.

After we let Coal loose, I knew I needed to get back to the

cabin. I had no idea what time it was and hoped it wasn't past six. I thanked Dean again for the riding lesson. He told me to come back up the next day.

"Really?"

"Yeah, I'm up here most afternoons working on the horses. Come on back."

The thought of riding again and hanging out with Dean had me smiling. "I'll see you tomorrow."

He tipped his hat. "See ya then."

I felt Dean's gaze linger on me as I turned to go. I waved one last goodbye. After my hand fell, my eyes flickered around, but as hard as I tried to find Aaron, it was like he disappeared.

CHAPTER THIRTEEN

I walked slowly back to the cabin. My thighs protested the entire way. About halfway down the hill, footsteps sounded behind me. A mental picture of Aaron flashed through my mind. It was of him raising his hand to strike me down. Instinct took over. I whirled around, placed my feet farther apart and brought my fists up.

But it was only Flint.

He stopped a few feet away and held his hands up. "What's wrong?" His tone was hard.

I paused. "Ah, it's nothing." I dropped my fists. "I thought you might be Aaron."

"And that makes you frightened?"

"Yeah."

"Why?"

"His cloud's dark."

Flint put his hands on his hips. An expression grew on his face. He didn't seem happy. He was also dirty from a morning on the ranch and incredibly attractive in the sun. I wanted to kick myself for noticing.

"I wondered as much," he said. "I could tell you were

bothered by something when you met him. I haven't been able to figure him out, but I don't trust the guy."

"You shouldn't. I'd stay away from him if I were you."

"It's not myself I'm worried about."

I balked at his gruff tone.

He raked a hand harshly through his hair. "Are you going to make it back to the cabin?"

I figured he noticed my less than graceful walk down the hill. "Yeah, I'll be fine."

"Do you know where Aaron is?"

I shook my head.

He frowned again. "I'll walk with you."

Before I had a chance to reply, he started walking which forced me to follow. I half expected him to stay ahead. Instead, he slowed his step and walked by my side, matching his longer stride to mine.

The sun shone upon us. Fresh, clean air swirled around. Neither of us said anything. I was acutely aware of the awkward silence.

"What did you think of Dean?" Flint asked abruptly. He still stared straight ahead.

"Um, I like him. He seems really nice and genuine – generous too. He spent a long time teaching me about horses this afternoon."

"He certainly did." Flint's tone was gruff, and he ran a hand through his hair again.

Silence stretched. I was about to ask him something really witty, like, *did you have lunch*, when he said, "You did well on that horse."

His compliment took me by surprise. "Um, thanks."

"Do you think you've ridden before?"

"I have no idea. Maybe?"

"Di and I talk about that a lot, about what we've done in our lives and what we haven't. Like driving. Di and I are pretty competent behind the wheel, but Jacinda's an accident waiting to happen, and I'm pretty sure Jet doesn't know where the brake is."

I laughed.

For a moment, I thought he was going to smile. He didn't.

"So are we going to try to get permanent jobs on this ranch?" I asked.

"Did Di tell you that?"

"Yeah."

"Something like that is the plan."

I was about to ask him another question when he nodded ahead. "Looks like someone's waiting for you."

Di and Jacinda stood no more than ten yards away. I'd been so caught up in Flint, I hadn't noticed we were almost to the cabin. I hastily took a step away from him. Unconsciously, I'd inched closer and closer to him since we'd walked down the hill. I hoped Di hadn't noticed.

"Lena," Jacinda called. "Come on, we're going to be late."

"You better get going," Flint said.

I didn't want to leave. I liked being near Flint. I liked it too much. "Yeah, thanks for walking with me."

He didn't reply, but when I turned to go he said, "Lena?"

I actually shivered at the sound of my name on his lips. "Yeah?"

"Stay away from Aaron, okay?"

"I will."

"And tell Di and Jacinda about him. They need to know."

I TOLD DI and Jacinda about Aaron's cloud when we walked to the main house. Jacinda's eyes widened. Di merely pinched her lips together.

"Is he the only one here with a dark cloud?" Di asked.

"I don't know." Since coming to the ranch, I'd been lulled into a feeling of safety. Between the effects Flint had on me, always being in a group and getting to know Pete, Val and the guests, I'd never felt threatened. Beside the cowboys, I hadn't checked anyone's clouds.

"Then that's what I want you doing tonight. Assess everyone, and I mean everyone. Report back to me what you find," Di ordered.

I swallowed uneasily. "Um, okay."

By seven that night, everyone was in the dining room, including Flint and Aaron. I tried not to let Aaron affect me. He kept watching me, as if *I* was his meal. Biting my lip, I glanced at Flint. Safety once again engulfed me even though he ignored me. A part of me felt confused. This afternoon, Flint had seemed worried for me, but tonight, he hadn't said hello.

I sighed. Turning, I walked back to the kitchen. Di stood at the counter, helping with dessert.

"What'd you see?" she asked quietly.

"No one's dark. I don't think we need to worry about any of them."

Di nodded tightly. "So, it's just Aaron."

"Yeah, just Aaron." Although, that *just* didn't make it any better.

Once back in the dining room, my eyes darted to the cowboy's table again. Dean sat beside Tyler, and across from him, Aaron. The other cowboy I hadn't met yet sat beside him. He had black hair and looked Native American. I figured he must be Jessie.

Against my better judgment, I shifted my vision. Aaron's cloud readily appeared. Ugly, black, jagged edges darted around his skull and neck. It was unsettling to watch. With difficulty, I swallowed a grimace.

A few minutes later, Dean pushed his chair back from the table. The scraping sound echoed above the din. When he passed me on his way out, he smiled brightly and stopped.

"It'll be fun to do another riding lesson tomorrow," he said. "I'm looking forward to it."

I smiled back. "Yeah, me too."

"I bet you'd make a good cowgirl. Maybe you could join

Mica and the rest of us instead of working in here."

I shrugged uncertainly. "Well…I'm not sure if we're fully employed. We're just helping out right now."

Dean smiled. "You will be. I heard Pete and Val talking. They're going to offer you all jobs. They said something about you not having any plans, so maybe you'd want to stick around for a while."

"Really?" A part of me was dumbstruck. Was that Di's plan all along? To let Pete and Val think that *they'd* come up with the idea of hiring us? It was an incredibly manipulative tactic that Di seemed to have pulled off flawlessly.

"Lena?" Dean said.

"Oh, um." I glanced toward the kitchen. I wondered what Val would think if another one of us disappeared to the outdoor work. "I'm not sure Val would approve if I left. She needs the help in here."

Dean grinned. "Right, what was I thinking. A woman's place is in the kitchen." He winked.

I laughed at his joke. His eyes lighted up even more. We spoke for a few more minutes before he left. When he finally disappeared out the door, a strange sensation flowed in the air. My body followed the feeling on its own accord.

My eyes locked with Flint's. I realized that strange power sensation was coming off him again. He averted his gaze. Abruptly, he stood and stalked out the door. My breath came out in a whoosh. I hadn't realized I'd been holding it.

With Flint gone, the strange power slowly dissipated. I jolted back to my surroundings. My eyes flashed to each table. Everyone carried on eating, talking and laughing. They all seemed oblivious to the heavy energy that just flowed through the room like invisible syrup.

"You want to give me a hand, Lena?" Di held up a tub full of dirty dishes.

"Right, of course." I shook myself.

I joined her in the kitchen. However, I still couldn't shake off whatever had just transpired in that room. How was it that nobody felt that energy off Flint? It was so strong at times, it took my breath away.

DEAN WAS RIGHT about Val and Pete. The next day, they offered us jobs until the season was over. Di's plan had worked.

Consequently, Di, Jacinda and I began working in the kitchen. Since Val only needed two of us we had a number of days off, also like Di anticipated. Over the next week, we fell into a steady routine as we waited for the new girl. It was pretty much the same each day. Our day started at six. We'd help Val with breakfast and then clean cabins all morning. After that, we made lunch, did dinner prep and then we had off until six at night. It was a split shift but I didn't mind. We were off during the nicest part of the day.

The other routine I'd fallen into? Every afternoon, I joined Dean for a riding lesson. A few times I considered asking Di or Flint if I could join them when they ventured to internet cafes, but I didn't. Being around Flint and seeing the closeness he shared with Di hurt too much. I felt weak because of that. I wished I could force those feelings away or bury them in some hidden chest deep within my mind, but every time I saw Flint – those feelings exploded. I had no control over them. Besides, Di and Flint seemed to work well together. Maybe it was best to leave them up to finding answers. The rest of the group seemed to have done just that. Still, that didn't sit well with me. I wanted answers more than anything and passively waiting for them didn't suit my personality.

Riding and joking with Dean, however, helped keep my mind off Flint and our strange situation. It was the only thing that stilled the longing in my heart, or at least, allowed me to ignore it for a brief amount of time.

"Afternoon, Lena!" Dean's cheerful voice called. I'd just finished the steep climb to the barn. Once again, he waited for me at the top.

"Hi, Dean."

"You ready?" His hazel eyes shone brightly, a big smile plastered on his face. "I brought Coal into the barn for you to saddle. I already brushed 'im."

"You did?"

"Yeah, I was thinkin' maybe we'd do somethin' fun today. How 'bout a trail ride?"

"Really?" We'd never done that before.

"Sure, I'll show you some of the ranch that you can't see on the guest trail rides. You've learned enough you'll be just fine, even if Coal gets spooked. It's a great afternoon to go out."

I glanced at the sky. Nothing but endless blue.

After we had our horses ready, we walked them out back and mounted. The air was warm. I tied my jacket around my waist anyway. One thing I'd learned was that the weather in the mountains could be entirely unpredictable.

"Have you ever gone back this way?" Dean asked, turning in his saddle. We walked past the maze of corrals and pens.

I shook my head. "No. I've only been on the group trail rides." Those usually went in the opposite direction and stayed in the lower regions. Dean seemed to be taking us up, not down.

Dean grinned. "I'll be sure to give ya a good tour then."

I smiled and sank deeper into the saddle.

We ventured slowly into the mountains. The black specs of cattle on the hills grew larger as Dean pointed out landmarks.

"You see that over there?" He nodded to a sharply pointed mountain. "That's called the witch's tit."

"The witch's *what*?"

Dean chuckled. "The witch's tit. And that," he pointed to an area of mountains and trees that were pointed at the top and fanned out at the bottom, "is called her broomstick."

"Why didn't they call the witch's tit the witch's hat?"

Dean grinned. "I dunno. It was named long ago by lonely miners. I'm sure you can guess where their minds were."

I laughed.

The ranch soon became a distant speck behind us. We dipped and turned around hills and cliffs. Birds sang. Chipmunks and squirrels ran along tree branches and fluttered under leaves. Scents of pine and horse filled the air. It was incredibly pleasant.

"It's so beautiful out here," I said.

Dean nodded. "This is God's country."

I smiled. For once, I didn't feel the anxiety that accompanied me since meeting Flint and learning how scary our situation was. It felt so good, freeing almost. If I had known the mountains could do this to me, I would have ventured out here sooner.

About an hour later, we passed through a shallow creek. I had no idea where we were in relation to the ranch, but Dean pointed to the ravine. "You ever get lost out here, ya look to see which way the water's movin'. This stream connects to a bigger river that's not far from the ranch. You just follow that, or any other stream you find, until ya get to it. Most of the creeks around here dump into that river."

I sincerely hoped I'd never get lost in this wilderness. This may be God's country, but out here, it was every man for himself. We trailed up another mountain. Dean pointed to a swamp of trees that were so dense it seemed impossible to enter. "Ya see that over there?"

I shaded my eyes. "Yeah."

"That place is called the Forbidden Hills. It's a good way to get lost and never come back. Many men have ventured into that forest to never return. The hills are too dark and the trees too dense. Even mountain men get turned around in there. It's best to stay away from it."

I swallowed uneasily. "Okay."

Dean laughed. "It's kinda like the Bermuda Triangle of Colorado. Scientists from all over the world have come to study it, but nobody can figure out why the crazy things happen in it. GPS's randomly won't work. Hikers swear they lose their bearin's within a few minutes of enterin' the trees. People have gone in and never come back." His joking words died, his face serious. "They're dangerous, the Forbidden Hills. I mean it when I say to stay out. None of the locals will go in there, but every now and then, we'll get a tourist lookin' for a thrill. They never make it far before they turn around and run out. Trust me. It's best to just stay away."

A chill ran through me. "I will."

A few hours later, the ranch appeared. It popped up so quickly I hadn't realized we were so close.

"We're almost back," I exclaimed.

"Less than a mile from here."

I nudged Coal forward until we were beside Dean and his mount. A smile grew on my face. "Race ya!"

Before Dean could respond, I kicked Coal into a gallop. The huge gelding sprang into action. We flew across the landscape. It was exhilarating to feel Coal's powerful hooves pounding into the terrain and feel the air whooshing past. I'd never gone this fast before, but it was almost a straight shot to the barn.

I heard hooves thundering behind me and glanced over my shoulder. Dean followed in hot pursuit, but he was still a few lengths back. Razz was doing his best to catch Coal, but the smaller stallion was no match for Coal's long legs. I urged Coal to go faster. We left them in the dust.

A few minutes later, we reached the pastures and pens behind the barn. A hundred yards after that, the barn approached. I sat up straighter, not realizing I'd been hunched over Coal's neck as we thundered across the land.

"Easy, boy." Coal instantly responded to my shifting weight. He slowed to a canter and then bumpy trot. I trotted in a circle and turned. Dean was still galloping at the last pasture. He slowed as he got closer to the barn.

"Damn, girl, you can ride!"

I grinned.

Dean smiled, an ear breaking grin that stretched across his face. "We better walk 'em."

We walked the horses to the end of the pastures and back again. By the time we reached the barn, both horses were cooled.

"That was a lot of fun," I said. "Thanks for taking me."

"My pleasure. We should do it again."

"Definitely." I swung my leg to get off Coal but paused. Something pulsed into my back. A wave of energy hit me. Looking awkwardly over my shoulder, I spotted Flint standing by the barn. His arms were crossed. Power radiated off him in hot waves. It was so strong, I physically felt it.

I tried to balance my boot in the stirrup, but another push of his power hit me. The next thing I knew, my foot slipped and I was falling. Before I could shriek, strong arms encircled me and a tight voice whispered into my ear.

"Just what the hell do you think you're doing?" Flint seethed.

CHAPTER FOURTEEN

Flint caught me so abruptly, the air whooshed out of my lungs. It took me a minute to catch my breath. "What...how..." I stammered.

Dean's voice interrupted. "Flint? Where'd you come from?"

The cowboy's head was cocked, a puzzled expression on his face. Flint still had his arms around me. They were so hard. I wondered if Dean had seen Flint's mind numbing speed as Flint raced the twenty yards from the barn to where I'd fallen off Coal. From the innocent curiosity in Dean's voice, I guessed not.

I still reeled from how fast Flint moved. Other than him rearranging the furniture that one morning, I'd never seen what he was capable of.

"Did you *fall?*" Dean asked incredulously.

I nodded numbly and tried to stand. Flint and I still huddled close to the ground. However, I couldn't get my tongue working. How could his arms be so hard? They felt like steel. Before I could get my knees to straighten, Flint stood and set me back on my feet. The ground, however, didn't cooperate. It swayed. Or perhaps, I swayed. My head spun from how close Flint stood.

"Thank you." I did a double take when I saw Flint's expression. Thunderous, was the first word that came to mind. His eyes shot sparks at Dean.

"Lena?" Dean said.

"Yeah?"

"We should probably put the horses away." His gaze didn't leave Flint's.

"Right. Excuse me." I sidestepped Flint and pulled Coal to the barn, but Flint's words stopped me.

"How far did you take her?" He stared at Dean.

Dean shrugged. "To the Forbidden Hills and back."

"You took her all the way to the Forbidden Hills?" Flint said, his voice rising. He placed his hands on his hips. Once again, raw power radiated off him. The force of it hit me like a wave. I gasped and stepped back.

Dean didn't seem to notice the energy pouring off Flint. Instead, he slid off Razz and put his hands on his hips too. Both men stared at each other. The stallion pawed the ground and flung his head. Apparently, I wasn't the only one feeling the charged atmosphere.

"Did you consider what would happen if she'd fallen off or gotten hurt out there?" Flint asked.

"She wasn't gonna fall," Dean said. "She's a solid rider."

"She just learned a week ago."

"Well, she's the most natural rider I've ever met!"

Both men now stood within a foot of one another. I briefly thought of a Clint Eastwood movie. I waited for guns to be drawn and a shootout to begin.

"Ah, excuse me. I'm still here, you know." I blew at an annoying curl that kept fluttering in front of my face.

Dean shook his head and took a step back. "Sorry, Lena."

Flint stayed put, his shoulders bunched. He still glared at Dean. "Did you think to tell anyone where you were going?

What if something happened? How would we have known where to look for you?"

By *we*, I assumed he meant himself and the other cowboys. Not *moi*. But instead of Dean coming back with a smart comment, something Flint said seemed to touch a chord in him. "We were never in any danger," Dean said, although his voice wasn't so sure.

"Yeah," I replied. "No danger at all. We were only walking in the woods."

"Walking?" Flint spun, facing me. The intensity of his gaze made me step back. I resisted the urge to take another step back when he leaned forward. "You call that neck breaking gallop into the barn, *walking?*"

I stood up taller and put my hands on my hips. "Well, yes, actually, we were walking. The entire time out there we were walking."

"Then how do you explain what I saw just a minute ago?"

"So we raced in, what's the big deal?"

"The big deal?" he said, his voice tight. "The big deal is that you could have fallen off and gotten hurt."

"So?"

"*So?*"

"Yeah, so? What's it to you, anyway?"

Something in his face changed but abruptly it disappeared. "You're my responsibility, that's why," he said gruffly.

I didn't think he could have said anything worse to hurt me. I was his responsibility. It was his duty to protect me, nothing more. My heart broke right there. That's all I'd ever be to him even though something about him pulled at me like gravity. Just his presence made me want to step closer, to touch him and feel his muscles bunch and tighten beneath my fingertips. My body was helpless to resist. It was impossible for me to ignore my attraction to him.

Not wanting him to see the tears that burned my eyes, I turned and stalked to the barn. Dean called out but I ignored him too. How could I have been so stupid? I'd actually hoped that maybe, just *maybe*, Flint cared for me. Maybe a little. But why would he?

Flint appeared at my side, hands in his pockets, head down. "Lena?" he said quietly.

I ignored him and kept walking. I couldn't speak. My voice would probably break. A breeze swirled around us. I pushed another curl behind my ear.

"Lena?"

If I didn't know better, I'd say there was an ache in his voice, but I *did* know better, so I knew I imagined it.

"Lena," he repeated, sounding exasperated. "I'm sorry."

I stopped. My chest rose and fell quickly. I was pretty sure my skin was even paler than normal. For some reason, that happened when I got hurt, angry, frustrated, and all of the other emotions I felt right now. I concentrated on the anger. That was the easiest to feel.

"Did you just say you were sorry?" I turned toward him and cursed the stupid, bright sun that made me squint when I looked up.

"Yes."

"Whatever for?"

He either didn't hear my sarcasm or chose to ignore it. "For..." he began, but then stopped.

I raised my eyebrows.

He didn't say anything. Something flashed across his face again. Those damned, fleeting emotions that never lasted longer than a second. I swatted at another curl, my frustration growing. Tapping my foot, I waited for him to continue. He didn't.

"Just forget it." I turned and walked the remaining steps to the barn. I half expected Flint to say something and secretly hoped he would. I waited for him to call out. He didn't. Nothing but a soft breeze whistling through the rafters reached my ears. I turned.

Flint was nowhere to be seen.

I spun around. Was he really gone? I ran to the end of the barn and then back to where Dean stood. There was no sign of him. "Have you seen Flint?" I asked Dean.

He shook his head. "No. Why, he leave?"

"I guess so."

Dean sighed. "Good." He turned back to his horse.

AFTER THAT INCIDENT at the barn, Flint went back to ignoring me. Unless it was required he talk to me, it was like I didn't exist.

I attempted to make myself feel better as I got ready for work the next night. I searched for one of the trendy tops Jacinda bought me. It was almost six in the evening. I didn't have much time so cursed when I couldn't find it. After digging through my mountain of clothes on the floor, I finally spotted it.

Jacinda insisted fashion was therapy. Beautiful clothes always made her smile. I had yet to experience that euphoria, but considering my mood today, I was willing to try.

Muted colors of green, lavender, gold and ivory flowed around me in the peasant style top. The material felt nice. I had to agree with that. However, a heaviness still hung in my heart. Just the thought of Flint was like tying an anchor to my mood. It sank.

A noise sounded in the hall. Jacinda stood outside my door, grinning. She held a finger up and told me to wait. She sailed down the hall and returned a minute later.

"Wear these with it," she instructed. She held up gold, hoop earrings. A hint of her jasmine perfume floated around me as she surveyed my legs. "Now, to go with the top…" She eyed my skinny jeans.

"No," I replied. "Don't even go there."

I picked up my favorite cut-off jean shorts from the floor and pulled them on before slipping on simple, white canvas sneakers. They were broken-in and comfortable for work.

Surprisingly, Jacinda clapped in approval. "Lena! You just put together your first cute outfit!"

I rolled my eyes but couldn't stop my reluctant smile. "Come on, we're running late."

Di was in a mood too, evident in the way she grumbled and paced in her bedroom. Apparently, the new girl changed direction again, opting for a bus heading for Arizona versus Colorado. In other words, she wasn't arriving this week.

Half an hour later, Jacinda and I were setting up the buffet. Jacinda's eyes still twinkled every time we bumped into one another. She didn't try to hide her excitement over my sudden fashion interest. I didn't burst her bubble that it was a one-off interest. So far, all the pretty top had done was get in the way when I tried to lift things. The damned top was too tight in the shoulders.

"Lena, you look great!" Dean called. His voice snapped my attention from the buffet. The cowboy stood at the side door, and for once, was early. The other cowboys, and cowgirl, stood behind him – Tyler, Jessie, Aaron and Mica. Jet, Jasper and Flint were nowhere to be seen. I avoided Aaron, even though I felt his eyes on me. To quell my unease, I locked my gaze on Dean.

"Thanks. Where are the other guys?" I asked.

"Still out working." Mica dusted her hat off on her jeans. "Pete sent them off to round up the last cows that wandered onto the north ridge."

I envisioned Flint and the twins on horseback wandering around the hills. Did that mean they wouldn't make it back in time for supper?

"You gonna join us for the meal tonight?" Dean asked.

I held up what I arranged on the buffet. "Gotta work."

Dean shrugged. "Worth a try." He squeezed my shoulder when he walked by. His hand was large, not as big as Flint's, but still, it swallowed my upper arm. I wanted to kick myself for liking the feel of Flint's hands more.

The cowboys and Mica followed Dean. They were all dirty, dusty and towered over me. I smiled pleasantly at everyone except for Aaron.

The next hour passed slowly. Dean was right about Jet, Jasper and Flint. They never made it back for supper. I still couldn't stop my eyes from going to the door every few minutes to see if they'd arrived. Since the incident at the barn, the only times I'd seen Flint had been in passing at meals. I couldn't help but feel he was avoiding me even more than usual.

The cowboys all talked and laughed throughout the meal, obliviously happy and content. My gaze scanned everyone in the hall, one by one. I hadn't realized I'd switched my vision until it passed over Aaron and his ugly, evil cloud rose like a tidal wave. It hovered above him, swimming around his neck and through his hair. The shifting ebony colors were like a gigantic eel that slithered against his skull. I snapped my sight back to normal and swirled out of the dining room. I couldn't get to the kitchen fast enough.

When the meal finished, Jacinda approached. "Hey, Little L? Val needs to go into town to get supplies and said that one of us can go with her. Do you want to go or stay here and clean up?"

From the sparkle in Jacinda's eyes, I knew she wanted to go. While she liked the ranch, at heart, she was a city girl and used every excuse to get into Little Raven, even though it wasn't a sprawling metropolis.

"You go," I replied. "I'll stay here and clean up."

"You don't mind?"

"Not at all." I didn't mention that I still felt like a freak in town. It didn't seem my first impression on the locals was wearing off anytime soon.

"Okay, we'll be back in a few hours." Jacinda flashed her supermodel smile. I knew she was ecstatic. I only got *that* smile when she was really happy.

After they left, I took my time with everything. By the time I finished, the dining tables gleamed and the floor was thoroughly mopped. Cleanliness always made Val happy.

I stepped out into the night and felt a little better. There was nothing like productivity to calm a heartbroken spirit. I took a deep breath. Scents of horse, grass, cattle and clean mountain air filled the night air. I was growing to love that smell.

It was chilly, so I took off at a brisk pace. Pete told me, way back on the day he'd picked me up, that the ranch's high altitude accounted for a number of crisp evenings, even during the summer. He hadn't been kidding. Goose bumps rose on my arms faster than a rabbit running from a coyote. I walked faster.

The farther I got from the house, the quieter the night became. All of the guest cabins were dark. It was then I remembered it was the night of the big bonfire down by the river. No wonder no guests were around. Smiling, I rubbed my chilled arms and kept walking.

Thump, thump, thump.

I abruptly stopped. The breeze tossed curls into my eyes. What had that been?

Scanning the darkness, I tucked a strand of hair behind my ear. Faint light from the main house shone in the distance. Other than that, I was surrounded by darkness. I still stood a fair distance from my cabin so scanned the area again. I didn't see anyone. I cocked my head, listening.

Just the nighttime sounds. That was it.

Shrugging, I began walking again. I'd only gone ten yards when the same sound came. I swirled around. There was *definitely* something behind me.

The hairs on the back of my neck stood up. I froze. I looked around but still didn't see anything. I looked left and then right. Nothing. But I felt...*something.*

"Is anyone there?" I called. I waited a moment.

Silence.

"Hello?" I said.

Nothing.

I waited a second longer, but I could still feel it. My sixth sense told me I wasn't alone. I started to breathe faster. *Someone is near and doesn't want me to know it.* I felt as certain of that as I knew the sky was blue.

Without another thought, I turned and sprinted. My feet scissored beneath me as a survival instinct roared to life. I bolted for the cabin as fast as I could go.

I couldn't be sure, but I thought I heard someone behind me. The *thump, thump* on the gravel was faster, more pronounced. That almost made me shriek, but then I saw the cabin. It was still far. The small building had only crested my view on the gravel drive, but the light was on in the living room. That small, shining light beckoned safety. I breathed harder and moved my legs faster. The breeze whipped across my face, all pleasant scents gone.

The distance closed. Forty yards. Thirty yards. Twenty yards. Ten yards! I was almost there when a dark figure stepped out in front of me.

I screamed.

The sound abruptly died when I slid to a careening halt. The sudden stop pitched me off balance. I almost tripped. The figure reached out and grabbed me. I screamed again, the sound pierced my own ears, but then I recognized a scent.

Spice, wood and tangerines.

Flint.

"It's just me." Flint's voice was gruff. Concern laced the edges. "Why are you running?"

He pulled me to a dark cabin a few cabins up from ours. It was empty. Tall grass tickled my calves. I panted from running and clung tightly to his forearms.

"Why are you running?" he asked again, more firmly this

time.

I could only breathe loudly.

"Lena?"

I took a staggering breath and struggled to get myself under control. His fingers grasped my chin and tilted my head up. In the moonlight, his angular features were sharp and severe, his eyes black.

"Jesus," he whispered. "What happened?"

I was still too stunned to speak.

"Did somebody hurt you?" He gripped my shoulders tighter. Hot energy rolled off him. I shook my head. Already, the fear I'd felt was rapidly disintegrating. *Safe, I'm safe*. Once again, that soothing, precious feeling flowed through me in his presence.

"Lena, what happened?" His breath was warm and sweet. It was hard to not lose all coherent thought.

"Nothing," I finally managed. "I don't know." I shook my head as I tried to figure out what *had* happened. A few other times, in Rapid City, I felt that someone was after me. It was usually at night when I was out wandering around. Both times it happened, I listened to my gut. I ran as fast as I could to a more populated area. I'd never know if those fears had been valid, but I trusted my gut. It was all I'd had.

"Did something scare you?" Flint asked.

All I could do was nod.

"What?" he demanded. Another huge wave of energy rolled off him.

"I heard someone. Someone was following me when I was about halfway back. I could feel that I wasn't alone, but nobody answered when I asked who was there."

"Where?" he asked, his tone clipped.

I explained where I was when I first heard it. I was about to mumble that I might have been mistaken when the air whooshed around me. My breath caught in my throat.

I was flying.

Before I could think two words, I stood on my cabin's porch.

Flint was gone.

It all happened so quickly, it took me a minute to process it. My eyes widened when I did. Flint just *carried* me up the road to my porch. I searched for him in the distance. He'd vanished into the night.

"Lena? Is that you?" A tapping sound made me turn.

Mica's face pressed against the glass. She was sitting at the kitchen table, visible through the window. She smiled and waved. I returned the wave as best I could before walking inside. The feeling of being chased, the sensation of being near Flint, and the incredible way he'd moved me ten yards in two seconds left me dumbstruck.

"What took you so long?" she asked when I stepped inside. She was reading a book. A cup of half-drunk juice sat beside her.

Instead of responding, I walked to the bathroom. I closed the door and placed my hands on the sink. I leaned into them. Harsh breaths escaped me. My fingers gripped the porcelain bowl tightly, the smooth basin hard and unforgiving.

A few minutes later, finally feeling in control, I looked up. My face stared back in the mirror. I was a little paler than normal. Other than that, I looked like myself. Dark red curls tumbled down my back. My green eyes were particularly alert but not out of the ordinary. I splashed cold water on my face and returned to the living room.

"Where's Jacinda?" Mica had moved to the couch, the book on her lap.

"She went to town with Val," I replied automatically. I sat beside Mica and pulled my feet underneath me. The couch's upholstery felt rough and worn. A second later, an abrupt whoosh of hair had me sitting straight up, but it was only Flint, barreling through the cabin's door.

"Nothing," he said. "I searched the whole area but didn't

find anyone." His eyes were like two, onyx daggers darting through me. I wondered how far he'd gone. With how fast he moved, he'd probably covered a few square miles.

"Okay," I replied. "Do you think I imagined it?"

"No." He didn't elaborate.

Mica fidgeted beside me just as Di appeared in her bedroom door frame. With wide eyes, Mica said, "What happened?"

Before Flint or I could respond, commotion sounded on the porch. Jacinda pushed passed Flint, carrying several bags.

"Hey, guys," Jacinda said pleasantly. She sailed to the small kitchenette and placed the bags on the counter. "I bought us some more coffee and that cereal you like, Mica. Lena, I bought you a new pair of earrings. I hope you don't mind." Her chatter died down. The rustling from the plastic bags died with it.

Jacinda frowned and surveyed all of us. Di, in her usual all black attire, crossed her arms. "Something's happened," Di said.

Flint nodded curtly. "Someone was following Lena."

"What?" Jacinda's face paled. "Are you serious?"

"Where?" Di demanded.

"On her way back to the cabin," Flint said.

"Do you know who it was?" Jacinda asked.

Flint shook his head.

Di eyed all of us. "Right, no one is to be alone outside at night anymore. Got it?" She turned back to Flint. "Are you going to tell the guys?"

"I will, but I don't think Jet or Jasper will be too worried. What's the likelihood of someone attacking a male?"

Di frowned and replied in a quieter tone, "Unless it has something to do with us." She made a motion toward her tattoo.

My eyes widened. I hadn't thought of that possibility.

"Hmm." Flint's lips tightened.

Di turned to the three of us. "I don't want any of us alone anymore at night. Okay?"

"Should we tell Pete?" Mica asked.

Di and Flint dipped their heads and started whispering. I couldn't hear what was said. I knew Jacinda did from the way she perked up. When they stopped, Di said, "For the time being, no."

I swallowed. They were obviously concerned enough about our situation to not want Pete and Val involved.

Flint eyed me. "Are you sure you're okay?"

"Yeah, fine."

His gaze lingered. Jacinda had sat beside Mica and I, her hands clasped tightly in her lap. Di on the other hand, stared out the window, looking deep in thought.

Only Mica seemed unperturbed. She picked up her book again. "Not many boring nights around here!"

CHAPTER FIFTEEN

When I walked up to the main house the next morning, I kept thinking about the previous night. Had someone really followed me? How likely was that? And could it really be related to what happened to us all those months ago? I shivered at that thought.

Since it was my day off, the dining room was in full swing by the time I got there. I grabbed a few slices of toast and a cup of coffee. Flint sat on the other side of the room with the cowboys. I tried not to stare. Something about him looked different.

It took me a minute to place it. Stubble lined his cheeks. Dark smudges blackened the skin under his eyes. He looked tired. That was a first. I'd never seen him as anything but clean-cut and alert looking.

Mica appeared just as I finished. "Is it your day off?"

"Yep."

"We're taking the guests on a nature walk. Wanna come?"

Since I didn't have anything planned, I nodded. "Sure."

As usual, Flint ignored me when I passed. Even after last night, nothing had changed. My heart sank.

A group of guests, most of them kids, were already waiting outside. I smiled at the kids and let the magic of being around people work through me. When I dipped down to talk to the little ones, I got a few giggles. That made me smile.

It was nice to be outside for a change. I was glad I brought my windbreaker, though. It had cooled considerably, and a low cloud cover was moving in.

"Nice to have you with us, Lena." Pete stood in the yard and smiled warmly before beckoning the kids and parents to join him.

"We'll be goin' on a nature walk today," Pete said. "We'll be talkin' about the plants of Colorado, specifically, the ones that grow around here. Now to start, can anyone tell me how plants are named?"

One of the girl's hand shot in the air. "They're named in an old language so everyone calls them the same."

"That's right," Pete said. "All plants are given Latin names and common names. The Latin names were developed long ago by…"

A famous botanist named Linnaeus. I reeled inwardly when the knowledge spewed out of my brain. *Here we go again.* Once again, random knowledge escaped from some unknown cavern deep within my subconscious. If only I could do that with my identity. I groaned inwardly. I was certain, more than ever, that I'd been educated at some point in my life.

A few hours later, we returned to the main house. Everyone climbed the steps just in time for lunch.

"What did you think?" Mica asked. Mica also helped with the tour. She knew all of the Latin names too.

"You did great," I replied.

"Really?"

"Did Pete teach you that stuff?" I asked as the last guest trailed inside.

"No, I already know it."

I sighed. "So we're all like that."

"Yep!"

We walked into the house. The door closed softly behind us. Mica stomped the mud from her boots on the rug.

"Do you think we all went to college?" I asked. "Or some advanced prep school?" Considering how much we knew, it didn't seem like your every day school program explained it.

"We must have, cause you have to admit, we know a lot. And it's not like I'm the smartest person in the world," Mica replied.

I also didn't think I was the next Albert Einstein. However, it was almost eerie at how much was crammed in our heads.

"Why do you think we can remember so much, but can't remember ourselves?"

Mica shrugged. "I don't know. Your best bet is to ask Flint or Di. They spend a lot of time talking about this stuff. Ooh! Pizza for lunch! Yum!"

She raced into the dining room. I sighed and followed.

Jacinda, Di and Val were hard at work when I entered the hall. I couldn't help but wonder if the three were having a hard time keeping up without me. There were two additional families at the ranch this week. No doubt the new girl would come in handy when she arrived, if Val and Pete were happy to hire her too. I wondered how we'd explain that one. It was kind of weird after all, to just randomly show up with another person, as if out of thin air.

I got a plateful of food and sat beside Mica.

"You okay?" Mica asked. She had almost half a pizza on her plate.

I forced a smile. "Just thinking about something."

"What?"

I pushed around the slice with my fork. "Do we all go to pick up the new girl?"

"Yep, or at least, that's what we've done so far. Flint doesn't like us getting split up for too long. He thinks it's safer that way."

Of course he does. That only made my shoulders slump further. Flint felt responsible for everyone. His interest in me had never been any different.

Jacinda sauntered over just as Mica stood to refill her drink. She pulled out Mica's chair and sat. Her expression seemed particularly coy today. "Talk to Flint much this morning?" she asked.

I shook my head and bit off a large bite of pizza. "No."

Jacinda rolled her eyes. "Really, Little L, do you have to chew with your mouth open?"

A blush crept up my cheeks. I didn't mean to have bad table manners. I forced my lips closed and tried to eat more daintily. It was hard. It didn't seem the starvation mentality I'd acquired those first few months was wearing off anytime soon.

"Sorry," I mumbled.

Jacinda leaned forward. "Back to Flint. I just wondered if you saw how tired he looked this morning?"

I thought about the dark circles on his too handsome face. "Yeah, I noticed."

"Any idea why that is?"

I shook my head and took another bite. I was careful to keep my mouth closed through the *entire* bite. Seriously, I would get good at this. Jacinda placed her forearms on the table. Her perfectly manicured nails curled around her elbows. "Do you know where Flint was last night?"

"No."

"Care to take a guess?"

I raised an eyebrow.

"Okay, okay. I was just asking." She sighed. "Well, just so you know, he spent the entire night outside our cabin. He didn't sleep a wink."

"Really?"

"Really."

"Why would he do that?"

"I think he was keeping watch, but he didn't want us to know he was there. Of course, I still heard him. He made a racket every time he did one of his rounds." She rolled her eyes, her delicate eyebrows rising.

"But *why* would he do that?"

Jacinda cocked her head. "I think to keep you safe."

"You mean from whoever chased me last night?"

"I think so."

That took me aback. "Don't you think he wanted to keep everyone safe?"

Jacinda bit her lip. "I don't think so."

"Why don't you think so?"

"That's what I'm trying to figure out. He's been weird ever since you arrived."

I tried to keep my voice even. "What do you mean?"

"The way he is with you. It hasn't escaped my attention that he's always avoiding you or only speaking to you when necessary. *And* he doesn't hang out with us anymore. Before you arrived, we all hung out. Now that you're here, though, he's completely distanced himself. But then he gets all irritated when one of the cowboys grabs your attention. Not to mention, I've never seen him go so crazy when he thinks you're in trouble."

My mouth dropped. I shook my head. "Wait a minute, he doesn't get irritated about the cowboys. What are you talking about?"

Jacinda smirked. "You think he likes how much time you spend with Dean?"

I had no idea what she was getting at. Flint didn't know I spent my afternoons with the cowboy. He had no idea what I did. Right? But then I remembered the incident at the barn, when he'd known I'd been on a trail ride with Dean.

"But Dean and I are just friends."

"Is that what you call it?" Before I could reply, she added, "You wouldn't know this, but Flint hasn't been the same since you arrived. He's moody and withdrawn – more so than usual. Even Di's noticed since he's snapping at her now. He won't tell her why, but personally, I think it's because of you."

Her words made me balk. "Jacinda, that doesn't make sense. Aren't he and Di *together*?"

"Together?" Jacinda's eyebrows rose clear to her hairline.

"Like dating or something?"

She grinned and then laughed. She pushed to standing when Mica returned.

"What are you guys talking about?" Mica held a full glass of lemonade and took a drink.

"Nothing," Jacinda said.

"So, are you gonna join us this afternoon?" Mica asked me. "Pete's gonna show the guests how to use a lasso."

I shook my head. My head was still spinning from all that Jacinda implied. "Um, no, I think I'll join Dean for another riding lesson." The truth, however, was that I wanted to get into the mountains. I needed some time to think. I couldn't do that during a lasso lesson.

"Oh," Mica said.

I turned to Jacinda. "You should go with Mica. You could learn how to rope calves."

Jacinda's nose wrinkled. "No, thank you."

"Are you sure?" Mica asked.

Jacinda looked like she'd rather drink paint than work with cows. "Not for me." She turned her gaze back to me. "Have fun with *Dean*."

I rolled my eyes. "Goodbye, Jacinda."

I followed Mica out of the dining room, but Jacinda's comments still lingered in the back of my mind. It also didn't escape my attention that she never replied to my question about Flint and Di.

CHAPTER SIXTEEN

Dean and I went on another trail ride. We spent a few hours meandering through the hills. I often wondered how Dean got any work done. He spent the majority of his afternoons with me. However, he continually assured me that he rose early and did most of his work then.

Jacinda's comments made me wonder, though. I studied Dean while we rode. He was being friendly because he was my *friend*. Or at least, I'd always thought so.

Scents of leather filled the barn as we wiped down the heavy, western saddles. "Want to sit together at dinner tonight?" Dean asked as he lifted his saddle to its post.

My hand stilled. It wasn't the first time Dean had asked me to join him. Of course, most days he asked I was working. Since it was my day off, however, I was free.

Still, I paused. "Uh, sure," I finally replied.

Dean grinned.

When dinner finally rolled around, I couldn't believe how nervous I felt. I inwardly cursed Jacinda. If it weren't for her, I wouldn't have thought twice about eating with Dean. As it was, my hands sweat like a glass of ice water on a hot summer day. I kept rubbing them against my jeans as I walked to the main house.

"This isn't a date. It's *not* a date," I whispered as I entered the dining hall. If it was a date, Dean would have picked me up at my cabin. He didn't. Therefore, it *wasn't* a date.

"Lena!" Dean called. He sat at a table.

Oh crap.

He'd obviously showered and was dressed in the nicest clothes I'd seen him in. Clean jeans and a clean flannel. I walked stiffly forward until I was at his side. A waft of cologne drifted my way. The dust and horse smells that normally clung to him were gone.

Even though this was feeling more and more like a date, I couldn't stop my smile. I'd never seen Dean without a cowboy hat. The tan on his face was pretty amusing. The upper half of his face shone white. The lower half was deeply tanned.

I swallowed a smile and sat beside him. "Hi."

He cocked his head. "What's so funny?"

I hurriedly coughed. "What? Oh, nothing."

His gaze twinkled. "Come on. I'm not letting you off the hook that easy."

I smiled again but this time couldn't stop my laugh. I pointed at his face. "That's an interesting tan you have there."

He reached up, as if not understanding. I brought my hand to my nose and placed it horizontally across my face.

It clicked. He chuckled and then laughed deeply. "Oh, yeah. It's from the cowboy hat."

"Figured as much."

"You should get a hat. Then you could look as cool as me."

"You're right. It is a pretty fashionable tan. I should look into that."

Dean laughed again and all of my nervousness melted away. Jacinda and her stupid comments. Of course Dean and I were only friends. This is how we always acted.

"You look nice," he said.

I glanced at my simple jeans, t-shirt and flip-flops. "Uh, thanks."

"Shall we?" He waved toward the buffet table.

"Sure."

Di was topping off the water pitchers at the end of the table. She eyed me curiously when Dean and I filled our plates. Jacinda was another matter entirely. I swear she kept approaching our table just to torment me. She winked when I mouthed at her to *go away* and snickered when she walked back into the kitchen.

Dean took a bite of his steak. "How do you like your job here?"

"It's good. I mean, we all really like it."

"How long are you staying?"

"Hmm…" I cocked my head. Country music floated through the air. Snippets of conversation from the other tables drifted to us. I spoke louder as the din in the room grew. "I know we're employed until October. Not sure beyond that."

"You know," he cleared his throat and set his utensils down. "They sometimes need help through the winter. Maybe you could stay on year round. We could spend the holidays together."

I almost blew water through my nose. I hastily set my glass down and grabbed a napkin. Coughing vigorously, I wiped my face. Had he really just said we could spend our holidays together?

Dean clapped me on the back, a frown on his face. "You okay?"

"Yeah. Yeah, I'm fine," I managed through the coughing.

Dean rubbed my back. The coughing had subsided but Dean didn't seem in any hurry to remove his hand. "You sure you're okay?"

Heavy energy abruptly pulsed through the air. I stiffened. Dean still rubbed my back, oblivious to who just entered the room. I didn't have to look. I knew Flint just walked in. His energy was so strong it felt like a hot ribbon wrapping around me, sliding along my limbs. I inched away from Dean, but Dean's hand stayed put.

"You want me to get you more water?" Dean's hand moved down to rub my lower back.

"No. I'm good."

I tried to inch away but it didn't help. Dean just smiled as he softly rubbed my muscles. He started saying something else but stopped. I wasn't listening anyway. Between Dean's hand and Flint's energy, my senses were overloaded.

Dean's gaze was trained on the door. I followed it. Sure enough, Flint was here. He stood by the door, staring at us. I switched my vision. His orange and blue cloud pulsed and grew around him. It seemed to double in size every second. I hurriedly snapped my vision back to normal.

My breath sucked in when Flint strode toward us. His steps were purposeful and strong, his shoulders tensed, his hands fisted. My gaze dipped lower. His shoulders tapered to a toned waist that was as hard as the rest of him. Desire flowed through my veins. It came out of nowhere. But seeing Flint like that, hot with rage, purposeful and strong, did something to me. It felt like fire licked my insides. My hands gripped the table tightly.

My senses flooded with his nearness and scent. Spice, wood and tangerines. His scent only made me want him more. I tried to keep my voice even. "Hi," I said a little breathlessly when he stood beside our table.

"Hi." He scowled at Dean before coming back to me. "Can I talk to you?"

I blinked. "Talk to me?"

"Yes."

Dean stopped rubbing my back but didn't remove his hand. "We're kind of having dinner right now."

"I'm aware of that," Flint replied tightly.

"What do you want to talk about?" I asked.

"Can we go outside?" Irritation lined Flint's words. His dark eyes bore into mine. For a fraction of a second, he let the curtain fall open. Deep emotion swirled in those inky irises. With a blink, it was gone.

Despite trying to control myself, I started to cave. I inched closer. I wanted to soften into him, to wrap my arms around him. My heart ached to *be* with him, if only for a second. All of sudden, I realized what I was doing. I abruptly straightened. I hated that I couldn't control these emotions, especially when he so easily ignored me.

"No, not right now," I replied.

"No?" His eyebrows shot up.

"Like Dean said, we're having dinner. Can we talk later?"

The power off Flint soared. He gritted his teeth, turned and stalked away.

The rest of the dinner was awkward, to put it mildly. Flint sat at a table over from us. Hot energy pulsed toward me the entire time. Dean chatted away and acted like Flint wasn't there. Meanwhile, I squirmed and fidgeted. All I wanted was to run to Flint. I knew, however, that I'd look like a pathetic girl falling all over her first crush. Not to mention, Dean and I were having dinner. If I left, that would be rude.

When dinner finally ended, Dean smiled. "There's another bonfire tonight. Want to go?"

Jacinda's head whipped toward mine. She stood over twenty feet away, cleaning up the buffet, yet I knew she heard him. She was trying to hide a smile.

Between how Dean's hand had lingered on my back and his now eager expression, the hundred percent certainty I'd felt that he and I were only friends dipped down to ninety percent.

"Um, I think Flint wanted to talk to me."

Dean's mouth tightened. He glanced toward Flint. Flint was currently attacking his steak. Literally. It was like he thought the thing was still alive from how he stabbed it. The knife's blade actually bent.

"Can't you talk to him later?" Dean asked.

"Ah, I guess so."

We stood. Our chairs scraped loudly. I felt Flint's gaze burn into my back on my walk out of the dining hall. Flint's energy grew to an entirely new level. It was seriously making my head spin.

Outside, I took a few deep breaths as the world returned to normal. I didn't understand how nobody else could feel what I so easily felt from Flint. Just now, it had been so strong, it felt like a living life force all on its own.

Oblivious to my turmoil, Dean smiled and reached down. His fingers brushed against mine. I stuffed my hands in my pockets.

Make that eighty percent.

"Um, I can't stay out too long. I'm got to...err..." I released a hand from my pocket to pull at a curl.

Dean just smiled. "I'll walk you home whenever you need to get back."

Dean led me down the pavers that cut into the front lawn. When we reached the gravel, the wind picked up. His cologne wafted toward me again. Another grin spread across his face as we started to walk.

"We should go to the creek tomorrow on the horses," Dean said. "There's a nice picnic area there. Maybe we could pack a lunch."

"Ah, I usually eat lunch in the kitchen while I'm working."

"Oh." His smile dimmed. "Maybe on your next day off."

Guilt pummeled me as we walked to the bonfire. Had Jacinda been right? Did Dean like me more than a friend? I chewed my lip. I hated everything about this. Dean had only ever been nice to me. Why couldn't I like him instead of Flint?

The smell of wood smoke filled the air the closer we got to the fire. It was also getting dark. I shivered as the temperature slowly dropped.

"Cold?" Dean asked.

I shook my head. "No, I'm fine." I plastered a grin on my face. Dean was already unbuttoning his flannel. A crisp white-t-shirt shown underneath. "Really, I'm fine."

"Oh, sure." He re-buttoned the top.

The next thirty minutes were entirely uncomfortable. It was the complete opposite to how I'd initially felt at dinner. I didn't know if Dean wasn't taking the hint or if he thought awkward side steps and mumbled responses were the norm on "first dates." I groaned inwardly. How had I gotten myself into this?

I was about to throw myself into the fire when I felt him. I stiffened and almost dropped the stick I roasted marshmallows on.

Flint's energy pulsed toward me. My head whipped around. When I couldn't find him, I switched my vision. His cloud gave him away. He stood off in the trees. A large oak almost hid him, but his shoulders were broad enough that it didn't hide him completely, and his pulsing orange and blue cloud glowed around him. I snapped my sight back to normal. Since it was so dark, he blended into the night. If it weren't for his energy and glowing cloud, I'd have never known he was there.

"Um, I should probably turn in." I hastily stuffed the marshmallow in my mouth.

Dean straightened. "I'll walk you back."

I forced a smile. "I'll be fine. Really."

Dean frowned. It was the first doubt I'd seen flash across his face. "I'd feel better if I saw you home."

I remembered Di's order for none of us to walk alone at night. Besides, Dean deserved better than for me to ditch him at the fire.

"Okay, thanks." I smiled genuinely.

He perked up and placed his hand on my lower back. He kept it there until we returned to the gravel driveway.

The entire walk to my cabin I felt Flint follow. I didn't know who he thought he was fooling. He was silent. I'd give him that, but I swear I'd feel his energy a mile away. At least when it was flowing this strong.

On my porch, I turned to Dean to tell him goodnight. His lips descended over mine and his arms encircled my waist before I knew what was happening. I jumped back as if I'd been burned.

Flint was at my side in a second.

"I think Lena's ready to turn in." Flint towered over me with fisted hands and tensed shoulders.

Dean hastily stepped back and blinked. The bewildered expression on his face made my guilt flow stronger.

"Flint?" Dean shook his head a few times, as if he wasn't sure if he was seeing things. Dean glanced around. "Where the heck did you come from?" The utter confusion in Dean's voice made my eyes widen. I couldn't believe Flint hadn't been more careful about his speed.

"He was on the hill, coming down from the barn," I said quickly.

"You were?" Dean asked.

"Yep, he was. Okay, then. I'm turning in. Night, guys!" I bolted through the cabin door and slammed it behind me before either of them could respond. Guilt made me cringe. It wasn't the nicest way to end the night with Dean, but I wasn't ready to face *that* conversation. Not yet at least.

Breathing heavily, I leaned against the door and sank to the floor. The hard wood pressed into my back and the tiled entryway was cold. I didn't care. All I knew was that I needed some time to figure out what the hell just happened.

Since it was dark and quiet in the cabin, I knew Jacinda and Di were still working. I didn't know where Mica was. Even though I usually preferred to be surrounded by people, at this moment, I was glad to be alone.

"What the hell was that?" I finally muttered. I was about to stand when I felt it again. Flint's energy. It came from *behind* the cabin. It was so strong I felt it through the wall.

Wide-eyed, I stood and opened the door. Cool evening air swirled into the cabin. Moonlight illuminated the porch.

With hesitant movements, I peeked out. Dean was gone, thankfully. I didn't see anyone else. Shivering, I crossed my arms and walked quietly down the porch and around the side of the cabin. Tall grass brushed against my legs. When I rounded the back corner, sure enough, Flint was there. He was sitting in the grass, aggressively pulling petals off some wildflower.

"Flint?" I said.

He bolted to standing. "Lena?"

His hair was a mess, like he'd been running his fingers through it repeatedly.

"What are you doing here?" he asked.

I balked. "What am *I* doing here? Uh, I live here."

He dropped the flower and raked a hand through his hair. "Oh. Right."

"What are *you* doing here?"

He looked down and shuffled his feet. The movement was entirely bizarre. I'd never seen Flint as anything but calm and cool. This was a complete one-eighty.

"I...ah..." he stammered. He didn't continue.

I raised my eyebrows. "You what?"

He stuffed his hands into his pockets and shrugged. A confused expression crossed his face. "I don't know."

I shivered in the cool night. His head snapped up. "Are you cold?"

"A little."

In a move so fast he was a blur, he stood beside me and was putting his jacket around my shoulders. The warm fabric fell around me before I could protest. In the next second, a cloud of spice, wood and tangerines wafted up to greet me. My head spun.

In just a t-shirt and jeans, he shoved his hands back into his pockets. Strong, muscled forearms peeked out. A rush of desire shot through me again. As before, it took me completely by surprise.

"What did you want to talk about in the dining room?" I asked. Hot, raw energy flowed out of him again. My pulse quickened.

"Nothing."

"Nothing?" I cocked an eyebrow.

He glanced away and ran a hand through his hair again. "It was just…" he made a noise in his throat, like a frustrated growl. *"Dammit,"* he seethed.

His frustration took me completely by surprise. "Is everything okay?"

He laughed humorlessly. "Oh yeah, everything's fine."

When I raised my eyebrows, he took a deep breath. It looked like it pained him to continue. "I don't know why I came up to you like that. I'm sorry."

"So…you didn't have anything you wanted to talk about?"

His dark gaze had that deep emotion in it again. In the moonlight, it practically swirled. Except this time, it didn't go away. "No, not really. I saw you sitting there with Dean. He was touching you, and I don't know…I kind of…"

The silence stretched.

"You kind of what?"

"I kind of lost it," he said quietly.

I waited for him to explain. He didn't.

"What does that mean?"

He raked a hand through his hair again. This time, he kept his gaze averted. "I wanted to get you away from him and telling you that I needed to talk to you outside was what I came up with."

That admission left me speechless.

Flint ran a hand through his hair *again*. It was practically standing up straight by now. I'd never seen him so unsure or embarrassed before.

"Oh, um, okay…" I murmured.

"So yeah…" He turned and took a step back. Raw energy still poured from him. It took me a second before I realized he was about to walk away.

"Wait!" I called.

He stopped dead in his tracks. Pushing a strand of hair behind my ear, I waited until he turned to face me. "I don't get it," I said.

His shoulders tensed.

I tentatively put a hand on his forearm. His muscles bunched, and his heat seared my skin. Another rush of desire, so strong it made my knees weak, shot through me. "So…you don't want me seeing Dean?"

He gritted his teeth. "No. I guess I don't."

"Why?"

He shook his head but didn't say anything.

"Flint. Please tell me what's going on."

He raked a hand through his hair again. "I don't know." He sighed harshly. "It's just…" His silence stretched.

"Just what?"

He refused to meet my gaze. "That first day when we picked you up…something…changed in me when I saw you."

For a moment all I could do was breathe shallowly. I still had my hand on his arm. I was acutely aware of his hot, smooth skin. "Is that why you ignored me when I got in the Suburban?"

He gave the barest hint of a nod.

"And that's why you barely speak to me, unless you have to?"

Another slight nod.

"Right." I dropped my hand and gazed out over the pastures. I couldn't think when I touched him. Nighttime sounds drifted to us. Crickets, the wind, a distant vehicle on the county road.

"I should probably go," he said.

My stomach sank. "Don't."

He tensed again.

"Talk to me. Don't leave like this."

He was about to reach his hand to his hair when I grabbed it. Energy exploded off him. "Whoa," I murmured. "You have no idea what's coming off you right now."

"What do you mean?"

"Your cloud is so strong. I can *feel* it. You're the only person I can feel like that."

"Really?"

"I could feel you at the fire, when you were hiding behind that tree, and I felt when you followed Dean and me back here. I knew you were there."

Flint groaned quietly. "Well, shit, that's embarrassing."

I laughed. I couldn't help it. Once again, I'd never seen him so unsure and I swear he just blushed. In the moonlight, his cheeks visibly darkened.

"It makes me feel better when I can feel you," I admitted.

"It does?"

"Yeah, you're not the only one who felt something when we met. I…ah…got a feeling off you too."

His voice deepened. "What kind of feeling?"

"When I first saw you, something came over me…I felt…safe. Like you'd never let anyone hurt me."

"I wouldn't."

"I know."

The silence stretched again. I let go of his hand even though I loved how it felt. Taking a deep breath, I finally got the courage to ask him something I'd been wondering all day. "Did you really spend last night outside our cabin?"

His forehead furrowed. "How'd you know that?"

"Jacinda."

He snorted. "Figures."

"She thought you were keeping watch – over me."

He didn't respond.

"Were you?"

"Yes."

"You mean you weren't concerned for *everyone's* safety?"

He smiled humorlessly. "I suppose I should have been. But no, if you want the honest answer, I was only worried about you."

"What about Di?"

"Di?"

"Isn't she your…girlfriend…or whatever?"

Flint's eyes widened. His mouth actually dropped. "Di? My *girlfriend?*"

I squirmed. "I just thought…I mean I wasn't sure since you two always hang out together."

"That doesn't mean she's my girlfriend."

"Oh."

"Lena, I think Di's my *sister.*"

Now it was my turn to look stunned. "Your sister?"

"Haven't you noticed how similar we are? We're both tall, have dark eyes and olive skin. Even our personalities are similar. Both natural leaders, keep to ourselves, don't always get along with others."

"Um, now that you mention it." A warm rush of relief washed over me.

He chuckled. We stood staring at one another for a moment. I was acutely aware of every second. Finally, he grunted, "So are you dating Dean?"

"No."

His energy noticeably subsided. "Good. Keep it that way."

The possessive tone in his voice surprised me. I wanted to ask him *why* he didn't want me dating Dean, but then I heard voices. Footsteps on gravel accompanied the voices and then the thump of people climbing the porch.

"Di and Jacinda are back," Flint said. A breeze ruffled his thoroughly mussed hair. I wanted to reach up and smooth it. I barely stopped my fingers.

"Yeah, I hear."

"It's late. We should probably turn in."

Disappointment swelled in me. I cleared my throat. "Yeah, of course."

We walked to the front of the cabin. Our arms brushed each other's. The slight contact sent desire racing through me.

At the bottom of the porch steps, he turned to face me. The porch light illuminated his dark eyes and that deep emotion that still swirled in them. He wasn't shielding anything right now. His energy had also picked up again, but it was more controlled, like soft waves instead of the fierce power it'd been earlier.

"What are you doing tomorrow night after work?" he asked.

His eyes and scent made my head swim. "Um, nothing, I don't think."

"Do you want to go somewhere with me? Just the two of us?"

I stopped breathing. "Yes."

He smiled, a small crooked smile that looked sexy as hell. "I'll see you then."

And with that, he was gone.

CHAPTER SEVENTEEN

The next morning, I woke early and lay in bed going over every detail from the night before.

Flint didn't want me dating Dean. He'd actually admitted that.

I turned on my side and stared at the wall. A sheetrock screw had popped. I picked at it and snuggled deeper under the warm covers. Flint had also *followed* me from the dining room to the bonfire. After that, he'd raced to my side when Dean kissed me. He'd been angry at the thought of me with Dean. That poor wildflower had taken the brunt of his aggression.

I muffled a giggle and smiled into my pillow.

By the time I got up, I had to scramble. Scents of brewing coffee wafted into the room. I knew Di was at the kitchenette. The blow dryer sounded in the bathroom. Jacinda was probably putting the finishing touches on her hair. As for me, I threw on the first thing I picked up. Jeans and a t-shirt. I almost fell over as I hurriedly stuffed my legs in the pants.

"Lena!" Di called from the living room. "Get moving. We gotta go!"

That's right. It was Val's day off today. All three of us were working. "Coming!" I tried to call quietly.

Mica grumbled in her sleep and buried her head under her covers. I nearly tripped trying to get out of the room. Mica was as messy as me. Our stuff lay everywhere.

When Di, Jacinda and I finally walked out the front door, the last thing I expected was what greeted us on the porch.

Flint sat on the swing.

One foot rocked the swing, while the other sat idle. He was staring at the sunrise, but his gaze honed onto me as soon as I passed through the door. I could tell his presence took all of us by surprise, although Di tried to act like it was perfectly normal as she turned to lock the door. However, Jacinda and I both stared, wide-eyed.

When my brain actually worked enough to do something, I looked out across the ranch. I didn't know what else to do. Flint was here, on our porch, but why? The sun burned on the horizon, the breeze cool. A blur of movement swirled the air at my side.

Flint stood beside me.

Startled, I anxiously assessed our surroundings, wondering if anyone had seen him move that fast. No one else was out. It always seemed Flint knew when he could and couldn't move at his speed. The times he did, not a soul could be seen. Well, except for last night, when he'd been unable to control himself after Dean kissed me. I smiled inwardly.

Flint's scent flowed like a soft caress across my skin. I resisted the urge to close my eyes and inhale. Peeking up at him, I mumbled, "Hello."

His response was to clasp my hand and pull me toward the steps. My heart stopped. It was only then I remembered we weren't alone. Di and Jacinda both watched, mouths open.

"Coming?" Flint called.

They kicked into action, and we all began walking toward the main house. Nobody said a thing. This was definitely going to be an awkward five minutes.

Jacinda broke the ice a few steps later. "Nice morning, don't you think?"

"Pretty sunrise," Di commented.

"Yeah, lots of colors," Jacinda said.

Flint's fingers curled around mine. They were hard, calloused, and warm. I couldn't manage a reply to the sunrise conversation.

Flint, of course, remained silent. Di and Jacinda eyed each other and took a big step forward, then another. Slowly, they got farther and farther ahead.

"You sleep okay?" Flint asked when we fell behind. Our arms brushed each other's. That small sensation sent tingles along my nerves. He was still holding my hand.

"Um, yeah, fine. You?" I replied.

"Really good."

I swallowed self-consciously. "Well…it probably helps that you didn't slink around our cabin all night."

He smiled. "I might have gotten up a few times to check on you."

My eyes shot to his. From the teasing glint in his gaze, I couldn't tell if he was serious or not. When we got to the main house, he stopped and faced me. I held my breath, unsure of what he'd do.

Another crooked smile greeted me. "Have a good day."

I tried to reply. All that came out was an unintelligible sound.

"See you tonight," he added. "I'll pick you up at nine." With that, he turned and walked away.

I SPENT THE entire day watching the clock. The morning crawled by. The afternoon wasn't any better. Since things ended awkwardly with Dean last night, I didn't go to the barn on my break. I felt guilty about that. I knew sooner or later I'd have to face him and try to smooth things over, but today wasn't that day.

Consequently, I practically paced the cabin for the entire four hours in the afternoon. My nerves didn't abate one bit when we went back to work at supper.

By the time eight o'clock finally rolled around, I was so anxious I ran back to the cabin. Given I still had an hour until Flint was due to arrive, I had enough time to mull over what to wear. Of course, Jacinda approved whole-heartedly.

With her help, I chose fitted jeans and a green sweater that matched my eyes. Since I figured we'd be somewhere on the ranch, I anticipated being outside. Mica suggested I tie my hair up in case it got windy. I hesitated. Fingering my curls would give my hands something to do.

"I think I'll keep it down," I replied.

"Suit yourself," Mica shrugged.

"What about shoes?" I asked.

"Definitely hiking boots." Mica lounged on her bottom bunk. "Then you're ready for anything."

Jacinda snorted. "Hiking boots? No." She rummaged through my closet and pulled out my lone pair of heels. "These would look great with skinny jeans, but we may need to change your top…" She bit her lip.

I snatched the hiking boots off the floor. "These will do!"

Running from the room, I escaped to the couch. Di merely quirked an eyebrow when I plopped next to her. The title of the book she was reading, *Amnesia – The Mystery behind the Secrets Within* was visible from where I sat. I was pretty sure Di had raided the entire medical section in Little Raven's small public library. Last week, she'd been reading, *The Science of Memory*.

I hurriedly pulled the boots on. I was about to ask Di if she'd discovered anything to explain our memory loss when a knock rapped on the front door. All of the blood drained from my face. My gaze flew to the clock. I gulped.

It was nine o'clock.

My heart pounded as I walked to the door. Out of my peripheral vision, I saw Jacinda and Mica take my place on the couch, which of course gave them an unobstructed view of the front door. Casting them an irritated look, Mica merely grinned.

"Well, don't keep him waiting!" she called.

Taking a deep breath, I opened the door. The second my eyes met Flint's, I stopped breathing. He lounged casually against the door frame and smelled freshly showered. That mix of spice, wood and tangerines wafted toward me. His chestnut hair curled at the ends. It was still slightly damp. A clean, flannel button up shirt stretched across his broad chest. Worn jeans hugged his lean hips, and an old tattered, wool blanket was tucked under one arm.

He stood at the threshold, not coming in. Instead, he held out his hand.

It took me a moment to understand I was supposed to take it. I was glad my back blocked my shaking fingers from view.

"Ready?" Flint asked.

"Bye!" I called over my shoulder.

Flint pulled me onto the porch. Just as the door closed, Mica yelled, "Have fun!"

A few muffled laughs followed. I gritted my teeth and tried to stop the nervousness that churned my stomach. My free hand was already pulling a curl.

The porch creaked as we walked to the steps.

"Where are we going?" I was glad I'd worn a sweater. The evening air was chilly.

"You'll see."

We hopped down the stairs and walked toward the upper barn. A few stars appeared amidst the wispy clouds. The air was fresh, scents of grass and milkweed on the breeze. Our feet tramped softly on the gravel. I wondered if we were going for a ride. I'd never done an evening horseback ride before, but just as we reached the big hill to the upper barn, Flint propelled me farther to the left.

"I was thinking we could go to this place I found," he said.

Night sounds drifted in the breeze. I tucked a strand a hair behind my ear. "Um, sure. What place?"

"It's a few miles from here."

Good thing I wore the hiking boots. "Sure, this way?" I angled my head to the left. I was about to start walking when Flint reached out. His hand closed over my forearm. Tingles immediately raced along my arm.

"It will probably take an hour to walk there. It'd be faster if I carried you."

"Carried me?"

"May I?"

I had no idea what he was asking so just nodded. Before I could blink, the air rushed around me and the next thing I knew, I was astride his back, piggyback style. "Whoa," I managed at the sudden movement.

"Can you hold this?" He handed me the blanket.

"Ah, okay." I placed it between us.

"Hold on." He wrapped my legs securely around his waist.

He wasn't kidding. A second later, we were flying.

I wrapped my arms tightly around his chest. His arms pumped at his sides. In no time, we were in the forest. I had no idea any human could move so fast. The night air flew by. Cool, fresh air burst across my face.

Surprisingly, riding on Flint's back was smooth, even when he leaped over logs or darted around trees. His joints were liked well-oiled hinges, his legs strong as steel. Steady breaths rushed in and out of his lungs. The incredible speed at which he ran seemed to barely affect him.

It couldn't have been more than five minutes before we came to an abrupt halt. The jolting stop almost pitched me over his shoulders. Luckily, he had my legs gripped tightly around him.

Carefully, Flint set me down. It appeared we were in a large clearing.

"Where are we?" My legs wobbled for a moment. He reached out to steady me before taking the blanket and spreading it across the long grass.

"About three miles west." His deep voice carried in the breeze.

"Are we still on the ranch?"

"Near the perimeter."

After the blanket was fully settled, he sat down. The fast run hadn't fazed him. Sweat didn't line his face. Harsh breaths didn't raise his chest. Flint reached up and held out his hand. "Care to join me?"

I tried to nod but couldn't breathe. How had he run that fast with me? And *how* could he seem so relaxed and confident when it felt like my stomach would flip right over? The picture he painted sitting on the blanket with his hand outstretched made my head spin. It seemed the cool, confident Flint I knew was back. It was like the nervous, unsure one from last night never existed.

"Lena?" he asked in that deep tone of his.

"Right, sorry." The instant my hand joined his, I was lying on the ground beside him. He'd moved like lightning again, picking me up and laying me beside him, like I weighed no more than a jar of Val's pickled green beans.

"Wow," I muttered. "It's a good thing I don't get motion sickness."

His eyes widened. "Sorry."

"It's okay."

As my eyes adjusted to the dark sky, the silence stretched. I played with my hair again. Flint lay only inches away. I felt his gaze on me.

"Um, so…how was your day?" I asked.

"Good. Just the usual, mending fences, moving cattle. You?"

"Yeah, good too. Same as you really, just the usual." I stumbled over the words and wanted to kick myself. I bet

Jacinda hadn't batted an eye on her first date with Huxley. I wished I could be more like her.

Flint was watching me with a smile on his face. Once again, the curtain was wide open. A deep emotion glinted in his irises.

"What?" I raised a hand to straighten my hair. Were snarls flying all over?

"Nothing, just you."

"Just me, what?"

His lips tugged up more. He shook his head. "You just have this way about you. One minute you've got a smart comment on the tip of your tongue, but the next you're nervous about your hair, or carrying on some silent conversation with yourself."

I made a face. "How do you know that?"

"Your expression changes. I can only imagine what you're thinking."

My eyes widened. "Oh, well–"

"I like that about you."

"You do?"

"Yeah."

"Oh, good. I think."

He smiled. A real smile this time. It was the first one I'd seen. His teeth flashed white, and he was so unbelievably sexy I stopped breathing. I had to look away. It was doing my head in.

"So…" I kept my gaze on the meadow that dipped down in front of us. It seemed to stretch forever. "Can I ask you something?"

"Yes."

"Is…uh…is this a date?"

A few seconds passed. "Do you want it to be?"

Yes. The thought came immediately. I didn't have the guts to say it, though. But the things he'd said last night…

"Tell me," he whispered.

The word flowed out of me before I could stop it. "Yes."

He seemed to breathe a sigh of relief. "Good, because that's what I want too."

His face was only inches from mine. I hastily glanced away and thought about that first moment we met, the way we both reacted to each other. More than anything, I was certain I'd once known him. It was like my body remembered what my mind could not.

Flint reached up and traced a finger across my cheek. The touch seared my skin, like a fire blazing a trail. "I want to know you better."

"What do you want to know?"

His eyebrows drew together. I thought he mumbled *everything*. "What kind of books do you like? Have you ever seen a movie? What do you do when you're not working? How do you like living on the ranch? Who's your favorite in the group? Do you–"

I held up a hand. "Hold on. Do you want me to answer all of those questions?"

"Yes."

I smiled. "Okay, one at a time then."

He shook his head. "Sorry. I feel like I've wasted so much time with you."

"Well, we've got plenty of time now."

"Do we?" His eyes darkened in the moonlight. I was about to ask him what he meant, when he said, "You're right. Of course, you're right. Why wouldn't we?"

Somehow, I managed to shake off that uneasy comment.

"So?" he said.

"So what?"

"Are you going to answer my questions?"

I bit my lip to keep from grinning. "Okay, well, I've only read a few books since that first morning, but I like to read mysteries. And while I seem to know when people are referring to movie quotes, or talking about an actor, I don't actually remember any movies from…before. The only movie I've seen in the past five months is *Ghostbusters*."

Flint raised an eyebrow.

"A couple I hitchhiked with put me in the back with their kids. They had a DVD player."

"Right."

"It was a good movie, but I think I was more amazed that I recognized some actor's faces. I mean, how could I do that, if I couldn't remember anything about myself?"

"It's like that for all of us."

That statement reminded me how unusual our circumstance was. The titles from Di's books flashed through my mind. Nothing about us, how we met, who we were, or what we could do, was normal. And none of us knew why.

"The not knowing drives me crazy," I said quietly.

"I know."

"And nobody will talk to me about it. Except Jet, and I'm not sure I want to talk to *him* about it."

"I take it you've heard his conspiracy theories that we're all aliens reincarnated?"

"Unfortunately, yes."

I caught his smile before his tone turned serious. "You can talk to me if you want."

"Really? I didn't think I could. That one time I went with you and Di to the library, I felt like a third wheel."

He sighed. "I know. I'm sorry for how I acted. I was trying to ignore you so I wouldn't have to address the emotions clawing up my insides."

Emotions clawing up his insides? I ducked to hide a smile. "Do you ever think we'll find answers?"

"I hope so. Di and I still spend most of our free time combing the internet, searching for articles throughout the country about missing people and hunting for any clue that could help identify us."

"I'm guessing you haven't found anything?"

Flint shook his head. "Not yet."

"But you have an idea about our tattoos?" I still remembered what he'd said that day almost three weeks ago when Jacinda and I went shopping.

"Yes." He picked up my wrist. His large finger traced my tattoo. I wanted to close my eyes as tingles ran up my arm, but his next word snapped me out of it. "Earth."

I shook my head. "What? Earth?"

"Yes."

"What does that mean?"

He held up his wrist. The circle with the arrow attached to it was barely visibly in the moonlight. "Mars."

It clicked. "They're planetary symbols."

"So far, yes. All of them are. We'll have to see what the new girl's tattoo is, but I bet money it's Mercury. It's the only symbol left."

"What the heck. What does that mean?"

"We don't know."

I bit my lip. When I thought about it, *really* thought about it, I wanted to scream in frustration. But it was more than that. It wasn't only frustrating, it was frightening too. I remembered what Jet said, that day the group told me who they were. *A bad omen.* He was probably right. Someone, somewhere knew who we were. And someone tattooed us with these symbols, but why?

"Hey," Flint nudged me.

I met his gaze. Worry flashed across his face.

"Sorry," I mumbled. "It's just," I paused. "It's scary."

He inched closer to me. "What about your free time? What do you like to do?"

I knew he was trying to distract me. The energy that always flowed around him picked up. My guess was worry caused it. Perhaps it wasn't only anger that made it peak.

"Um, well…" I shook myself mentally. He was right to change the subject. Getting wrapped up in fears about our beginnings wasn't how I wanted to spend our first date. We had plenty of time for doom and gloom later. "When I'm not working, I'm at the barn with Dean, which is pretty much every day."

The energy increased. "Hmm, Dean again."

I smiled at his tone. The possessiveness of it once again sent shivers through me. However, he didn't give me a chance to recover before he launched into more questions. For the next hour, I told him everything he wanted to know. All of the cities I'd hitchhiked to, which guests had made the biggest impressions on me, what my favorite foods were, who I liked hanging out with most in the group, what kind of music I enjoyed, if I was a morning person versus a night person, etcetera. He seemed endlessly curious and asked me more and more things. It warmed me considerably, since I guessed when it came to other people, Flint was not a curious person.

"Okay, my turn," I said after a while. "You won't let me get more than a sentence or two in."

"Sorry." He shook his head. His hair ruffled in the breeze. I wanted to touch a strand that fell across his forehead. Instead, I eyed the small distance between us. Only inches separated us.

"What did you want to ask me?" His tone grew deeper.

I cleared my throat. "Tell me about *you*. You know so much about me, but I know next to nothing about you."

"What do you want to know?"

"Well," I chewed my lip. "How about where you woke up, wasn't it somewhere unusual?"

"Yes."

"So," I prompted. "Where?"

"Yellowstone National Park."

"What?"

He chuckled. "I'm not lying. I swear."

"Beside a geyser or something?"

"Not quite that interesting."

"Then where?"

"In a cabin in the park, but it wasn't a luxury condo like everyone else."

"But you still had the money and IDs?"

"Yes."

I thought again about our strange situation. I couldn't help it. A chill ran through me. "I wonder who set this all up, and why."

"Your guess is as good as mine."

I gazed into his dark eyes. The moonlight dipped his face into shadows. "Does everyone *ever* talk about it? As an entire group? About what happened to us?"

"Initially, yes, it was all we could talk about for weeks. You have to remember that some of us were here for months before you arrived. During that time, we combed this area, searching for what drew us here. None of us could find anything. But as you may have noticed, some in the group find it too upsetting to talk about, so now it's just Di and me pursuing answers." He paused. "Di's still convinced we'll find answers eventually. Maybe here, maybe somewhere else. She sees us leaving eventually, as you know. As soon as the new girl arrives, we'll figure out what to do next."

"What do you mean, *do next?* Like go somewhere?"

"Exactly."

"Where would we go?" The John Hancock building flashed through my mind.

"If Di can't give us an exact location, we'll decide as a group at our next meeting where to go."

"We'll have a meeting?"

"We always have them before we pick up a new person. That started after we found Jacinda. And anytime we're contemplating a big decision for the group, we always have a meeting, and there's only one rule."

"Which is?"

"We all have to be in agreement when we make decisions.

If someone thinks we should go somewhere or do something, it has to be a unanimous vote. It's either all in or it doesn't happen."

I lay back down. The scratchy wool blanket tickled my ear as a stray curl flew over my face. Flint reached up and tucked it behind my ear. His finger lingered a second longer than necessary. That little intimate gesture made me lose all train of thought.

For a moment, I just lay there, studying him. Fire once again grew in my veins as I memorized his broad shoulders and muscled arms. I mentally slapped myself. "Um, so why does it have to be unanimous? Why not majority rules?"

"We decided early on that everyone needs to be okay with what's being asked of them. Control isn't something we have much of."

"Oh." I gazed at the sky so I could actually concentrate on the conversation. Watching Flint didn't allow that. "I guess that makes sense. Those first few months I felt completely out of control. The instinct, or pull or whatever you want to call it, pushed me for so many weeks. I was like an addict to a drug, too helpless to resist it. I wanted so desperately to know what happened to me."

Flint's heat and that energy that always surrounded him picked up again. I kept my gaze on the sky. Stars shone brightly above. Out of habit, I reached up and slowly traced a constellation.

"What are you doing?" Flint asked, a smile in his voice.

"Nothing." I dropped my hand.

He inched closer and reached down. He took my hand into his. My breath stopped when he lifted my arm back up. Cupping my palm, he stretched out my finger beside his and together we began tracing patterns in the sky.

"Polaris which traces into Ursa Minor," he murmured, guiding my hand.

"And sits above Ursa Major." I moved his arm.

He trailed our fingers along the stars. "Draco...Hercules...Serpens..."

"Caput...Ophiuchus..."

One by one, we named the summer constellations.

"You know them too," I whispered when we finished.

"Sometimes at night, I'll come out here to find the constellations. I didn't know you enjoyed backyard astronomy."

"I've always liked it, at least, what I can remember of it. Since I slept outside every night, before I met all of you, I spent a lot of time staring at the sky."

His energy picked up again. He cursed and raked a hand through his hair. "I hate thinking of you out there by yourself with nothing."

It took me a moment to calm my breathing. His energy still flowed full force. "Um, I was fine. Really."

"That was pure luck you were fine," he muttered. "What if some guy found you asleep on the ground?"

"I'm not completely helpless."

He sighed. "I know. I know. I just mean..." he paused and sighed again. "You're a woman, and you're so small. What if that guy didn't have honorable intentions? Then what?"

I muffled a smile that he'd actually said *honorable intentions*. "Well, that never happened. Most nights I slept off roads and highways in the ditch. Nobody knew I was there."

He muttered a sound. "And *that's* safe?"

I shrugged.

"What about the rides you took? What if one of those guys raped you or hurt you?" he demanded.

I sighed. He had a point. Those thoughts had plagued me too, but I also knew I had an advantage.

"I'm a pretty good judge of character. You know, that internal radar thing?" I tapped my head. "My clouds have never been wrong. At least, not that I know of." I briefly thought about Aaron and his ugly, black cloud. I hadn't seen him all week. I only hoped it stayed that way.

Flint traced a finger along my cheek. I shivered. His eyes darkened even more. "Despite your radar, I never want you doing that again."

"I don't intend to."

His finger stayed on my skin, tracing a line down my neck. Heat pooled in my core. I squirmed. "Um, I still don't know much about you."

"What do you want to know?" he asked softly.

"Well, what about what you asked me? Favorite food? Music? Who you like hanging out with the most? Morning versus night person?" I trailed off.

He cleared his throat and dropped his hand. "I'll eat mostly anything, but I do seem to be a meat and potato guy. My favorite music is rock, but I've grown used to the country Val and Pete prefer. Until now, my favorite person to hang out with was Di, and I'm a morning person. I'm usually the first awake in my cabin."

I quirked an eyebrow. "Di *was* your favorite? Who's your favorite now?"

"You." His tone implied that answer should have been obvious.

"Even though Di's your sister?"

"Even though she's my sister."

Warmth slid through me that had nothing to do with his body heat. I leaned back again. "So, Jet and Jasper are brothers, and you and Di are siblings," I said more to myself than him.

"We think we are," Flint added. "We don't have proof."

"You could get a DNA test."

He shook his head. "No tests."

"Why not?"

"Because we don't know why we're like this."

"What do you mean?"

"You know, our abilities or gifts or whatever. We're all different, and we don't know why that is. What if internally,

165

we're different too? Different blood work or different DNA? What do you think would happen if someone ran those tests and discovered that?"

I swallowed uneasily. "They'd probably want to do more tests."

"Exactly."

"So no tests."

"And no hospitals either, for the same reason."

His comments reminded me there were still a lot of unanswered questions. Things we may never know.

"Do you think it's possible that I have a sibling?" I asked. "If you and Di are related, and we know Jet and Jasper are definitely related, then maybe I have a brother or sister?"

I didn't know why, but the innate need to find my family was so strong. Initially, it's what I thought I'd find in Little Raven. For months, I thought the instinct was my subconscious leading me home. And then, when I'd had that reaction to Little Raven, I thought all I needed to do was find someone who recognized me and they'd tell me where I lived. Of course, all I'd ended up doing was scaring the locals and making a name for myself in town. Not a good name.

"Do you think it's possible?" I knew my eyes were pleading.

Flint's voice softened. "Anything's possible."

"Maybe this new girl? Maybe she's my sister?"

"I suppose she could be."

For a moment, I just stared at him, my eyes still pleading.

He abruptly leaned forward and pressed his lips into mine. He kissed me softly, fire burning in his touch. I felt his need, his desire and it took me so completely by surprise, I tensed.

He pulled back. "Sorry. It's just that look on your face…"

"Don't go," I whispered.

He didn't need encouragement. In one of his incredibly fast moves, he pulled me to him. He trapped me in his arms, pinning me to the ground. I wrapped my arms around him. My fingers threaded through his hair.

I had no idea if I'd been kissed before, but I didn't care. Any thought of whether or not I was doing it right, vanished. Flint's taste commanded all of my attention. My body felt alive under his. Tingles and heat raced through me. The energy off him exploded. Feeling his need only fueled my own.

After I don't know how long, Flint finally pulled back. It was then I became aware of a rock hard bulge pressing into my thigh. "We need to stop, Lena." His breath came out in harsh pants.

I could only nod.

He let go and rolled off. I missed him. The night air felt so cold. Wrapping my arms around myself, I shivered.

"Cold?" The concern in his tone made me smile. Being cold was something I'd grown used to. Sleeping outside wasn't exactly comfortable, and so far, being a little cold had never hurt me.

"I'm okay."

He grunted. "Right and I'm the King of England. You're shivering."

Before I could reply, he pulled me to him again. Snuggled up beside him, his heat flowed over me. "How is it that you're so warm?" I reveled in his tight, possessive embrace.

"Fast metabolism."

"Mmm," I murmured. I laid a hand on his chest. His breath sucked in.

"You have no idea what you do to me," he growled. He clasped my hand and brought it safely between his. He thumbed my tattoo while he stared up at the night sky. I was tempted to remove my hand and reach lower. The distinct bulge in his pants was still glaringly obvious.

Instead, I watched him as he gazed at the stars. The feel and smell of him created a hot, heady feeling in me. My core still ached and yearned for more, but I knew now wasn't the right time.

Snuggling closer, I heard his heart beat strongly within. The sound, smell and feel of him so closely against me stirred something deep in my mind. I felt it happen. Like a book cover that cracked, revealing a deep, intricate story that promised to captivate. I knew without a doubt that something dormant inside me, buried deep within my subconscious, had come back to life.

CHAPTER EIGHTEEN

We lay on the blanket until the wee hours of the morning. It was only when I started to nod off that Flint gently picked me up.

"I should get you back," he said.

I murmured something halfway intelligible. I knew I was somewhere between asleep and awake but couldn't rouse myself completely. The feel of his arms around me, his scent and that ever present feeling of safety beckoned me to sleep.

Rustling sounded and then the scratchy, wool blanket covered me. It tickled my face. I merely snuggled closer to him as he began to walk. I must have truly fallen asleep on the way back to the cabin. The next thing I knew, Flint was laying me on my top bunk. Soft snores from Mica filled the room.

"Night, babe," he whispered.

Soft lips pressed into mine. I moaned and leaned closer. He took a deep breath and firmly, yet gently, pushed me back. A second later, a door closed.

I woke to the smell of coffee and the sound of a distant shower. Groggily, I opened my eyes and sat up slowly. I was back in my bedroom.

Rubbing my eyes, I tried to remember returning with Flint. It was hazy, like a dream that disappeared upon waking. The sights, smells and memory of it vanished. Only a good feeling lingered. It made me want to snuggle under my covers and try desperately to hold onto it.

"Well, good morning, sunshine," a voice called.

My eyes snapped wide open. I peered below. Mica lay on her bed, awake. She grinned brightly. "Have fun on your *date*, last night?"

I rolled my eyes and threw my pillow at her.

"Hey, just asking." She dodged the blow. "You were out pretty late. It's only natural to be curious."

I yawned and stretched.

"Gonna tell me about it?" she asked.

I pictured Flint's broad shoulders, strong chest and how he'd felt and tasted. A wave of possessiveness rolled through me. I didn't want to share that with anyone.

"Nope."

Mica made a noise that sounded very similar to an audible pout. "I'd tell you if Jasper kissed me."

"Jasper kissed you?"

"Well...no, but if he did, I'd tell you."

I jumped down from my bunk. Sounds came from the living room. Di and Jacinda were talking. It was probably time to get going. All three of us were working again today. Like yesterday, Val had the day off.

"Hmm, well that's nice," I said.

Mica harrumphed. "Fine, don't tell me."

When Di, Jacinda and I walked to work, Jacinda's gaze was very similar to Mica's. "You're certainly in a good mood."

It was only then that I became aware of the ridiculous grin on my face. "What do you mean?"

She winked. "I think you know what I mean."

I rolled my eyes but kept grinning.

"What'd you two do last night?" she asked.

A door banged. One of the guests stepped onto his porch, a steaming mug in his hand. I smiled and waved. He waved back.

"Are you going to tell me?" Jacinda asked.

"Tell you what?" I asked sweetly.

She sighed and smoothed her perfectly ironed shirt. "All right, all right. I'll stop asking."

"Oh!" Di abruptly fell to the ground. Both Jacinda and I careened to a stop. I winced when the sound of gravel crunched into Di's knees. For a second, Jacinda and I just stood there, but then Jacinda kicked into action and rushed to Di's side.

She kneeled beside her as Di panted quietly. Alarm raced through me. "Should I get help?"

Down the drive, the guest on his porch stood from the porch swing. He made a move like he was going to run to us.

Di shook her head, panting quietly. "No, no, I'm fine. It was just a vision, but a strong one. She's coming. *Tomorrow!*"

I waved the guest back. "She's fine!" I yelled. "Just tripped!" The guest sat back down.

Jacinda and I helped Di to her feet. *She's coming.* That only meant one thing. The new girl.

"So you're not hurt?" I asked. The knee in Di's black pants had ripped. A smear of blood trailed along the fabric.

Di shook her head furiously. She winced when she fully straightened her leg. "No. It's just...that vision was powerful." Di's face was practically white as she rubbed gravel and dirt from her pants. "She just changed course. She'll arrive in Colorado tomorrow. I'm sure of it. I saw a plane. She's on it."

"Does that mean she's flying into Little Raven?" Jacinda asked.

Di shook her head and fingered her temples again. "I don't know. Maybe. Or maybe not." She groaned. "I hate when my visions are like this. So strong but still cloudy. It's incredibly frustrating."

It was the most I'd ever heard Di talk about her gift. Laying a hand on her arm, I said, "Don't worry. We'll find her."

Di smiled weakly. "We better get to work. We'll have a meeting to discuss it tonight."

Jacinda and I flanked Di's sides and held onto her. Di walked steadily after a few steps, but I didn't want her tipping over if another vision pummeled her. The three of us moved silently to the main house. However, the farther we got the more irritated Di seemed.

"I'm fine," she hissed. She brushed our hands off. Jacinda and I eyed one another but allowed Di some distance.

THE DAY PASSED slowly. My thoughts meandered between Flint and the new girl arriving. When two o'clock finally rolled around, Jacinda and I went in search of Mica, the twins and Flint. They needed to know about the new girl, and they needed to know to return early tonight for the meeting. Di, meanwhile, returned to the cabin to try and see her.

Jacinda headed off to the guest barn, and I trudged up the hill to the work barn. I knew I'd probably see Dean. I sighed heavily. Ignoring him wasn't being fair. Even though I was looking for the twins, Mica and Flint, I should probably clear the air.

Sure enough, Dean was working on one of the horses when I entered the barn. A grin flashed across his face when I stepped inside.

"Hey, Lena." He straightened and dusted his hands off. A leather apron covered his clothes. "I didn't see ya yesterday. I think that's the first time we've missed a ride since you started workin' here." He cleared his throat and smiled awkwardly.

I stuffed my hands in my pockets and kicked at non-existent pebbles. "Yeah, it was a busy morning. I decided to stay in the cabin for the afternoon."

His eyebrows rose. "Err…sure."

I twirled a strand of hair between my fingers. "Have you seen Mica, Jet, Jasper or Flint?"

"They're at the lower barn with Jessie."

"Oh." *So Jacinda's probably found them.*

"Everything okay?" he asked.

"Yep, everything's fine." Since I didn't need to find them, I knew I should probably get this conversation over with. I stuffed my hands in my pockets. "So…about the other night. I…well…I just wanted to say that I really like you, but—"

Dean held up his hand. He wouldn't meet my gaze. "You don't need to say anymore."

"I don't?"

His mouth tightened. "I get it."

"Oh."

At least ten seconds of awkward silence passed. I wrung my hands. "Dean, I really like you a lot. You're one of my best friends."

He laughed humorlessly and turned back to shod the horse. "Best friend, huh?"

I winced. "I'm sorry. I just don't feel any more than that."

Scraping sounds filled the barn. "Does this have anything to do with Flint?"

My cheeks flushed. "Why would you think that?"

More scraping sounded. Dean continued to file the horse's hoof. "I'm not an idiot, Lena. The guy goes crazy every time he sees us hangin' out, but since you never said you two were together, I thought ya were fair game."

I awkwardly clasped my hands together.

"So that ain't true?" Dean asked. "You guys are actually together?"

"Um, well, I don't know. We weren't before, or anything like that, but now," I paused, thinking about last night. "I guess we kind of are."

"I figured as much." He stood and grasped the horse's lead rope. When he tried to walk by me, I grabbed his arm. His muscles bunched underneath my fingertips.

"I know this is really cliché but can we still be friends?"

For a second, I didn't think he was going to reply. He stared over my head, his mouth a tight line. I shuffled from foot to foot.

He finally met my gaze and sighed. A sad smile spread across his face. Pulling me into a hug, he sighed. "Yeah, of course. We can still be friends."

Embraced in his strong arms, his scent surrounded me. Horse, sweat and some kind of cedar deodorant. It wasn't an intoxicating scent that made me want to close my eyes in bliss, but he didn't stink.

I hugged him back. He held me a bit longer than a "friend" would but I let him. When I finally pulled back, he let go reluctantly. I stuffed my hands in my back pockets.

"Do you want to go for a ride today?" I asked.

A wistful expression covered his face but with a blink, it was gone. He took a step back. "Yeah, of course. Just let me finish up in here."

BY THE TIME the evening rolled around, I felt better about everything with Dean. We'd gone on our usual ride. He'd been friendly and joking, just like he usually was. A few times I caught him watching me, his eyes soft, but each time he smiled and said something funny. I knew things would be weird between us for a while, but I hoped with time he'd see that Flint and I were serious about one another.

At least, I thought we were serious.

I frowned as Jacinda, Di and I walked back to the cabin following the supper meal. It was already getting dark. Surely Flint and I were more than friends now. Right?

"What time are the guys and Mica done tonight?" Di asked.

"Any minute," Jacinda replied. "Flint said they'd come straight down from the barn. Have you had more visions of her?"

"A few. Not as strong as the one this morning, but I'm feeling more and more confident that she's arriving tomorrow."

"Do you know what time?" I asked.

"No." Di fingered her temples. "Let's get back to the cabin. I want to try and see her again. Hopefully I can find out."

We reached the porch and climbed the steps. I sat down on the porch swing. "I'll wait here."

"Waiting for someone?" Jacinda winked.

I rolled my eyes.

She laughed and walked inside with Di.

I leaned back on the swing as the door closed softly behind them. The wooden seat boards were hard and not entirely comfortable, but I liked how the seat swung easily and the gentle creak it made.

A few minutes later, Flint, Mica and the twins appeared in the distance. They were all talking and laughing as they walked down from the barn. Correction, Mica and the twins were talking and laughing. Flint wasn't.

Striding toward me, Flint looked so strong, sexy and serious that I actually stopped breathing. A feeling that was becoming all too familiar coursed through me. It was like someone had hooked me up to a generator. An electric jolt of awareness followed by a hot feeling of lust slid through me. It felt like my senses were on fire.

Nobody had ever affected me like he did.

He was about ten yards away when he finally realized I sat there, watching him. I felt his energy pick up. It rolled toward me in steady waves. A smile tugged at his lips.

When the four of them climbed the porch, Flint walked over and sat beside me. The other three stopped by the door. Jet winked when I caught his gaze, a knowing glint in his eye. I would have blushed, but the envious expression on Mica's face stopped it. She glanced at me and Flint and then Jasper. A hunger appeared in her gaze as she stared at the twin. It wasn't the first inkling I had that Mica was interested in Jasper. Her look now, though, confirmed it.

"How was work?" I asked.

Jet shrugged and leaned against the door frame. "Nothing earth shattering."

A tapping on the window sounded. Jacinda beckoned everyone to come in.

"The goddess calls." Jet pushed away from the door and walked inside. Mica and Jasper followed. I made a move to stand, but Flint stopped me.

"They can wait a minute," he said.

My heart rate increased at his deep tone. I lowered myself back beside him. He brushed a strand of hair from my face. The contact sent tingles along my spine.

"Have a good day?" He leaned closer.

My heart slammed against my ribs. "Um, yeah," I said a little breathlessly.

His lips were nearly touching my skin. Flint inhaled and then stiffened. I barely noticed. He was millimeters away from touching me, but then he leaned down and smelled my shirt. And then he smelled my shoulder.

Energy exploded off him. "Care to tell me why you smell like *Dean?*"

It took me a moment to snap out of my dazed state. "What? Dean?"

A muscle ticked in Flint's jaw. "Yes, Dean. You smell like him."

"I do?"

Flint inhaled tightly. "It smells like he's been all over you."

"Really?" I leaned down and sniffed my shirt. Lingering scents of horse, sweat and Dean's deodorant indeed clung to my clothing. It finally clicked. "Oh, right. He gave me a hug this afternoon. That's probably why I smell like him."

"A hug?" Flint's nostrils flared. "Is that all he gave you?"

I almost laughed but then realized he was serious. I bit my cheek to stop from smiling. "Yes. I promise. That's all."

Flint leaned back, that unreadable expression on his face again. He took a few deep breaths, his strong shoulders rising and falling. If it hadn't been for my gift, I'd have no idea how he was feeling right now. But since my clouds didn't lie, I felt the anger pulsing off him. Anger he was trying desperately to get under control.

After a minute, he sighed heavily and raked a hand through his hair. "You're gonna be the death of me, woman."

Another shiver ran through me. Something told me I wasn't going to mind Flint's possessiveness at all. In a way, it was incredibly arousing. "Are you okay?" I asked.

He took another deep breath. "Yeah, just give me a minute."

It seemed to take him at least that long to calm down. When he finally did, he rubbed his face in his hands. "I hate the thought of you with another guy," he muttered. "Sorry for going all alpha male on you."

"I think I like it. It's kind of hot."

His eyes darkened. "Kind of hot, huh?"

I smiled.

He shook his head and grinned. "Come on, let's go inside. They're waiting for us."

Heat cascaded between my thighs. "Right. Of course."

A knowing glint gleamed in his gaze when we finally stood to join the others.

THE CHAIRS AND couches were all in a circle when we entered the living room. Flint and I sat on the free couch just as Di strode into the room. She wore clean black yoga pants and a long-sleeve black shirt.

"She's definitely coming tomorrow," Di stated. "I'm thinking she'll be somewhere in Gunnison." Di sat on the free chair and scooted it closer to the group.

"So we go to Gunnison," Flint said.

Di nodded. "All in favor?"

Everyone immediately voiced their agreement. "Lena?" Di glanced in my direction. "Do you approve?"

I sat up straighter. "Oh, yes."

"What time are we leaving?" Mica asked. "And how are we gonna all get off work? I don't think Pete's gonna like that."

"Or Val," Jacinda added with a frown.

Di glanced at Flint briefly before turning to the group. "I think it's best if most of us stay here."

"What?" Mica said. "Why? We always go."

"This one's different," Di said. "She always seems frightened and is never talking to anyone. Not like Lena."

My mouth dropped at her teasing tone, but Di just carried on, her face serious again. "One interesting thing about this girl, is she always has an animal with her. At least a dozen times now, I've seen her with a stray dog or cat. Once, I saw her with an iguana." Di shook her head. "I think two, three max, should get her. And we definitely need a woman in the group. I have a feeling if it's all men, she'll run."

"I'll go," Mica volunteered.

"And almost blow it like you did with Lena?" Jet replied. "I don't think so."

"I didn't blow it," Mica retorted.

Jacinda patted Mica's hand. "You were pretty close. A few times you almost gave us away."

"I did not," Mica protested but not as loudly this time. I watched Mica's growing irritation and thought back to what she'd said to me when we'd first met. I couldn't recall exactly *what* was said, but I did remember others interrupting her.

"So Mica's out," Di said matter-of-factly. Mica crossed her arms. "Jacinda?" Di added.

Jacinda shook her head. "I think Lena should go. I mean, look at her. She's about as innocent as they get."

"What does that mean?" I asked.

"Good point," Di said. "Okay, Lena, you're going."

"I am?"

"Yes," Di replied. "Now, should another girl go? Or a guy?"

"Since Mica's out, and since Lena's going, I think a guy should go," Jacinda said. "Val won't be happy if two of us disappear from the kitchen."

"That makes sense," Jasper agreed.

Di clasped her hands. "So what guy is going?"

"I'll go," Jasper said. "And Jet can stay here. That way if we need to talk to you all, I can tell him, and he can relay the message."

Jacinda's eyes brightened. "Good idea, Jasper."

"Yes, that makes sense," Di agreed. "Okay, so Lena and Jasper will go."

"I'll go too," Flint said.

"Big surprise," Jacinda murmured and winked at Jet. Jet chuckled. Mica crossed her arms even tighter across her chest. Her gaze glued to something on the floor.

"Okay so Flint, Jasper and Lena?" Di said. "All in favor?"

Everyone agreed, except for Mica and me. Mica's reaction made me hesitate. Finally, I said yes. Mica still didn't say anything. The entire group stared at her.

"Mike?" Jacinda elbowed her gently. "Come on, we need you to agree."

Eventually, she mumbled her agreement.

"So that's settled," Di said. "Now, we have to work out how you three are going to get her into the Suburban…"

THE MEETING CONTINUED well into the evening. Everyone, other than Mica, chipped in ideas on the best way to approach the new girl and lure her back to the ranch. It was also agreed that we would stay on the ranch until someone remembered something prior to the first morning we woke up.

Either that, or until Di received a vision that gave us a direction to follow.

About halfway through the meeting, Flint raced up to the main house to speak with Pete and Val about a few of us missing work. Since it was Di's scheduled day off tomorrow, she agreed to switch shifts with me. Only Flint and Jasper would miss work. When Pete and Val asked why they needed to miss work, Flint made up some story about an old friend of ours getting in contact with us. He said we'd only just heard from her and that she was arriving into Gunnison the next day. She was hoping to join us on our travels and was willing to work on the ranch until we carried on.

Luckily, the Henderson's bought the story and were willing to give the new girl some part time work. They didn't ask any other questions, thankfully. It had been a lucky break. If the ranching couple had been adamant none of us miss work, or hadn't been willing to welcome the new girl, we all would have had to pack our bags and sneak out during the night. I didn't like the thought of that, especially since that's how their previous help left.

By the time the meeting finished, it was pitch black outside. The dim light from the two lamps in the living room cast a somnolent glow.

"Meeting adjourned?" Di asked.

Everyone stood. Jet groaned loudly with a stretch, while Flint leaned down and whispered, "Going to bed?"

"I guess."

He trailed a finger along my cheek. "We could go for another walk. It's not that late."

I smiled.

Everyone was preoccupied with rearranging the furniture and chatting about the new girl. No one seemed to notice when Flint and I sneaked out.

CHAPTER NINETEEN

We took off at a brisk walk. I unconsciously headed toward the barn. Flint followed.

"What do you want to do?" he asked.

I shook my head as I realized where I was going. "I always go to the barn when I leave the cabin. Habit."

He smiled. "We can go there."

We walked quietly across the grass. I knew Flint slowed his speed, since he almost ambled beside my hurried pace. He didn't swing me up on his back. I was glad. The butterflies flapping in my stomach were hard enough to swallow and the fast walking helped.

"What are you thinking about?" he asked when we reached the base of the hill.

"Butterflies."

He raised his eyebrows.

"Metaphorically speaking."

He just shook his head and smiled.

As we climbed the hill, I breathed heavily. Flint wasn't even winded. At the top, I took a deep breath and wiped sweat from my brow. "I don't think I'll ever get used to that hill."

"I could carry you."

"I'm not that incapacitated."

Chuckling, he reached down and clasped my hand. "Do you want to go into the barn or out back?"

His question took me a minute to process since all of my thoughts focused on the feel of his fingers. "Um, out back."

He tugged me in that direction.

We wandered to the back of the barn. I walked toward the gate, but Flint pulled me to the nearest fence. "This will do."

Before I could ask what he meant, his hands locked around my waist. A sailing sensation took my breath away. A second later, I was dropped on the other side. I shook my head. "You like doing that, don't you?"

He shrugged. "Maybe." With a bend of his knees and a rush of air later, he stood beside me. He'd jumped the fence as if it were only a foot tall.

I gazed at him in amazement. "I don't know if I'll ever get used to that either."

He just chuckled and clasped my hand again.

We walked down the pasture along the fence railing. Tall grass brushed along our calves, making a swishing sound. The horses stood in a huddle on the other side of the field. Moonlight washed over their broad backs. Flint pulled me toward the center of the pasture and stopped at a large boulder poking up from the earth.

"Here okay?" he asked.

"Sure."

He cupped my waist and lifted me onto the rock. At least this time, he did it at a normal speed. My head didn't spin when he set me down. Once I was settled, he easily climbed up beside me.

Spreading his legs, he pulled me to him so my back snuggled against his chest. I closed my eyes. The feel of his hard abdomen and steely arms looped around my middle made heat flare in my veins. He brushed my hair away from my neck, his fingers trailing along my skin.

My eyes flashed open. "Is it in the way?" I reached up to move my hair.

"Yes, but I like that. Leave it."

His dominant tone made me shiver again.

"Cold?" Flint murmured.

He seemed to mistakenly think the breeze was the cause of my shiver. "No."

Flint pulled me closer. His scent was everywhere. Need clenched in my belly so deep, I had to make myself sit still. I wanted to grind into him. More than anything, I wanted release.

He growled. That sound only made my blood heat more. "Is there something I can help you with?" He pulled my hair back again and planted a kiss on the base of my neck. He bit slightly.

I actually moaned. Goosebumps sprung on my arms. The way his lips felt along my skin made concentrating on anything impossible.

Flint just growled and swiveled me around until we faced each other. His lips found mine. Once again, emotions completely took over when he kissed me. It was like a fire burst to life deep in my belly and the longer his lips explored mine, the larger the fire roared.

When he finally pulled back, I was breathless. We sat like that, only inches away from one another. The mountain air flowed around us, scents of milkweed and grass carried in it, the soft knicker of horses in the distance. Our breaths puffed and swirled together.

"Do you think we knew each other, before?" he asked quietly.

I gave a small nod. It was all I could manage.

He grunted and kissed me again. This time, I could feel that he held nothing back. I met him every step of the way, not caring that we were out in a field, on display for anyone walking by. My entire world became him and me on the rock. The energy around him grew, pulling me into its power. It pulsed and throbbed, as if in sync with our desire.

He abruptly stopped, his breathing harsh. I squirmed, wanting more.

"Damn, woman. You're going to make me forget that we're in the middle of a field."

I was breathless when I replied, "The grass is pretty tall. Nobody would see us if we laid in it."

He chuckled and nipped my ear. "I'd love that, and I'd do that right now, except for one, tiny detail."

"What?" My eyes closed again when his lips blazed a trail down my neck.

"I don't think I'd be able to stop."

"Would we need to stop?"

He groaned. "Damn, woman."

I wiggled closer to him. He stilled my hips. His large hands pressed hotly into me. I could practically feel his heat through my jeans. "Not here. Not like this."

I almost groaned in frustration. "Why not?"

"The first time I take you, it'll be somewhere we can enjoy it for hours. Not some hurried romp in a field."

His words only made me hotter. "Then you better stop talking about it, or I'll be dragging you down there whether you like it or not." I wiggled against him again.

His eyes closed tightly as a muscle clenched in his jaw. A sudden rush of air and blur of movement later, and he stood twenty feet away from me.

He did it so fast, I blinked a few times. The rock felt hard, cold and entirely empty. "Come back," I said.

"Give me a minute."

I waited in the chilly breeze until he returned. With one powerful leap, he sat beside me again. My eyes widened even though the field appeared empty.

"How do you know nobody can see when you do stuff like

that?" I asked.

"Because we're alone up here."

"Are you sure?"

"The guests know this barn is off limits and all of the cowboys finished for the day when we did."

"I never knew this place was off limits." I thought about the day I'd climbed the blasted hill and met Dean. Technically, I wasn't on staff at that point.

"That's because you didn't read the guest handbook."

His tsking expression made me laugh. "And you did?"

"Cover to cover."

I rolled my eyes. "You and Di with your rules."

He pinched me gently in my side which got a squeal out of me. He chuckled deeply. "At least one of us has to keep you out of trouble."

Flint draped his arm around my shoulders. Another spark of desire flowed through me, but I made myself ignore it. Slow, steady pushes of his energy still pulsed into me. I knew I wasn't the only one having a hard time reining in my need.

We both obviously needed a distraction.

"So…what do you think the new girl will be like?" I asked.

He took another deep breath and then another. Slowly, his energy subsided. "Not sure."

"Di hasn't told you about her visions? When she sees her?"

"Yes and no. She tells me when she sees her, but she doesn't give me details, not real details anyway. Only the generalized stuff, like what she told us at the meeting."

"Oh." I thought for sure Di told Flint everything. "Why not?"

"Di's a very private person."

"But aren't her visions something we should all know?"

"Not really. Di sees people at all times of the day. Sometimes she sees people in situations most wouldn't want to be seen in. She takes her visions seriously and feels it's a betrayal of that person's privacy if she divulges every detail."

I hadn't thought of it like that. "Is that why she's always so serious?"

He shook his head. "That's probably because she's always stressed. Di feels a lot of responsibility for our group. If she wasn't able to locate all of us, none of us would have found each other."

I chewed my lip. Again, I hadn't thought of it that way. "I never considered that." We were quiet for a moment and then I said, "What did she say when she saw me? Did she tell you anything?"

Flint smiled.

"What?"

"She didn't tell the rest of the group anything other than what they needed to know, but she told me a few details. More details than she usually does. Such as you had long, red hair. *Wild and the color of fire*, were the exact words she'd used. She also said you were dirty and very thin." His tone changed, growing rougher. "I think that's why she opened up to me. She couldn't figure you out. After she told me more about you, we figured you were naturally a thin person, not realizing you were homeless and starving, but neither of us knew how thin you'd be. We couldn't figure out why you were so dirty, though."

I remembered my homeless days all too vividly.

"She also said you were always talking to people. Lots of people."

"Meeting people was the only thing I enjoyed in my travels."

Flint grunted. "When you started hitchhiking, Di got really confused. She kept seeing you with a new person every time she saw you. Since it never occurred to us you wouldn't have money to travel, we figured you sought people out and liked the company. We never guessed, or even considered, that you were hitching rides."

"Well, there is some truth in that. I *did* like the company."

"I know." His energy picked up again. A hot wave rolled over me. "I still never want you doing that again."

I put my hand over my heart. "Promise."

"Good."

WE CONTINUED TALKING well into the night. When we walked back to the cabin, Flint offered to swing me up on his back. In the black night, I knew no one would see, but nerves churned inside me anyway.

"We'll be fine," Flint whispered. "If I move fast enough, I'm a blur. Then no one can see me."

He wasn't kidding. When we reached the cabin, I felt sick. He'd run much faster than he had the previous night. "Are you okay?" He gently lowered me down.

I sank onto the porch step. "So much for not getting motion sickness."

He frowned and sat beside me. "I'm sorry. I didn't realize. Do you need something? A drink or a cool rag?"

I took a deep breath and shook my head. "No, I'm okay. Just took me by surprise."

He winced. "Sorry."

"It's okay, really."

He helped me stand and then led me inside. It was dark and quiet. Everyone was asleep so we tiptoed into my room. Mica snored softly. I almost giggled when she started talking in her sleep, mumbling about horses and Jasper.

Flint smiled. "Is she always like that?"

I shrugged. "No idea. I've never heard her talk before, so if she is, I probably sleep through it."

I walked to the bunk bed. Flint followed silently behind. "Do you need to get undressed?" he whispered.

Bright moonlight flooded the room, making shadows around us. He leaned against the wall and crossed his arms. Hot energy rolled toward me. With a start, I realized he planned to stay that way.

My eyes bulged. "You want to watch?"

He nodded.

A burst of self-consciousness fired through me, but the heat in Flint's gaze melted it away. He found me sexy. I could feel it. His energy couldn't lie.

Taking a deep breath, I started doing something I'd never done before.

A strip tease.

Considering I had no practice doing it, I still felt self-conscious, but the way Flint's eyes widened and his breath became more rapid, made any insecurity I had fly out the window.

Unbuttoning my jeans, I slowly shimmied them down my hips, letting them fall to the floor. I kicked them to the side before moving to my top. Inching it up, I took my time, letting Flint look his fill until moonlight washed across my abdomen. Silently, I felt thankful for all of the abundant food. I no longer resembled a skeleton.

Soft skin and smooth curves had replaced the bony prominences and muscled planes that had been there only a month before. I felt one hundred percent sexy woman. It was a heady feeling.

I let my sweater catch on my breasts. While they weren't large, they were soft and round. Flint groaned when I gave a little hop to get it off, making my breasts bounce.

"Do you want me to keep going?" I let my shirt fall behind me.

"Yes. Please, don't stop," he said huskily.

I reached behind me, unclasping my bra. For the first time, I was thankful for the shopping trip Jacinda insisted on. I wore a lacy bra with matching panties. They were deep navy with lime green trim. The material brushed against my breasts, making my nipples hard. A shiver of desire ran through me. Flint growled. I held the bra against my skin, rubbing it over me.

Flint's entire body tensed. His harsh breaths became audible. "Lena…" He stepped closer.

"I'm not finished yet." I stepped back.

Stomping down my last insecurity, I let my bra fall to the floor. Moonlight washed across my naked breasts. They jutted forward, hardening in the cool air. I lifted my hands and cupped them.

Before I could move to my panties, Flint was on me.

I was in my bunk, him on top of me, pinning me to the mattress while kissing and grinding against me before I could take a breath.

"Goddamn, woman," he groaned. His head dipped. Hard kisses raced down my neck, until he hovered over me, staring down at my naked breasts.

I crossed my arms over my chest. A flash of movement, and he was pushing them down.

"Don't, you're beautiful," he whispered.

His rough clothing rubbed against my bare skin while his scent made my head swim. I splayed my hands across his chest, marveling at the strength flowing under his skin. I could feel it. It was like a river, a current almost, always there but varying in its intensity. At times like this, when his heart raced with desire, it increased. The raw energy exploded around him, like a raging whitewater until it grew out, almost pulsing in a sphere around us. I gasped at its intensity.

As if knowing what I sensed, he leaned down and tilted my chin up. "You have no idea how much I want you."

His lips locked against mine, and suddenly, he was everywhere. My fingers threaded through his hair as all coherent thought left me. His hands caressed, gripped, and pulled me tightly against him. I gasped at the sensations rolling through me, like wave after wave of desire and energy balled into one. His mouth never left mine as his hands explored and roamed over every inch of my skin. I felt on fire, that I could be consumed right there.

It was only when Mica groaned from below that we stilled. Flint's mouth tore from mine, his breathing ragged in the quiet room. My eyes bulged as I realized what we'd been doing. I hastily pulled a sheet over me.

"Damn," Flint breathed. He raked a hand through his hair and it was only then I felt the massive, hard bulge pressing into my thigh. I rubbed against it. I couldn't help myself.

Flint's breath sucked in. With a firm grip, he stopped me.

"Lena," he growled. He put a few more inches between us. His energy encompassed us, pulling me into its strength. It was an incredibly heady feeling. It felt like the entire world vanished when we were wrapped in his sphere. No wonder I'd forgotten about my roommate.

"Is she awake?" I whispered.

Flint glanced over the edge. Soft snores floated up again when he pulled back. "Doesn't appear to be."

My cheeks heated as I realized what we'd been doing.

Flint pulled me tightly to him and ran a hand up and down my back while taking deep, steadying breaths. "You have no idea what you do to me," he said quietly.

I laughed humorlessly. "Oh, I think I do. It's pretty much the same you do to me."

He grunted softly before nipping my ear. "I should go." He kissed me softly once more.

"Yeah." We'd already pushed our luck by how much we'd done. As erotic as it had been, I didn't want to get caught. That would be mortifying.

"Goodnight," he whispered, kissing me again.

"Night," I murmured. And with that, he was gone.

I WOKE AT four in the morning, a thousand thoughts flying through my head. Between what Flint and I had done last night and finding the new girl today, my mind wouldn't stop. It was like a wash machine stuck on spin cycle. It kept going around and around and around. Even though I'd only slept a few hours, I didn't feel tired. How could so much be happening all at once?

Flint and I were seeming more like a couple every day, we were picking up the new girl today, and then…

It was possible answers lurked just around the corner. The answers I'd so desperately hoped to find for almost five months.

When the sun finally crested the horizon, I was ready to go. Normally, I would have grumbled at already being up for hours. However, since I was still buzzing, I itched to move.

Mica and Jacinda sleepily waved goodbye from the living room. Given Mica's unremarkable expression, I guessed she'd slept through Flint's and my extracurricular activities last night. My cheeks still flushed when I met her gaze. She may not have known what happened right above her, but *I* did.

Pulling my sweatshirt on, I stepped outside. Fresh morning air greeted me on the porch. Di followed. She still wore her pajamas. Black yoga pants and a black t-shirt. Even at night, she wore all black.

She stood with me on the porch, shivering, until Jasper and Flint emerged from their cabin. My eyes locked with Flint's.

He smiled knowingly.

My heart beat erratically as I watched him walk down their steps. Broad shouldered and lean, he made me want to wrap my legs around him right there. His lips tugged up when he caught me watching him. I swear he knew what I was thinking.

Di gripped my arm before I could join them. "Are you sure you know what to do?"

"Yes. I won't mess up."

Her grip tightened. "You're sure?"

I almost rolled my eyes. "I'm sure."

Jasper, Flint and I climbed in the Suburban, all of us silent. Knowing Flint would be driving, I sat in the front. Jasper buckled into the backseat, the loud click echoing. Cold air swirled around. The temperature couldn't be above forty. I zipped my sweatshirt all the way to my throat and pulled the hood over my head. A few strands of my hair escaped, tickling my face.

Flint started the vehicle. The engine purred to life, breaking the peaceful mountain quiet. Di leaned down to talk through Flint's open window.

"Do you all remember what you need to do?"

"We'll be fine, Di," Flint said.

Di leaned to the side to see Jasper better. "And you'll call Jet if anything happens?"

"Yep," Jasper replied.

"Are you all *sure* you know what you're doing?"

Jasper sighed. "Di, chill out, we'll be okay."

She continued to gaze at us. "Call Jet if anything happens. I'll tell him to call you if I see anything change."

Flint gripped the steering wheel. "You still don't have any idea what time she's arriving?"

Di bit her lip. "No, but the sun's always bright when I see her, so it could be mid-morning, this afternoon, or even early evening. Just whatever you do, don't leave Gunnison airport without her."

Flint put the Suburban into drive. "We'll be in touch."

Di stepped back from the door, her arms crossed. "Let me know when you have her."

Flint waved and with a spin of tires we were off. Cool air blew in through Flint's window as we flew down the gravel driveway. I crossed my arms tightly over my chest.

"Cold?" Flint asked.

"A little."

He rolled up his window. The electronic sound hummed. I let my hood fall back. He reached over and tucked a long strand of hair behind my ear.

"I had fun last night." His gaze gleamed.

I smiled. Memories from the time in my bunk clouded my

thinking. I took a deep breath, trying not to squirm. "Me too."

"What'd you guys do?" Jasper asked.

"Oh." I sat up straighter and cleared my throat. "We went to the barn and hung out in the pastures."

"Uh-huh." That one word said exactly how much Jasper believed that.

Once we reached the end of the driveway, Flint steered toward Little Raven. We drove languidly on the county road. It would take around two hours to get to Gunnison, and considering how early it was, Flint didn't hurry.

When we reached the outskirts of Little Raven, Flint slowed. "Coffees?"

Jasper and I answered enthusiastically.

After finding a coffee house, a lone vibrant oasis in an otherwise sleepy town, we climbed back in the Suburban, lattes and mochas in tow. I wrapped my fingers around the cup. It was wonderfully warm.

As we left the small town, the Suburban hummed quietly. Flashes of trees and mountains zoomed past. I watched until Little Raven disappeared. It was hard to believe that only three weeks ago, I'd arrived in this small town, full of hope at finding my family and lost home. How wrong I had been.

For all I knew, I didn't have a family, possibly, I never had. The only family I had were the six strangers who picked me up. Under different circumstances, that might have brought a smile to my face, but given we were on our way to pick up *another* stranger – my thoughts twisted and turned with all the reasons for why that was.

I raised my arm, rested it against the door and cupped my chin in my palm. Flint set my coffee in the console and squeezed my free hand. The small gesture grasped my attention. Just the feel of him brought the inevitable feeling of safety. The anxiety and sadness that had been growing in me abated. I squeezed him back.

He cocked his head. The early sun played off the natural

highlights in his hair, turning his brownish locks into teasing specks of gold. I could tell he knew something was up.

"Are you okay?" he asked quietly.

I nodded, even though that wasn't entirely true. I wanted to know what happened to us, *needed* to know, but then a wave of despair settled over me. We all knew it was possible we'd never have answers. It was possible I'd die not knowing who I was.

He squeezed again.

I settled for fingering his palm as the trees zoomed by. An hour ticked by, and we reached Gunnison.

"Everyone clear on the plan?" Flint asked as we cruised through the streets. It was the first time any of us had spoken. I almost jumped.

"Yes," I replied.

"Jasper?" Flint eyed him in the rearview mirror.

"Yeah," he replied.

As we got to the western edge of town, where the airport sat, I wondered how many planes flew into it each day. I guessed there couldn't be a lot. From the distance, the airport seemed tiny.

Flint pulled onto the road leading to the entrance. "Ready?"

I nodded curtly. "Yes."

"Good." His voice was brusque and businesslike, very similar to how Di's could sound. He pulled up to the main entrance and stopped.

"We'll wait at these doors after we park, and don't forget this." He handed me the suitcase from the back. It was empty, but the new girl would never know that.

I took a deep breath. "Okay." I eyed Jasper. His bright, blue eyes glowed with excitement. I forced a smile. "See you in there."

"Good luck," Jasper called.

"Thanks."

I stepped out and was about to close the door, when Flint reached over and caught my hand. "Remember, if it doesn't work, just meet us at the entrance."

I tried not to think about how whether or not our current plan worked depended entirely upon *me*.

"You'll be fine." He squeezed me again.

I somehow managed a tight smile. "See you soon."

CHAPTER TWENTY

I closed the door, and they drove off. I knew I wouldn't see them until I found the new girl, so I concentrated on what Di told me. The girl was supposed to be short, around my height, with brown hair and brown eyes. Di described her as "cute" and said she always appeared scared.

Okay, so I'd just have to find a small woman who resembled a rabbit cornered by a python. Easy right? I chewed my lip as my nervousness grew. It reminded me of the times I'd felt this before, while I waited on highways and interstates, wondering who I'd ride with next. The unknowing, the what if's, the...

I stopped short. *Of all the times I felt this before.*

Grinning, I entered the airport. I knew exactly how I'd find her.

Two hours later, I still ambled around. I hadn't bothered to connect with Flint or Jasper. I knew they'd be waiting by the entrance, since our arranged meeting time wasn't until seven in the evening if I never found her. I had quite a few hours to kill until then.

I once again retraced my steps when I reached the end of a

hall. I pulled out a granola bar to abate my hunger. As I passed a few travelers, I murmured hellos to those I made eye contact with. Now that I was cleaned up and presentable looking, some readily greeted me in return. It wasn't like it'd been in my homeless days. Then, most people had avoided me like the plague.

An elder gentleman stopped to ask me where the restroom was, and since I already passed it around three dozen times, I easily gave him directions. Other passengers filtered through the corridor after him. A flight must have just arrived. The sparsely populated terminal suddenly had several dozen passengers milling about.

I turned and searched for her. What I saw at the end of the hall stopped me in my tracks.

It was her.

I knew it was her. It was so obvious. I had the ridiculous urge to run toward her and drag her back to Jasper and Flint, like a prized stag. I actually closed my eyes and took a deep breath to calm down.

She appeared as Di had described. Small and petite, with a short but stylish pixie cut of dark brown hair and large, luminous eyes. Cute was a good word to describe her. Terrified was another. She clutched a bag closely to her chest, like she expected someone to pounce on her at any moment.

If she only knew.

I approached her slowly. When I was within a yard of her, I stopped. She must have noticed because she turned and stared directly at me without saying a word. I smiled and hoped my hair wasn't too wild. That could always make me appear a little insane.

"Hi," I said.

Her wide eyes darted around. I thought she might run but instead, her tensed shoulders relaxed.

"Hi," she replied in a small voice.

"Did you just get here too?" I made a point of swinging

the empty suitcase I carried.

She eyed my luggage. "Yeah."

"Me too."

"You're alone?" Her eyes darted around again.

"Yep, just me. I came here for a summer job. I'm from South Dakota."

"Oh." She frowned. "But it's September."

Crap. "Yeah, well it's kind of a summer/fall job."

She was silent for a moment but then shrugged. I breathed a sigh of relief and studied the cloud that surrounded her. It was a beautiful indigo color mixed with the same blue everyone else in our group had. It stood out like a topaz gem in a sea of black and white.

It'd been so easy to find her. All morning, I'd been walking around with my eyesight permanently fixed in its altered state. When I saw her, I'd known right away that she was number eight.

"I'm Lena, by the way." I waved my free hand while smiling. I could tell she still wasn't sure what to think of me, but she hadn't run yet. I took that as a good sign.

"I'm Amber." She clutched her bag tighter.

"Nice to meet you, Amber. Where are you from?"

She bit her lip. "Err, Lubbock, Texas."

I grinned brightly. "Do you have any more bags?"

"No."

"Do you have someone picking you up?"

She hung her head, her eyes on her toes. With a deft movement, she shook her head. "No."

"So you're driving yourself? Or taking a cab?"

She didn't reply.

I walked closer until we were at eye level. "So what are you going to do here?" I made sure to keep my tone friendly.

Instead of answering, she shrugged and continued staring at her toes.

"So you don't have anywhere you need to be?"

She looked up. Tears welled in her eyes, but instead of acknowledging them I grinned. "Because that's great news. You could come with me!"

Her gaze widened, and she blinked back the tears. *"What?"*

I continued grinning, feeling like a real idiot, but keeping it up anyway. "I just accepted a job on a cattle ranch, and they've been looking for help, so if you need a job you could come with me."

I knew it was a preposterous thing to offer a random stranger, but since I knew her background, I knew she didn't have anywhere to go. We'd all agreed this tactic *might* work. But that might, was a big might. It could backfire. Any second, she could scuttle away and then what?

"Oh," she replied. She seemed about to run, and I felt a moment of panic, but then she mumbled, "I don't know if that's a good idea. I...I have...somewhere to be."

"Okay, but it's a short term position, only for a few more weeks until the tourist season ends. Not to mention, you get to ride horses every day and help with the cattle. But if you have some place to be..."

Her head snapped up. "Horses?"

"Oh yeah, horses, cows, dogs and cats too. It's a ranch, so there are a lot of animals."

"Really?"

"Most definitely, tons of critters."

"I like animals."

I know. "Well, if you don't have any immediate plans, you could always come with me. They're still looking for more help. They need someone to help outdoors with the livestock."

She paused, frowning. Her eyes were so big they reminded me of a doe. "Well, I don't know. I'm kind of..." but she stopped.

"You're kind of what?"

"Well...I'm looking for..." but she stopped again.

"If you're looking for work, it's a great job." I played

stupid. "And like I said, it's only short term."

"Hmm."

"But if you need to be somewhere…" I added, just so I wouldn't sound too desperate.

She shrugged. Tears welled in her eyes again. Before I could stop myself, I stepped to her side and put my hand on her shoulder.

"Hey, it's okay, don't cry." Her shoulder tensed when I touched her, but she smiled when my hair tickled her cheek.

"Sorry," I pushed it back. "It's always getting in the way."

"It's pretty. I wish I had long hair."

"It's overrated. Not very practical."

"I bet boys like it," she said in that small voice again.

I cocked my head. "Yeah, some do." I thought about Flint. "Especially some of the cowboys on the ranch. A few of them like it."

"There's cowboys there?"

I let my hand fall from her shoulder. "Yeah, quite a few." I watched, puzzled, as a new interest grew on her face.

"So there are real cowboys and lots of animals on this ranch?"

"Yep."

"And this job's only for a few weeks?"

"If that's what works for you."

She gazed at me and slowly, for the first time, smiled. Shiny white teeth emerged between her pert mouth. "If they don't hire me, I can come back here?"

"Of course."

"Um, I guess I could go."

"Really?" I felt as stupid as I sounded. Had it really been that easy?

She smiled again. "Yeah, let's go."

I bit my lip in puzzlement as we began walking. "We just have to find Flint and Jasper."

"Flint and Jasper?"

"Yeah, they're two cowboys from the ranch. They'll give us a ride."

"Are they cute?"

"Ah, yes," I replied hesitantly.

She grinned.

Unease settled in my stomach, but I ignored it and told myself to be grateful she was coming. We meandered toward the entrance where Flint and Jasper waited. Jasper stood leaning against the wall, his arms crossed, but Flint was pacing. The minute our eyes connected, he stopped.

"I'll be right back," I said to Amber. She was already staring at Jasper and Flint. I walked as quickly as I could to the guys.

When I was a yard from Flint, he said, "What's wrong?"

"Relax, she wants to come."

"Are you serious?" Jasper pushed away from the wall.

"Completely serious."

Flint smiled, shaking his head. "Di and Jacinda were right."

I shrugged, not too sure how much I had to do with it. I glanced over my shoulder and motioned Amber over. She hurried to my side.

"Amber, this is Jasper and Flint."

"Hi," Amber eyed Jasper first and then Flint. "These are the cowboys?" Her gaze lingered a bit longer on Flint than I thought was necessary.

"Are you ready?" Flint reached down and took my empty suitcase.

"Here," Jasper reached for Amber's bag. "I'll carry yours." She smiled prettily, and he grinned at her a little too broadly. I wanted to kick him, but then realized Amber seemed to enjoy the attention. I frowned again and followed Flint.

The sun shone brightly when we stepped out of the terminal. Five minutes later, we were climbing in the Suburban. Amber buckled herself beside Jasper, who in no time, turned on the charm. A small giggle escaped the latest newcomer when we exited the parking lot. The happy sound for some reason grated on my nerves.

"Hey." Flint nudged my leg. "Are you okay?"

I forced a smile. "Yeah, just tired."

The journey back to the ranch was quite different from the journey in. Amber's coy smiles and batting eyelashes had Jasper practically drooling. The few times she'd engaged Flint in conversation a white hot, searing jealousy flashed through me.

I clenched my hands into fists when we turned onto the ranch's gravel driveway. Just what exactly had we gotten ourselves into?

CHAPTER TWENTY-ONE

Jacinda shook out her kitchen rug on the porch. "So what do you think of Amber?"

Amber had been with us for two full days, yet each day had felt like a year.

"Oh, I dunno, she's okay I guess." I slapped the braided rug harder.

Jacinda quirked an eyebrow. "You guess? Are you saying you don't mind how she flirts with Flint?"

"Oh, that. Well…"

We'd told Amber yesterday morning who we were. She'd taken it pretty well. To say she now thought she belonged in our group put it mildly. The timid, meek girl Di saw in her visions had entirely disappeared. A flirty, bodacious young woman had taken her place.

She still loved animals and spent most of the last forty-eight hours with the cowboys and cattle, although half of that reason seemed to be *because* of the cowboys. I'd warned Amber on day one about Aaron, but I wondered if she realized how dangerous he may be. She flirted with him too.

I clenched my teeth and slapped my rug harder.

"I knew you didn't like her," Jacinda teased.

I eyed Jacinda. She just laughed. It was me, Jacinda and Amber in the kitchen today. Val had requested Amber work with us which didn't go over well with the newcomer. She pouted and said I promised she could work with the livestock. But after Di reminded her that Pete and Val were our bosses, she relented, however the pouting continued.

"We better go in." Jacinda rolled up her rug.

I reluctantly followed her inside.

Di was enjoying her day off, but I wished it was me having a free day. My morning hadn't exactly gone well. I spilled orange juice all over myself during breakfast after Amber declared she was joining Flint in the afternoon for a ride. Burning anger and disbelief had taken control, and since I only saw red, I didn't see the buffet table on my way back to the kitchen. I walked right into it, and the pitcher of juice I'd been carrying ended up all over my jeans.

I told myself repeatedly that what Amber said couldn't possibly be true. While Flint and I had never declared ourselves together – we were. Right?

Amber was still in the kitchen when we entered, although Val seemed to be doing most of the work. Amber sat propped on the counter with her legs crossed daintily beneath her.

"So, Dean's single too?" she asked Val.

Val continued mixing something in a bowl. "I suppose so, m'dear, but I'm not sure. I guess you'd have to ask him."

Familiar country music floated through the air. Some woman sang of losing her man and nursing a broken heart. Prophetic? I hoped not.

When Amber saw us, she smiled. "Hey girls, those rugs done?"

"Yes." Jacinda set them back on the floor.

"Is there anything else we need to do?" Amber jumped off the counter gracefully.

"Just the tables to wipe off, but you go on. I'll do it," Val replied.

"Really?" Amber asked.

I scowled at Amber. "I'll do it, Val."

Grabbing the bucket, I filled it with soapy water. Amber's large, pretty brown eyes followed me when I passed her. I avoided her questioning gaze. I also ignored her twitching nose. Amber's ability was her incredibly heightened sense of smell. She could also smell emotions. It was why she was so good with animals, since she could smell how they felt.

I could only guess what scent she got off me right now.

Her tattoo, on the other hand, was exactly as Flint predicted. It was similar to Di's but different – a half circle attached to a full circle with a cross on the other side. Like Flint had guessed, it was the symbol for Mercury.

Eight tattoos. Eight planets. Eight individuals. We were all together now.

Di and Flint had also been right about her last name. On Amber's fake identification, her name read Amber Williams. Another top last name in the U.S. And, like the others, she'd also woken up in a luxury condominium with tons of money. The city she'd woken in was Lubbock, Texas. Another random location.

I plunged into work and scrubbed the first table I reached with more force than necessary. I didn't want to think about our strange situation anymore, or more upsetting, what Amber said about Flint. I returned to the bucket to rinse out the washcloth as another pair of hands dipped in beside mine. A strained smile covered Jacinda's face when I glanced up.

"With two of us doing this, we'll be done in no time."

I frowned. "Where's Amber? Isn't she going to help?"

Jacinda shrugged. "Ah, no, she left."

"Where'd she go?"

Jacinda hastily wiped down a table, not meeting my eyes. "Not sure."

"She's going on a ride with Flint, isn't she?"

Jacinda muttered something under her breath and turned to face me. "Who knows, Lena. Really, don't worry. I see how Flint looks at you. You have nothing to worry about."

"But she said she was joining Flint for a ride?"

Jacinda made a face. "Yeah, but–"

"But nothing. Let's just finish up here."

I walked away before Jacinda could say anything else. I didn't stop until I was clear across the dining room so she wouldn't see the tears brimming in my eyes. The rational part of my brain knew Amber could be lying. It could all be made up. But the emotional part of my brain? Inside, I was crumbling to pieces.

Even if Amber had lied, the question was why? Why would she do that? Wasn't it obvious Flint and I were together? Why would she want to break that up?

Suddenly, I hated Amber. Hated her with such ferocity it stunned me. I tried not to picture her cute face and wide luminous eyes, or how she walked so confidently among the cowboys. I'd never seen Flint look at her the way Tyler and Aaron had, but that didn't mean he hadn't.

No! He wouldn't do that! The Flint I knew would never do that.

My hand slammed down on the table as I viciously scrubbed every inch of it. I kept telling myself over and over that Flint would never date Amber *and* me at the same time, but still, a seed of doubt had planted. All it needed was a stray thought or two that doubted his sincerity and it bloomed to life.

Jacinda, bless her soul, remained quiet. She didn't say one word after we finished and returned to the cabin. Di was in the living room when we entered, but I was in no mood to talk to her either. Instead, I stalked straight to my room and slammed the door.

I paced back and forth a few times, too restless and angry to stop moving. Before I knew what I was doing, I changed into my riding jeans and walked back to the living room to look under all the tables and chairs.

"What do you need?" Jacinda asked. She and Di sat on the couch. Both watched me with puckered brows.

"Have you seen my cowboy boots?" I picked up my sweatshirt. It was lying on the floor. I tossed it back in my room.

"By the door," Jacinda said. "You left them on the porch last night. I pulled them inside so bugs wouldn't crawl in them."

"Thanks." I turned before she could say anything else. I hauled my boots out to the porch and sat on the swing. The stiff leather didn't slip over my heel right away which flared my annoyance.

"Lena, where are you going?" Di asked.

She and Jacinda stood in the cabin's doorway. Their puckered brows had deepened.

"I don't know." And I didn't. All I knew was that I needed to get out of this place. I needed to go somewhere. Anywhere. If I stopped moving, my mind would fill with pictures of Amber riding with Flint, talking with him, kissing him. My breath choked in my chest. It didn't matter that it could all be a lie. The pain radiating through me was unbearable. I stood and bolted down the porch steps.

"Lena, wait!" Di yelled.

I ignored her and ran blindly across the ranch. It wasn't until my breathing became so labored that I realized I was huffing up the hill to the barn. Unconsciously, I'd escaped to the one place I felt best. When I finally crested the hill, I stopped for a minute. Nobody was around. Even Dean was gone.

I strode into the barn and walked past the stalls. I didn't find anyone lingering about which suited me perfectly. After grabbing a grooming bucket and saddle, I walked unsteadily out to the back pastures, trying to carry everything all at once.

It didn't go well.

I dropped the saddle at one point, and the bridle's reins slipped all the way down and almost tripped me. I cursed each time I was slowed. With a sharp whistle, I called Coal. I didn't see any movement or hear any thundering hooves. I whistled again.

Nothing.

Dean must have taken him. I kicked the fence post. Surveying the pasture, I looked for a different horse and spotted a stout bay gelding. In record time, I had him saddled and was mounted. We trotted down the pastures before breaking into a canter. Just as I reached the last corral, I heard something behind me. I turned my head. Two figures stood by the barn.

I knew who they were, even from the distance. Di and Jacinda. For whatever reason, they'd followed me.

Instead of circling back to them, I nudged the gelding into a gallop. His thundering hooves drowned out their yells. I glanced one last time over my shoulder. Di was waving both of her arms overhead. The gelding and I crested the hill. They disappeared from view.

I kept up the gallop until the ground became too uneven and then slowed us to a trot. When we reached the trees, I easily navigated the stout horse through the dips and turns. I wasn't following any particular path. I just wanted to get away and was in a hurry to do it.

Eventually, I slowed us to a walk. We were truly miles from the ranch now and had nothing but the birds, marmots and chipmunks for company. The trees were thick and the air cool.

We kept moving, almost aimlessly. I concentrated on listening to the sounds of the gelding's hooves clopping on the forest floor and smelling fresh pine in the air. When we reached a steep ravine, I stopped. Hills climbed sharply on both sides. The only way through was straight ahead. I had no idea where it led.

For a moment, we just sat there. Stopping only made tears well in my eyes.

Since taking off on the horse, I'd managed to think about nothing at all, but now that we stood still, I wondered if Flint and Amber were together at this exact moment. Maybe one hill over from here. Or maybe, I'd passed them in my rushed gallop from the barn. For all I knew, they'd been curled up on a blanket having a picnic right in the pasture.

No! I took a deep breath. *You're just being ridiculous. Flint would never do that.*

I slid off the horse and tied his reins to a branch. He lowered his head to eat grass, and I sank on the ground beside him. The soft sound of his chews and the smell of the fresh mountain air helped. I actually started to feel better. Well, a little. It wasn't until a sharp crack from a twig sounded that my head snapped up.

What I saw made me choke.

Aaron.

He stood ten yards away, his horse behind him. He must have come from within the ravine.

"Hey, Lena," he said.

He walked slowly toward me. I bolted to standing and shifted my gaze. A scream rose in my throat when his ugly, black cloud came into focus. It was pitch black and swirled around his shoulders. His cloud was even blacker than normal and swelled and pulsed with every step he took. He'd already advanced a yard. Each step had caused his cloud to grow in diameter. I'd never seen that before, but my gut told me what it meant.

He planned to hurt me.

"What are you doing way out here?" he asked, smiling.

Instead of responding, I grabbed my horse's reins. I was never one to ignore my instincts, and I wasn't about to start now. As I leaped onto the horse's back, I knew without a doubt that Aaron had been the one to chase me that night on the gravel driveway.

Adrenaline infused speed into me. My feet still hung by the stirrups when I kicked the horse into a gallop. I felt something brush my leg. Aaron's hand was reaching for my calf, his cloud pulsing into me, but he was too late. I'd already wheeled the horse around and we were off.

I held onto the saddle horn as if my life depended on it, which it very well may have. The gelding ran blindly down the canyon. My terror panicked the horse which I only realized when we almost skidded off an embankment around a sharp turn.

Get a grip, Lena!

I lay low against the horse, my breath labored from exertion and fear. Air whipped across my cheeks. I had to steer us several times to avoid getting hit by a tree branch. I dared a look behind us but didn't see Aaron. I had no idea where he was or if he was after me or not. The air whooshed past me at frightening speed. I turned around. My eyes widened when I realized we were headed straight for a log.

I sat up at the last second, but I wasn't fast enough.

The gelding jumped. The movement set me off balance and then air sailed around me.

Only air.

I saw the tree before I hit it. Then everything went black.

CHAPTER TWENTY-TWO

"Lena! Lena! Can you hear me?"

The words sounded through a fog. My body floated. Darkness surrounded me. It was peaceful. Nice.

"Lena!"

I wanted to swat the voice away. It was annoying. I didn't want to move.

"Lena! Open your eyes!"

"Here, let me try something. Move out of the way," another voice said.

Something rough rubbed on me, like a grating saw against my sternum.

"You're hurting her," the first voice growled.

"I'm testing her consciousness and she just responded to pain. Did you see it? She winced."

"Of course I saw it. Do you really think that's necessary? Don't you think she's hurt enough?" The first voice became hard, edgy almost.

I didn't know who the voices belonged to or why they were arguing. I wished they'd go away. This vacant floating place was soothing and tranquil, yet slowly it became filled with pain.

Sharp, searing pain. Dull, throbbing pain. "Ah!" someone moaned.

"Lena? Lena! Please open your eyes, babe. Please look at me!"

Not only was there pain and coldness but also fear.

"No," someone moaned. "No!" The voice sounded pitiful. But as the pain and coldness continued, I realized that the pain was *my* pain and that the coldness was *my* coldness.

My eyelids fluttered open. Bright light instantly shone into my eyes. I flinched, drawing back.

"Dammit, Di!"

I recognized that voice. Flint.

"Her pupils react to light. That's a good sign." Something clicked and the bright light disappeared.

A heavy weight settled against me. It was warm and firm. A smell fluttered to my senses. I'd recognize that scent anywhere. A feeling of being safe cloaked my skin.

"Flint..." I breathed. My eyes fluttered open again. It was dark, cold, and whatever I was lying on was moist and bumpy. The moon shone through leaves above. "Flint, where am I?"

"Lena, thank God!" Flint choked.

I'd never heard him like that. He sounded panicked, out of control, so unlike the Flint I knew. Big, warm fingers gently pushed tangled hair and leaves from my face. His movements were gentle, but I still winced when they touched my temple. I became aware that my head was pounding.

"My head hurts," I moaned.

"I know, babe, I know."

Aaron!

A horrible fear engulfed me. Why had I thought of Aaron?

"I'm so cold," I whispered. My teeth chattered. The next thing I knew, something fuzzy and warm pressed against my skin. A blanket. Flint lifted me from the ground. I cried out in pain.

"I'm sorry, babe. We'll get you back to the ranch and then

everything will be okay," Flint whispered in my ear. I barely heard him. I was slowly falling into nothingness again, but an image appeared in my mind. Aaron in the ravine. Aaron coming after me.

"Aaron," I whispered. "Aaron…"

"Shh," Flint said. "Don't worry. Everything's going to be okay."

That was the last thing I heard before everything went black again.

IT WAS DAYTIME the next time I woke. Bright sunlight pierced my eyelids. Trying to get away from it, I rolled into something heavy.

I opened my eyes. It appeared I was in a bed, and the heavy thing I'd rolled into was Flint. "Hi," I managed.

"Hi. Are you hurting?" His gaze darted across my face.

"Yeah." My head pounded, and my body felt…broken. I didn't know how else to describe it. I coughed. "Ow, what the…" I grabbed my side. "My ribs really hurt."

Flint frowned. "A few are cracked."

"They are?"

"I'm going to get Di. I'll be right back."

In one of his lightning fast moves, he was gone. The movement was so quick and agile it barely disturbed the mattress's springs. I was grateful, since the little movement it had caused hurt my throbbing side.

A few minutes passed before Di appeared in the door frame. Flint stood behind her.

It was then I realized I wasn't in my cabin. Instead, I was in the guy's bedroom. Their cabin was smaller than ours, just one bedroom with a queen bed and a set of bunk beds. Jet and Jasper were nowhere to be seen. I guessed they'd slept here, though. The bunk bed sheets were mussed.

Di approached. Flint hovered behind her. Di kneeled by the bed and placed a bag beside her. From it, she withdrew a syringe and a vial. "Flint said you're in pain."

I nodded.

"I have pain meds."

"What are they?" I tried to lean forward. Bad idea. I winced and lay back.

"Morphine, but if that doesn't do the trick, I also have Fentanyl. We'll use these for a few days while I start you on a regimen of oxycodone and acetaminophen. Once your pain subsides enough, we'll only do oral meds."

I vaguely wondered how she got the drugs or knew how to use them. I didn't ask. I hurt too much to be curious. With a deft movement, Di filled the syringe and the pungent smell of alcohol filled my nose. She scrubbed something sticking in my arm with an alcohol swab.

"What's that?" I asked.

"An IV cannula. It makes it easier to administer drugs and fluids."

"But why..." My voice trailed off as the pain slowly subsided.

Di tossed the syringe into a plastic box in the bag. It bounced off something. I wondered what else she had in there. "Feeling better?"

"Yes," I sighed as a blissful numbing sensation filled me.

"Good." Di fingered my wrist and felt my pulse before pulling out a stethoscope and listening to my chest. "Your pulse and respirations are good."

I tried to sit up but felt so weak. Flint was on the bed before I could blink. He easily repositioned me until I sat upright. He then fluffed the pillows behind me.

I frowned and surveyed the room again. "Why am I in your cabin?"

"Because," was the only reply I got.

Di stood from her kneeling position and began assessing me. Or at least, that's what it felt like. She started at the top of my head and worked her way down. She looked in my mouth, flipped down my bottom eyelids, inspected my ears and felt along my jaw and neck. After that, she pulled back the covers and did everything from listening to my chest and back, to palpating my stomach and tapping her fingers all around.

Next, she asked me to move to the edge of the bed and dangle my feet. She made me do all sorts of funny things – I had to follow her finger with my eyes, flip my hands up and down on my lap, touch my nose and then touch her finger, squeeze her fingers, flex and point my toes against her hands, follow her finger with my gaze.

It almost felt like a game, but after a while I just felt tired.

She took a few more things out of her bag, and after taking my blood pressure and temperature, she put me back into bed. I stared at her for a moment.

"Di, are you a doctor?" I asked.

She shrugged and arranged the covers around me. "I don't know, but it seems I might be. Now, tell me, what do you last remember? Do you know what happened or what day it is? And more importantly, do you know who you are and where you are?"

I frowned. "Um, yeah, I know who I am. My name's Lena, and I don't know what day it is, but I'm in the guy's cabin." Flint put his arm around my shoulders and squeezed. A grim smile covered his face.

"It's Friday today," Di said. "You went for your ride two days ago and didn't come back. Do you remember any of that?"

"Ride?" I exclaimed.

Suddenly, the damn broke loose. Running away from the ranch on the bay gelding, wandering through the mountains, stopping in the ravine, encountering Aaron, galloping away, flying off the horse. The tree.

Fear consumed me.

"Aaron…he… he followed me….into the mountains. I don't know how, but he…he tried to attack me."

A hot wave of energy rolled out of Flint. He took a few deep breaths. I could tell he was trying to control his rage.

Despite the angry emotions emitting from him, I felt nothing but safe. *Safe, I'm safe. I'm with Flint.*

A warm, relaxing feeling settled over me.

Di scowled. "I thought something like that happened. After you left the cabin, I got a vision. It was of you and Aaron in the forest. You were frightened. That's when Jacinda and I chased after you."

I vaguely recalled seeing them before I left the barn, but it was hard to decipher what was what. I felt so tired. Leaning forward, I rested my head between my hands, but that made my ribs ache despite the morphine so I leaned back.

"What's wrong with me?" I asked. "Everything seems so fuzzy."

"You have a concussion," Di said. "From how we found you on the ground, I'm assuming you collided with that giant tree you were leaning against?"

Her words brought back a sharp memory: sailing through the air when the horse jumped and my head colliding with a tree. "I think so."

"You were knocked unconscious," she continued. "You're lucky. You could have broken your neck."

"Hmm," I muttered.

"But that doesn't explain what happened out there," Flint said. Hot energy still poured out of him. His efforts to subdue it weren't working. He pulled me back against him. "What did Aaron do to you?"

"He, well, nothing really." I paused. I remembered Aaron advancing on me, but I had no idea why. "I remember riding into a ravine, getting off the horse, and then he was there."

A picture of his ugly, black cloud entered my mind. I shuddered. "His cloud was black and pulsing when I saw him. I think he was there to hurt me."

Heat exploded off Flint. "What? He was *there* to hurt you?

He followed you out there intentionally to hurt you?"

"I think so."

"I'm going to kill him."

"Flint," Di said in a stern tone. "We can't do anything rash. Besides, he hasn't shown up yet and considering how he chased Lena, I'd be surprised if he did."

"What?" My head snapped toward her. I regretted the movement. "He hasn't come back?" I rubbed my neck.

"No." Di crossed her arms. "No one's seen him."

"Then where did he go?"

"Your guess is as good as mine," Di replied.

Flint fumed silently beside me. He took a deep, steadying breath before he asked quietly, "What were you doing out there anyway?"

The memory rushed back for *why* I'd run so impulsively from the ranch. I glanced at Flint. He waited for my answer with an unreadable expression on his face. Was it because he felt guilty? Denial crushed me with its weight. *No, he wouldn't have gone on a date with Amber.* Or had he?

"Um, I was upset," I replied.

"About what?" He pulled me closer.

I glanced at Di. I wasn't sure I wanted to have this conversation in front of her. Ignoring him, I said, "How'd you find me anyway?"

"Amber found you," Di said.

"Amber?" I stiffened and pulled away from Flint.

"She followed your scent," Di continued. "And the scent of your horse, which stood patiently waiting a few yards away from you, in case you were wondering."

"Was everyone there or just you and Amber?" I asked.

Di shook her head. "No, Jacinda, Jet and Flint were there too. When we realized you were truly missing, we sent Val, Pete, Mica, Jasper and the other three cowboys looking for you in the opposite direction of where Amber thought you were. She was fairly certain she could track you, but we didn't want the other cowboys or Pete and Val there. They'd ask too many questions."

I frowned. So Amber had found me and possibly saved my life? I wasn't sure how I felt about that. I pushed that thought aside. "How are Pete and Val?"

"Okay, now that you've been found," Flint answered. He was frowning. I'd put at least six inches between us. "Pete's had a few guests over the years go missing when they've wandered off. He said a guest once got seriously injured and almost died before he was found."

I raised my eyebrows. Guilt pummeled me for putting Pete and Val through that. "And everyone else, how are they?"

"Currently, everyone's at work," Di replied. "Jacinda's worried since you hit your head so hard. She and Amber are up in the kitchen while the twins and Mica are out working with Pete. The cowboys are doing their usual thing."

I licked my lips. My mouth felt like the Sahara. "Is there any water?"

"Of course." Di stood and left the room. With her gone, the bedroom turned into an echoing void. The silence hung. I felt Flint staring at me, but I refused to meet his gaze. A second later, Di returned.

"Here." She handed me a large glass of water.

After I drained it, I placed it on the nightstand. The movement bumped my ribs, causing my breath to hitch.

"Ouch," I muttered. I wanted to rub them but knew that wouldn't do a thing. I rubbed them anyway. "How badly am I injured?"

Di's brow furrowed. "Without an x-ray, it's hard to say, but I believe you have a cracked rib, if not several cracked ribs, thanks to that tree you collided with."

"So cracked but not completely broken?"

She frowned. "I'm not sure, but I think so."

"Oh." That didn't sound promising. "Why didn't you take me to the hospital?"

"No—"

"That's right," I said. "No hospitals. I guess it's good you're a doctor."

She shrugged. "If I'm not, I know enough to help you."

"But where'd you get all that stuff?" I nodded toward her bag.

She frowned. "Well…we…or rather…"

"I stole it," Flint said.

I turned to him with wide eyes. "You *what?*"

"I stole it."

"But how?"

"Little Raven's outpatient clinic isn't very hard to break into," Flint replied.

I gaped. "But what if you get caught?"

"I didn't leave any prints, and I only took what was needed. It won't be obvious anything is missing. They probably won't know until they do an inventory."

I shook my head. This was all getting to be too much. "So you know how to break into a building?"

"It seems so," he replied.

"And you're a doctor?" I said to Di.

"Perhaps," she replied.

"Yet we still have no idea *how* we know any of these things," I finished.

"Correct," Di said.

It was all too much. My head felt incredibly heavy. "I'm tired," I complained.

"You will be for quite some time." Di arranged the covers around me again. "Head injuries take a while to heal, and it's important that you tell me if you start having uncontrollable headaches, dizziness, nausea with frequent vomiting, increased confusion…"

She spewed out a list of symptoms that I assumed meant my head injury was getting worse versus better. To be honest, I only half listened. My eyelids felt like lead again. I couldn't believe how tired I felt.

"Enough," Flint interrupted. "She needs to sleep."

Di smiled. Somehow, the expression didn't seem right on her, like a badger trying to look meek. "Right, sorry. Go to sleep."

I had no idea what time it was but felt that was good advice. I sank into the pillow and barely felt when Flint gently caressed my hair and softly kissed my cheek.

"Sleep babe, I'll be here when you wake up," he whispered.

CHAPTER TWENTY-THREE

Flint was indeed there when I woke up. I questioned if he moved. He still sat propped against the headboard, his long frame stretched out in front of him. Dressed in the same clothes, with a book propped on his lap, I wondered if he slept at all.

Daylight spewed through the sheer curtains. I guessed it was morning. The light shone muted gray and had that dusky glow that only came with sunrise.

"Hi," I mumbled.

The book flopped to Flint's side. In a flash, he leaned over me. "You're up."

"How long did I sleep?"

He glanced at his watch. "From six last night till now. It's six in the morning. Twelve hours."

"Oh." I glanced toward the bunk beds. "Where are Jet and Jasper?"

"Working. They left half an hour ago."

I fumbled with the covers. "Excuse me, I'll be right back."

Before I could pull the covers off, he was at my side, lifting them. My movements were stiff and clumsy. I groaned when a breath sliced through my ribs like a hot knife. At least my head no longer pounded.

"Here, take these." Flint's brow furrowed. He picked up two pills from the bedside table, laid them in my palm and gave me a glass of water.

I didn't ask what they were. I guessed it was Di's regimen of pain meds. I washed them down with a quick swallow and tried to stand.

"I'll carry you."

Before he could sweep me up, I shook my head. I was surprised I beat him to it. "No, I'll walk. I'm fine."

As much as I loved the feel of his arms around me, I didn't want to be carried to the bathroom. Besides, I still didn't know how I felt about everything. For the first time since meeting him, the safe feeling he evoked didn't pacify my nerves. Was his concern genuine or out of guilt? That unreadable expression from last night flashed through my mind.

Flint frowned when I took a hesitant step. His face was masked with so much worry I actually smiled. He was like a fretting mother hen. "Flint, I'm fine."

He just frowned further.

When I reached the bathroom, I managed to close the door without falling over or jarring my ribs. I finished my business and went to the sink. At least my toothbrush was here. While brushing my teeth, I looked in the mirror.

I wished I hadn't.

The sight wasn't pretty. Cuts littered my face like a bad cross-stitch. A bump on my head resembled a misshapen egg, and my hair was, well, I won't even go there.

I lifted my shirt. An ugly, purple bruise bled across one side of my chest. I was a sight.

With less enthusiasm, I hobbled back to the bedroom. Flint waited for me. He tried to help me into bed. I refused and dumped myself rather unceremoniously onto the mattress which only made me yelp.

"I never was very graceful," I muttered.

"If you'd let me help you, it wouldn't hurt." Flint pulled the covers over me despite my protests. "Are you hungry?"

"Starving."

"Be back in a minute."

Of course, he was back in roughly thirty seconds. When he sat beside me, he presented me with a steaming mug of coffee and a large, warm caramel roll. My mouth watered.

"Where'd you get this?" I bit into it. Caramel oozed along my tongue. Delicious.

"Val made a pan this morning and brought them down. She knows how much you love them."

"Yeah, they're great," I mumbled between bites. The doughy goodness hit the spot. When I finished, he took my plate and laid it on the table. I settled back into bed.

The silence stretched.

I'd only seen Flint's room a few times. In general, the group rarely hung out in the guy's cabin, and the few nights Flint and I had been together, we were outside. I chewed my lip. Had Amber seen his bedroom?

I reminded myself I still hadn't heard his side of the story.

"I've been staying here since Amber found me?" I asked.

The worry was back on Flint's face. I wasn't sure if it was from my tone or something else. Guilt maybe? I arranged the covers, refusing to meet his gaze. "Why am I not in my cabin?"

"I didn't want you away from me. Just in case—"

"Just in case Aaron came back?" I finished. My heart inadvertently raced. What if Aaron *had* caught me?

"Something like that." Flint pulled me to him. I didn't realize I was shaking until he touched me. Despite my will to put distance between us, I momentarily sank into him. Once again, my body betrayed me.

"It's stupid. He didn't do anything," I whispered.

"No, but he could have." His skin grew warmer. Energy pushed off him like the tide coming in. With each passing second, I not only relaxed but felt safer and safer, but then I thought about Amber and pushed Flint away. I still needed answers.

Flint sighed harshly and raked a hand through his hair. "Lena? What's going on? You said you rode off because you were upset. What were you upset about?"

I stared at my toes.

"Tell me. What's going on?" His voice was tight, laced with demand.

I met his gaze. I needed to see his reaction when I told him. His eyes didn't lie, not when the curtain was wide open like it was now. I took a deep breath. "It was because of you...and Amber."

Genuine surprise glowed in his irises. "Me and Amber?"

"She said you two were going on a date."

"*What?*"

"She said you two were going on a ride together, the day I went missing. Were you?"

His mouth tightened. "No, she *asked* me the previous day if I wanted to go on a ride with her, but I declined."

"You did? So she *did* lie?"

"Yes, she lied," he replied icily.

I crossed my arms tightly over my chest. Wincing, I lay them back at my sides. I didn't know what to feel. Happy that my worry had been for nothing? Or anger that Amber had made it all up?

The anger won out.

"Stupid, Amber," I muttered darkly.

Flint, however, seemed to care less about Amber. "Lena, there's something we need to clear up."

"What?" I asked warily.

He tilted my chin, forcing me to look him right in the eye. "I want to get one thing straight right now. I was never with Amber, have never been with her, and have no desire to ever be with her. You got that?"

"Okay…"

"And I don't know what she told you, but don't believe any of it. Don't believe anything she says. I'm with you and only you. You got that?"

"You are?"

He sighed harshly. "Lena, I want you to be *mine*. Don't you see that?"

"Yours?"

"My girlfriend."

I just stared at him.

Worry grew on his face while the energy around him increased.

I bit my lip as it suddenly dawned on me why I'd been so quick to assume Flint might change his mind about me and why I thought he may have gone on a date with Amber. "So you're not going to start ignoring me again?"

His head snapped back. "No, never."

"You're sure?"

"Yes, I'm sure. I thought we cleared that up? I ignored you when we first met because I didn't know what else to do. It was stupid. I know that now."

I took a deep breath. He was right. We *had* cleared this up, but obviously, deep down I'd still been worried.

"Lena?" he said. "Will you?"

I finally nodded. "Okay."

"Okay what?"

"Yes, I'll be your girlfriend."

A smile spread across his face. "Good."

"But you have to promise me one thing."

"Anything."

"Don't ignore me again. Don't ever treat me like you did before. I couldn't bear it."

His smile vanished. "I won't."

"Promise?"

"Promise."

I let out a relieved sigh and settled against him as comfortably as I could. Deep down, I knew I should have gone to him first and asked him his side of the story. If only rational thought was my strong suit. I may have only known myself five months, but impulsiveness seemed to be my specialty.

"I'm sorry," I said. "I should have talked to you first."

He grunted.

I felt stupid for feeling so insecure with him, but it was like a part of me still expected him to ignore me at any second. Like the fragile bubble we'd created around ourselves could burst at the slightest breeze.

He reached up and pushed a lock of hair from my face. "Lena, when we found you…" He stopped and took a deep breath. "Seeing you like that, on the ground, not moving." He shook his head. The raw pain in his words was so evident.

"Flint…"

"No, let me finish. Lena, I can't lose you. Don't you see that? I don't know what this is growing between us, but I have a feeling it's something deeper than either of us can understand. And I don't know why, but you mean everything to me. You do. You always have. From that first moment I saw you, that was it. I was yours, for as long as you'll have me."

I wanted to say something. My lips wouldn't move.

"I love you," he grumbled. "Don't you see that?"

"You do?" I smiled slowly. "I think I love you too."

He chuckled. "You think, huh?"

Pulling me closer, he slowly tilted my chin up. I wrapped my arms around his neck as his mouth met mine. His lips were hot, firm and he tasted so sweet.

The brief twinge in my ribs was drowned out by a hot surge of desire. I threaded my fingers through his hair, loving the feel of it. Like soft silk. I didn't care when pain shot through my ribs again. His words sparked fireworks in my veins.

He abruptly pulled away. The magic disappeared.

Everything felt empty.

"Dammit," he muttered. "You're going to make me forget you're injured."

A commotion of voices filled the hall outside the door. The first voice I recognized was Mica's excited babble, then Jacinda's soft voice, followed by Di's direct tone. When I heard Amber's pert words, I made a face, but then remembered since she saved me, I shouldn't be mad at her. Well, at least not for too long.

The door burst open and everyone piled inside.

"Lena!" Mica exclaimed, rushing to the bed.

Jet and Jasper shrugged apologetically. "We tried to stop her," Jet said.

Jacinda joined Mica. The tall beauty seemed about to cry. "Oh, Little L, look at you!"

Everyone crowded around the bed. I grinned. I couldn't help it. For the first time, I felt like I belonged somewhere and that I had a family. A real family.

I glanced at Flint. He still watched me with fire in his eyes. Love radiated inside me as Mica took my hand and began babbling about how worried she'd been. Her words poured around me, but I barely heard them. Flint's gaze held my attention. Flint loved me. He said he always had.

I couldn't believe I'd ever doubted him.

CHAPTER TWENTY-FOUR

As the weeks progressed, I slowly healed. Because of my injuries, we stayed on the ranch. Staying stagnant didn't matter since Di's visions kept changing. She saw us in more than one city, but rarely got a clear picture, just snippets of us in different places. It wasn't enough to act upon since nothing was consistent.

A few images repeated themselves, though. She kept seeing a desert and at one point, she thought she saw the Golden Gate Bridge, but since it was a very foggy vision, she couldn't be sure. Jet joked it probably hadn't been a foggy vision, merely actual *fog* around the bridge. Regardless, she didn't feel confident enough to move us.

To pass time as my ribs healed, I helped with research. I spent a few hours every day at the library or internet cafes in Little Raven. A few hours was all my injured brain could handle, but I did my best to search for the cities Di described. Other than San Francisco, I wasn't able to find a specific city that matched her visions.

It was frustrating to put it mildly. It didn't help that it took almost a month for my plaguing tiredness to go away. Of course, my ribs took longer. It was entirely annoying, especially since it felt like everyone catered to me. Val clucked her tongue if she saw me doing something I wasn't supposed to. Not to mention, she gave me the easy chores when I finally returned to work. Jacinda wasn't any better. She constantly tried to help me with everything. She'd even tried to dress me the first few days after I'd returned to my cabin. That was entirely mortifying.

Flint, however, was a completely different story.

From sunup to sundown, he only left my side to work. It was like he thought Aaron would pop up at any second to finish what he'd started. No one ever did find out what happened to the deranged cowboy. His horse wandered back without him the day after he'd followed me, with no sign of him. Pete contacted the local authorities to report the incident, but since an actual attack never happened, it got backlogged to the filing cabinet of never-seeing-the-light-of-day-again.

In other words, I'd most likely never see Aaron again, and he definitely wasn't getting arrested.

As always, the days continued despite our growing frustrations. The guest ranch closed at the end of September which lightened our workload indoors, but the workload outdoors increased. By the time mid-October rolled around, I was finally, completely whole.

It felt good to be myself again, but like everyone else in the group, I was antsy. We'd been on the ranch for over two months, yet had no idea what brought us to this region in Colorado. Sooner or later, we knew we'd have to make a decision on where to go from here. Regardless of Di's unpredictable visions, each day it became more obvious that waiting for answers was leading to nothing.

IT WAS A crisp, beautiful autumn day when everyone met in the barn for the last roundup of the season. Bitter sweetness followed. Our employment was almost done. I wasn't sure how I felt about that. In a way, this ranch was the only home I'd ever known, but at the same time, our staying put while waiting for memories to return was doing nothing but stagnating us.

It was just after eight in the morning. A nip hung in the air that hadn't been there a few weeks ago. Everyone was going out for the round-up, even Val, which Pete said only happened once a year. Their daughters: Shelby, Fiona, Haley and their families had returned home for the occasion. Apparently, it was something the Henderson daughters never missed.

"You wanna ride Coal?" Dean asked as we haltered the horses in the back pasture. Tyler led two quarter horses back to the barn, a lead rope in each hand. Mica and Jessie did the same.

"Don't you want to?" I replied.

Dean grinned. "I know it's gonna be one of your last chances to ride 'im. Unless you stay that is."

The twinkle in his eyes made me smile despite his words. Dean had hinted on and off over the past few weeks of me staying through the winter despite Flint and I being a couple.

Flint's eyes met mine when Dean and I returned with Coal in tow. The large gelding breathed heavily through his nose, his breath carrying scents of sweet hay and grass.

"You're riding Coal?" Flint asked.

I snapped the gelding's halter into the cross ties and picked up a brush. "Yep. Dean offered."

"I'm sure he did," Flint replied.

I bit back a smile. Flint was tolerant of Dean and his persistent affections, although *tolerant* put it graciously.

Cool air flowed around us when everyone mounted. The entire Henderson family, Jacinda, Di and the twins were riding on four-wheelers, while Flint, the cowboys, Mica, Amber and I opted for horseback. Amber sat prettily on a young mare. Her horse was part thoroughbred and a beautiful black color. Together, they made a stunning pair.

We all waited for the go-ahead from Pete. Amber eyed Jasper and smiled suggestively. Mica fumed.

Amber and Jasper had formed a rather unusual relationship over the past month. The two hadn't declared they were together, yet the way they flirted, and the amount of public affection they displayed, hinted at something way beyond friendship. Amber however, didn't seem the least bit perturbed by Mica's jealousy. In fact, she seemed to revel in it.

"All right, listen up," Pete said. "We've got eighty-eight cattle to find today. With any luck, we'll have 'em all by sunset. Work together, follow your leader's instructions, and don't get lost." He said the last bit while gazing at Amber. "I'll radio Tyler when we're heading back to the barn. Let us know if you run into any trouble. We all clear?"

Everyone nodded or tipped their hats. Those on the four wheelers would take the lower parts of the ranch that weren't so hilly and full of trees. The rest of us on horseback were heading deep into the mountains.

"Tyler, did ya test your radio?" Pete asked.

Tyler was the one leading our group. "Yeah, I tested it this morning."

Pete nodded. "Keep in touch. Good luck."

Pete tipped his hat into place and climbed on his four-wheeler. The rest in his group did the same. When they drove off, Jacinda winked at me from under her hat before she raced to catch up with Haley. The two were quickly becoming friends, probably because Haley was the first person Jacinda had encountered who loved city life as much as she did.

"Ready?" Tyler asked the rest of us.

Everyone voiced agreement. Tyler reined his bay horse north and kicked him into a canter. We all squeezed our horses and followed, setting out on familiar ground.

When we reached the end of the corrals, the group slowed to a trot. It was the fastest way to cover ground without tiring the horses. The cold, crisp air swirled around. At certain angles, the wind bit into my cheeks enough to make tears sting my eyes. It was hard to believe just over a month ago, I'd worn a t-shirt.

"Think the weather will hold out?" I asked Flint. I had on thick gloves, a GoreTex jacket and fleece lined jeans.

"I think so," Flint said. "Forecast for the day is clear."

"That's a relief."

Dean rode up to my other side and smiled. "How's your ribs?"

"Good as new."

Dean smiled brighter. "I'm glad to hear it. It's good to see you on a horse again. I've missed our daily rides."

"Yeah, me too."

Dean seemed about to say something else but then glanced at Flint. "Well, err, see you." He nudged Giselda into a gallop and rode off.

I glanced at Flint. The scowl on his face vanished but not before I saw it. "Was that necessary?" I asked.

"What?" he said innocently.

"Scaring him off like that?"

Flint shrugged. "We compromised on this, remember? I'm okay with you two being *friends*, but it doesn't mean I have to like it."

I rolled my eyes. "I think Dean got that message when I was bed ridden and he tried to visit but wasn't allowed within five feet of me."

"Whatever are you talking about?" Flint grinned wickedly.

"You know what I'm talking about." I tried to sound stern, but a smile broke through anyway. While I was healing, Flint had stayed by my side every time Dean visited. He had also practically growled every time Dean came near me. The poor guy had felt so uncomfortable, he'd ended up sitting in a chair…by the door.

As the distance passed beneath us, Amber continually moved to the front of the pack. As usual, she wanted to be the center of attention. Tyler didn't seem overly perturbed, but Mica did. A scowl seemed permanently etched on Mica's face.

"Interesting crew," Flint murmured.

"I'll say," I replied.

During the next hour, we wove deeper and deeper into the mountains and moved in a progressive line northwest. By mid-morning, Pete radioed Tyler to say they'd found thirteen cattle and wondered about our progress. So far, we'd only found twenty-eight. We decided to branch out more.

"Dean, you and Jessie take the southwest ridge," Tyler instructed. "Flint and Mica – you come with me. We'll take the north cliff. Lena and Amber, do the midline section scanning from east to west."

Everyone murmured their agreement, but Amber plucked a hand on her hip. "I don't want to do the midline, that's boring. Can't I go with you?" She pouted prettily, but for once, Tyler didn't seem charmed.

He shook his head. "You don't know this terrain well enough to take the cliff. Stay down here."

She pouted further. "Why does Mica get to go but not me?"

"Because Mica's been riding on this land for a lot longer than you," he retorted.

At that response, Mica grinned. Amber's nostrils flared. "Fine!" She spurred her horse and took off down the valley.

I sighed. "I guess I'll do the babysitting today."

Jessie shook his head. "She should have gone on a four-wheeler. We don't have time for this."

"Sorry, Lena, will you be okay with her?" Tyler asked.

"Yeah, don't worry." I glanced at Mica. She was still grinning.

"Let's get a move on," Dean said uneasily. "I don't like the looks of those clouds on the horizon."

We all turned. A wall of gray hung to the west. I hadn't noticed it. It was like it came out of nowhere. "I thought no snow today," I murmured.

"There won't be," Tyler said confidently. "It's supposed to stay north, but just to be safe, I want everyone to move. We don't want to get caught in a storm."

Everyone split up. Tyler and Mica cantered away, but Flint nudged his horse closer to mine. We were momentarily alone in the clearing.

"Be careful," he said.

I pushed a long strand of hair out of my eyes. The wind was definitely picking up. "I will."

Flint sat still, staring at me. I knew he hated to leave my side, especially in the mountains. "Flint, I'll be fine," I added softly.

He continued to stare, but eventually took a deep breath. "Okay."

I knew it would take time for him to not feel so worried, especially since Aaron had disappeared without a trace. "You be careful too," I added. "It's more dangerous where you're going versus staying around here." I waved a hand at the sheltered valley.

He smiled and leaned away from his horse to kiss me softly on the mouth. "Love you, babe."

As always, those words left me breathless, not to mention, wanting more. I watched him go, a flurry of man and horse thundering across the landscape. When they disappeared from view, I turned to find Amber.

There was no sign of her.

I sighed. I was supposed to be finding cattle, not some spoiled teenager. I took a deep breath. "Typical," I muttered and nudged Coal forward.

I found her not long later. As much as Amber liked to think she was a competent cowgirl, she didn't actually know north from south. I could tell from her expression that she was already lost.

"Lena!" she called when she saw me. Wild worry glazed

her eyes. For a second, I felt sorry for her. According to Amber's driver license, she was the youngest in our group. I believed it. Even though she turned nineteen last May, she acted a lot younger. I knew I should cut her some slack. I reminded myself that half the time she probably didn't know any better than to act how she did. Hopefully, she'd grow out of it someday.

"Don't worry." I reined Coal beside her. "We just need to move west, and then turn back and go east when we reach the fence. Follow me."

She jutted her chin out. I ignored her. With another look at the gray clouds, I knew that Tyler was right. We didn't want to get caught in a storm. We needed to move.

It took us a while to reach the property line, but along the way we found eight more cattle. Slowly, we herded them back to the others and then moved east. The cattle we had found throughout the morning stayed in a circle and slowly, our herd grew, but we still needed to find several dozen more.

The progress was slow. I could tell that Amber wasn't enjoying herself, but when snow flurries began to fly, the least of my concerns was her enjoyment. We didn't have any way of talking to the others since only Tyler and Jessie had radios.

"Lena, let's go this way," Amber called. She turned and led her mare into the forest.

"We're supposed to go east!"

"I think I saw a cow over here!" she yelled over her shoulder.

I rolled my eyes and nudged Coal forward.

"Amber!" I called, but she kept moving and grew out of sight. Snow flurries drifted up and down in the wind, and if I wasn't so nervous, I would have enjoyed it. It was the first snowfall, and the flakes were large and coarsely scattered in the wind. Nothing accumulated on the ground, but I knew in the blink of an eye that could change.

I progressed farther into the woods but still didn't see

Amber. "Amber?" I yelled again.

"Lena, up here!" her voice called in the wind.

My brow furrowed. I wasn't sure which direction her voice had come from but nudged Coal forward anyway. "Do you know where she is, Coal?"

He moved a foot left, but then waited for me to tell him where to go. I didn't know what to do for a moment but then pushed him through the growing swamp of trees. It was weird. The air felt...different in here, like it moved. I shook that feeling off. That didn't make any sense.

We rode forward with no sign of Amber. What I did find were multiple *No Trespassing* signs. I was beginning to realize we'd wandered off Pete's land. I gritted my teeth and cursed Amber, but I kept going. It was either that or leave her out here to freeze to death, as tempting as that was.

Every now and then, a fresh hoof print would appear on the ground, letting me know I was still on the right track. My uneasiness, however, grew. The trees were so dense and that strange dizzying feeling remained. I didn't recognize anything.

"Amber? Where are you?" I yelled. When I didn't get a reply, I screamed again. "Amber!"

A few minutes later, I heard her response, but it was faint. "Lena! Over here!"

I glanced over my shoulder. No sign of her. But wasn't that where she'd yelled from?

Swallowing the dread in my throat, I halted Coal. All around, the forest grew denser. I didn't recognize any of my surroundings. It felt like I'd already been riding for over an hour with no sign of her. But it couldn't have been that long — could it?

"Amber!" I yelled again.

"Lena! Over here, quick, come see!"

I wished that I had Jacinda's hearing. Being able to see a person's cloud didn't help. "I can't see you Amber!"

"Down here, I'm down here!"

It sounded like she was moving farther and farther away. My uneasiness turned to fear. I had no idea where I was. It looked like behind me had been in front of me, but I knew that couldn't be correct because we hadn't turned. Right?

"Amber, where are you!" I screamed.

"Lena?" Amber's voice called. It was louder this time. I exhaled a breath of relief.

"Amber, *where are you?*"

"Look to your left."

I did. She stood no more than twenty feet away. Her horse was tied to a tree. *What the heck, how come I didn't see her?* My uneasiness vanished as anger took its place.

"Amber we don't have time for this! I thought you said you saw a cow–" My voice died.

A cabin, painted the color of the trees, stood dark and foreboding only ten yards away. If we hadn't been right beside it, I never would have seen it. It was camouflaged that well.

Amber excitedly ran to the side. "I found a way in over here!"

Annoyance flashed through me. "Amber, no! We don't have time for this. We need to find the rest of the cattle and get back to the barn. Haven't you noticed a storm's coming in?"

"Yeah, I know," she called. "But you've got to see this! You won't believe all the cool stuff in here!"

"That's breaking and entering."

"Come on, Lena! Just one quick look!"

"Amber," I groaned. I slid off Coal and tied him beside the mare. I'd pull Amber kicking and screaming from the cabin if I had to. We didn't have time for sightseeing or trespassing. I glanced toward the northern skyline, or at least where I thought the northern skyline was, and pictured Flint. Was he safe up there?

"Lena?" Amber's muffled voice called.

She peered through a window. Amber was already inside.

She waved but then disappeared from view.

I stalked to the back of the home. Trees surrounded the cabin on all sides. A few areas around the cabin had homemade chairs and tables. Another area had rocks at just the right height for sitting. Squinting, I thought I saw something else.

My eyes widened when I spotted a small barn about twenty yards away. It was barely visible through the growing snow. Like the cabin, it was perfectly camouflaged. Around it was a small fenced enclosure. *Why would someone want a barn all the way up here?*

Maybe whoever owned this place rode their horses to access it. Turning back to the cabin, I uttered a sound of disgust. Amber had left the door open. Cold air blew inside. I walked up the porch, my steps loud on the wood planks. I inspected the lock on the front door. Triple deadbolt. There was no way she'd have been able to break into this place. That only meant one thing. It'd been unlocked.

While that didn't surprise me, most folks in this area didn't bother locking their properties, it didn't add up. Why would someone leave their door unlocked yet have so many bolts in place?

I stepped inside. Once in the entryway, the wind died down and the words that were on the tip of my tongue vanished. I was speechless for a moment. The cabin was huge, much bigger than I'd thought. A large kitchen was off to the right. It was simple and rustic yet had actual appliances. Cabinets lined the walls and a table that could seat ten sat in the middle. The entire room was clean. I stepped closer and slid my finger along the counter. No dust.

Frowning, I walked to the sink. My eyes widened when I saw a bowl in it. Milk and a few bits of cereal floated in the dish. It wasn't rancid smelling and no mold was present. My heart stopped. That only meant one thing.

Someone, today or very recently, had been here. Probably

the person who lived here.

I raced from the sink and yelled for Amber. "Amber! Get down here, now! This place isn't abandoned!"

"Lena, come see!"

I stalked across the wood floors into a living area. The living room held three, large sofas with plump cushions. Several tables and chairs lined the windows. Each table had board games on them. On the far wall, by the massive fireplace, was an entire wall of shelves. Rows and rows of books covered them. I tried not to pry but couldn't help but notice the titles. There were classics and current fiction, but also non-fiction. On the bottom row, it was all textbooks. Math, science, history, art, astronomy, physics...the list was endless. It appeared to go on for the entire length.

As much as I knew we needed to leave, curiosity won. Pulling one out, I lifted the stiff cover. The edition date was within the last five years. I flipped through the pages. The margins were filled with hand written notes. Whoever this belonged to he, or she, had read the entire thing. I carefully put it back.

"Lena, would you get up here!" Amber called. I spun around to see her at the top of a ladder. The cabin was two stories. To the side of the living room, a ladder climbed up to a loft area. Amber waited at the top.

"There are bedrooms up here!" she cried.

"Amber, we really need to go." My annoyance flared again. "Somebody lives here! Don't you see that?"

Of course, she ignored me.

I stomped up the ladder. On the second floor, there was a short hallway. Several doors lay on either side. I walked to the first. It held a bedroom. It was small, only holding a single bed and desk. A lone window revealed snow flying outside.

"Amber?" I turned away. The second room held three beds, also single beds, like the first room, but this room was decorated. Hand drawn pictures of machines, solar systems, chemical structures and landscapes hung on the walls. They were intricately drawn. Whoever had done them had taken their time.

"Lena, I found something!" Amber called.

I fled from the room to the last door in the hallway. As I rushed in, I unconsciously realized it was the biggest room of the three. Two sets of bunk beds, and one single bed lined the walls along with two big dressers. There were also two desks and a large shelf of books.

Amber sat in the middle of the floor and paged through a notebook. There were pages and pages of animal drawings. Horses, birds, mountain lions, wolves, otters, bears, it was an endless collection.

"This entire notebook is full of them!" she said, smiling. Her cowboy hat sat to the side, and her legs were curled daintily underneath her. It seemed for all intentions she had settled in for the afternoon.

"Amber, we need to go," I said sharply. "There's a blizzard brewing outside, and this isn't our place. Somebody lives here and could be back any minute. Get up! We're leaving!"

"But look at this," Amber exclaimed and jumped up. She walked to the shelf and pulled out a book. At first, I thought it was an old folder of some kind, but when she opened it – it held a variety of fashion magazines.

"These are all from last year," Amber stated. "Whoever lived here, or lives here," she said when she saw my expression, "must keep up on current stuff."

"That's nice, but we have to go." I walked to the window. Snow flew everywhere. My stomach sank. How were we supposed to find our way out?

"We really need to go. This blizzard is getting worse. So, put everything back and–"

Amber was gone. The drawings lay scattered on the floor.

"Amber!" I hurried out of the room and searched the other two bedrooms. No sign of her. When I got to the ladder,

I could easily see that she wasn't in the living room. I almost tripped in my haste to get down. I yelled again.

No answer.

Cursing, I walked back into the kitchen and then back to the living room. There were other rooms. Doors lined the back of the living area. There had to be more rooms on the first floor. I raced to them and began opening the doors one by one.

The first was a closet. The second held a full bathroom. So this cabin had running water. Surprising. I closed the door and moved onto the next.

The third door held a stairwell.

My mouth dropped. Inky blackness greeted me. "Amber?" The sound echoed in the dark void.

I fumbled on the wall and found a light switch. Amazingly, it hummed to life when I switched it on. So this cabin had power too. The light revealed smooth concrete stairs and concrete walls. At the bottom was another hallway, but I couldn't see where it led. It was shadowed in inky darkness.

I glanced over my shoulder, but still didn't see Amber.

"I'm going to kill her," I whispered and took the first step.

CHAPTER TWENTY-FIVE

I slowly descended, my footsteps echoing in the stairwell. The air grew colder and colder. When I reached the bottom, another door stood to the left. It was solid and felt heavy when I turned the handle. It opened with a rush of stale air.

The second the door swung open, a light flicked on. I stared at the small room. My confusion grew. The walls were still concrete. A single, modern light illuminated the tiny room. Along each side were benches. Hanging above the benches were hooks on the wall. Several of the hooks held white suits.

Frowning, I stepped closer and felt one. I lifted a sleeve. Each had a hood with a plastic face shield.

"Biohazard suits?" I whispered incredulously. What the heck would someone have these for?

Under the benches were boots and in cubbies above were latex gloves and masks. At the end of the small room, there was another door no more than eight feet from me. Breathing shallowly, I stepped closer. The door had a window, but whatever lay on the other side was hidden in darkness.

My chest rose and fell painfully fast. I reached out, grasped the door handle and tried to turn it. It wouldn't budge. I then noticed the key pad off to the right. The door was password protected. "How odd," I murmured.

But my jarring the door triggered something. Lights flooded the barricaded room. My mouth dropped as I stepped closer to the glass and peered inside.

"What the hell…" I stared into the room, too stunned to move.

"Lena?"

"Amber!" I whirled away from the window and raced back up the stairs. Amber stood just outside the last door, the fourth one. The one I hadn't had a chance to open yet.

"Come see this." Her voice shook.

"Amber! What are you doing?" I raced into the room, my eyes wide with panic. Amber stood in what appeared to be an office. Papers were strewn everywhere. When my gaze rose to her face, my anger and confusion vanished. Tears shimmered in her luminous eyes.

She held up papers with shaking hands. "Look. These were lying here."

I took a tentative step closer. Amber gave me the papers and then balled her fists to her mouth. A soft wail escaped her. I leafed through the papers' contents, my eyes widening with every page, my chest rising and falling faster with each new sheet.

"No!" I whispered. "How can this be?"

Amber whimpered as tears rolled down her face. "What does it mean?"

I shook my head. Between this and the room downstairs, I didn't know what to think of this place. It certainly wasn't a vacation retreat.

"I don't know, but we need to get out of here!" I folded the papers and stuffed them in my pocket. "Come on." I reached down and clamped hold of her wrist.

I dragged Amber through the cabin and out the back door. A part of me half expected someone to appear, like we were being watched, or followed. An image of the cereal bowl flashed through my mind.

Once outside, I propelled Amber to the horses. I hurriedly brushed snow from our saddles, my movements jerky. Already, an inch of white powder sat on the ground.

The feeling of being watched grew. I didn't know if it was my imagination going crazy, or if it was a valid concern. For a second, a buried image of Aaron surfaced in my mind. I shuddered, forcing the memory down.

I mounted Coal and heard a soft wail. Amber stood by my side, crying. "Amber," I said sharply. "Get on your horse!"

She just cried harder.

I closed my eyes and took a deep breath. In a softer tone, I said, "Amber, honey, we need to go. Just untie your mare and we'll meet the others." I held my breath, not sure what she'd do, but then with stiff movements, she mounted her horse.

"Good," I said. "Now, follow me." I led us back into the woods, but after a few minutes realized I didn't know which way we'd come from. I swiveled around in my seat. Amber followed right behind, her eyes wide. I glanced to my left, right and then straight ahead. Snow fell all around. I wasn't sure where to go.

"Um," I mumbled.

"Are we lost?"

I shook my head. "No, we'll find our way back."

I nudged Coal forward. Flurries flew everywhere. The farther we got from the cabin, the safer I felt, which didn't make any sense, since it'd probably dropped another ten degrees. At least the cabin would provide shelter. We weren't dressed or prepared for winter weather.

Coal's huge hooves made deep imprints in the snow. He calmly waited for me to guide him. I floundered. I didn't know where we were, and I was all turned around. I had no idea which way was north, south, east or west. Frantically, I looked up, but the sky was no help. It was one vast gray ceiling.

"You don't know how to get out of here, do you?" Amber asked.

I answered honestly. "No, I don't. I don't know where we are."

Panic filled her face.

We both stood there, and for the first time since we left the group, I felt the gravity of our situation. We were deep in the mountains, at high altitude, with no protection other than our jackets. We had no way to find the ranch, and a blizzard was brewing.

"What should we do?" I asked.

She shook her head. Tears sprang into her eyes. "I don't know!"

"I guess we keep walking forward." Maybe we could find a stream. That's what Dean said to do if I got lost. I swallowed and turned around before nudging Coal again. We walked farther but I felt convinced we had moved deeper into the forest. Once again, I stopped.

"I'm sorry, Amber," I called loudly over the wind. "I don't know what to do."

"Neither do I!" she wailed. We both stared at each other. I reached out and grabbed her hand as snow flew around. As our fingers wrapped around each other's, Amber's gaze snapped wide open. "Wait! I do know what to do!"

"You do?"

"Or, at least I think I do," she replied. I had no idea what she was talking about, but instead of telling me her plan, she closed her eyes and lifted her head. She sniffed the air and then exhaled deeply before sniffing again. Her eyes flashed open. "This way."

She nudged her mare forward. I followed.

We meandered through the forest, the sky darkening while more and more snow fell. I had no idea how long we walked. It seemed not only direction, but time, became jumbled in this part of the forest, but each time I felt certain we were more lost, Amber lifted her nose and smelled the air.

"Are you sure you know where we're going?"

She didn't answer. Deep concentration lined her face. I continued to follow, not at all convinced we'd find our way out, but eventually, the trees thinned. Thirty yards after that, an opening appeared. Out of nowhere, I spotted a cow. As we got closer, the entire herd appeared. I'd never been so happy to see anything in my life.

"Amber, you did it!" I exclaimed.

Her eyes snapped open. A triumphant grin broke across her face. "It worked!"

"How'd you do it?"

She smiled. "I followed their scent." She nodded toward the cattle. "They have a strong stench."

I almost hugged her, but then realized I'd probably fall off Coal so settled for grinning happily.

"Lena!" Flint's voice called in the distance. A figure galloped toward us from across the snow ridden field. "There you are!" he called when he got closer.

The rest of the group huddled together at the edge of the herd, about a hundred yards away.

"Where have you been?" he demanded. He stopped his huffing mount inches from mine. His eyes were dark and wild. I wondered how long they'd been waiting.

"Searching for cows." I knew now was not the time to bring up the cabin, or the papers...or the basement. I gave Amber a hard look so she'd keep her mouth shut.

Flint glanced toward the forest we'd emerged from. "Did you come out of *there?*" His eyes grew even crazier. "Lena, do you know what that is?"

I shook my head. From Amber's frightened expression, I guessed she didn't either.

"Those are the Forbidden Hills! Are you crazy? What made you go in there?" Flint cried.

I eyed Amber. "I don't know, but we're fine. We made it

out."

Flint took his hat off and raked a hand through his hair. "Come on. We need to get down. The snow's coming in too fast."

Guilt followed me down the mountain. The panic in Flint's gaze, and the way he stayed close to my side for the entire ride back, told me he'd been more than worried. He still seemed panicked, even though I rode beside him. Of course, I didn't tell him that his worry was valid. If Amber hadn't been able to sniff our way out of the Forbidden Hills, we'd no doubt still be there, maybe forever. I shuddered.

The wind howled around us. The sky was darker than midnight. "Let's get the horses cleaned off. When you're done, go to the main house," Tyler instructed as the barn's lights came into view.

"So much for no snow," Dean said with a forced smile. I knew he'd been worried too. When he'd seen me and Amber ride up with Flint, a look of huge relief had crossed his face.

I slid off Coal. The papers in my pocket crinkled. I stuffed them deeper into my jeans. "We better get these horses unsaddled."

Everyone groomed and blanketed their horses before putting them into stalls. One of the cowboys mixed together hot bran mash which each horse readily inhaled.

My feet sank into the snow with each step back to the house. Flint kept his hand firmly locked around mine the entire way. At the main house, Val had hot cocoa, coffee, tea and cinnamon rolls waiting. From the other smells coming from the kitchen, I guessed there'd be a huge feast for supper.

"You all took your time," Jacinda commented when I walked into the large living room. She sipped a cup of tea while lounging on one of the huge sofas. Di sat across from her, reading a book. Haley sat on the end chair, reading an issue of *Vogue*.

"How'd it go?" Di asked.

247

"We got all of them," I said, referring to the cattle. I hung my wet jacket beside the roaring fire. The heat coming off it felt so good. I held up my cool fingertips.

"Where are the guys?" Jacinda asked.

"In the mudroom."

The guys and Mica were still discussing the cattle with Pete, and Amber was in the kitchen chatting nervously to Val and her other daughters.

I eyed Haley. When she caught me watching her, she smiled. I forced a smile back before I caught Di and Jacinda's attention. I nodded stiffly to the door. *I need to talk to you,* I mouthed.

Di frowned and stood. So did Jacinda. They followed me into the hall. No one was around.

"We need to have a meeting, *now,*" I said in hushed tones.

"Why?" Di asked.

"We just do. Can you gather everyone?"

"Yes." She spun on her heel and disappeared.

Jacinda and I hurried back to our cabin, the wind biting into us. Everyone else followed. When Jet entered our tiny living room, he closed the door behind him.

"This better be good," he said, dusting snow from his jacket. "Pete just pulled out the whiskey."

I gave an exasperated sigh. "It is."

"Well?" Di crossed her arms and tapped her foot. Her eyes practically gleamed.

I pulled the papers from my pocket. "Look."

Holding them out, I let everyone see what was on them. Drawn in intricate detail were all of the symbols tattooed on our wrists.

The symbols of the solar system.

DI SNATCHED THE papers from my hands. "Where did you get these?"

I eyed Amber. "Do you want to explain or should I?"

"I will." Amber held her head higher. "Let's all sit."

Everyone pulled the chairs and couches into our familiar circle and then Amber launched into a tale. She told the story of how we'd been searching for cattle. About how we'd broken away from the group and then wandered into the Forbidden Hills because she had a *feeling* something was in there. I rolled my eyes at her exaggerations while Jet and Jasper's mouths actually dropped. Amber remained oblivious. I wondered if she knew about the reputation those hills had. Probably not.

When she got to the part about the cabin, everyone grew silent.

"So you found these papers in that cabin?" Di finally said. She held them in her hands and studied them closer. An aggrieved expression settled on her face. "I don't understand. What does it *mean?* That whoever owns that cabin knows about us?"

"Maybe," I replied.

She passed the papers around so everyone could see them better. Each sheet held a hand drawn picture of a planet from our solar system. Someone had painstakingly etched each one in pencil, along with a detailed description about what the planet consisted of. It was all done in tiny, precise writing. The amount of information was staggering. The planet's description was written in a neat column beside the picture. It included the planet's size, mass, atmosphere, what its core was made of, its distance from the sun, its revolution and rotation time, and other tidbits that were unique to each celestial body.

But it wasn't the writing or pictures that caused everyone's eyes to widen. It was the symbols drawn in the middle of each planet. The symbols tattooed on our inner wrists. Jacinda's face whitened when she saw her tattoo in the middle of Uranus.

"So these are planetary symbols?" she finally said.

Flint nodded. "Di and I knew that. This isn't new information, but the fact that whoever lives in that cabin had these drawings is suspicious. Definitely suspicious."

Jacinda clasped her hands tightly together.

Di's brow furrowed and a sound of frustration emitted from her throat. "I didn't *see* any of this coming. Why is that?"

"You can't see everything," Mica shrugged.

Di still didn't look happy. She leafed through all of the papers again. "My symbol is Venus."

"And I'm Mars," said Flint.

"Earth," I chipped in.

"Mica's Neptune, Amber's Mercury, and Jacinda's Uranus," Di said.

"And we're Jupiter and Saturn," Jasper commented, nudging his brother.

"So what does this mean?" Di set the papers in her lap.

"That we're aliens from these planets?" Jet said.

I almost slugged him in the shoulder. "Serious answers only please."

"But we could be." Jet's eyes gleamed. "I mean think about it. We could have—"

"No." Di held up her hand. "Just read the descriptions on these planets. No humans can inhabit these places. And we're all *human.*"

"But do we actually know that?" Jet said.

Di sighed. "Yes."

"What this could mean, is that the cabin you found is part of our pasts," Flint said. "Either that or the owner has an obsessive interest in astronomy."

I thought about Flint's and my backyard astronomy hobby. I then thought about the bedrooms with the three beds in one and five in the other, and the animal drawings and fashion magazines.

"I'd bet money that cabin is part of our pasts," I said, frowning. I thought about the room in the basement. I still hadn't told anyone about it. I wasn't sure I liked that room being a part of *anyone's* past.

"There's more," I said.

Di stood and put her hands on her hips. "There is?"

"There was this room, in the basement." I paused. "It was…unusual."

Amber eyed me, her gaze questioning.

"What kind of room?" Di asked.

"I'm not sure exactly. It looked like a laboratory."

"Seriously?" Jet said.

"Seriously," I replied.

"We should go back," Mica said. "And check it out."

"Yes, we should go back," Di agreed, "but will we be able to find it? The Forbidden Hills are notorious for people getting disoriented in – right?"

Amber's eyes lit up. "I can find it. The cabin had a unique smell. I think I can track it." The twins grinned. Mica actually cheered.

"Wait," I said as everyone's excitement grew. "Someone lives there."

"What?" Di spun toward me. "Someone *lives* there?"

I described the cereal bowl. "Someone has been there recently. At least in the last day or two."

Di pursed her lips and paced a few times. "Why would someone live there?" She tapped a finger to her mouth. "I didn't think anybody lived in the Forbidden Hills."

"Well, if you're our alien master you might," Jet said.

"Here we go again," Mica muttered.

"Do you think whoever was there knows us?" Amber asked.

"It's possible," Di said.

"So when do we go back?" Jasper asked.

Di paced again. She stopped and put her hands on her hips. "Right after supper. Since Pete and Val are expecting us back, we need to have dinner with them. If we don't, they'll look for us. We don't want to risk anyone following us."

"Let's head back to the main house now," Flint said. "We'll tell everyone goodnight after we eat, say that we're tired and turning in. With the blizzard, nobody's going to be out. They won't know we're gone."

Di nodded tightly. "Let's go."

Everyone stood to leave. In a hurry, Di bumped into Jasper. The bump made her lose hold of the papers. They fluttered to the floor. "Damn," she murmured.

She reached down to collect them. They lay scattered in a half circle. I stared at the symbols. My eyes widened. I scanned them again and stopped her from picking them up.

"Wait! Just hold on a minute." My eyes darted back and forth across the symbols. A second ticked by. Then another. I raced into my bedroom.

The room was a mess. Between Mica, Amber and I, clothes were everywhere. "Dammit," I muttered. I reached down and fumbled through everything. My backpack had to be in here somewhere.

Flint appeared at my side. "What are you looking for?"

"My backpack."

I didn't need to say anything else. He whipped into action. A blurred second later, my backpack was in my hands.

"Thank you."

He just nodded. "What did you think of?"

I unzipped the bag and pulled out my map. I fingered the rough paper. I'd never actually used it. In fact, I'd never even opened it, since, in the end, the instinct had led me entirely on its own. I'd bought it nonetheless before leaving Rapid City, just in case.

"Follow me," I replied.

We joined everyone back in the living room. I unfolded the map on the floor and stared at it. "Has anyone thought about where we woke up?" I asked excitedly. "About the cities we woke up in?"

Di rolled her eyes. "Of course. Flint and I have looked at them from every angle. What states they were in, the names of the cities, how they were spelled, if they had similar histories, population sizes, demographics. Everything. But we couldn't find a connection."

"Yeah, but did anyone look at them on a *map?*" I asked.

Di glanced at Flint. He hunkered down at my side.

"No," Di said grimly.

I flattened the map more. "Maybe there's some kind of connection with where we woke up and these symbols."

Di kneeled at my side. Lines of highways, interstates and outlines of the forty-eight states lay before us. "Does anyone have a pen or something I can write with?" I asked.

Flint rushed from the room and returned two seconds later with a ballpoint. I grasped the pen and scanned the map, circling the cities as I went. "Okay, Rapid City, South Dakota; Yellowstone National Park; Salt Lake City, Utah; Las Vegas, Nevada; Phoenix, Arizona; El Paso, Texas; Lubbock, Texas; Wichita, Kansas."

I studied the dots. Reaching down, I drew an imperfect circle, connecting all eight cities. I grinned.

Jacinda leaned forward. She studied it for a few seconds. Her eyes widened. "It all goes in order."

Di frowned, assessing the cities again.

Jacinda's eyes glowed excitedly. "Lena woke up in Rapid City. You woke up in Wichita, Di. Amber woke in Lubbock, Mica in El Paso, me in Phoenix, Jet in Las Vegas, Jasper in Salt Lake and Flint in Yellowstone!" Her voice grew more animated with each second.

"You see it too!" I cried.

Di's eyes widened. "Our tattoos! Mercury, Venus, Earth, Mars, Jupiter, Saturn, Uranus and Neptune."

"They go in order with our cities and tattoos," Flint stated.

"Yes! My tattoo – the symbol for Earth is Rapid City. That's just northeast of Yellowstone, where you woke up, Flint, and just northwest of Wichita, the city you woke in, Di. Venus, Earth, Mars – our three cities sit on the circle in correlation with our tattoos. Just the order they correlate with in our solar system."

"Yes!" Di studied the map. "It's too uncanny to be a coincidence."

"They do almost fall in a perfect circle with each other." Jasper eyed the map.

"Yeah, it's pretty close," Jet agreed.

"It's too much of a coincidence," Di stated. "These have to be clues."

"And at the center of it all, is *exactly* where we are." I pointed at the center of the circle. It was near Little Raven.

"Which is probably why we were drawn here," Flint murmured.

"But we haven't found anything," Jacinda said. "If we are where we're supposed to be, how come we don't know anything?"

"Because we're not *exactly* where we're supposed to be, just close to it," I replied.

"Are you thinking what I'm thinking?" Flint's energy grew. A steady push pulsed into me.

I nodded. "It's not just Little Raven and this ranch that are near the center of the circle. That cabin is too."

CHAPTER TWENTY-SIX

We hurried through supper. I'm sure everyone noticed our strained conversations and inhaled eating. Luckily, since the Henderson daughters and their families were here, Pete and Val had others to capture their attention. The cowboys, however, all eyed us curiously. Especially Dean. I avoided his questioning glances as the eight of us threw our coats back on and trudged out the door.

Once back in our living room, Di wasted no time issuing orders. "Everyone get their warmest clothes on. We'll also need flashlights and a crowbar. If whoever lives there isn't back, I'm breaking into that lab."

We all flew into action.

I eyed Amber as she and I finished getting dressed in our room. A sliver of fear snaked through me.

"Are you sure you can find it?" I asked. We walked out of the room to join everyone else. For a moment, Amber's brow furrowed, and she bit her lip.

"Do you know what will happen if you *don't* find it and we get lost in the Forbidden Hills?" I hissed.

Jacinda flashed us a worried look but pretended she hadn't

heard my questions.

Amber jutted her chin out, a determined expression growing on her face. "I'll find it."

IT WAS A cold, dark ride back into the hills. Bitingly frigid wind stung my face. Nothing but white flew around. The snow was already six inches deep which made for slippery footing. The horses didn't seem fazed, but I gripped my legs tightly around Coal as we climbed the hills behind the barn.

When we finally reached the Forbidden Hills, a dark mass of nothingness stood in front of us. My toes were mostly numb, and I was pretty sure my cheeks were red from the cold. I could practically feel Amber's nervousness, but once again, she closed her eyes and slowly nudged her mare ahead.

We followed her deeper and deeper into the trees. Moving in a single file line, we kept each horse nose to butt so we wouldn't lose track of anyone. Every now and then, we did a count. Everyone had to state their name and where they were in the group so no one got lost.

As I ducked my head at the last minute to avoid a tree branch, I figured that the chances of us losing each other were slim despite the dark night. With all of us together, our gifts made us quite formidable.

After another solid hour of riding, maybe more, maybe less – it was hard to tell in this forest, the cabin appeared. It was like before. It was so well blended into the landscape and designed in such a way as to not draw attention that I would have walked right past it if Amber hadn't stopped us.

Dim moonlight filtered through the clouds. We all stopped and circled around. Everyone stared at the vacant windows. Mica jumped to the ground and ran to the porch. I, however, didn't feel nearly as excited. The room in the basement flashed through my mind.

In the night, with snow flying, there was just enough light to see the old, wooden siding which was painted to mimic leaves and trees. It was eerie and ominous looking, like someone had a secret hidden deep within this place. A secret someone didn't want anyone to find.

I briefly wondered if whoever lived here had built this cabin or simply fixed it up. Perhaps this house had been around for a hundred years, but then I remembered the concrete foundation. It couldn't be that old.

"So, this is it," Di said. Her voice was quiet, yet eager, and snapped me out of my reverie.

We corralled the horses in the small barn. From there, Amber led us to the cabin door. Inside, Flint whipped around the house at lightning speed until every light was switched on.

"I take it no one's here?" Di asked when he returned.

He shook his head. "It's empty."

I returned to the kitchen. The cereal bowl was still there. Someone *had* been here. The evidence lay right in front of me. I joined the others as they all stared. It was like they were afraid to move anything, as if it would evaporate with the slightest touch.

"Does anyone remember *anything* about this place?" Di asked.

Everyone shook their heads.

"Show me the basement," Di said.

I took a deep breath. The group followed me downstairs. Coldness grew as we descended. Everyone gazed in puzzlement at the strange suits at the bottom.

"Why would these be needed?" Mica picked up a sleeve.

I shrugged. "Maybe things can't get contaminated in there." I nodded toward the other room.

Di walked to the door with the window, but it still wouldn't budge when she tried the handle.

"It's password protected." I pointed to the keypad.

She tapped her fingers against it and frowned. Like it had earlier, light flooded the room on the other side. I guessed it had movement sensors. Di stared inside when the room was completely lit.

"Unbelievable," she murmured.

Everyone else moved to take a turn at the window. One by one, we all stared wide-eyed.

On the other side of the door, was a huge modern lab. It was one large room with rows and rows of counter space. On the counters were beakers, petri dishes, shelving and endless amounts of machinery. Several cabinets looked like refrigerators or freezers and held jars and dishes of different liquids and solids. They were a variety of colors. I once again stared in amazement. I didn't know what any of it was.

Di whirled around. "There's no way we can get in there?"

"Not unless you break the window," Flint said.

"Good luck," I murmured. I didn't know why, but I had a feeling it was bullet proof.

"Come on." Flint put his arm around his sister's shoulders. "Let's look at the rest of the house." She grudgingly let him pull her away.

We spent the next several hours filtering through everything. For a split second, I felt guilty about that, but my need to find answers took precedence. If this place could answer what happened to us, I'd turn it inside out if need be.

Flint stayed with me while we dug through drawers and scrolled through bookshelves. Jacinda and Mica spent most of their time in the biggest bedroom with all of the bunks, while Amber, Jet and Jasper stayed in the other bedrooms and living room.

Di, on the other hand, became obsessed with the lab. She returned to the door and spent the entire time trying different numerical passwords. Of course, none of them worked. The crowbar didn't help either. The door wouldn't budge.

"It doesn't make any sense," I complained to Flint. We stood in the living room, going through books. I pulled out a text on the history of ancient Europe. The cover showed a picture of a decaying castle. I studied it before putting it back on the shelf. "If this place *does* hold something in our pasts, why don't we remember it? Surely something would trigger a memory in one of us?"

A lock of chestnut hair fell across his forehead. He was kneeling at the bottom shelf and put away a memoir from a Civil War veteran. "Yeah, you'd think one of us would remember something."

By the early hours in the morning, we all came to the conclusion that there was nothing left for us to find. While there were endless books to read, drawings to admire, games to play and lab doors to bang our heads against, the general consensus was that there was nothing else that alluded to our identities.

"At least, we know about the symbols and the connection to our cities," Mica said as we stepped onto the porch. Cold wind greeted us. We walked to the horses who sat huddled together.

Luckily, Amber didn't have any problems navigating us back to the clearing, although we all agreed that our senses were completely upside down and inside out in the Forbidden Hills. I could see why they were called that. It was like time stood still and space took on its own dimension. If I hadn't been surrounded by everyone, I probably would have freaked.

By the time we reached the barn, tended to the horses and made it back to the cabin, a good eight inches of snow sat on the ground. I was mostly frozen. The clocked chimed five in the morning, and the space heaters were turned on full blast when we all collapsed, exhausted onto the couches.

"There's got to be another clue!" Di's dark eyes were almost wild. The cool, composed Di I'd always known had vanished. "We're just not seeing it!"

Jet shook his head and rested back in his chair. "Di, there was nothing else at that cabin. No names on any books, no initials on any drawings, no papers stating the deed of ownership…there was nothing. What do you expect us to come up with?"

"Yeah," Jasper agreed. Amber sleepily nodded from the crook of his shoulder.

"We should go to bed. Everyone's too tired to think of anything," Jacinda yawned, but Di held firm. She insisted we stay up until something revealed itself.

Consequently, all of our eyes were bloodshot and gritty by the time the sun rose. It was only when I dozed off in Flint's lap that he gently nudged me awake. Without a word, he carried me to bed. Flint's obvious disregard for Di's manic request was enough for everyone to follow suit.

"Come back!" she yelled. "We just need to think harder!" The sounds of doors opening and closing as the others wandered off to bed was the only response she got.

"You okay?" Flint whispered when he lifted me to my bunk.

"Yeah, I'm fine," I mumbled sleepily. "You?"

"Yeah. Sorry about Di. She can be rather hard headed when something gets in her mind."

I smiled. "Sounds like her brother."

He chuckled and kissed me softly on the lips. When I pulled him in for a deeper kiss, he growled. Amber had fallen asleep with Jasper on the couch. Mica was currently in the bathroom. In other words, we were alone.

"I assumed you were too tired for that," he said.

"I'm never too tired for that. Besides, it's been too long." Since my accident, we'd managed to get away from the group a few times, but each time was hurried and quick since one of us had to work or someone was expecting us somewhere. Every time, we kissed and touched, and while clothes came off we'd never had sex. Birth control was not something we had. Hence, mounting frustrations.

"In that case…" he murmured.

A whoosh of air and he was on top of me. I pulled him eagerly into another kiss as he pushed my shirt up. Cool air washed over my abdomen. My nipples hardened which caused a murmur of appreciation from him. Since we had no idea when Mica would be back, it was another hurried moment where we explored one another as fast as we could while making sure to keep most of our clothes on in case someone burst through the door. I could feel Flint's desire. Once again, raw, hot energy poured off him. His need consumed me, making me long for him even more as the familiar ache grew between my thighs.

When voices sounded outside the room, Flint pulled back. I huffed in annoyance and smoothed my shirt back in place.

"Are they coming in?" I asked quietly.

"Not sure."

It sounded like the twins but eventually the voices passed. They'd obviously moved on.

Flint sighed harshly. "I need to get you alone, in a hotel, for a week, before I'm going to feel like I've had enough of you."

He climbed off the bunk. Bringing up his forearms, he rested them on the frame. I admired their deep, tawny color and the way his muscles rippled beneath them.

"Only a week?" I teased, tracing a finger along his skin.

"Minimum of a week, and that's just to work out the initial frustration."

"That sounds better," I mumbled sleepily, my eyes closing. "Count me in."

He was kissing me softly when Mica entered. Wet hair dripped down her back as she clutched a towel around her. An annoyed grumble was her greeting before she stalked to her dresser. Flint took the hint.

"Goodnight," he whispered and disappeared out the door.

PETE WOKE US around lunchtime. He didn't comment that it was past twelve and all of us were either in bed or sprawled on the furniture. Well, except for Di.

I stumbled out to the living room when I heard the commotion. Bright sunlight streamed into the room. Pete stood by the door, his hat in his hands. A light dusting of snow covered the floor around him. Di stood by the window, staring out into a sea of white. I wasn't sure if she had let Pete in or not. She seemed almost catatonic.

Amber yawned and rubbed her eyes. Jasper sat beside her on the couch, doing the same. Jacinda was the only one presentable. In a long silk nightgown with her hair perfectly styled, she stood at the small kitchenette making coffee. I could only imagine what I looked like. The stray snarls of hair curling around my face resembled a poorly constructed beehive.

Fresh scents of coffee soon filled the air. Pete cleared his throat. "Well, the reason I came down was to make sure all of ya were all right. And also to let ya know the girls are takin' off today." Pete addressed Jacinda. "Haley's gotta get back to work and Shelby and Fiona need to get their boys back to school. Haley was hopin' to see ya before she left."

Jacinda smiled. "Of course. I'll get dressed and be right up."

Pete turned and tucked his cap back on his head. Warm air flowed through the door when he opened it. It had to be at least fifty degrees. It seemed the freak blizzard weather had ended.

I watched through the window as he trudged up the drive. At least a foot of snow sat on the ground. The entire outdoors blazed brightly, like a white frosted quilt had settled over the landscape. It was so bright it actually hurt my eyes.

Squinting, I turned to the bathroom only to see the door close. Jacinda had beat me to it. In other words, I wouldn't be getting in there for at least an hour.

"Did you sleep last night?" I asked Di.

She still stood at the window, not moving. I had to ask her again before she turned.

"Oh, yeah, a little," she replied quietly.

With crossed arms, she continued gazing out the window. A slamming door from somewhere outside sounded. A moment later, Flint and Jet appeared through the window, walking in the snow toward our cabin. Flint hadn't bothered with a jacket. Clad in only a t-shirt and jeans, he trudged through the snow. Tawny forearms and broad shoulders made my pulse quicken. I made myself take a deep breath.

They entered without knocking. Another warm breeze trailed inside.

"Morning," Flint said to everyone.

Jet pointed at the clock. "I believe the technical term is *afternoon*."

Flint ignored him and glanced at Di. With a furrowed brow, Flint approached me. "Hi." He leaned down and kissed me softly on the mouth.

My hands clenched his t-shirt as he pulled away.

"Sleep okay?" he asked.

"Yeah, but coffee still sounds good."

In lightning fast moves, he poured cups for everyone. It was a miracle it didn't spill, although the liquid did slosh a few times.

"Di?" Flint nodded toward the bedroom she shared with Jacinda. "Can I speak with you?"

She followed him mutely. I sipped my coffee, watching them disappear behind the closed door. I had a fairly good idea what they were talking about.

The cabin.

WE JOINED THE Henderson family and cowboys for a late lunch. Tears were shed and lots of hugs went all around when Pete and Val's daughters left with their families. When the last vehicle drove down the driveway, we all waved.

"When will they be back?" Jacinda asked. Her long hair flowed around her shoulders in the warm breeze.

"For Thanksgiving and Christmas," Pete replied. "We're

fortunate to have all our girls close. The McCormacks, they own the ranch west of here, only see their kids once a year if they're lucky. Their kids have all gone and moved outta state."

Flint put his arm around me. I settled against him as thoughts of our families and beginnings once again sneaked to the front of my mind. The cabin in the Forbidden Hills held something in our pasts. I was sure of it. Now, it was just a matter of finding out what.

"I've got coffee and tea brewing," Val said. "Let's all move back inside." She bustled everyone to the front door.

As soon as the door closed behind us, Flint nodded in the direction Pete had gone. Before I could ask what was going on, he and Di left the entryway. The rest of us were still kicking snow off our boots.

"When's our last day here?" Mica asked. She hung her jacket on the coat rack.

"Tomorrow." I slipped out of my boots and did my best to avoid the wet puddles on the floor.

"Already?" she replied incredulously.

"Yep." With the last roundup done, our seasonal employment had come to an end. Pete had hinted a few times about keeping two or three of us through the winter. Dean's eyes had alighted on me each time that subject came up. So far, none of us had responded to those hints. We couldn't be split up. Now, however, with our finding the cabin so close to Pete's land, I wasn't sure what we'd do. Maybe it'd make more sense for some of us to stay working so we'd have a way to venture there more often.

"Mmm," Mica said. "You smell that? Val's cooking something."

She trailed off to the kitchen. Jacinda, Amber, the twins and I followed.

An hour later, we were all sitting around the kitchen table playing cards when Di and Flint finally reappeared with Pete. The cowboys had joined in our game. I was losing badly.

Apparently, I didn't know a thing about poker.

Tyler added a five dollar bill to the pot. Jasper sighed and folded.

I glanced away from the game. Pete held out his hand to shake Di's hand and then Flint's. "We'll sure miss all of you. You've been a great help. I'm not sure what Val and I would have done without ya."

"We appreciated the opportunity," Di replied. "It made for an interesting break in our travels."

I frowned as those words sank in. *We're leaving?*

Dean tensed beside me, his ears perked toward the conversation. I knew Flint had noticed how closely Dean sat beside me. Flint's energy slowly pushed toward the table.

"We'll pack tonight and head out tomorrow morning." Flint crossed his arms. My eyes glued to his strong forearms.

Val wiped her hands on her apron. "It's a pity to see you all go. We've really loved having you."

Mica, Jacinda, Amber, the twins and I all glanced at one another. If we were leaving tonight, how would we make trips to the cabin?

"SO WHAT'S THE plan, Captain?" Jet asked as we walked through drifts of melting snow.

"We pack when we get back and clear out in the morning," Di replied.

"And go where?" Mica asked.

Di strode purposefully forward. "The cabin. Someone was there and that place holds answers. Therefore, that's where we'll be staying until whoever owns it shows up again."

"But how are we going to get there?" Jasper asked. "It takes hours on horseback and come tomorrow morning, we won't have any horses to borrow."

Di glanced at Flint. "We'll hike there."

"*Hike* there?" Jacinda almost stumbled but caught herself just in time. "As in *walk?* On foot?"

"That's generally what hiking means." Jet clapped her on the back.

"What about all of our stuff?" Amber asked. We reached the cabins and everyone stomped snow on the porch steps before piling into the living room.

"We don't have that much stuff," Di said. "What we do have, we'll take with us."

"So we're hiking *and* carrying our bags." Jacinda fluffed her hair after taking off her jacket. "I certainly hope we don't do this more than once."

"Like Di said, we'll stay at the cabin until whoever lives there shows up again," Flint replied. His hair stood out on all ends when he took his hat off. It looked funny and sexy at the same time.

"My suitcase won't be easy to carry," Jacinda huffed.

"I'll carry it," Flint replied. "And whatever else everyone isn't able to carry themselves."

"Ah, to have the superman gene," Jet sighed. He sat down on the couch, his broad shoulders widening as he settled his arms over the couch back. "And all I got was *The Voice*."

Jasper brought his hand to his chest. "I'm touched at your regard for our special gift, brother."

Jet snorted a laugh.

"Let's pack," Di said, putting her hands on her hips. "I told Pete we'd also clean these cabins from top to bottom."

"In other words, we have a lot of work to do," Jacinda sighed.

WE SAID OUR goodbyes the next morning. Tears stung my eyes when I hugged Pete and Val. I had no idea our departure would affect me like it did, but in a way, saying goodbye to Hideaway Hills was like saying goodbye to the only identity I'd ever known. Even though I still knew nothing past six months ago, here on this ranch, I'd become someone.

Dean knew me as the girl who enjoyed horseback rides

through the hills. Val as the worker who was always happy to help. Pete as the girl who eagerly greeted the guests and joined in the group activities.

Prior to coming here, I'd been a lost, homeless girl on the streets, desperately searching for answers that I had no way of finding. But now, I had an identity, at least a new one, and I clung to that the way a drowning person clings to a raft.

"We'll sure miss you." Val wiped tears from her cheeks and hugged me fiercely.

I hugged her back and blinked rapidly. "I'll miss you too."

The sun warmed my back as we stood on the porch. Humming from the Suburban, as it idled in the driveway, intermingled with the rustling from our jackets as we hugged everyone goodbye. The cowboys shuffled their feet, hands in their pockets. When I approached Dean, a fleeting look of sadness passed across his face before he covered it with a grin.

"So you're leaving us after all," he said.

I felt Flint watching us, but I reached out and hugged Dean tightly. Despite Flint's jealousy, the cowboy had been a true friend to me. I wouldn't forget that. Dean's arms wrapped around me as he pulled me into his warm embrace.

"Take care and tell Coal I'll miss him," I said in muffled words into his shoulder.

Dean's arms tightened. Scents of hay, horse and sweat surrounded me. "I will." He paused yet he didn't seem in a hurry to let me go. "I'm gonna miss ya, Lena." His voice was gruff.

"I'll miss you too."

When I pulled back, I glanced self-consciously at Flint. He stood at the edge of the porch, watching us. An unreadable expression covered his face. I could feel his possessiveness in the energy that rolled off him, but he didn't make a move to stop me and Dean. Love swelled in my chest. I knew Flint hated the closeness Dean and I shared, yet he'd never asked me to stop talking to Dean or stop seeing him. He put up with it because he knew I cared for the cowboy.

"You take care, ya hear?" Dean said. He cleared his throat and stuffed his hands in his pockets.

"I will. You too."

By the time we all piled in the Suburban and waved our last goodbyes, it was mid-morning. Everyone was quiet as Di drove down the driveway.

Our one security disappeared behind us like a dream upon waking. We drove ahead, not stopping, not looking back. I could only hope the hidden cabin in the Forbidden Hills held the answers we so desperately craved.

CHAPTER TWENTY-SEVEN

We drove from the ranch to a remote area in the National Forest and parked off an old logging road. From what Di and Flint had been able to piece together on the map, it was the closest area to the hidden cabin in the Forbidden Hills. At least, where we thought the cabin was.

That didn't mean it was close. Flint guessed it was at least a twenty mile trek through the mountains, and from the topography on the map, the going wouldn't be easy. I just hoped we'd find it.

When we stepped out of the Suburban, fresh pine scents and singing birds surrounded us. Melting snow dripped from the trees, the occasional drips sounding on the forest floor.

"Forecast is for warm weather all week," Jasper said. "With any luck, this snow will be gone in a few days."

"And then we'll have mud to hike in." Jacinda sighed. "How lovely."

Mica double knotted her boots and slung her pack over her shoulders. Between the eight of us, we carried enough food for a week.

"Let's get a move on," Di said. "With any luck, we'll get

there by sundown."

THE HIKE THROUGH the forest was pleasant for the first couple hours. I wasn't used to carrying a heavy pack, but I didn't mind it as I got caught up in the sounds and feel of the forest. Slushy snow crunched underfoot while our quiet breathing puffed around us amidst the singing birds and scampering chipmunks.

It was mid-afternoon when we entered the Forbidden Hills. I knew when it happened. That funny feeling again took hold, like time stood still and everything felt upside down. I now understood why scientists traveled from around the world to study this area. In a way, it felt like we stepped into another dimension.

"I wish I had a camera," Mica said at one point in the afternoon. Flint walked ahead of her. Between the backpacks he carried on his back and chest, and the two huge suitcases he carried in each hand, it did look rather impressive.

"You really don't get tired?" she asked him. He'd been walking like that all day, not once complaining.

Flint shrugged. The movement should have been awkward, considering what he carried, but he managed to make it look graceful and easy. "Not really."

"Are we there yet?" Jacinda huffed. She stopped and braced a hand against a tree. Her chest rose with each breath. We'd been hiking for over two hours since we stopped for lunch yet I had a feeling we'd be lucky if we were halfway there.

Jet clapped her on the back. "Nope. Not even close."

She glared at him which only got a laugh out of the twin.

If it weren't for Flint and Amber, I'm not sure if we'd have made it to the cabin. Amber tracked the cabin's scent, keeping us from getting lost in the crazy hills. While Flint carried the heavy bags as if they weighed nothing at all.

By the time Amber found the hidden home, the sun had

mostly fallen, and I was more than ready for the hike to be over. My legs ached in a way that reminded me of my homeless days when I'd walked for miles and miles if I wasn't able to get a ride. A sharp twinge plagued my side, and my shoulders felt stiff.

I grinned in relief when the trees thinned and the camouflaged cabin appeared. Amber stopped sniffing.

"Finally," she said.

Jasper hugged her. "I knew you'd find it."

Jacinda, however, collapsed against a rock and let out a loud sigh. "I…never…want…to do…that again," she said in between breaths.

I bit back a smile but couldn't stop my muffled laugh. Jet laughed too and then Jasper joined in. Before long, we were all laughing as packs fell from our shoulders and shoes flew off. Nobody seemed to care when muddy, slushy snow squished between our toes. In a way, it felt good and refreshing. It soothed my swollen feet.

"No lights are on," Di commented after our laughter finally died down.

"Looks just like it did when we left it," Jasper replied.

"Let's get inside." Di shrugged off her pack. "I don't know about the rest of you, but I'm starving."

THE CABIN INDEED looked the same since we'd left. The cereal bowl still sat in the sink, only now the milk smelled curdled and bits of film stuck to the sides. Jacinda rinsed it out and cleaned it before putting it with the rest of the dishes.

Nobody said much as we ate a simple meal and got ready for bed. The long hike and tearful morning seemed to take its toll. I could barely keep my eyes open when we climbed the ladder for bed. The guys went to the room with the three beds while the five of us went to the larger bedroom. It wasn't until all of us pulled back sheets and burrowed under the covers that I realized something.

"We all just climbed into a bed as if we knew exactly which one was ours," I said.

I lay on the top bunk. Mica had the one beneath me. Across from us were Di and Jacinda. Amber was in the single.

"You're right." Di's dark eyebrows drew together. "All the more reason to stay here until the owner returns. Maybe we've slept here before."

I buried myself under the warm blankets while moonlight filtered through the curtain. Had this been my bed once? Had I lived here at one point? It was frustrating yet exhilarating. Once again, it was like my body remembered something my mind could not. I knew this bedroom. I knew this cabin. Only for some reason, my mind couldn't remember.

THE NEXT TWO days, nothing happened. We hung out at the cabin and jumped every time we heard the slightest sound. Each time it would only be a tree scraping against the house or a bird landing on the roof. Not the cabin's inhabitant.

To pass time, we played games, read books and hung out outside. In a way, it felt like we were at a secluded retreat. However, there was nothing relaxing about waiting for the cabin's mysterious owner to return. At times, it felt like I'd jump right out of my skin I was so anxious.

"Do you want to go for a walk?" Flint asked.

We sat outside on the porch step. I'd been tapping my foot nervously and only stopped when I realized what I was doing.

"Yes!" I jumped up. Sitting around was killing me.

"I'll tell the others we're leaving in case we get lost." Flint sprinted inside and returned with a device in his hand.

"What's that?" I asked.

"A GPS I found. We'll see if it works."

"And if it doesn't?"

"I asked Amber to find us if we haven't returned within an hour."

We set out through the trees. It had to be mid-morning by

now. It felt good to move again. I was still stiff from our arduous hike to the cabin. Exercise was exactly what I needed.

Warm, autumn air swirled around. Temps in the fifties had melted most of the snow. Only the shaded areas held traces of the October blizzard.

"Do you hear that?" I asked as we tromped through the trees.

Flint cocked his head. "Hear what?"

"It sounds like a helicopter."

Flint shrugged. "It's probably a rancher rounding up the last of his livestock."

We carried on. I slowly relaxed into the hike. "What are we going to do when we run out of food?"

"Amber and I will hike out, and whoever else wants to come, to do a grocery run."

"I bet Jacinda will go."

Flint chuckled and held up a branch so it wouldn't hit me in the face. "She does seem to love hiking."

We meandered through the trees, and despite the crazy feelings these hills evoked, I didn't feel fear. In a way, it felt like home. My breathing relaxed into a steady pace, my legs moved steadily beneath me. Flint and I soon fell into easy banter.

It wasn't until we stepped into a small clearing that I stopped short. All happiness and tranquility the hike created – vanished.

An older man walked toward us, his head down, a device in front of him that he seemed to be studying intently. Before I could say two words, Flint grabbed me and flew us behind a rock. We hunkered down, our breathing heavy.

"Do you know who he is?" I whispered.

Flint shook his head, his mouth tight.

I straightened just enough to see over the rock. The man continued to walk toward us, his head still down. He didn't seem to know we were there. I switched my vision. His cloud appeared, and my mouth fell open.

"What is it?" Flint asked. His energy pulsed into me.

I didn't answer. Instead, I watched, mesmerized by the cloud flowing around the older man's shoulders. It was...strange. I didn't know how else to describe it. A rainbow of very faint colors danced and flowed above his body. Red, violet, magenta, green, indigo, pink, gold, orange, silver, navy, yellow. The list went on.

At least twenty colors intermingled in his cloud. All of those colors were faint, like they'd been washed out in a spring rain. The oddest part, however, were the two *bright* colors in the faint rainbow: blue and pale green. Those two bright colors, mixed with the fainter ones, made it the most beautiful cloud I'd ever seen. It was also the most perplexing aura I'd encountered.

I switched my vision back to normal and rapidly assessed everything else about him. The man looked ahead now. I frowned and tried to remember or recognize something about him. He had a normal face, from what I could see of it. Sharp hazel eyes stared straight ahead. Deep wrinkles lined the corners of his eyes. Gray hair covered his head, slightly wispy at the top. He moved quickly and strongly.

From the gray hair and wrinkles, he had to be in his fifties or sixties. For all intents and purposes, he looked like somebody's grandfather. Harmless, benign, your average normal older man, albeit fitter than most.

My frown stayed put. I knew he was anything but normal.

"Lena," Flint hissed quietly. "What's wrong?" His energy pushed into me again.

The man stopped. His head cocked as if listening. I frowned. There was no way he could have heard Flint. He was still ten yards away.

"He's different," I whispered.

The man turned in our direction. His gaze scanned the trees.

I hunkered back behind the rock. Was it a coincidence that

a man with a rainbow cloud was walking in the Forbidden Hills? It didn't take a rocket scientist to know it wasn't.

I stepped out from behind the rock before Flint could stop me. "Hello," I called.

The older man's eyes widened. "Galena!"

Galena?

The man dropped the device he was carrying and hurried to me. I again marveled at how swiftly and easily he moved. Dressed in tan hiking pants, sturdy boots and a lightweight jacket, he looked like a hiker out for a stroll, yet he was here, in the Forbidden Hills. Nobody hiked in the Forbidden Hills.

Before he could get within ten feet of me, Flint blocked him. I peeked around Flint's side since his broad back was about six inches from my face. The man had stopped, his eyes widening even more.

"Flint!" the man breathed.

Flint's shoulders tensed. Hot, raw energy poured off him. "How do you know my name?"

The older man's gaze swung around the clearing, worry lines deepening his wrinkles. "What about the others? Are they here too?"

"What others?" Flint said through clenched teeth.

"Diamond, Jacinth, Mica, Amber, Jet and Jasper. Are they here too? Are you all together?" The man stumbled over his words. Despite my heart hammering, I wanted to reach out and comfort him. He seemed so worried.

"How do you know our names?" Flint asked tightly.

The man took a deep breath and then another. "Of course," he said. "I'm sorry. You have no idea who I am."

An image of the cereal bowl flashed through my mind. The bowl that someone had eaten from the other day. I switched my vision again and watched the beautiful cloud surrounding the older man's shoulders.

I knew without a doubt that we'd just found the owner of the mysterious cabin.

"I'M NOT ASKING again," Flint said. "How do you know our names?"

The older gentleman shook his head. He took a few more deep breaths, as if composing himself. When finished, he held out his hand. "Let me introduce myself first. My name's Conroy Fielding, or Dr. Fielding to some, but I prefer Conroy."

Flint arms stayed at his side.

Conroy dropped his hand. "I've known you all for a long time. That's how I know your names."

I squeezed Flint's arm and tried to push him aside. He didn't budge. If anything, he stepped farther in front of me. His body felt like a hot rock, hard as stone, yet brimming inside with fire. I sighed and sidestepped him. I knew he was suspicious of this man, but his cloud was similar to ours. I didn't think Conroy would hurt us.

"You've known us for a long time?" I asked.

"Yes." Conroy glanced around again. "Now please, tell me. Is everyone else with you? Are all eight of you together?" His tone sounded so worried. "Please, tell me. I promise to explain everything."

Flint's jaw clenched. I put a hand on his arm.

"Yes," I replied. "We're all together. Everyone else is back at a cabin we found. I'm guessing it's your cabin?"

Conroy sighed, his shoulders relaxing. "Yes. I own the cabin."

"Are you going to explain now?" Flint said through gritted teeth. "You still haven't said how you know us."

"Yes. Yes, of course. This must be very confusing." Conroy walked back to his device to retrieve it. "Let's go back to the cabin and I'll explain everything to all of you." He began walking and waved us to join him.

I pulled at Flint. He didn't budge. "Flint, his cloud's like ours," I whispered.

That got a raised eyebrow. "It is?"

"Yes, please let's go."

Conroy stopped when we didn't follow him. He watched us with worried eyes.

"Please, Flint. He's not going to harm us. I feel fairly certain of that."

Flint's energy continued to roll off him. "Okay, but stay behind me."

We followed Conroy through the woods. None of us said a thing. A few times, I wanted to ask Conroy about how his gadget worked. It didn't look like a normal GPS, but I kept my mouth shut. From the hot energy rolling off Flint, I knew small talk wasn't something he'd appreciate.

When we approached the cabin, I spotted Di and Jacinda. Both were seated on the porch. They jumped to standing when they saw us.

Conroy smiled, another relieved sigh escaping him. "Diamond, Jacinth."

Diamond? Jacinth? That's what he'd said before when he named us.

Di glanced at Flint, a questioning look in her gaze while Jacinda merely cocked an eyebrow. "Do you know this guy?" Di asked.

Flint shook his head. "No, but he seems to know us."

Di tensed. "Who are you?"

Conroy didn't reply. "Where are Amber, Mica and the twins?" A worried expression again appeared on his face. He seemed constantly concerned for our whereabouts despite me telling him we were all together.

"Probably inside," I replied.

Di shot me a look.

I shrugged. "I think he's harmless." I inched closer to her and whispered, "His cloud's like ours."

Di frowned suspiciously. "Who are you?" she asked again.

The strange man held out his hand. "Dr. Conroy Fielding."

Di merely stared at him.

Jacinda studied Conroy curiously just as Amber, Mica and the twins barreled through the door.

"I just beat these three at cribbage!" Mica exclaimed. "And I'm thirty dollars richer for–" her words died when she saw Conroy. "Oh, hello," she said.

Conroy smiled, a relieved expression on his face. "It's good to see you all well."

"Okay, you've got to stop that," Di said, although her voice wasn't quite as stern. "Who are you really? Not just your name. Tell us now."

"You're right," Conroy said. "I'm sorry. I know you don't remember me, so this is probably very confusing. Let's go inside, and I'll explain."

Di turned stiffly. The rest of us followed.

We entered the cabin. Scents from breakfast lingered in the kitchen. Dirty dishes lined the counters. Conroy didn't seem fazed that we'd made ourselves at home.

When everyone was in the living room, we all sat. "Okay, tell us who you are," Di demanded.

Conroy sat near the fireplace. "Like I said, my name is Dr. Conroy Fielding. I'm a biomedical researcher. I used to work for O'Brien Pharmaceuticals."

We all stared.

"And that's supposed to mean something?" Jet said dryly.

"I'll start at the beginning," Conroy said.

Jacinda clasped her hands and leaned forward. "Please do."

"I've known all of you since you were young children." Conroy addressed Di. "We found you and your brother," he said, nodding toward Flint, "When you were around eighteen months old, and Flint was about two and a half. Your mother never knew when we took you. She'd leave you by yourself for days at a time."

Di's head snapped back. Neither she nor Flint had time to respond before Conroy turned to Jacinda.

"We took you and Galena when you were around eighteen months, and Galena a few months old. The next day, your mother died from a drug overdose."

Jacinda and I glanced at one another, both of us frowning. Took us? Our *mother*?

"Jacinda and I are sisters?" I blurted.

"Yes, partly," Conroy replied. "Same mother but different fathers, so technically you're half-sisters."

"And you, Mica," Conroy said. "You were maybe seven months old, your mother a prostitute, afflicted with horrible mental illness and addicted to meth. And the twins," Conroy said to Jet and Jasper. "You were both around twelve months, often left for days by your mother without anything to eat or drink. And lastly, Amber. You were just a month old when we took you from an alleyway. You were frequently left there when your mother worked. She was a homeless prostitute and would do anything for her next hit. Once, she tried to sell you."

Amber's mouth dropped.

"So, that's how it all began," Conroy continued. "When you were infants or small children, O'Brien Pharmaceuticals stole you from the monstrous homes you were born into. We rescued you from parents who abused you horribly and cared more about their next hit than their own child."

"You kidnapped us?" Jasper said.

"Yes," Conroy replied. "Our job was to locate children in different areas of the U.S. who were born into horribly abusive circumstances. From there, we transferred you to O'Brien Pharmaceuticals. We called you the lost children."

Lost Children?

"But why would you do that?" Amber asked.

"To experiment on you," Conroy said.

A few of us gasped.

Mica crossed her arms and leaned away from him. "Why would you experiment on us?"

Conroy hung his head. "I can't believe I ever thought anything good would come from what we did."

"Which was?" Mica raised her eyebrows.

"I used to belong to a powerful group that conducted legitimate business in the pharmaceutical world. We also had a private sector that very few in O'Brien Pharmaceuticals knew about." Conroy shook his head. Guilt laced his words. "Our group decided thirty years ago to experiment on children. The ultimate goal was to create a drug that resulted in the perfect specimen. A perfect human being. One capable of so much more than nature created. At the time, I dreamed of endless possibilities. Drugs that would give us the ability to cure blindness and deafness, while also enhancing aspects of the brain that controlled strength and speed, or tapping into dormant areas of the mind we do not use. Areas that create psychic connections. It was incredibly powerful." He paused. A pained expression crossed his features. "Ultimately, however, this group was not what I expected. When it became apparent that the experiments would be undertaken at all costs, I got out. And I took all eight of you with me."

My mouth dropped. Was this guy serious? We were taken from parents who didn't care if we lived or died, and then brought to some drug company that experimented on us like lab rats? It seemed too monstrous and entirely too preposterous to believe.

"Is that why we can do special things?" Amber asked.

"Yes," Conroy replied. "Our drugs gave you your abilities."

"Is this a joke?" Jet said.

Conroy shook his head. "I wish it were."

At least a full minute passed in which no one said a thing. My heart pounded. We were drugged? *Kidnapped?* Some pharmaceutical company gave us these abilities?

My head spun. It couldn't be true.

"Do you have proof you did this?" Di broke the quiet.

"How do we know we can believe you?"

"No, I don't have proof," Conroy replied. "I understand if you don't believe me."

"But how could something like that happen?" Jasper demanded. "How can you steal kids off the streets and experiment on them? Surely, *someone* looked for us after you took us? If not our parents, than the authorities or child services? Wouldn't someone catch you?"

Conroy shook his head. "Sadly, no. Part of the reason you were all chosen was because we knew nobody would ever look for you. All of you were born at home, if you can call filthy apartments or under bridges, homes. None of you have birth certificates. None of you have social security numbers. None of you exist according to the U.S. government. No trace of you will ever be found in a Social Service database, because the only people who ever knew you existed were your mothers and fathers, and all of them are long dead."

"You're saying that our parents never contacted the authorities after we went missing?" Di said. Disbelief lined her words.

"That's right," Conroy replied.

It seemed everyone else was processing this faster than me. I was still trying to get my head around Jacinda and me being sisters, and that all of us had once had families, real relations. Although, I'm not sure family would be the right term if what Conroy said was true. Families protected one another. I had no idea where that moral came from, but I felt it to my inner core. However, according to Conroy, our blood families did everything but protect us.

"How do you know our parents never looked for us?" Mica asked.

"We monitored all police activity," Conroy said. "And one parent, Jacinda and Lena's mother, died from an overdose before she knew we took you. Since your fathers were never in your lives, there was nobody to contact the authorities in your case."

Coldness swept through me. Had my mother really cared so little for me?

Flint put his hand on my thigh. He'd been suspiciously quiet. "How do you know her mother died?"

"Surveillance. We needed to make sure our group wasn't compromised."

"But how do you know *all* of our parents are dead?" Amber asked.

"Again, surveillance," Conroy replied. "We followed them all until their deaths."

"But why would you ever do such a thing in the first place?" Jacinda demanded. "To take children and experiment on them... That's horrific!"

"I know," Conroy said quietly. "Believe me, I know that now. However, at the time, I truly believed we were giving you a better life full of gifts and abilities, but I mistook the ambition of my colleagues. It was too late to stop them by the time I realized their intentions."

"What were their intentions?" Flint asked. Power rolled off him. It was hot, but I inched closer to him anyway. My body felt chilled.

Conroy's gaze clouded over. "To experiment on you at all costs."

Mica swallowed audibly. "What costs?"

"To the death."

My eyes widened.

A heavy sigh raised Conroy's shoulders. He wouldn't meet our questioning gazes. "Originally, there were three groups of ten children. However, two children in your group died. They were too old when I administered their drug. That's why there are only eight of you now."

Jacinda gasped. "They *died* because of what you did to them?"

Conroy gave the barest hint of a nod. "We didn't know

then that over the age of three, the human brain is too developed to adapt to the alterations the drugs demanded. Those older than three usually died from encephalopathy. If I had known that would happen, I *never* would have done it."

Silence followed that revelation. All I could do was stare.

"That's why you took us from our mothers and fathers when we were so young," Di said quietly.

"Yes." Tears clouded Conroy's eyes. He blinked them back and cleared his throat. In a shaky voice, he said, "If I could take back everything I did..." He paused. "I can't undo what I've done, and I can't take back the contributions I've given to O'Brien, but I *can* try to make it right. That's why I took all of you away from there many years ago. If I'd been able to take the other two groups, I would have, but transporting eight children as it was without being detected was almost impossible."

"Where did you take us?" Amber asked. Her voice was so small and frightened. Jasper tightened his grip around her.

"Here, to this cabin," Conroy answered.

I remembered last night. How we'd all climbed into beds as if we knew which one was ours.

"I'd heard about the Forbidden Hills and how people rarely ventured into them," Conroy explained. "It seemed like the perfect place to hide, so I bought this land and had this cabin built specifically for us. We all lived here together in hiding until six months ago."

"We did?" Mica exclaimed.

"Yes," Conroy nodded. "It was too risky to live in the normal world. O'Brien has searched for us since we disappeared over fifteen years ago. Hiding was our only option."

"Fifteen years?" I gaped. "We lived in this cabin in hiding for fifteen *years*?"

"Yes, it was the only safe option."

"How old were we when you took us from O'Brien?" I

asked.

"You were five, Galena. And you, Flint," Conroy said, his gaze shifting, "you were eight. Being the oldest in the group, you had the hardest time adjusting. You had seen and been through so much by the time I got you out of there."

Flint stared at Conroy, not saying a word. His energy, however, picked up a notch.

"How old are we now?" I asked.

"Your ages? You're twenty-one, Galena, and Flint," he said, his eyes shifting, "You're twenty-four. Diamond, Jacinth and the twins you're all twenty-three, Mica you're twenty-one but will be twenty-two next month, and Amber you're nineteen. You're the youngest in the group."

So the ages on the driver licenses were correct. However, I'd never had a license. I'd never known my age. Until now.

I'm twenty-one.

A huge sense of relief flowed through me. I had no idea how much not knowing my age had bothered me until that very moment.

Jasper leaned forward, his brow furrowed. "But *why* can't we remember any of this? How come everything past six months ago is blank?"

"Because my drug failed," Conroy said.

"Your drug?" Amber's head cocked.

Conroy nodded. "Did you use your tattoos to find this place?"

Amber's eyes widened. "You know about our tattoos too?"

"Yes. I tattooed them on all of you – six months ago, just in case."

Confused expressions sprouted on all of our faces. "Just in case what?" Di asked.

"In case my plan failed," Conroy replied. "Tell me, how did you all meet one another?" A keen interest lit his eyes.

"We all woke up in various cities but inevitably felt a pull to this area," Di said. "After several weeks to months, everyone arrived in Colorado in more or less the same place. I was able to see everyone and pull us together."

"So you all eventually arrived close to this cabin?" Conroy asked.

"Yes," Di replied.

"Yet none of you remembered your identities or that you once lived here?"

"Correct," Di nodded.

Conroy leaned back. "So your identities never returned, but something in your subconscious was triggered that led you back here." He paused. "I knew it was possible the drug wouldn't work, that memories might surface or something could trigger your subconscious. The fact that you're all here verifies that's exactly what happened. How interesting."

"Really?" Flint cut in. His energy grew hot again. "You call that interesting? Eight people left on their own in unfamiliar cities with no sense of who they are, and you call that *interesting?*"

Jacinda leaned forward and clasped her hands. "You keep mentioning a drug, Conroy. What drug are you referring to?"

Guilt flashed across Conroy's eyes. He wouldn't meet our gazes when he said quietly, "The drug I administered to all of you six months ago. The drug that made you forget."

CHAPTER TWENTY-EIGHT

"You drugged us?" Jet gaped. *"Again?"*

I thought about the lab downstairs. Conroy's lab? Where he created this drug?

"I know that sounds awful, but it was the only way I could see a safe future for all of you," Conroy said. "You have to understand, with Amber being nineteen you were all well into adulthood. And over the years, all of you voiced wanting to leave to start a real life. Only a few of you," he eyed Di and Flint, "were content to stay living in hiding. The rest of you wanted to live in and explore the world. But it was too dangerous to let you leave together. I knew I'd have to find a way to make it safe. After all, what right did I have to keep you any longer? And there was an incident last year, that made me reconsider staying—"

"But why drug us?" Flint interjected. "What was so dangerous that made you do that?"

Fear entered Conroy's eyes. "O'Brien."

Jacinda's eyes widened. "What do you mean?"

"They're still looking for you. If O'Brien ever spotted one of you, you'd unwittingly lead them to the others. I couldn't let that happen."

"What would they do if they found us?" I asked hesitantly.

"I honestly don't know," Conroy said. "I'm not sure I want to know."

"So you drugged us so we wouldn't remember each other and then you split us up?" Di said. "And you did all of this simply so we could live in the normal world?"

"Yes," Conroy replied. "Individually, you stood a better chance at not drawing attention. Even if one of you was spotted, there's no way you'd be able to lead them to the others if you couldn't remember anything. Especially, if you didn't know one another existed."

I leaned into Flint. "Which is why you took our memories away."

"Yes, it was the safest option I had."

"Did we agree to be drugged and split up?" Flint asked.

"You never would have agreed to be split up. You're family, even though you're not related," Conroy replied quietly.

Flint's grip tightened on my thigh. "So you obviously didn't ask our permission before you drugged us again." His jaw clenched. Once again, heat and that powerful feeling rolled off him.

Conroy clasped his hands together. "No."

"I didn't think so." Flint put his arm around my shoulders, pulling me closely to him. "So I suppose you don't know that something went wrong with whatever you did to Lena. She was homeless in Rapid City. Did you know that? That she had to hitch rides to Colorado when she felt the urge to return to this place?"

Conroy's head whipped up. "Homeless? But how? I gave you all money and homes."

"Well, you must have forgotten Lena," Flint seethed. "She had nothing."

Conroy shook his head. "No, no I didn't. She was left in her condo, just like the rest of you."

"That's not where she woke up," Flint persisted.

"Where did you wake up?" Anxiety laced Conroy's words.

"An alleyway, outside," I replied.

"Without anything, except the clothes on her back," Flint added.

A horrified expression crossed Conroy's features.

"So that wasn't where I was supposed to wake up?"

"No!" Conroy exclaimed. "I never would have left you somewhere like that. Never!"

"Then why did she wake up there?" Flint demanded, his voice tight. "Another one of your experiments failed?"

Conroy shook his head, appearing lost in thought for a minute. "The only explanation I have is that you sleep walked out of your condo. You have a history of sleep walking, Galena. That's the only way I can explain it. You must have left your home in your sleep, and since you didn't know it existed, you wouldn't have known to return to it." He covered his face with his hands. He looked almost sick. "No wonder I was never able to track you."

"You tracked us?" Di asked.

"Yes, with the cell phones I left all of you. I was able to follow all of you until your signals abruptly vanished. From the directions you were moving, I knew most of you were coming back here."

Di eyed Flint. "We were right." She glanced back at Conroy. "We destroyed them. We knew it was a way to be tracked."

Conroy smiled humorlessly. "Then I taught you well."

I was still reeling that I'd sleep walked out of the home I'd owned in South Dakota. I thought about all of the times during the summer where I sleep walked from ditches or rest stops. Usually, I woke up within a block of where I'd gone to bed. I remembered that alleyway in Rapid City. A condominium complex had been on the other side of it. Is that where Conroy had left me?

Di's next question pulled me back into the conversation. "But how did you do it all? How could one man drug eight individuals, and deposit them in eight different cities all over the country, without anybody seeing or knowing about it? It doesn't seem feasible."

"I had help," Conroy replied.

"From who?" Mica asked.

"My lawyer and pilot."

"What?" Mica said.

"They helped me carry each of you when you were drugged and unconscious," Conroy explained.

Silence again hung for at least a minute.

"But that still looks kind of suspicious, don't you think?" Jet remarked. "To be carried into a condo or brought up in the elevator? What'd you do, chopper us to our condo's rooftops?" he said sarcastically.

Conroy nodded. "Yes, in the bigger cities, that's exactly what I did."

My eyes bulged. "What? You *helicoptered* us around the country?" I remembered the faint sound of a helicopter this afternoon. Is that how Conroy had returned to the Forbidden Hills?

"It's my main form of transportation," Conroy said. "It's the only way I've ever left these Hills. Believe it or not, it's the most discreet way to get in and out of these mountains."

"But how did you get a helicopter?" Amber asked.

"I own it," Conroy replied.

Jet's eyebrows shot up. "You own it?"

"So you have money," Di stated. "Lots of money, obviously, if you're the one who left us the funds in our bank accounts."

"Yes," Conroy answered.

"But if we've been living in seclusion, how did you get the money?" Di drummed her fingers on the end table. "If what you're saying is true, you couldn't work living in seclusion out here. So where'd you get the money to fund all of this?"

Conroy cleared his throat. "I did work actually. I never stopped working. That's why I had the lab downstairs created so I could continue my research, but I also come from a wealthy family and have invested well over the years. Money has never been an issue in my life. Ever."

"But money leaves a trail, right?" Jasper said. "So if this so called group of yours, was really looking for you, couldn't they track it? Through money withdrawals or whatever? Surely they could have found you that way."

"My investment firm handles everything for me," Conroy replied. "That and most of my funds are kept in off shore accounts. They're not as easy to track."

"How much money do you have?" Jacinda asked. "If you don't mind my asking."

Conroy shrugged. "More than any of us could ever need."

"But that still doesn't explain how you got us out of the cabin, into a helicopter, with only the help of your lawyer and pilot," Di replied. "That's eight of us versus three of you. Surely we would have fought when you tried to drug us? Or did you slip it in a drink or something?"

Conroy shook his head. "No, neither of them helped get you out of here." He hung his head for a minute. "I'm not proud of this, but I lied to you all. I told you we were going on a trip. I took you all to one of my homes in Montana and drugged you there. After that, it was merely a job to carry you back to the chopper, which is when my lawyer and pilot stepped in. We took you all to your various cities from there."

Everyone stared at him, silent. "I guess money really can buy anything," I said.

"Yes, Galena," Conroy said. "It really can."

The heat off Flint escalated. A muscle clenched in his jaw.

"By the way, why do you keep calling me that?" I blurted. I put my hand on Flint's thigh, hoping the change in topic might distract him from his almost palpable rage. "My name's Lena."

"Lena's short for the name I gave you, which is Galena," Conroy answered.

"And you named Di, Diamond and Jacinda, Jacinth?" I asked.

"Correct. We never knew your birth names, or if your parents ever named you, so the group gave you names. Your section was named after natural elements. Diamond, Flint, Jacinth, Galena, Amber, Mica, Jet and Jasper. Your names are all derived from rocks, minerals and gems. I named you all."

"Oh," I replied, stunned. That was another clue we'd never put together. I hadn't realized our names were connected.

Everyone else remained quiet, brooding expressions on their faces.

It was a lot to take in.

Leaning back, I crossed my arms. Switching my vision, I again studied Conroy's cloud. It was so colorful and vibrant. However, like all colorful clouds, I couldn't firmly read it. Was Conroy really as honest and kind hearted as he proposed to be?

I remembered my initial reaction to him in the clearing. My gut had told me to trust him. Had my gut ever been wrong?

No.

If what Conroy said was true, he had only ever meant us well. He took us from homes in which we surely would have died from neglect, or been so horribly abused we would have been shells of the people we were now. And as soon as he found out what his O'Brien group was truly capable of, he took us from them too, even though it'd meant giving up his own life in the process.

Flint's energy pushed into me. A dark expression covered his face. I could tell he wasn't reaching the same conclusions as me.

I listened to my gut feeling again. It told me that Conroy was good. He meant well.

Uncrossing my arms, I relaxed back into the couch. Conroy *had* spent fifteen years in hiding with a group of sensory enhanced kids. Fifteen years away from everything he'd ever known, simply in hopes of keeping us safe. And while giving us a drug six months ago to make us forget wasn't ethical, I agreed with Flint on that one, Conroy had once again only had our best interests at heart. He was trying to protect us and give us back the lives stolen from us.

Di stood and paced a few times. "Is our situation really as dangerous as you claim? Everything you've done has been so extreme. Are we really in that much danger?"

"You're all living proof of the unethical and illegal activities that transpired within O'Brien," Conroy said. "So yes, our situation really *is* that dangerous."

Di stopped and stared at him. "So you created your memory drug, hoping we'd make safe lives in the real world?"

"Yes."

She put her hands on her hips. "Were we supposed to survive off that money you left us?"

"That was there as a backup. However, you're all educated and have exceptional gifts. I taught you all myself. If you'd chosen to get a job, that wouldn't have been a problem."

Flint snorted. "Without a diploma that seems doubtful. How would we get jobs?"

"Jobs were arranged for all of you, if you chose to take them," Conroy said. "You all would have received a letter stating your new positions of employment if you'd stayed in your cities."

"But we didn't stay," Di said. "All of us felt an urge to return to Colorado. Something inside all of us led us back here."

"I realize that," Conroy said. "Which is also why I tattooed you. I gave you the clues necessary to find me and this place if needed."

"And you've been living here ever since?" Mica asked.

"Yes," Conroy replied.

Jet smirked. "What were you planning on doing, retiring

here?"

Conroy frowned. "You're not the only one O'Brien's looking for, and my lab's here. Essentially, my life is here and has been for the last fifteen years. It was easy enough to stay and keep working, and I knew when all of your tracking devices went blank, except for yours Galena, that I had to stay until I found all of you again. I couldn't leave here if there was a possibility any of you would show up. I kept the door unlocked every day in case I wasn't here when one of you returned."

I thought about the triple dead bolt on the door. No wonder it hadn't been engaged.

Jet raised an eyebrow. "Why didn't you implant GPS locators under our skin? Wouldn't that have been easier?"

Conroy either chose to ignore his sarcastic tone or didn't pick up on it. "I considered it, but I couldn't risk it. If O'Brien ever found any of you and found a GPS device under your skin, they could potentially derive a way to track the devices and hunt the rest of you. I figured cell phones were the safest option."

That matter-of-fact comment made everyone go silent. It almost didn't seem real what Conroy was telling us. It was like our lives were plucked right from a science fiction movie.

"So now what?" I finally asked. "What do we do from here?"

Conroy eyed me with a grim expression. "That is a very good question. Only it's a question I don't have an answer to."

CHAPTER TWENTY-NINE

The eight of us talked long into the night. After lots of arguing, discussing and more arguing, we eventually decided we had two options. We could either continue living in hiding for the rest of our lives, essentially staying in this cabin and going back to the lives we'd left. Or we could leave and face the consequences of O'Brien hunting us.

The next morning, a somber mood hung in the air, similar to the gray clouds that rolled in overnight. Distant thunder sounded.

Di stood by the fireplace, arms crossed. "We can't keep running, and we can't spend our lives in hiding."

Flint and I sat on the couch. I curled my legs tighter underneath me while Flint tensed at my side. From the way Conroy described O'Brien, it was like they had spies all over the country, but that wasn't possible. Or was it? I thought about Conroy choppering us out of the Forbidden Hills, about the unlikelihood of that. It seemed a lot of impossibilities could be done with money.

"What do you suggest?" Flint asked his sister.

Di placed her hands on her hips. "We have to find out

what they'd do to us and whether or not other lost children are still alive."

Everyone grew silent.

"Won't they kill us if they find us?" Amber's fingers clenched the couch pillow tightly.

"But we can't stay in hiding forever," Jasper said. "We've done nothing wrong. Why should we have to pay the price?"

"Even if that price is our lives?" Jacinda said. "Don't get me wrong. I'm ready to get out of Timbuktu and get into a city, but that was before I knew all of this. I quite like being alive."

"Even if it means we're prisoners inside our own home?" Di countered. "For the rest of our lives?"

Jacinda frowned. "Maybe. I don't know. I wish I knew more about this group."

"Exactly!" Di said. "We need to learn more about them. At the very least, find out what they want."

"But how?" Jasper asked.

"Conroy," I replied. "He knows who they are and where they are."

Flint scowled heavily. He put his arm around me and pulled me close.

"But will he help us?" Mica asked. "It seemed like he wanted to stay under the radar. I can't see him walking through the front doors of O'Brien, asking where his old buddies are."

"No," Di agreed. "But if he's too afraid to go back than we'll have to. Or at least I'm going, even if none of you are."

That statement made me grow cold. We'd never done anything without the entire group agreeing, but now Di was saying she'd go alone if she had to. I chewed my lip. Our lives were about to change. I knew none of us would agree to be split up. We were in this together, come what may.

"Does that mean we're going back to O'Brien?" I asked.

"How about we handle it like we always do, with a vote?" Di said. "Those in favor of finding this group, raise your hand." She, of course, was the first to raise hers. I was the second.

Flint inched closer. "I go where you go." He raised his hand.

"We're in," said the twins.

"No way I'd miss this." Mica's hand came up.

"Jacinda, Amber?" Di asked. Fat rain droplets fell against the window. The sound drummed through the room. "Are you in?"

Jacinda glanced at Amber with raised eyebrows. Amber nodded, wide-eyed. "Okay, I'll go."

"Me too," Jacinda responded.

"Go where?" Conroy asked. He stepped out of the bathroom, toweling his hair off. Steam rolled into the living room.

"Back to O'Brien," Di replied. "And you're going to take us there."

Conroy dropped the towel. His face turned ashen.

I sank against Flint. I needed the secure and safe feeling his presence evoked. We were going back to where it all began, no matter what we may find. I felt Flint's gaze on me. For the first time since I'd met him, something in his gaze made me pause. The protective look he always had was still there, but fear now lingered as well.

The rain fell harder. It pelted against the windows, sounding loudly in the room.

"Are you sure you want to do this?" Flint whispered into my ear.

"What choice do we really have?"

He stared at me, an anguished expression on his face. He wrapped both arms tightly around me. We sat like that for a minute as everyone continued talking around us. But it was like everything became a blur. I closed my eyes, listened to his heartbeat and cherished his unique smell as the rain drummed down on the roof.

I clung tightly to him and wondered if there'd come a day when I'd no longer be able to feel him like this, love him like this.

He squeezed me harder, as if he'd been wondering the exact same thing.

FREE E-BOOK!

Join Krista Street's Newsletter and receive a
FREE copy of *Awakened*

Book 0 – A Novella Prequel – The Lost Children Trilogy

www.kristastreet.com/contact

BEFORE YOU GO…

The best way to support indie authors is to leave a review. If
you have time, please consider posting a review on Amazon
and Goodreads. Krista would really appreciate it!

TO FOLLOW KRISTA STREET ON
SOCIAL MEDIA

ACKNOWLEDGMENTS

There are a lot of people I need to thank. First and foremost, my family, for supporting me and encouraging me to pursue my writing dream. Especially my sister, Marla, who's been with me every step of the way. She told me she loved my stuff even when it was awful (seriously, truly, horribly awful!). That encouragement was what I needed while I figured out how the heck one writes a book.

Thank you to my husband and mother-in-law for letting me disappear into coffee shops for hours and hours while they watched the kids. Without them, I wouldn't have been able to mentally check out when I was neck deep in a story.

Thank you to my parents for their support, especially my dad for his expert attention to detail and ability to pick up inconsistencies that a dozen critique partners missed. To my sister-in-law for offering her time and graphic design talents even though we didn't go that route in the end, and to my brother for encouraging me to pursue self-publishing.

To my friends and beta readers: Jaime Lea, Kirsten and Meg. Your willingness to read my stuff, give honest, *salty* and thought provoking feedback, helped shape *Forgotten* into what it is today. I'll be forever grateful to each of you.

Thank you to Tony W., Mike K., and Tony E. for your publishing expertise and willingness to answer my never ending publishing questions. You all helped immensely. Thank you for putting up with my endless emails and sharing your wisdom.

To my writing group: your collective talents and advice

improved my writing immensely even when I thought I had a polished product. To Mike, Jen, Teresa, Lisa, Melissa, Jessi, Eric, Tony E., Amy, Tony W., Kirsten, Ben, Brian and the others who helped critique my work every month. Your feedback has been invaluable and enlightening. You've all made me a better writer and pushed me to improve month after month. Thank you!

And lastly, thank *you* for reading my book. Without you, I'd have no reason to publish. Thanks for reading!

ABOUT THE AUTHOR

Krista Street is a Minnesota native but has lived throughout the U.S. and in another country or two. She loves to travel, read, and spend time in the great outdoors. When not writing, Krista is either spending time with her family, sipping a cup of tea, or enjoying the hidden gems of beauty that Minnesota has to offer.

REMEMBERED

The Lost Children Trilogy
Book Two

TURN THE PAGE FOR A SNEAK PEEK!

CHAPTER ONE

"What do you think will happen if O'Brien catches us?" Mica's brown eyes narrowed when she glanced at Conroy.

I tensed from where I sat in the backseat and tucked a long strand of dark red hair behind my ear.

Conroy's hands tightened on the steering wheel. His gaze stayed trained on the road ahead. High mountain desert landscape flew by as we traveled down the interstate. Soft road noise hummed in the cab. Northern Arizona was beautiful. Pine forests and rolling hills intermixed with desert. It wasn't a bad place to escape to as we planned our return to O'Brien Pharmaceuticals.

"They'd kill us, wouldn't they?" Mica persisted.

"I think they may," Conroy finally replied. "It's why hiding is safest."

"But we've decided *not* to hide. If we do, the other lost children will never be free." Mica picked up her bag and rummaged through it.

Conroy took a deep breath and gripped the wheel tighter. His knuckles turned white.

The lost children.

That's what the men in Conroy's old group, Project Renatus, named us when they stole us from our parents almost twenty years ago. It was ironic in a way. None of us were lost. They'd kidnapped us and experimented on us like lab rats. Yet to them, that's what we'd become. The lost children.

Now, the eight of us living on the outside of O'Brien Pharmaceutical's walls were grown adults. All of us were in our early twenties, and all of us were fighting to be free from the corporation.

Nerves churned my stomach. How much our lives had changed in twenty-four hours. Meeting Conroy in the Forbidden Hills in Colorado. Learning about him and his part in Project Renatus. Discovering that men from that project, governed by O'Brien Pharmaceuticals, wanted us captured or dead.

It seemed too crazy to be true.

Flint's hand rested on my thigh. He squeezed my leg as I leaned closer to him. The rough fabric from his flannel brushed against my cheek. With it, came his subtle scent. Spice, wood and tangerines. I inhaled and clung to that scent. I needed the safe feeling it always evoked.

Mica pulled a bag of trail mix out of her pack and began munching. "Di will have a plan to get the other lost children back. She always has a plan."

Conroy didn't reply.

I wished I could adopt some of Mica's endless optimism. Dread followed me since we left the cabin in the Forbidden Hills. As much as I tried to leave that foreboding feeling in my wake, I couldn't help but feel bad things were to come.

I glanced over my shoulder. The rest of our unlikely family followed in the Suburban. Even from a distance, Di's face was visible as she held the wheel. From her grim expression, I guessed she mulled over everything Conroy had revealed to us two days ago. Either that or the twins were driving her crazy.

"When are we gonna stop for a bathroom break?" Mica

polished off the remaining peanuts, her crunching chews audible.

Conroy nodded to a sign that flashed by the window. "There's a gas station a few miles ahead. We can stop there."

"Good." Mica brushed crumbs from her top. "I feel like I'm gonna burst."

"Lena and Flint?" Conroy's gaze drifted to the rearview mirror. "Does that work for you?"

"Sure." I dog-eared the paperback mystery that lay forgotten in my lap. "I could use a stop too."

"When will we reach your house?" Flint's words were clipped.

I winced. Unlike some of us, Mica and I included, Flint hadn't been so easily won over by Conroy.

"We're a few hours away. We should be there by nightfall." Conroy always replied politely to Flint. The older scientist didn't seem fazed by Flint's hostility.

I wondered if Flint and Conroy had always had a rocky relationship. Of course, I'd never know. Memories of my life only went back six months. Frustration bubbled up inside me. While I now understood why I had no memories, thanks to the drug Conroy administered to me and everyone else six months ago, I still hated that I didn't know who I was.

Flint leaned forward. "So how do you know this house of yours is safe?" Sunlight glinted off Flint's chestnut brown hair, making it appear streaked with gold.

"I know it's safe because I purchased it a month ago, under one of my aliases. The only person who knows I own it is—"

"Let me guess," Mica cut in. "Your lawyer?"

Conroy nodded. "Exactly."

"Humph." Mica cocked an eyebrow. "I still can't believe everything we've learned. It's kinda crazy you know."

"Which part?" I asked. "Where O'Brien Pharmaceuticals stole us off the streets when we were babies from our drug addicted, prostituting parents or how O'Brien kept us locked up while we were experimented on?"

Mica chuckled as a strong push of energy hit me. Flint's jaw tightened. I laid my hand on his thigh. His warmth seared through his jeans. Right. Maybe it was a little too early to joke about that stuff.

"When you put it like that, it sounds rather barbaric," Conroy said.

Mica's eyebrows shot clear to her hairline. "How could you ever think it *wasn't* barbaric?"

Conroy sighed. His hands tightened on the steering wheel again as we sailed around a turn. "If you could have seen the conditions in which you were born." He stopped, his voice growing quiet. "I'm not saying it justifies what we did, I see that now, but at the time, I was young and hopeful. I'd been passionate about science since I was a boy. The possibilities of untapped chemical creations fascinated me. You have to understand, I was very young when I joined O'Brien. I was naïve and blinded by my ambitions to better the world. At the time, I truly felt like I was doing the right thing. I thought I was helping all of you. That I was making your lives better."

Mica cocked her head. "I know I just met you, so I can't believe I'm saying this, but I believe you."

"I do too," I said.

Conroy's hands relaxed. A smile lifted his cheeks.

"Well, *I* don't believe you," Flint muttered. He glared out the window.

Conroy's gaze drifted to Flint in the rearview mirror. His smile dimmed.

If only Flint could feel what I did. I switched my vision, activating the part of my brain that was dormant in others. Conroy's cloud appeared. The beautiful rainbow of dancing colors billowed around his shoulders. It was unlike anything I'd seen before. Some of the colors mirrored colors in our clouds: red, pink, orange, yellow, green, indigo, violet and gold.

However, other colors mixed in it too: magenta, silver, navy and at least a dozen more. All of Conroy's colors were faint like they'd been washed out in a spring rain. All except for two bright colors: blue and pale green. The blue matched the blue in our clouds. However, none of us had pale green.

As always, I couldn't explain why we had colors. I also couldn't get a firm read on Conroy's cloud. The rest of the population had some form of white, gray or black. The whiter the cloud, the more kind a person was, the darker, the eviler. Nobody else had colors. And as for why Conroy had so *many* colors, I had no idea.

However, my gut told me Conroy wouldn't harm us. And if there was one thing I always listened to – it was my gut instinct.

"So how'd you make the memory drug you gave us in April?" Mica asked.

"It was something I created last year, in the lab back home," Conroy replied.

By *home*, I assumed he meant the hidden cabin we'd left in the Forbidden Hills.

"But how did it work?" I asked.

"The drug targeted specific cells in your brains. Upon reaching those targeted cells, it severed all neuronal activity to your long-term memories. Basically, your memories are still there. However, you don't have access to them."

I sat up straighter. "They're still there?"

"Yes."

How does he know that? "So this drug must be different from the one you gave us as babies?"

"It's much safer. Age doesn't affect it."

That comment reminded me of the two oldest children in our original group of ten. I'd never met that older set of twins since they died from the drug Conroy administered to them. I swallowed uneasily. If I'd been older when he gave me my drug, I could have died too. Luckily, I was only a few months old when he stole me – plenty young for my brain to adapt.

Mica squirmed in her seat. "I still gotta go to the bathroom. How much longer?"

"Just ahead." Conroy put his blinker on and glided the Pathfinder off the interstate. I glanced behind us. Sure enough, Di followed.

"I gotta *go!*" Mica squealed. She bounded out of her seat the second we pulled into the gas station.

Conroy followed Mica. Cool air swirled into the car before he slammed his door. I unbuckled my seat belt, but Flint made no move to leave.

It had been a long day of driving. Conroy's original plan had been to helicopter us straight to his reclusive Arizona home, but after a brief discussion, none of us wanted to leave the Suburban behind. Call us sentimental, but when one's life is as erratic as ours, familiar things have greater meaning. However, none of us considered what keeping the Suburban entailed. That sentimentality had resulted in a nine-hour drive. It also meant Conroy had to purchase a vehicle since nine of us in the Suburban was too crowded.

"We better get to the bathroom." I opened my door. "Who knows when the next stop will be."

Flint grabbed my hand before I stepped out. His sudden grip made the charm bracelet I wore jingle quietly. The charm – a heart with an inscription reading *Love You Forever* – glinted.

"Lena, we don't have to go with Conroy. You know that, right?"

The urgency in his voice made my stomach sink. I settled back beside him. A strong gust swirled into the car from my still open door. It whipped my long dark red hair around my face. I tucked a strand behind my ear.

"I think we should," I replied.

"But we don't know if we can trust him."

He gripped my hand tighter. His palm was so warm. Another steady push of energy rolled off him.

Feeling Flint's energy was something I'd grown used to during the past two months. For some reason, the power inside him radiated out. It was hard to miss, at least for me. The drug Conroy gave me as a child resulted in my unique ability to see auras around people or clouds as I called them. It told me if a person was good or bad. However, it went a step beyond that with Flint. I could also *feel* his. When he was angry, aroused or felt any other strong emotion, the power rolling off him increased. The strength of it right now was enough to tell me he was very serious about ditching Conroy.

I slammed my door closed. Jacinda and the rest of the gang were getting out of the Suburban. I knew none of them would be able to hear us, except Jacinda that is, thanks to her enhanced auditory sense.

"We can't leave Conroy."

"Why not?" Flint demanded.

I tightened my grip on him. His palm was calloused and rough. "I know you don't believe it, but I know that Conroy would never hurt us. Just like I knew when *we* first met in August that you'd never let anyone hurt me. Those gut feelings we've all had about things? They're our subconscious trying to break through. Don't you see that?"

He gazed out the window, his expression brooding. "Then why don't I trust him?"

I swallowed uneasily. *That's a very good question.* "I don't know."

A sharp knock on the window made me jump. Jet and Jasper's faces plastered against it. Amber hung just behind them, grinning.

"Hey love birds, you two coming in?" Jasper called.

I forced a smile. "Let's go."

With stiff movements, Flint opened his door.

The twins and Amber had already sauntered away. Laughter trailed in their wakes. As usual, the twins' jokes prevailed, even in our current circumstances.

I inhaled the evening air. Already, it had cooled. Flat desert landscape surrounded us. The sky blazed purple from the setting sun. Distant mountains hovered on the horizon, hinting at colder temps to come.

"Chilly here." I shivered.

Flint reached inside the vehicle and grabbed his jacket. He slipped it around my shoulders before I could protest. The parka practically swallowed me.

Flint leaned down and kissed me softly on the neck. His lips lingered. Another push of energy rolled into me. Worry lined its edges.

"Are you two coming?" Jacinda stood by the door to the gas station. Her long blond hair trailed down her back. I hadn't realized she was waiting for us.

"Come on." I tugged Flint.

Our footsteps slapped the pavement. Flint glanced over his shoulder several times, his gaze curious. According to Conroy, we needed to be cautious in public. He claimed O'Brien *still* had eyes all over the country, people paid to watch out for a group of eight individuals matching our descriptions. I wasn't sure any of us believed him, though. The eight of us had been together for two months, granted it was on a secluded ranch, but still, there had been no sign of men watching us anywhere.

"How has it been riding with Conroy?" Jacinda asked.

"Good." I had to look up to address her. It still amazed me that we were half-sisters. I figured our fathers must have been complete opposites. Her dad a Norwegian Viking and mine an Irish midget. "Interesting too. Conroy's been telling us about the drug he gave us. It targeted our long-term memories."

"Is that right?" Jacinda cocked her head causing her long, blond hair to fall over her shoulder.

Flint held the door. A large shelf of candy bars greeted us the second we stepped inside. I eyed the Snickers with interest but Jacinda steered me away.

The travel center was large and clean. Scents of hot dogs and nacho cheese drifted in the air when we walked by the food station. Navajo art and souvenirs hung on display throughout the aisles. Halloween decorations draped from the ceiling. One ghastly ghoul looked particularly disturbing with its black, vacant eyes and open tooth filled mouth. The normalcy of this lone travel stop was exactly what I needed.

Some of the nerves left my stomach as Jacinda pulled me to the back of the gas station. An array of sandwiches lined the refrigerated section. They beckoned to me. Even though I'd been well fed for the past two months, my days as a homeless vagabond when food was precious, still lingered.

"Bathroom first." Jacinda rolled her eyes.

I grumbled but followed.

When we stood at the sinks, washing our hands, I asked, "How long do you think it'll be before we leave for Chicago to search for other lost children?"

Jacinda's hands stilled on her paper towel. With a start, she resumed drying them. "We'll have to see what Conroy discovers about his old group. It would be foolish to leave immediately."

"Jacinda! Lena!" The bathroom door banged open.

Di stood in the doorway. She wore her usual all black attire which mirrored her midnight hair and dark eyes. "Come on, we're leaving."

"Already?" I threw my paper towel in the trash. "But we've only been here five minutes, and we haven't bought anything to eat."

"Then hurry up." She glanced over her shoulder before stepping into the restroom. The door closed softly behind her. Looking past us, her eyes darted to the bathroom stalls. She lowered her voice. "Is anyone else in here?"

Jacinda glanced at the empty stalls. "No, just us."

"Good," Di said. "Because we need to get moving."

My heart rate increased. "Why? Did something happen? Did someone spot us?"

Di shook her head curtly, her short hair swaying with the movement. "No, but Conroy has something for us at his house. He just told me about it."

I gave Jacinda a questioning look.

Jacinda merely raised an eyebrow and shrugged. "This is news to me too."

"What is it?" I asked Di.

Di smiled. Her eyes carried the manic gleam I was becoming to recognize all too well. "Another drug he wants to give us, but this drug will make us *remember*."